PECULIAR WOODS

PECULIAR WOODS

∽ The Ancient Underwater City ∽

Andrés J. Colmenares

Andrews McMeel
PUBLISHING®

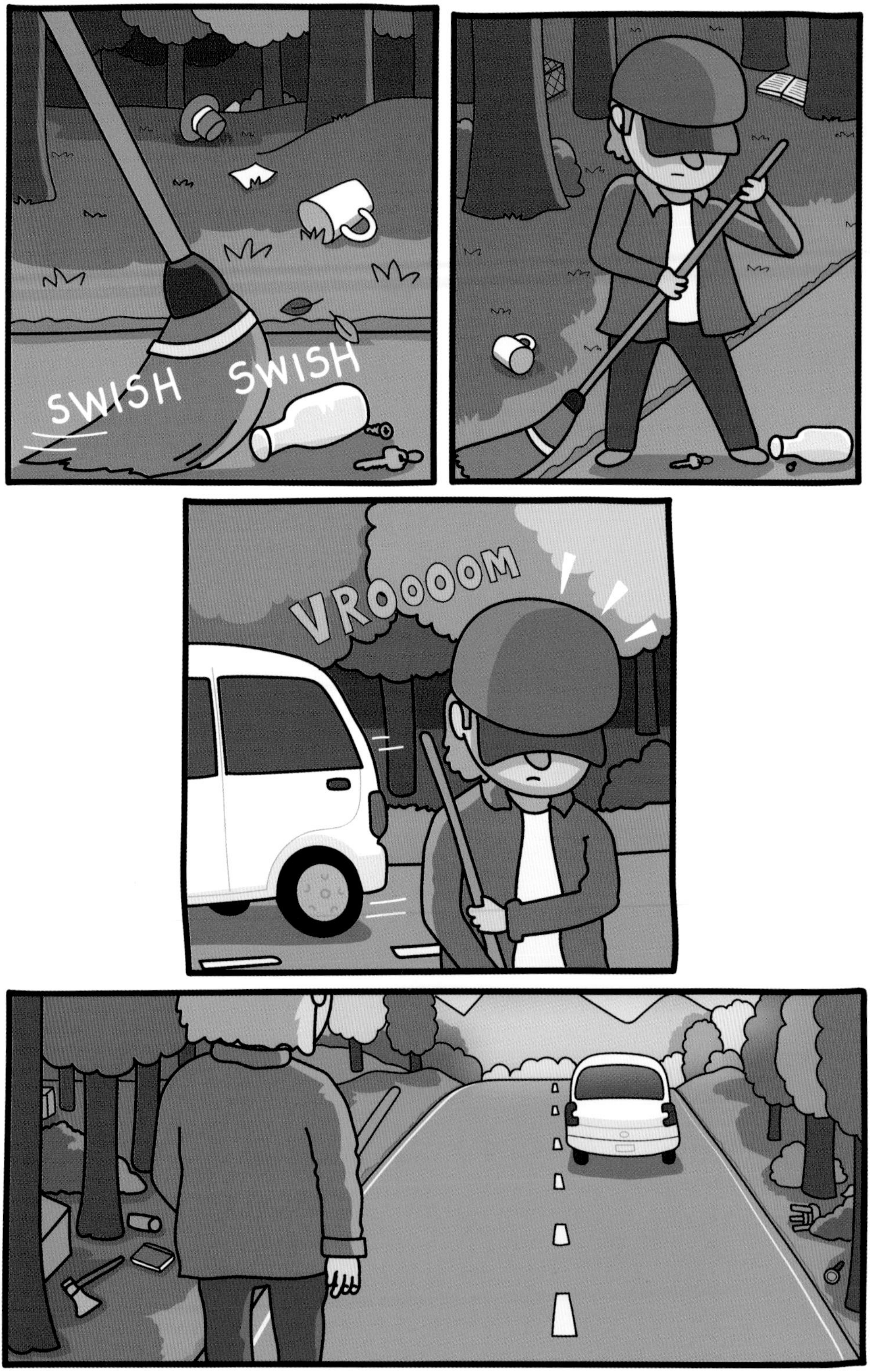
SWISH SWISH
VROOOOM

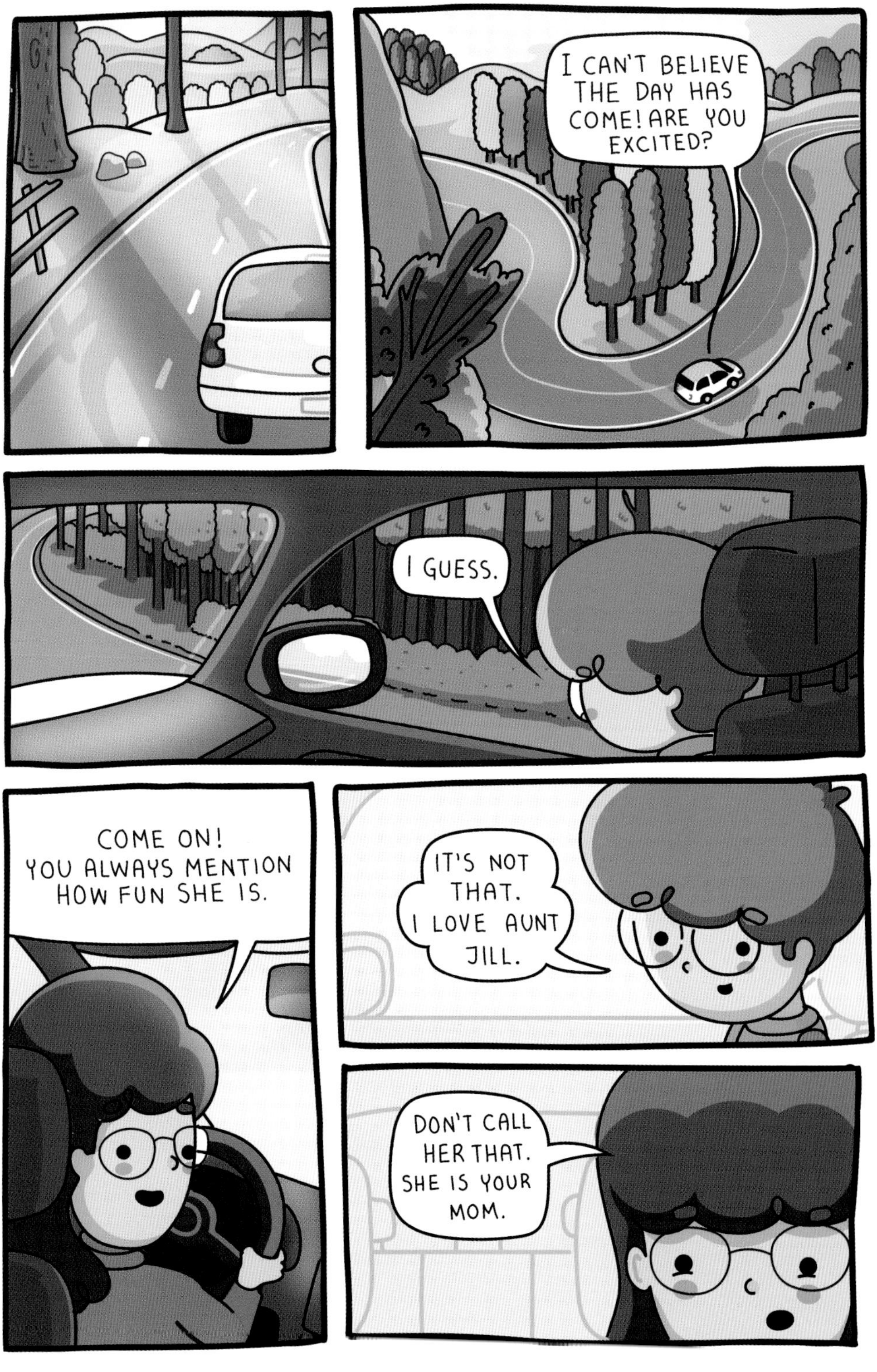
I CAN'T BELIEVE THE DAY HAS COME! ARE YOU EXCITED?
I GUESS.
COME ON! YOU ALWAYS MENTION HOW FUN SHE IS.
IT'S NOT THAT. I LOVE AUNT JILL.
DON'T CALL HER THAT. SHE IS YOUR MOM.

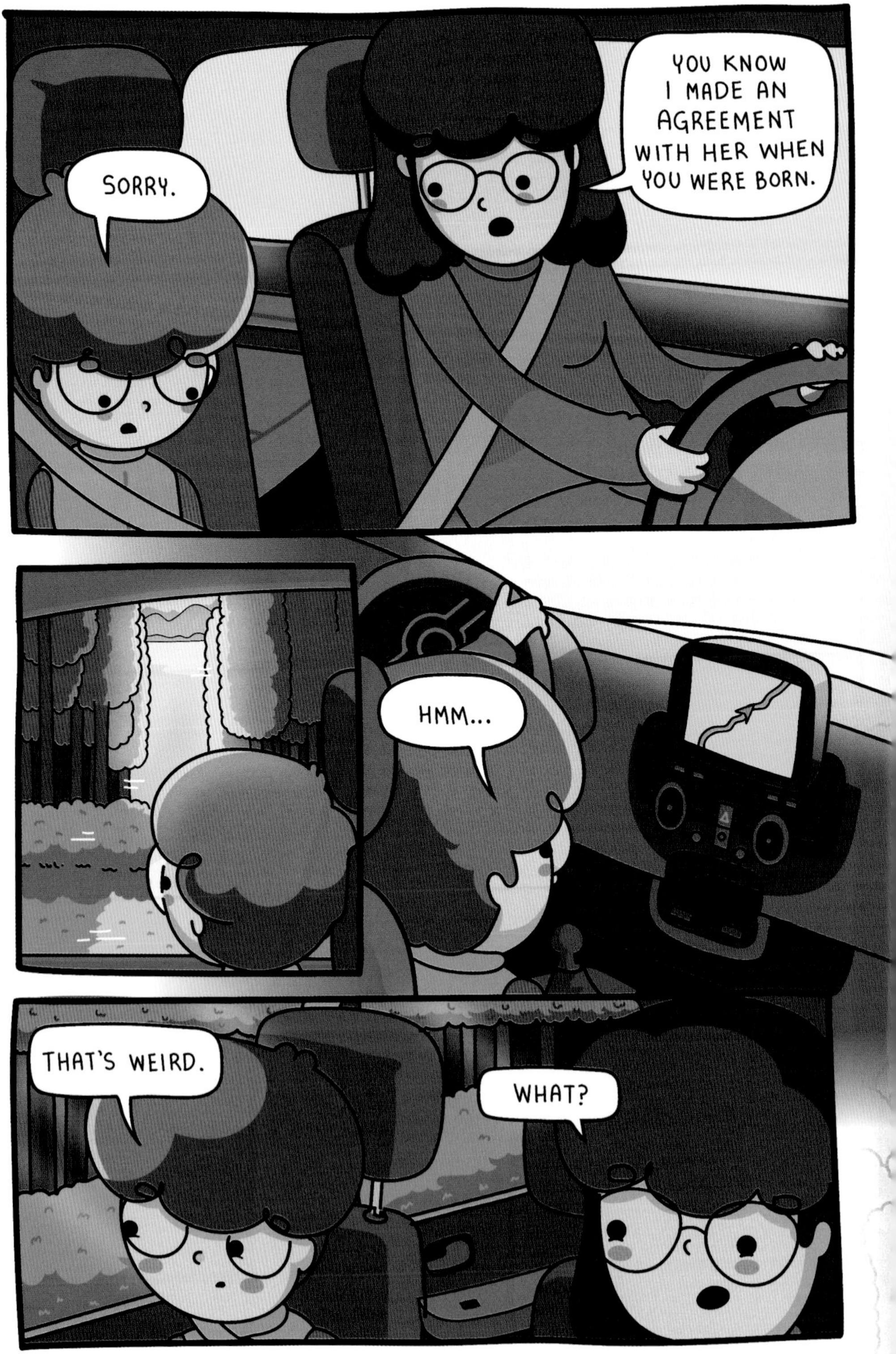
SORRY.
YOU KNOW I MADE AN AGREEMENT WITH HER WHEN YOU WERE BORN.
HMM...
THAT'S WEIRD.
WHAT?

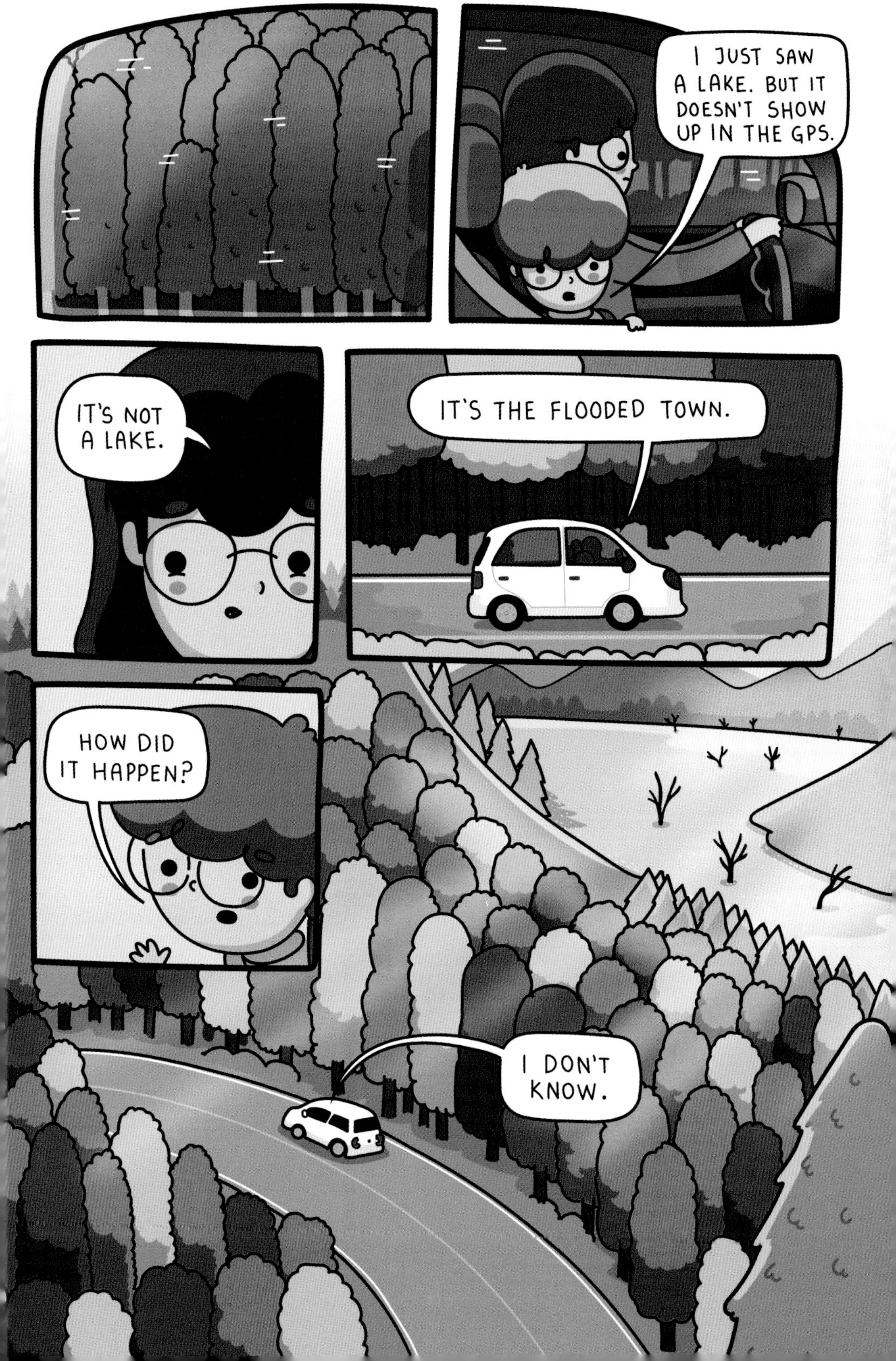
I JUST SAW A LAKE. BUT IT DOESN'T SHOW UP IN THE GPS.
IT'S NOT A LAKE.
IT'S THE FLOODED TOWN.
HOW DID IT HAPPEN?
I DON'T KNOW.

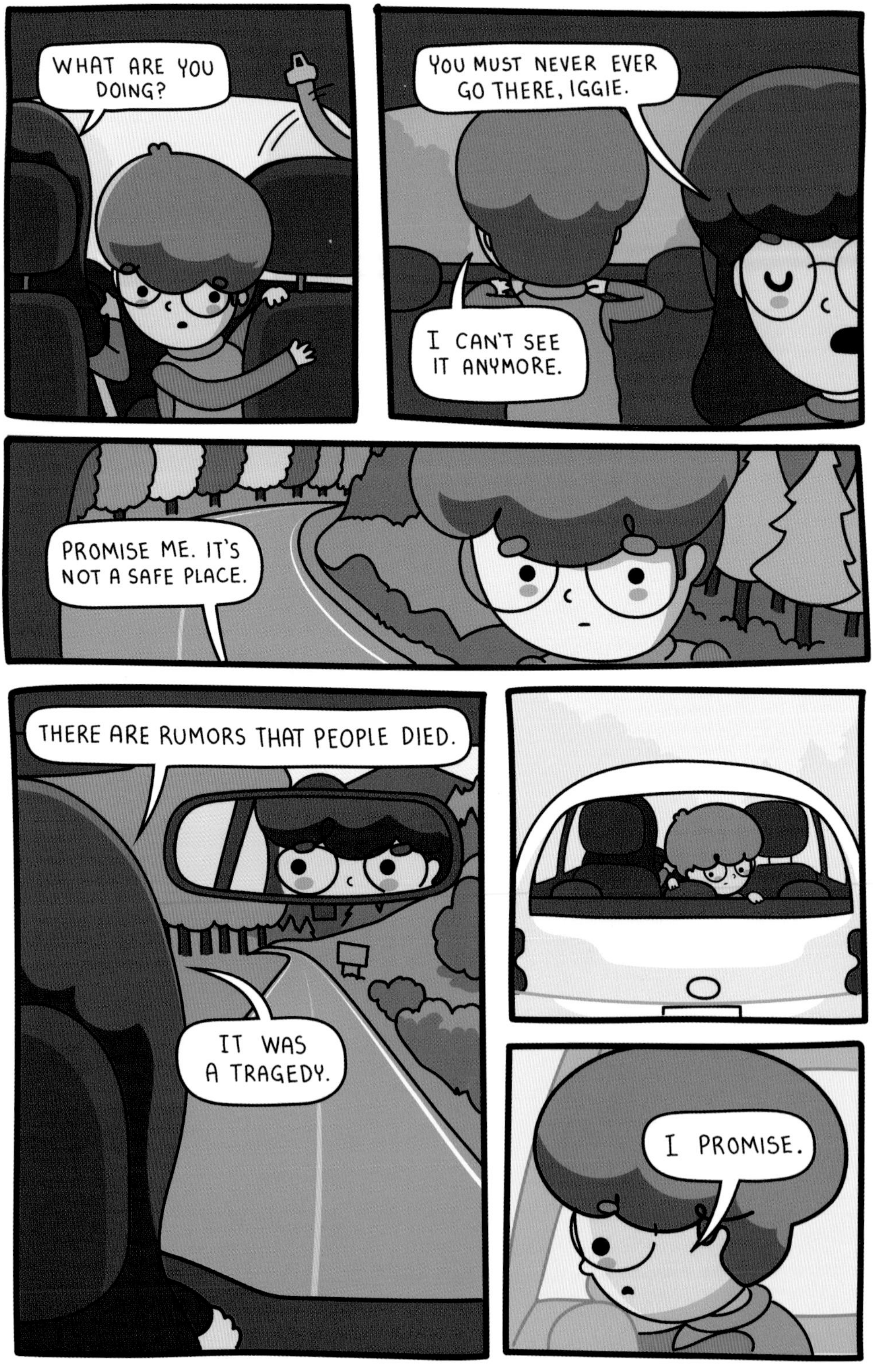
WHAT ARE YOU DOING?
YOU MUST NEVER EVER GO THERE, IGGIE.
I CAN'T SEE IT ANYMORE.
PROMISE ME. IT'S NOT A SAFE PLACE.
THERE ARE RUMORS THAT PEOPLE DIED.
IT WAS A TRAGEDY.
I PROMISE.

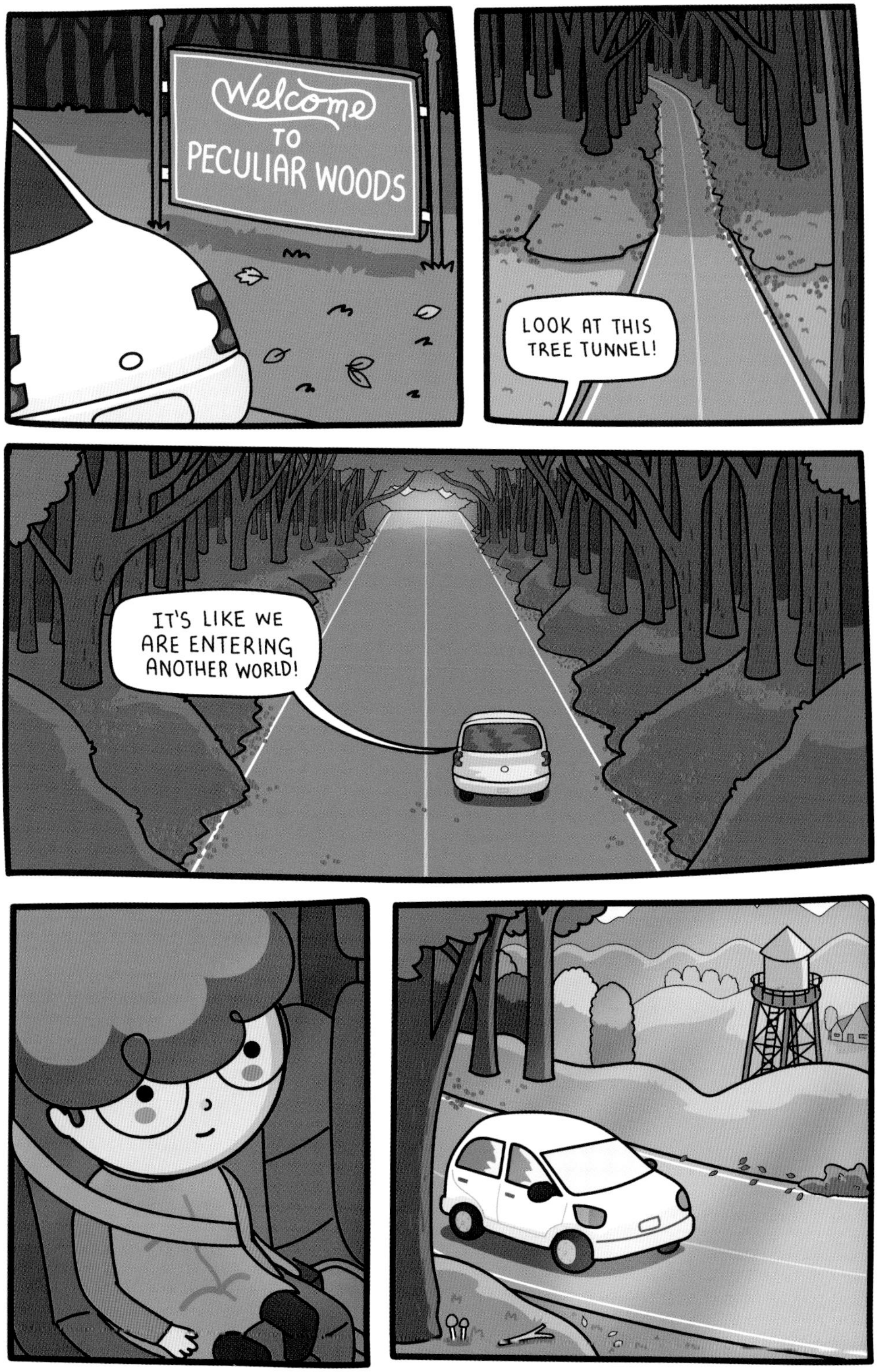
Welcome TO PECULIAR WOODS
LOOK AT THIS TREE TUNNEL!
IT'S LIKE WE ARE ENTERING ANOTHER WORLD!

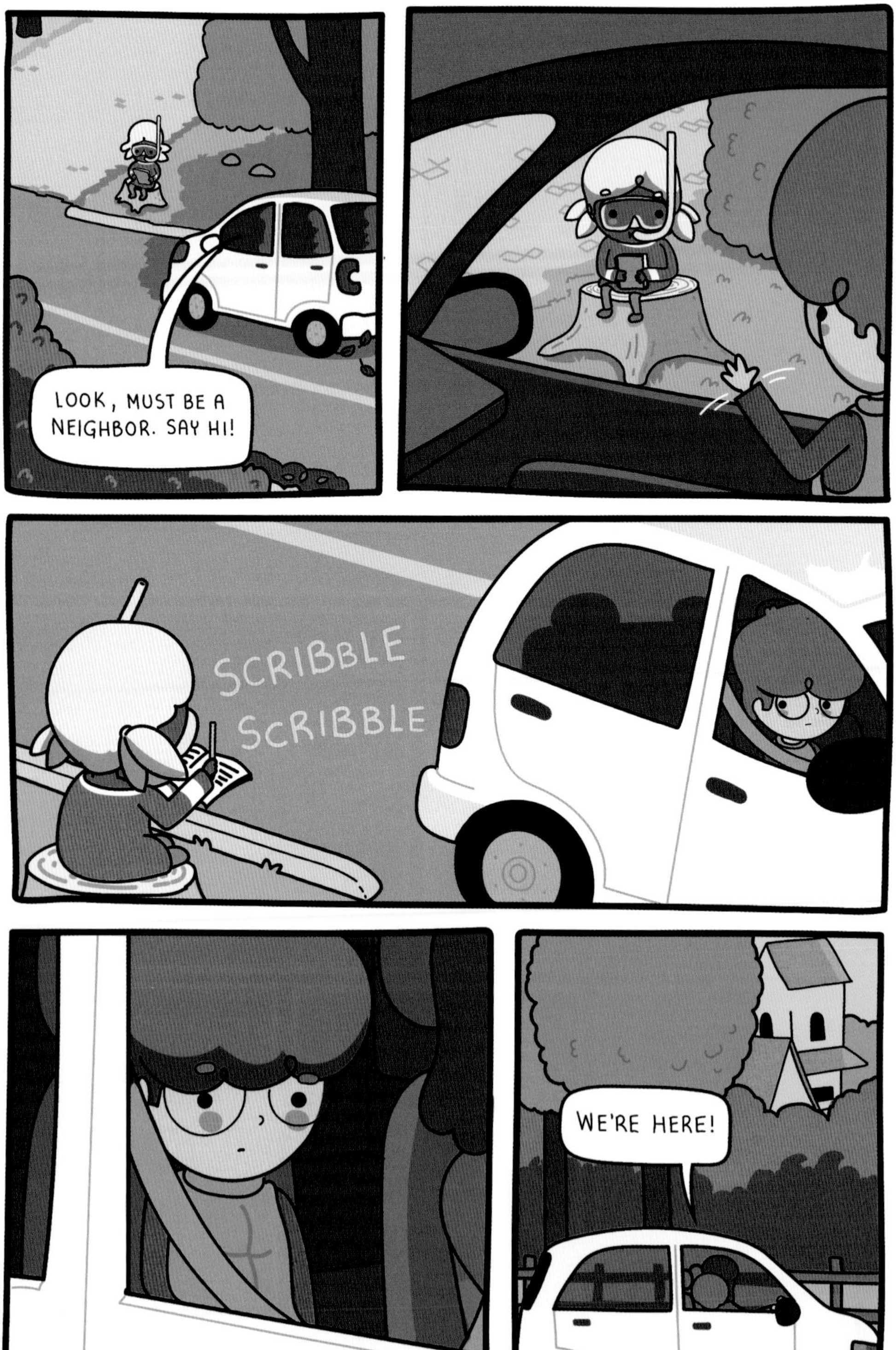
LOOK, MUST BE A NEIGHBOR. SAY HI!
SCRIBBLE
SCRIBBLE
WE'RE HERE!

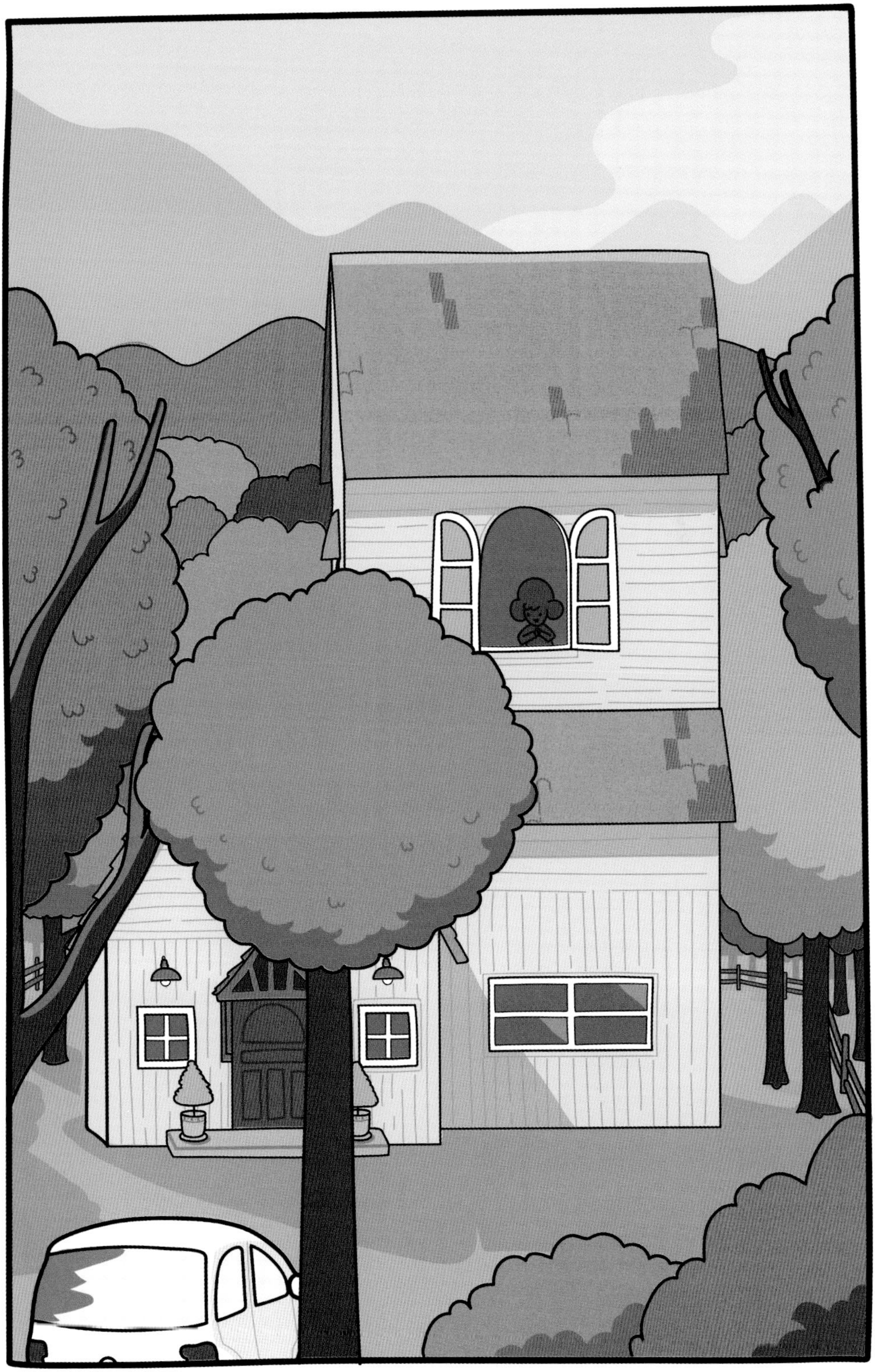

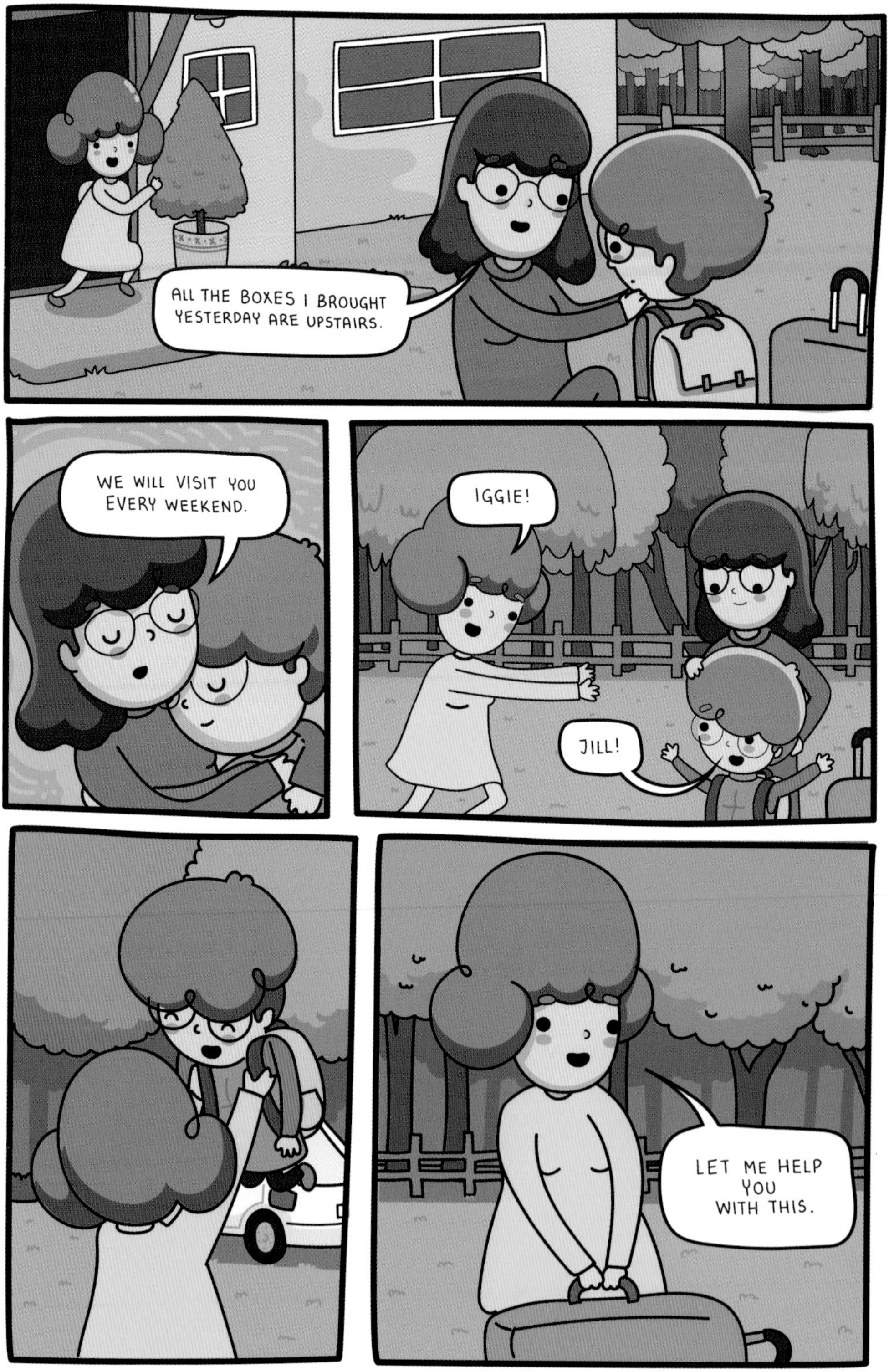
ALL THE BOXES I BROUGHT YESTERDAY ARE UPSTAIRS.
WE WILL VISIT YOU EVERY WEEKEND.
IGGIE!
JILL!
LET ME HELP YOU WITH THIS.

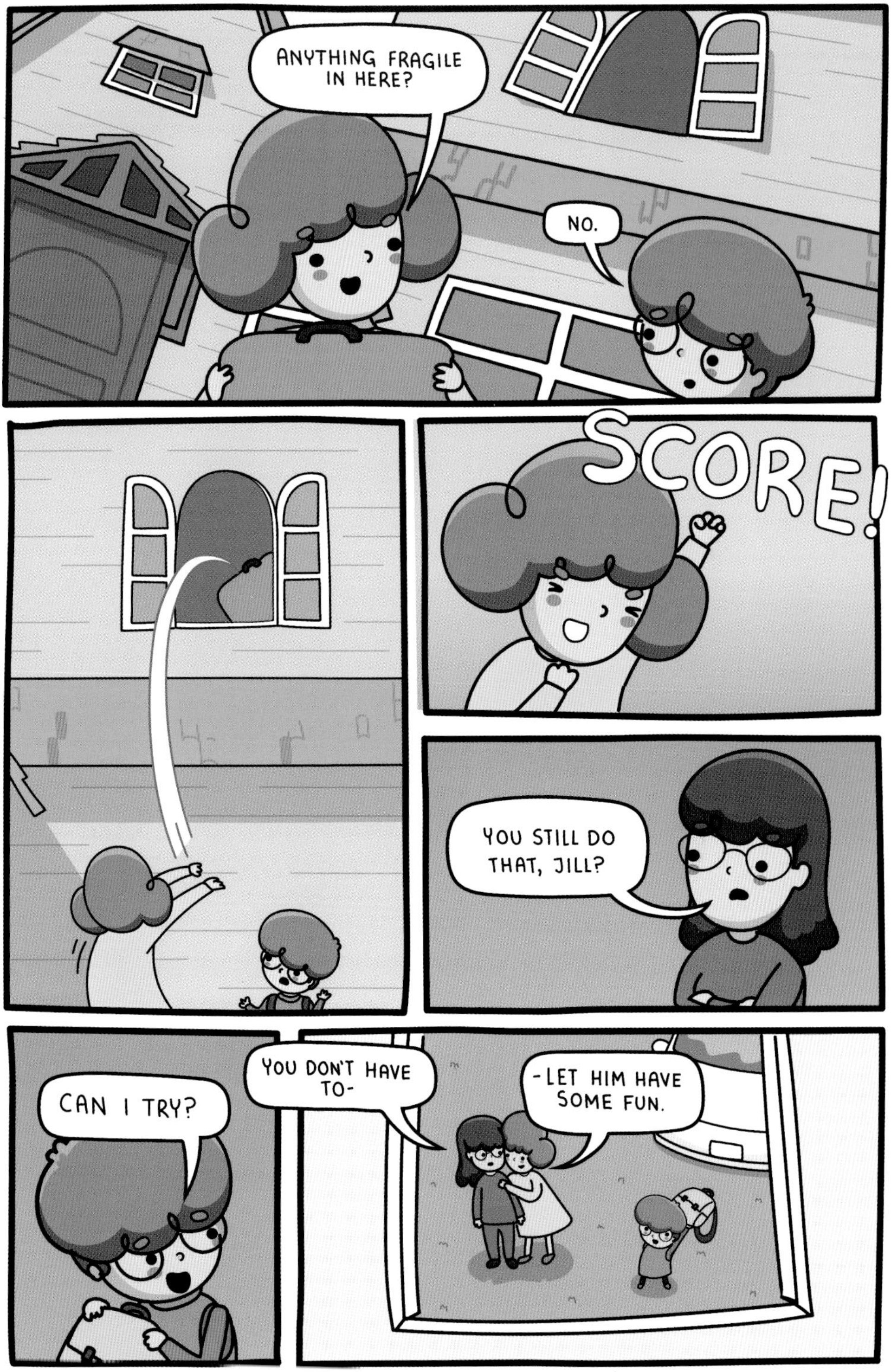
ANYTHING FRAGILE IN HERE?
NO.
SCORE!
YOU STILL DO THAT, JILL?
CAN I TRY?
YOU DON'T HAVE TO-
-LET HIM HAVE SOME FUN.

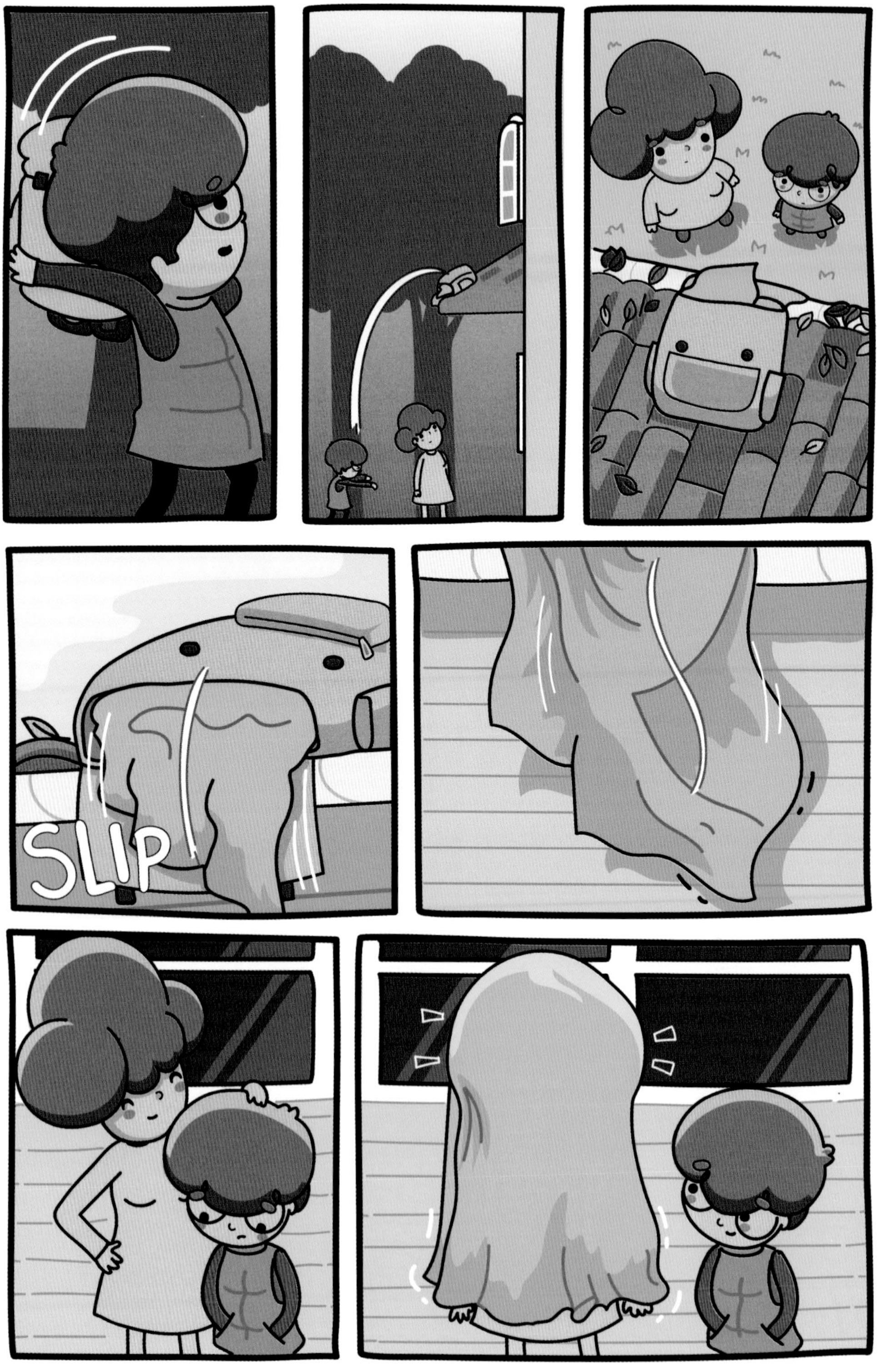
SLIP

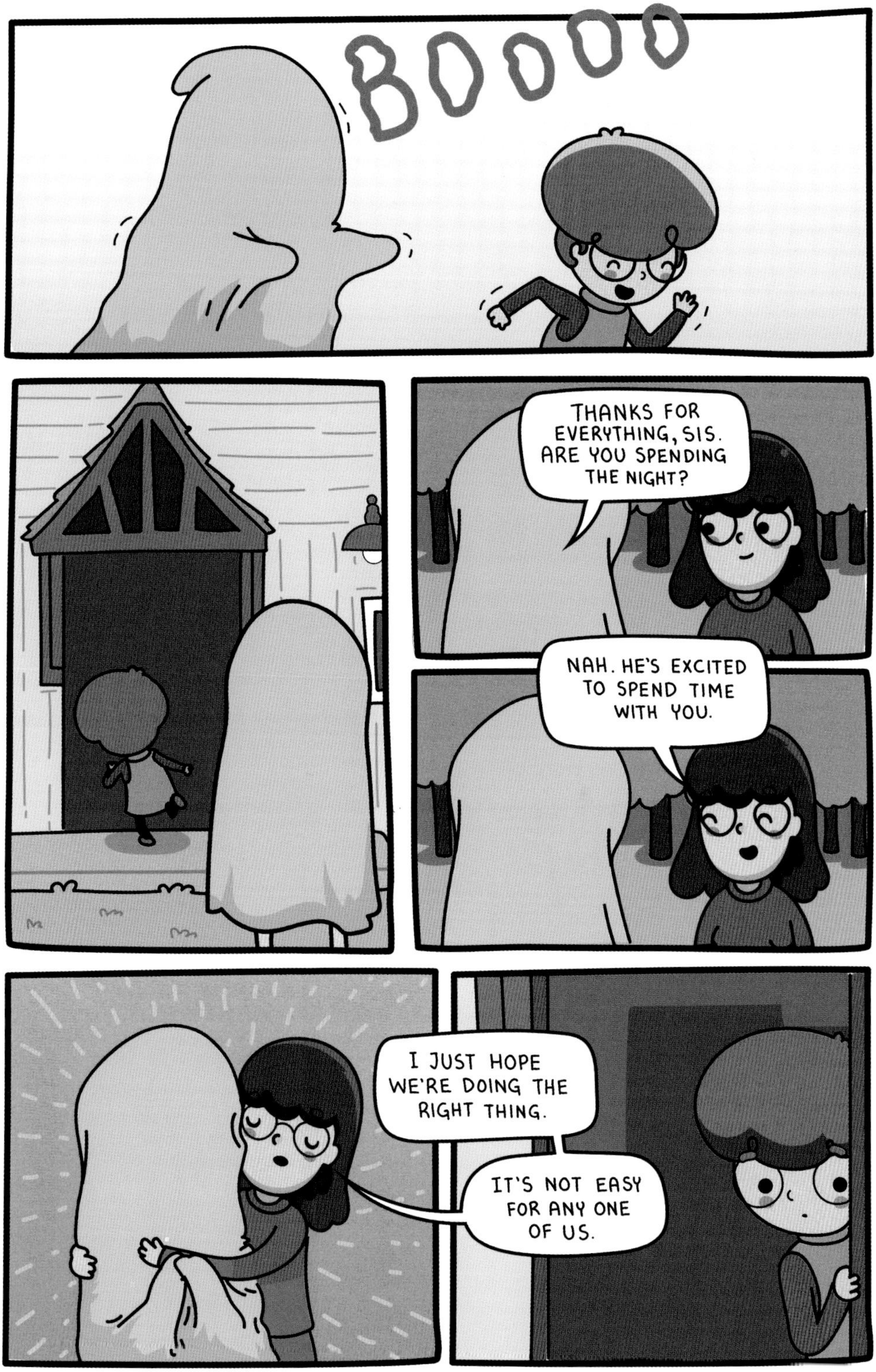
BOOOO
THANKS FOR EVERYTHING, SIS. ARE YOU SPENDING THE NIGHT?
NAH. HE'S EXCITED TO SPEND TIME WITH YOU.
I JUST HOPE WE'RE DOING THE RIGHT THING.
IT'S NOT EASY FOR ANY ONE OF US.

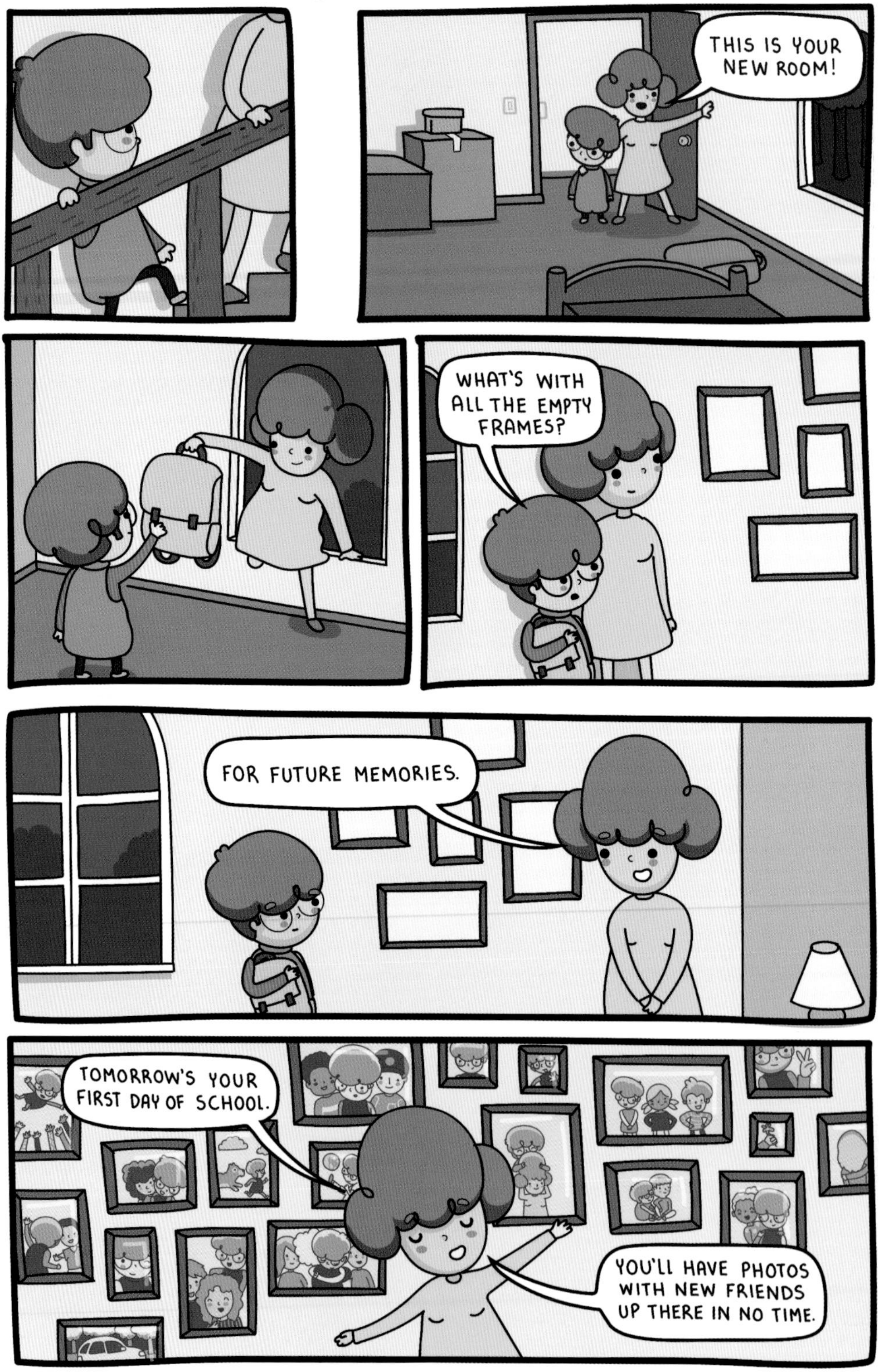
THIS IS YOUR NEW ROOM!
WHAT'S WITH ALL THE EMPTY FRAMES?
FOR FUTURE MEMORIES.
TOMORROW'S YOUR FIRST DAY OF SCHOOL.
YOU'LL HAVE PHOTOS WITH NEW FRIENDS UP THERE IN NO TIME.

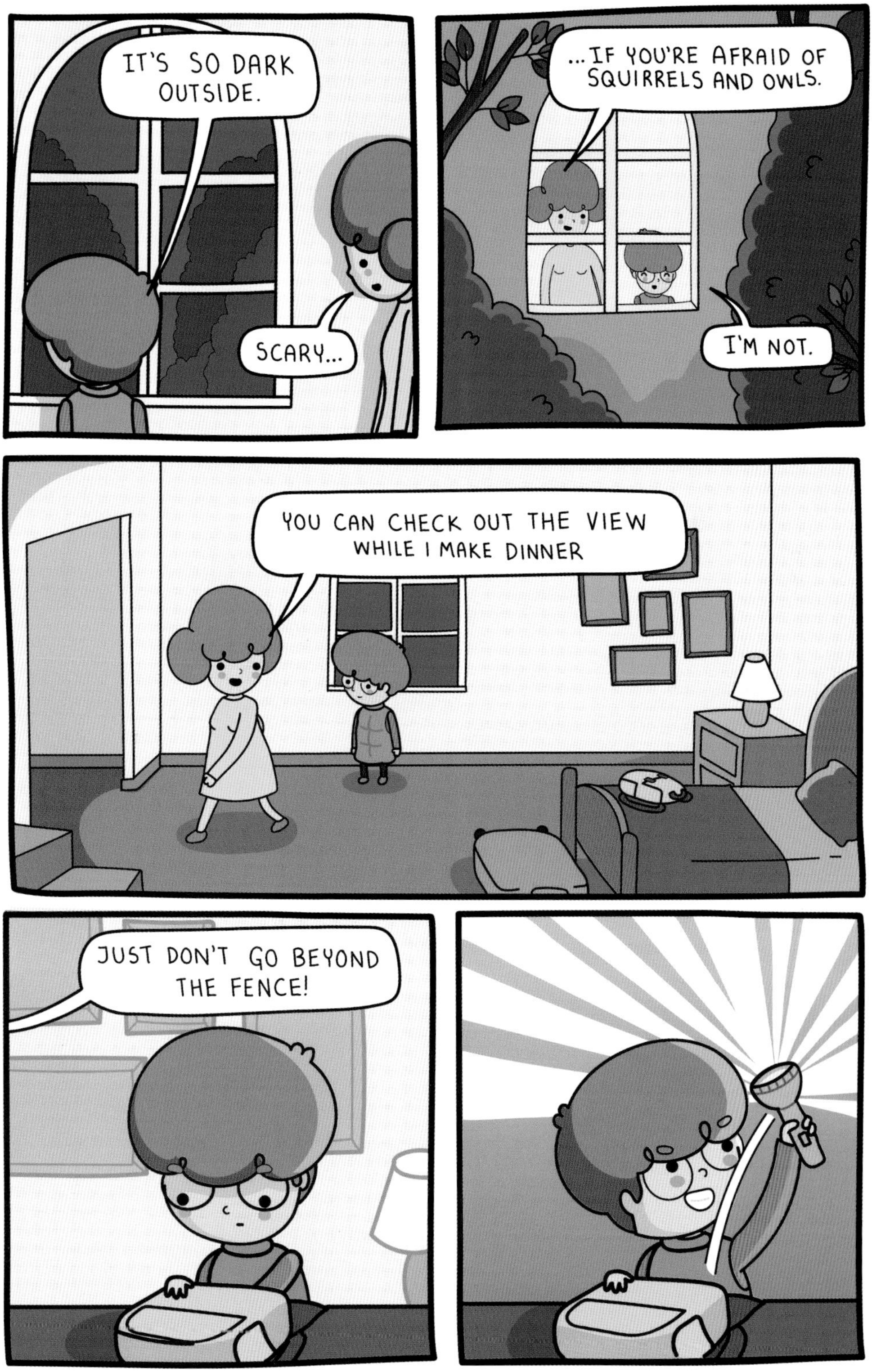
IT'S SO DARK OUTSIDE.
SCARY...
...IF YOU'RE AFRAID OF SQUIRRELS AND OWLS.
I'M NOT.
YOU CAN CHECK OUT THE VIEW WHILE I MAKE DINNER
JUST DON'T GO BEYOND THE FENCE!

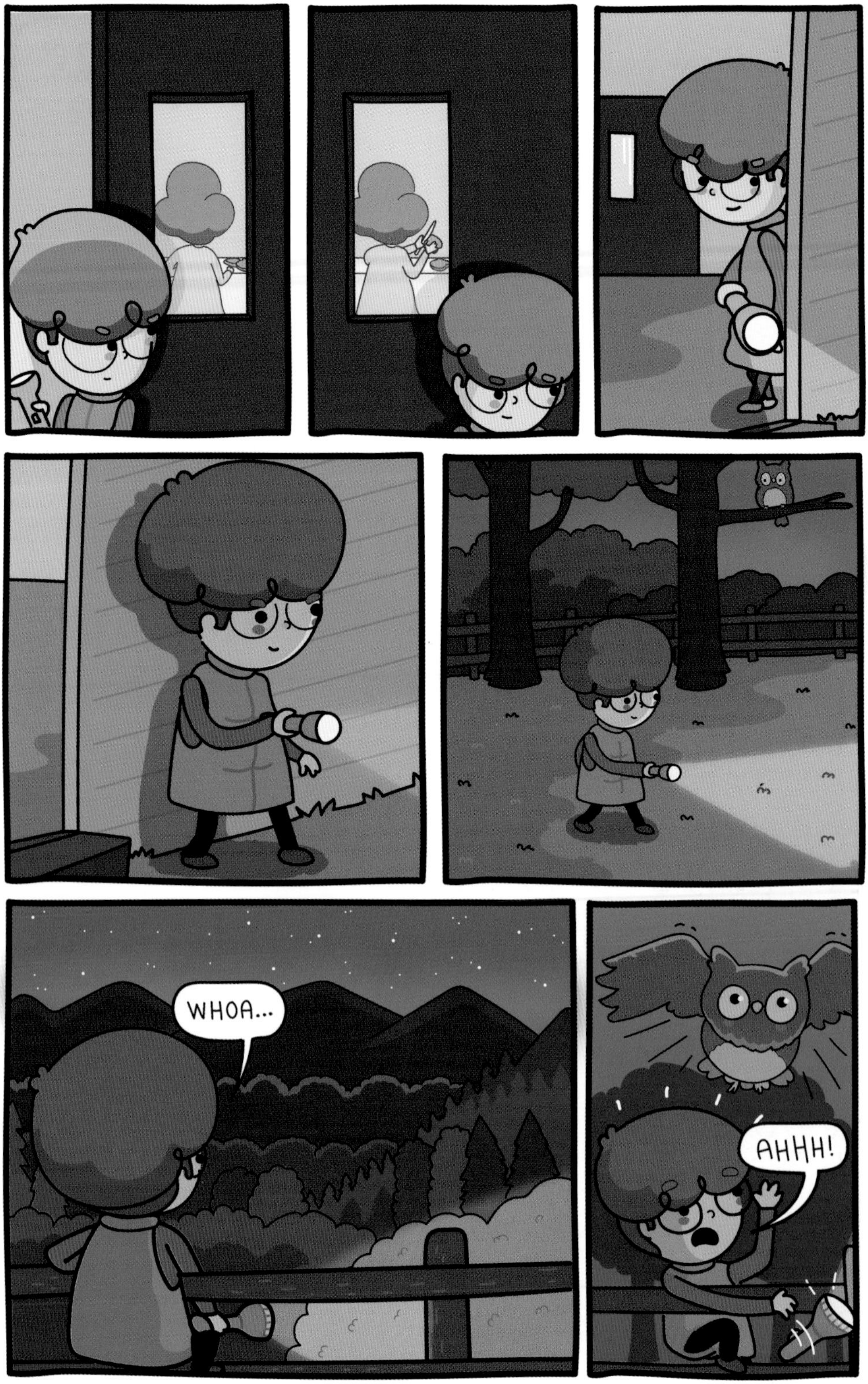
WHOA...
AHHH!

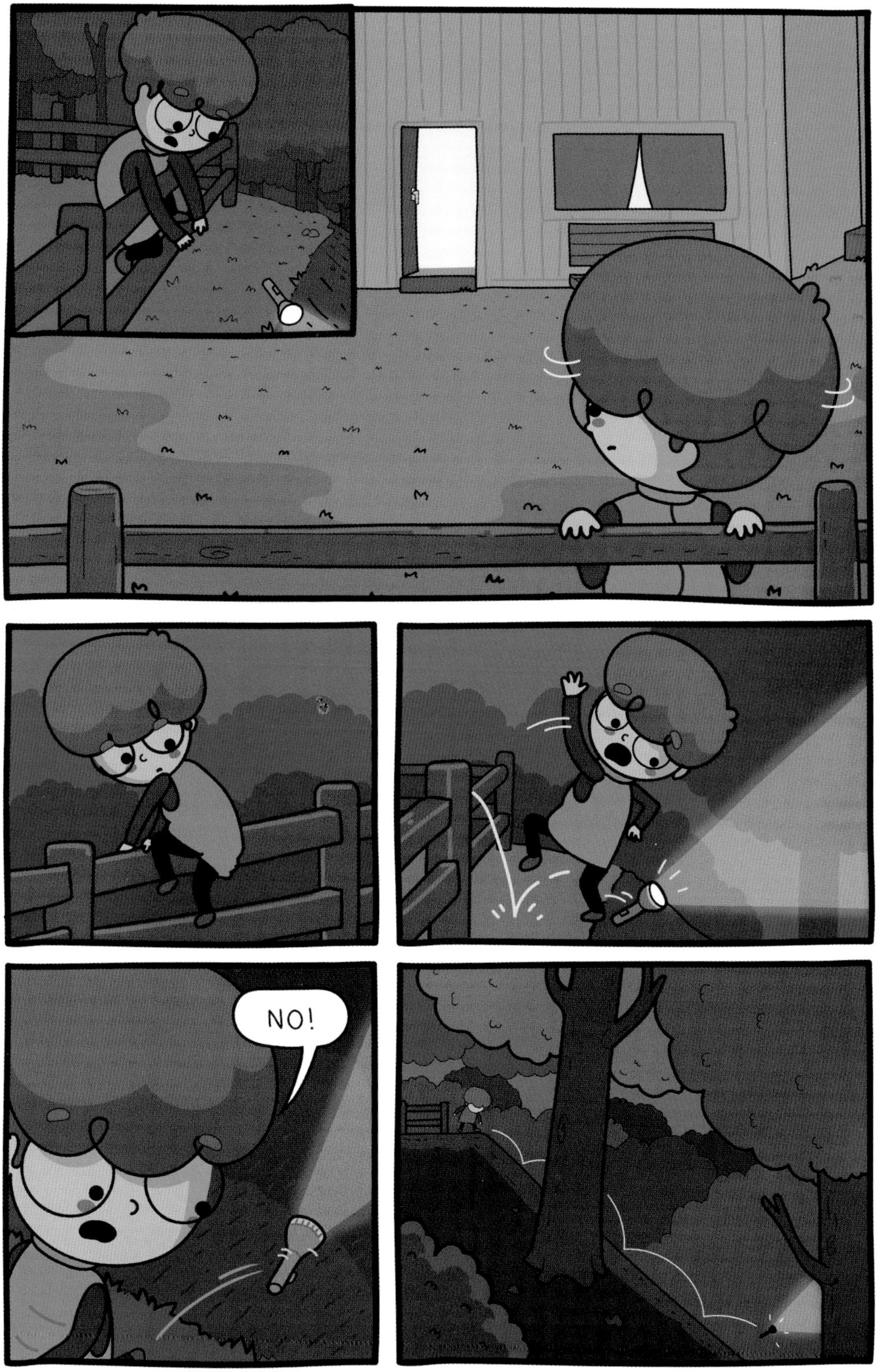
NO!

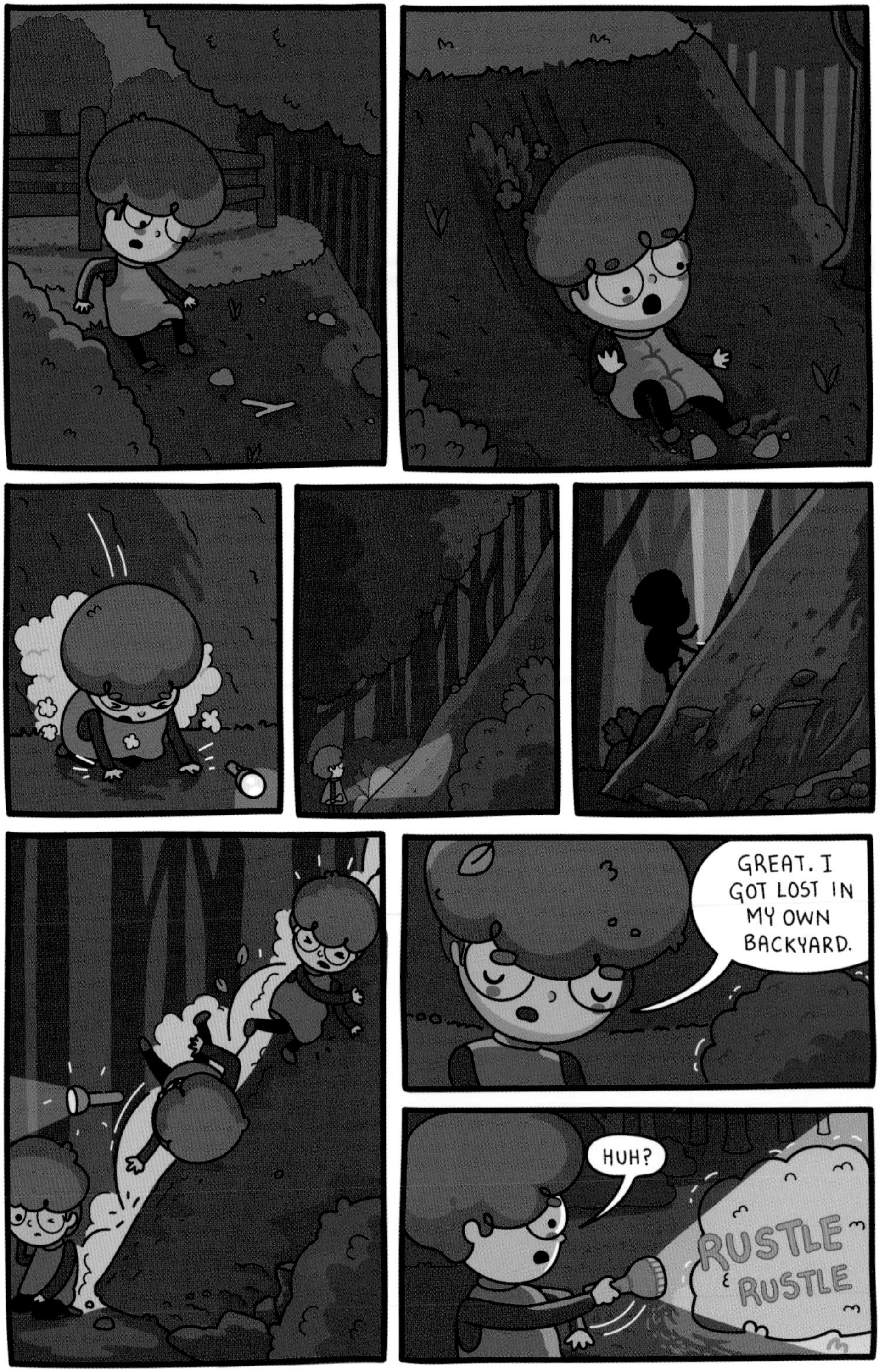
GREAT. I GOT LOST IN MY OWN BACKYARD.
HUH?
RUSTLE RUSTLE

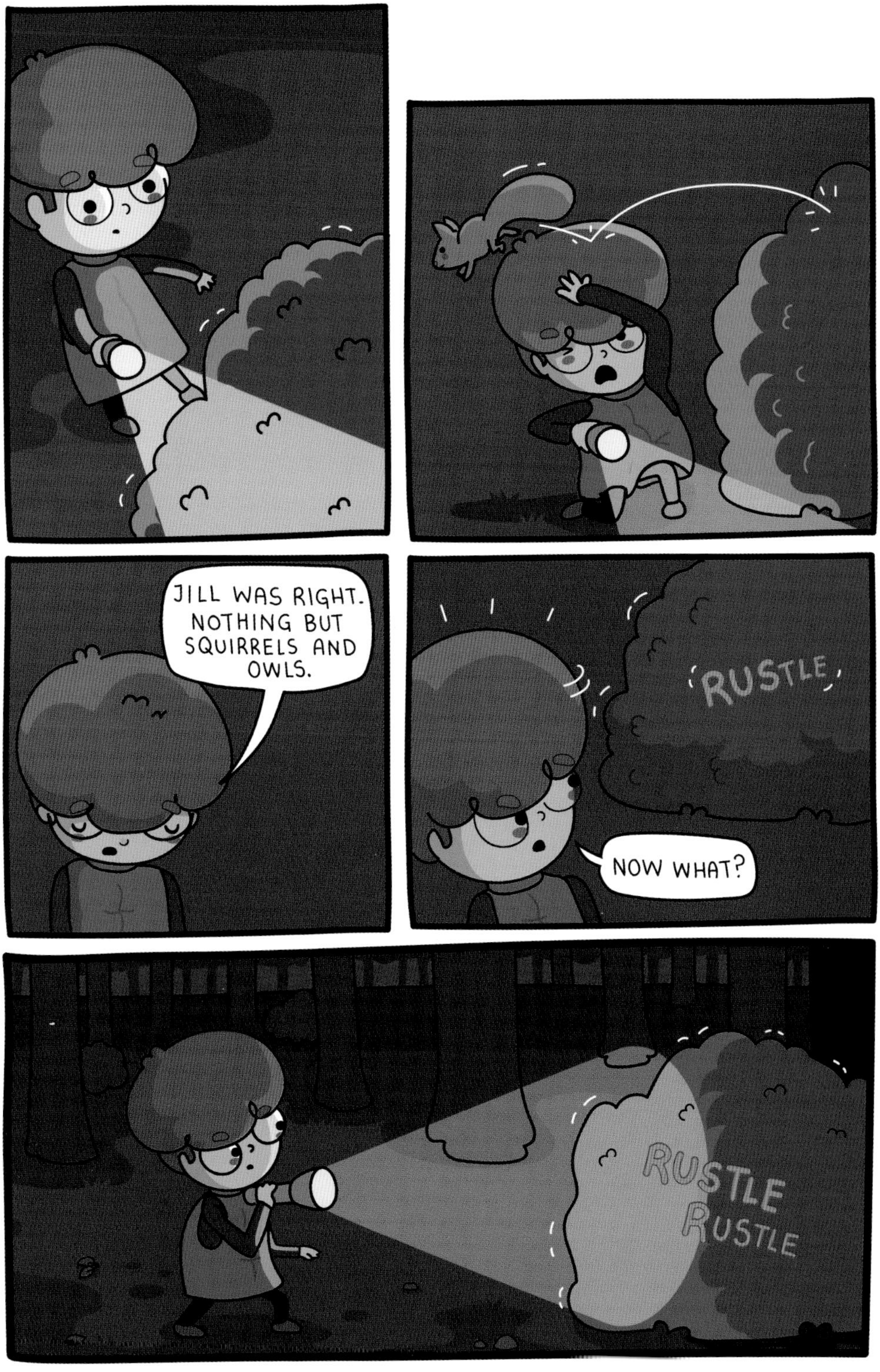
JILL WAS RIGHT. NOTHING BUT SQUIRRELS AND OWLS.
RUSTLE
NOW WHAT?
RUSTLE
RUSTLE

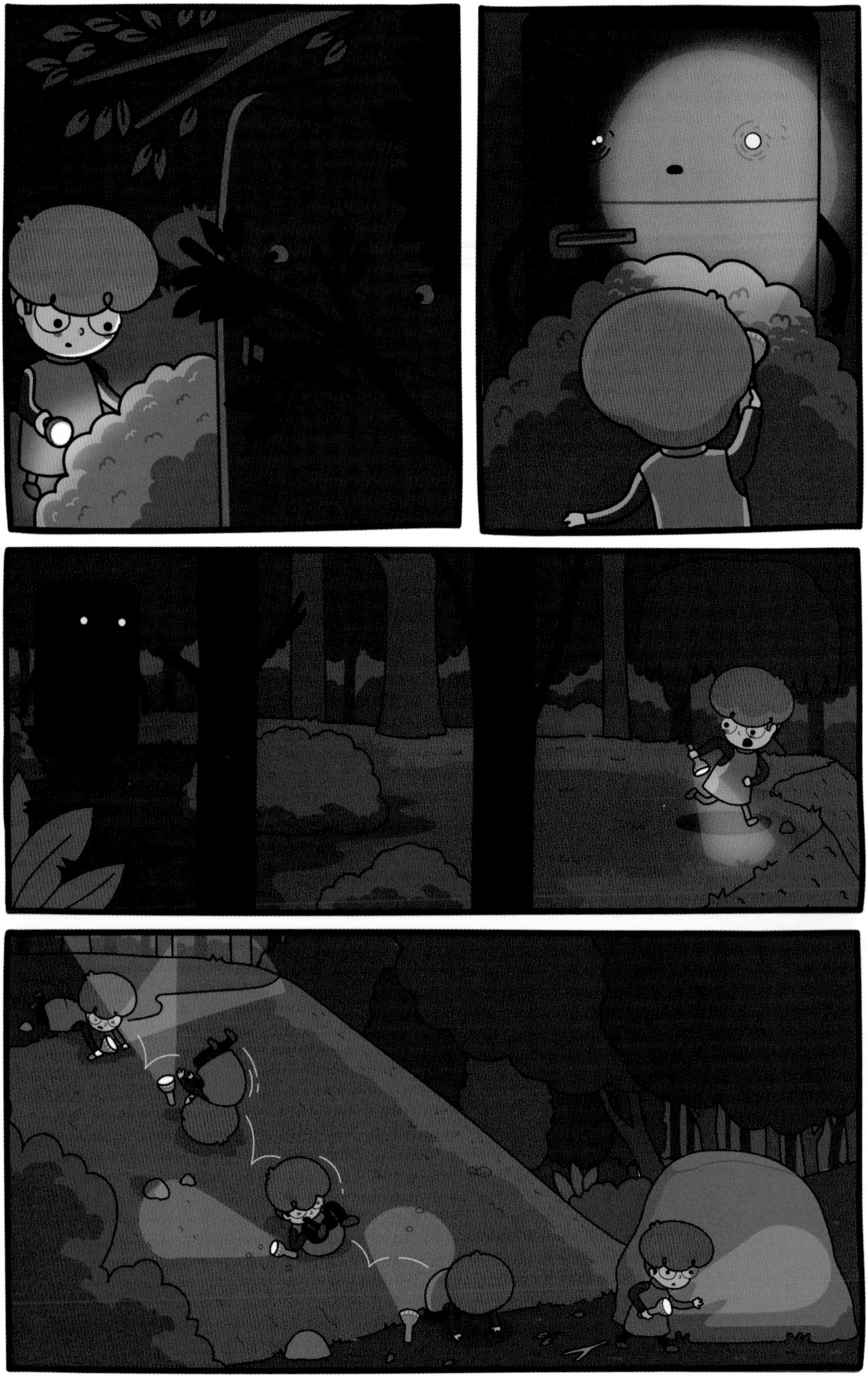

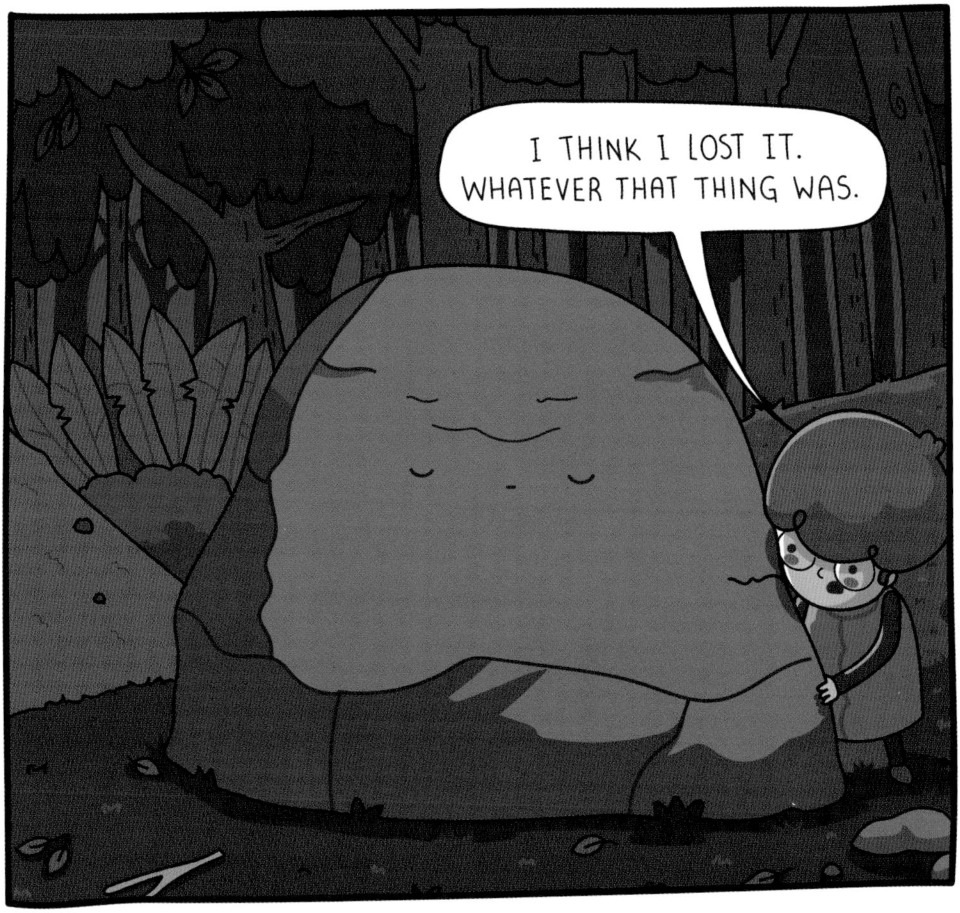
I THINK I LOST IT.
WHATEVER THAT THING WAS.

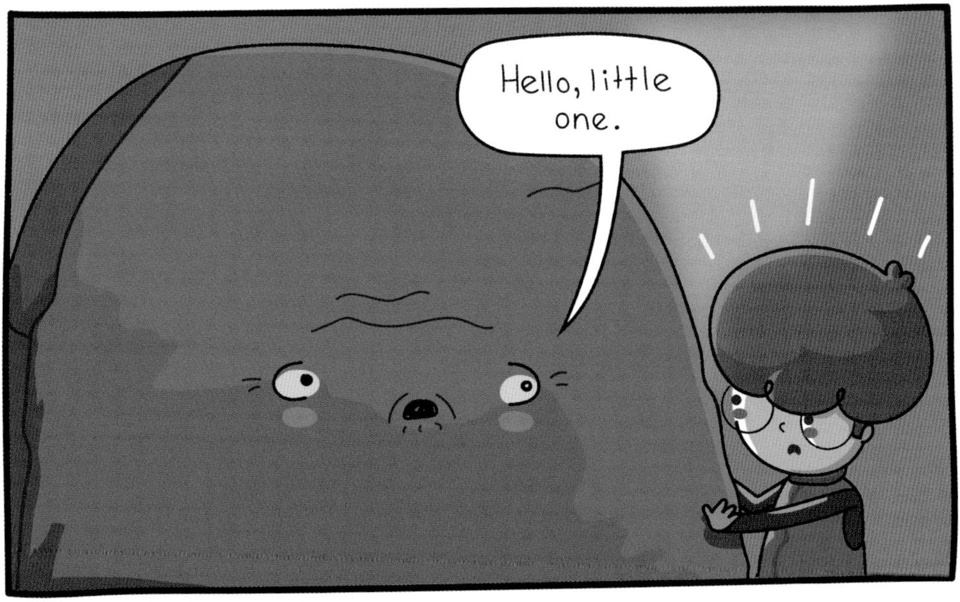
Hello, little one.

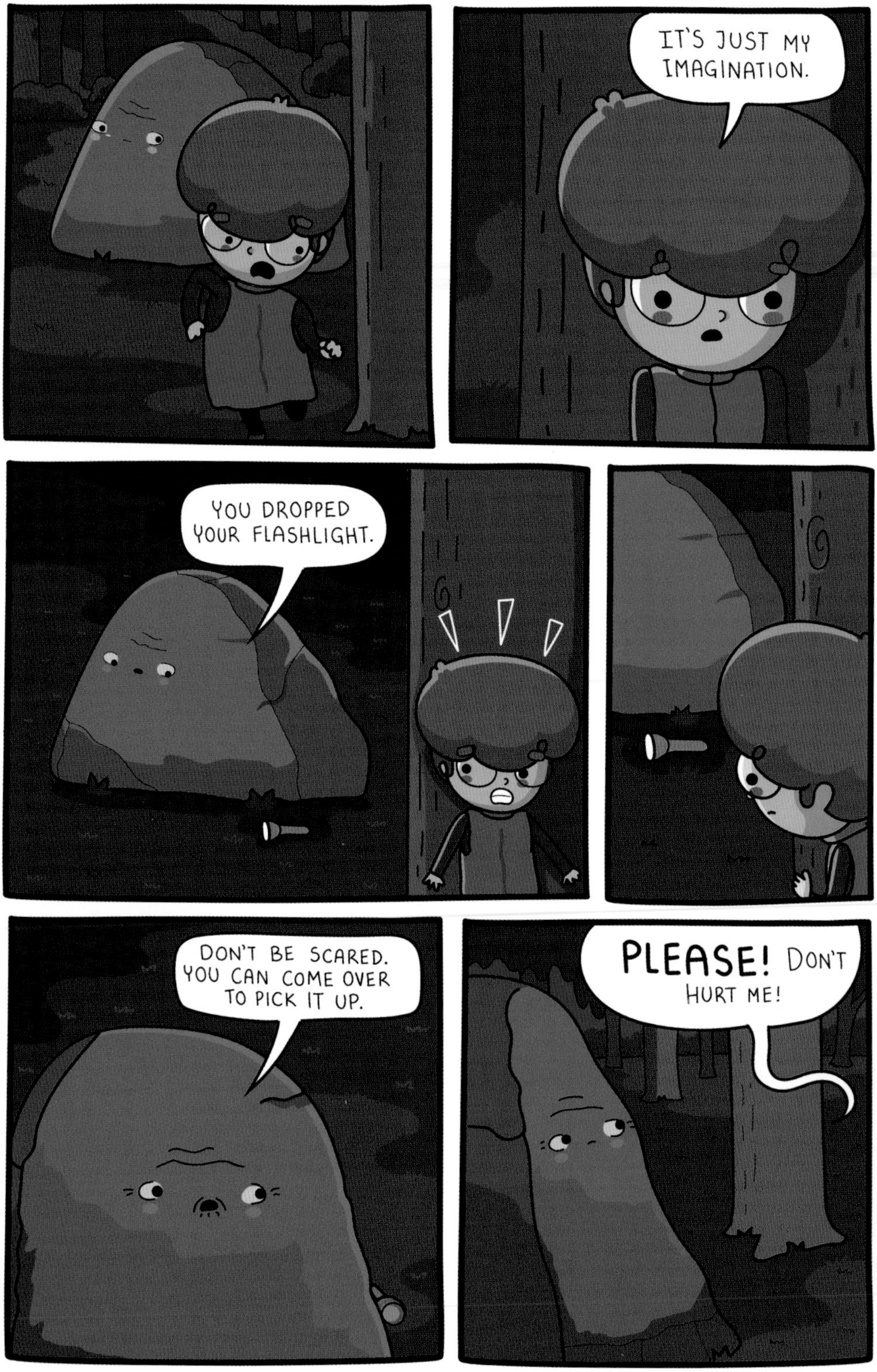
IT'S JUST MY IMAGINATION.
YOU DROPPED YOUR FLASHLIGHT.
DON'T BE SCARED. YOU CAN COME OVER TO PICK IT UP.
PLEASE! DON'T HURT ME!

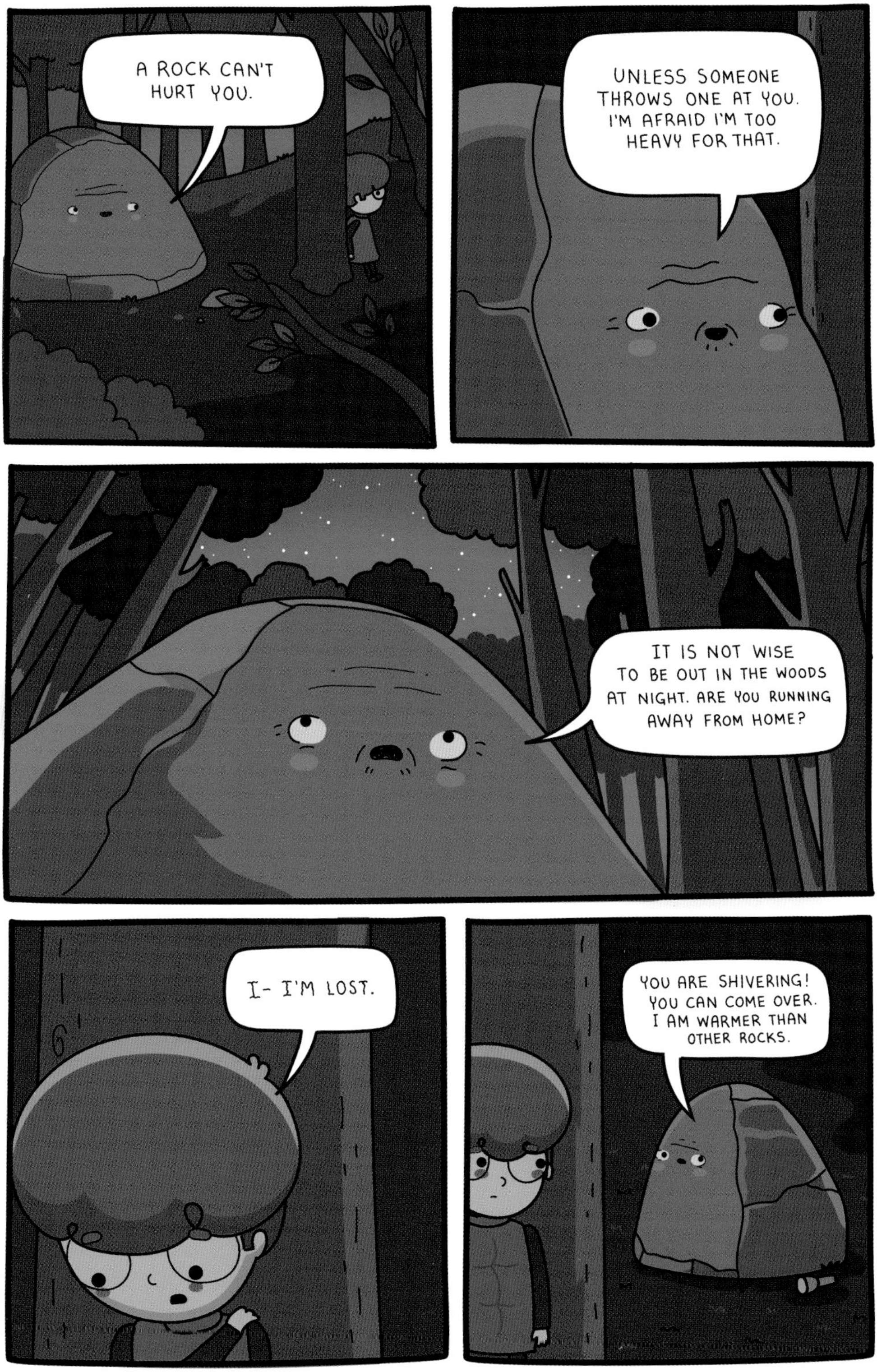
A ROCK CAN'T HURT YOU.
UNLESS SOMEONE THROWS ONE AT YOU. I'M AFRAID I'M TOO HEAVY FOR THAT.
IT IS NOT WISE TO BE OUT IN THE WOODS AT NIGHT. ARE YOU RUNNING AWAY FROM HOME?
I- I'M LOST.
YOU ARE SHIVERING! YOU CAN COME OVER. I AM WARMER THAN OTHER ROCKS.

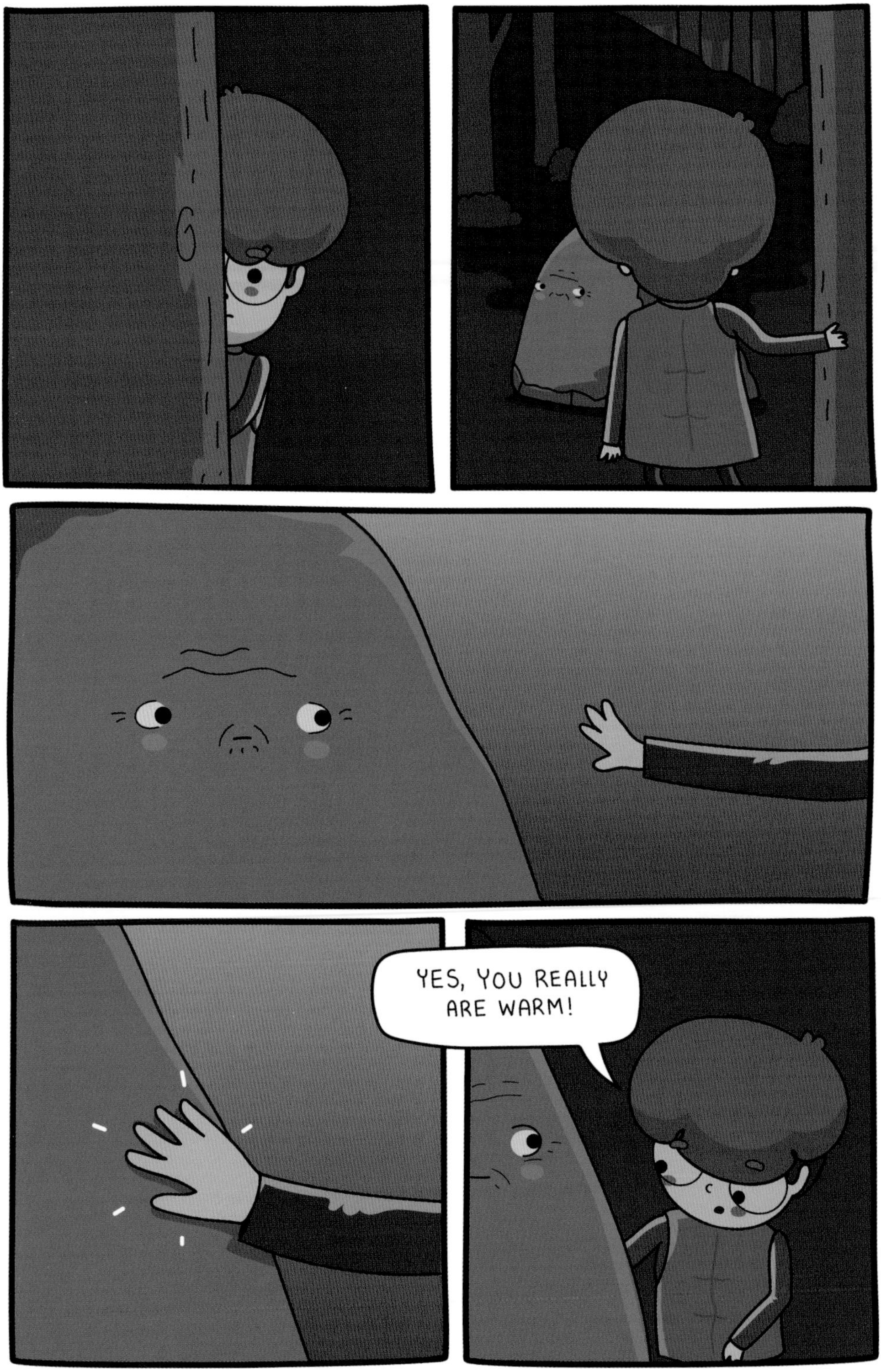
YES, YOU REALLY ARE WARM!

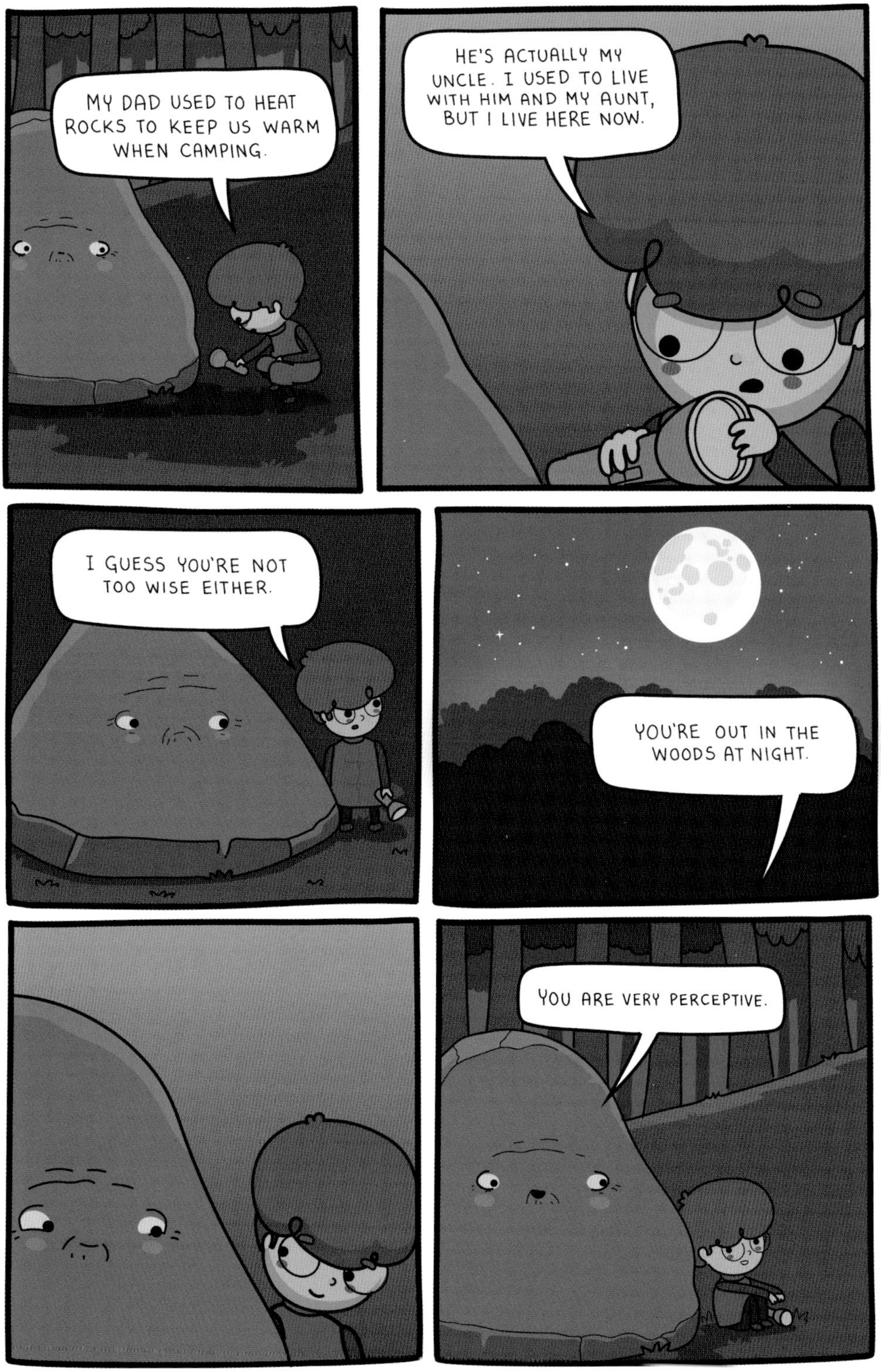
MY DAD USED TO HEAT ROCKS TO KEEP US WARM WHEN CAMPING.
HE'S ACTUALLY MY UNCLE. I USED TO LIVE WITH HIM AND MY AUNT, BUT I LIVE HERE NOW.
I GUESS YOU'RE NOT TOO WISE EITHER.
YOU'RE OUT IN THE WOODS AT NIGHT.
YOU ARE VERY PERCEPTIVE.

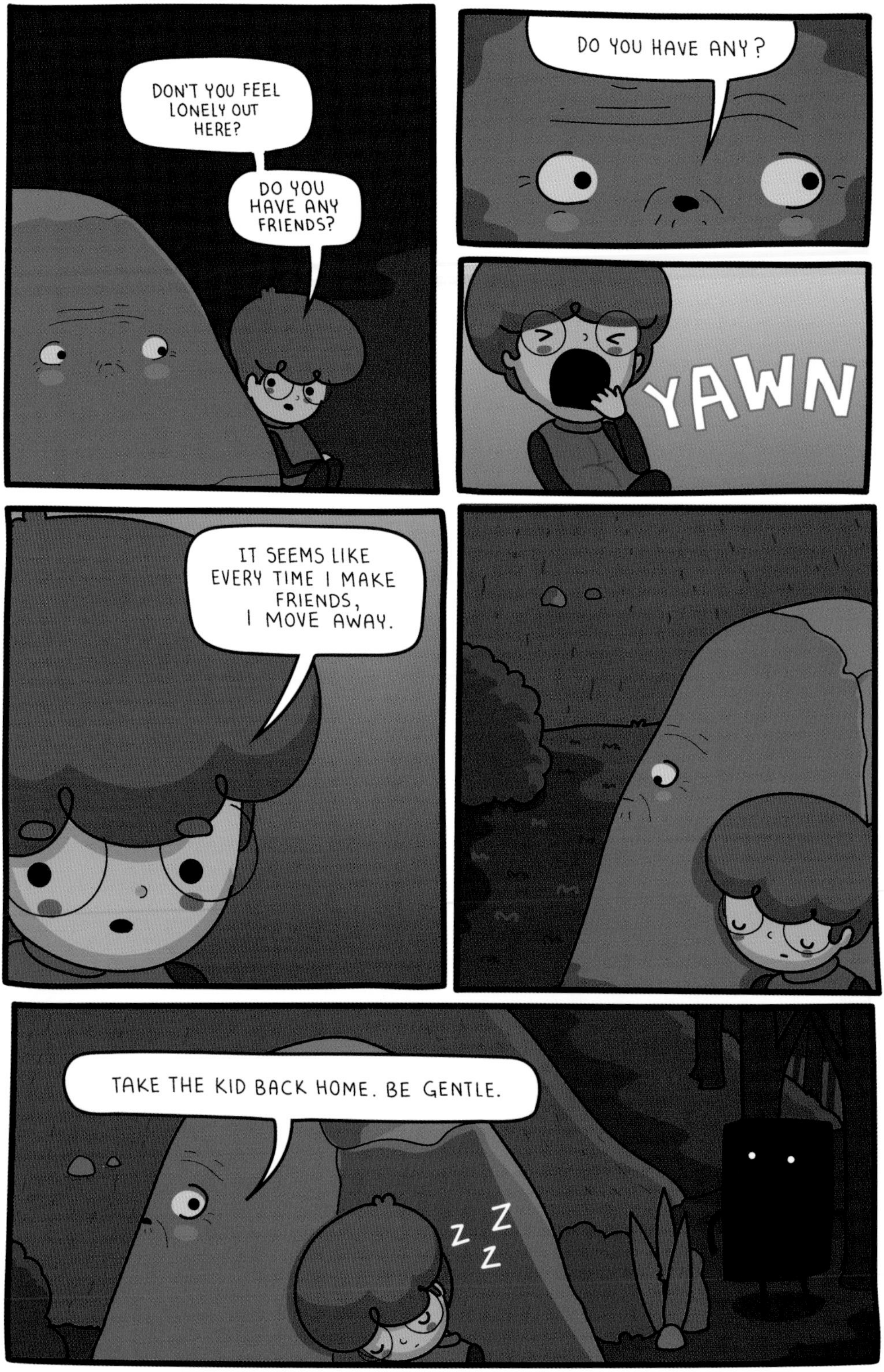

DON'T YOU FEEL LONELY OUT HERE?
DO YOU HAVE ANY FRIENDS?
DO YOU HAVE ANY?
YAWN
IT SEEMS LIKE EVERY TIME I MAKE FRIENDS, I MOVE AWAY.
TAKE THE KID BACK HOME. BE GENTLE.
Z Z Z

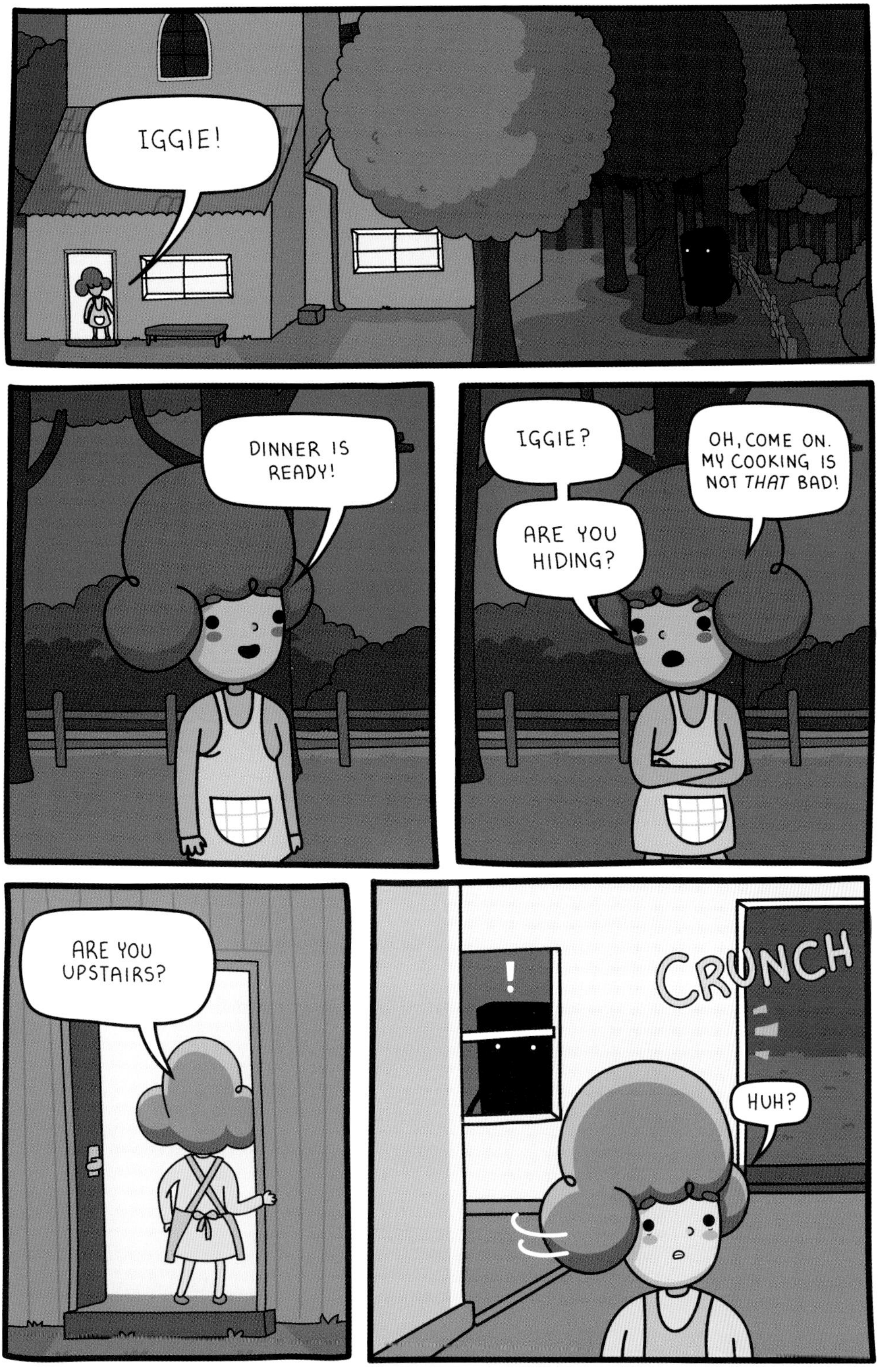
IGGIE!
DINNER IS READY!
IGGIE?
ARE YOU HIDING?
OH, COME ON. MY COOKING IS NOT *THAT* BAD!
ARE YOU UPSTAIRS?
!
CRUNCH
HUH?

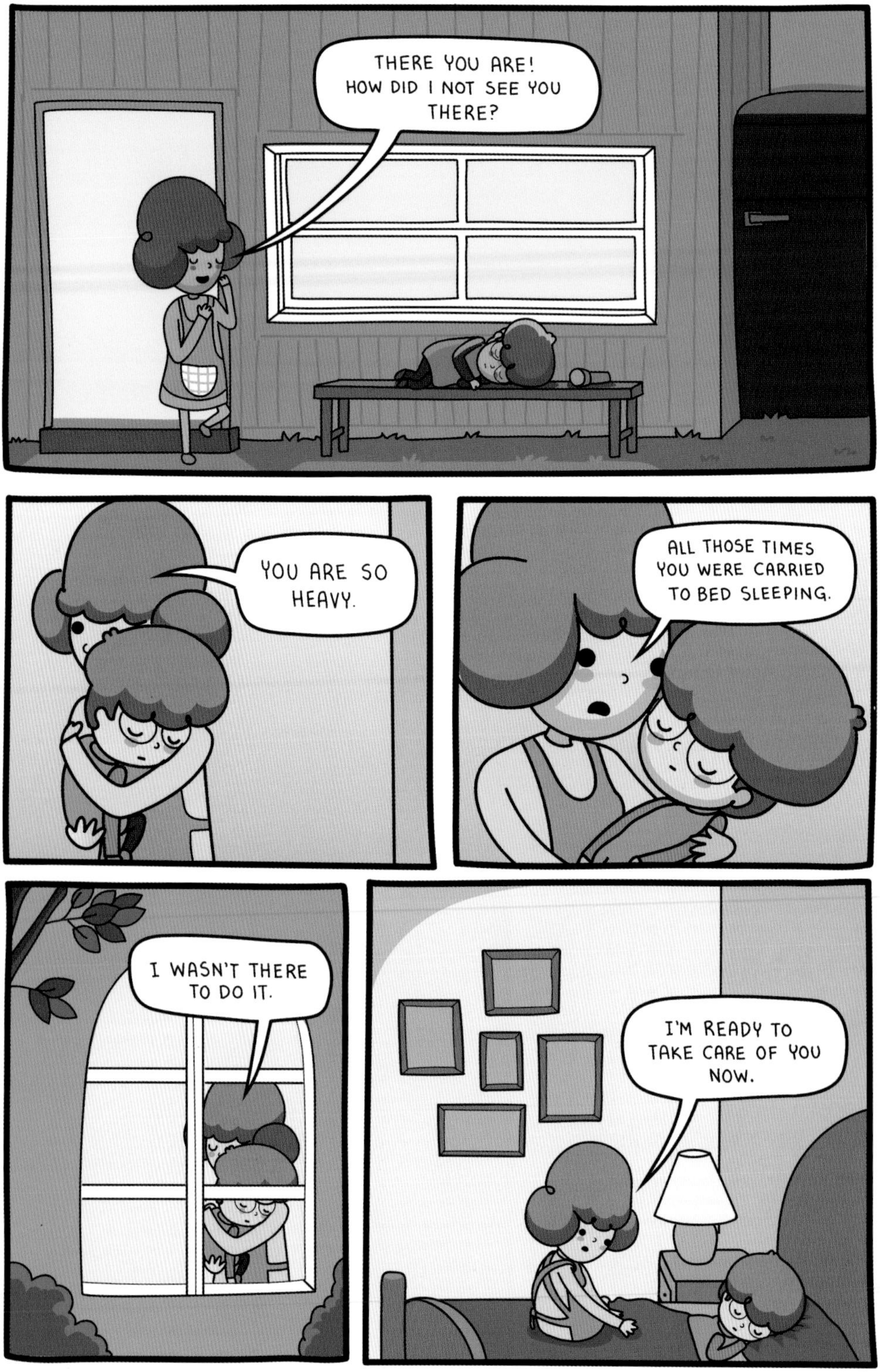
THERE YOU ARE! HOW DID I NOT SEE YOU THERE?
YOU ARE SO HEAVY.
ALL THOSE TIMES YOU WERE CARRIED TO BED SLEEPING.
I WASN'T THERE TO DO IT.
I'M READY TO TAKE CARE OF YOU NOW.

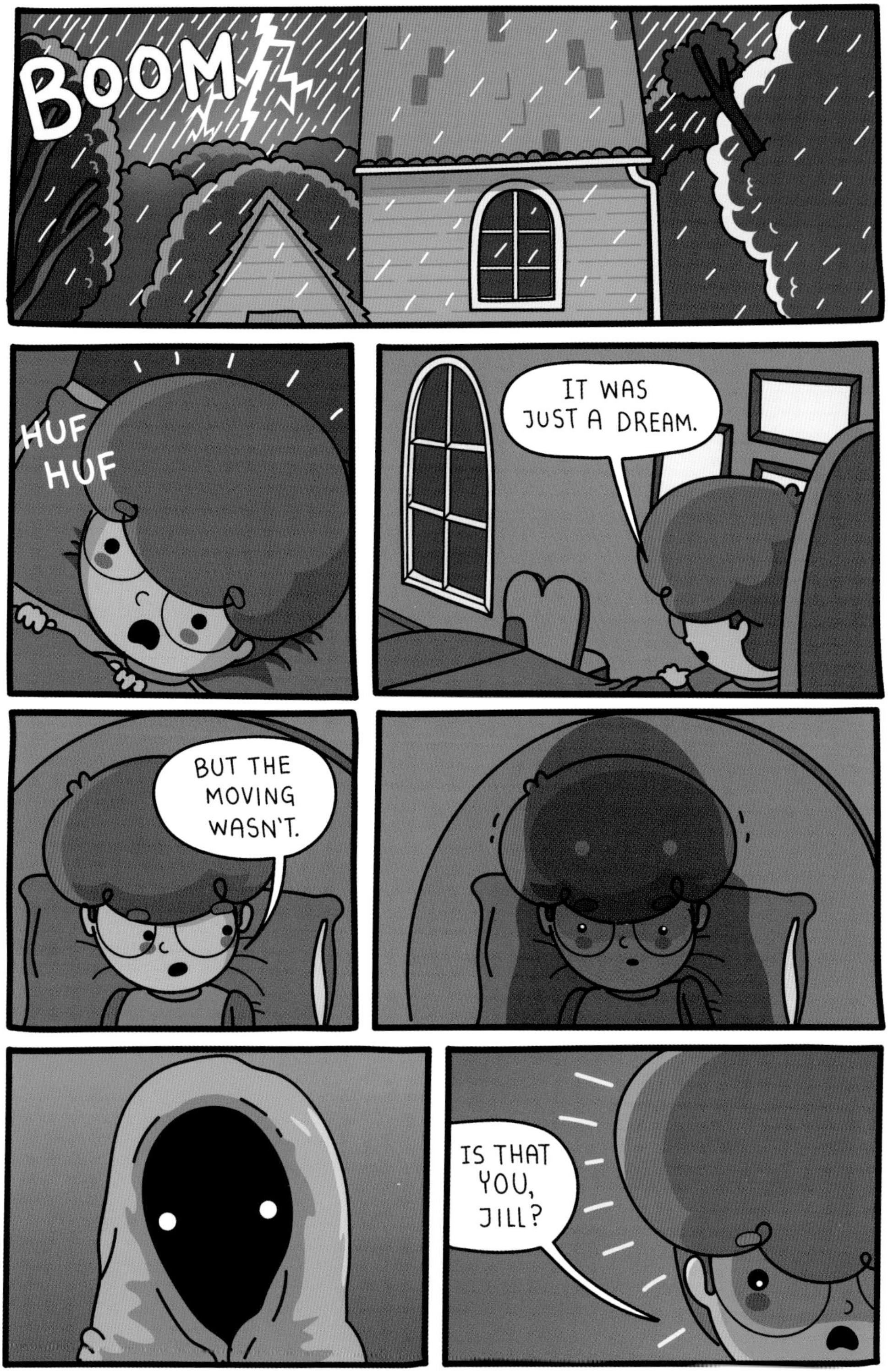
BOOM
HUF HUF
IT WAS JUST A DREAM.
BUT THE MOVING WASN'T.
IS THAT YOU, JILL?

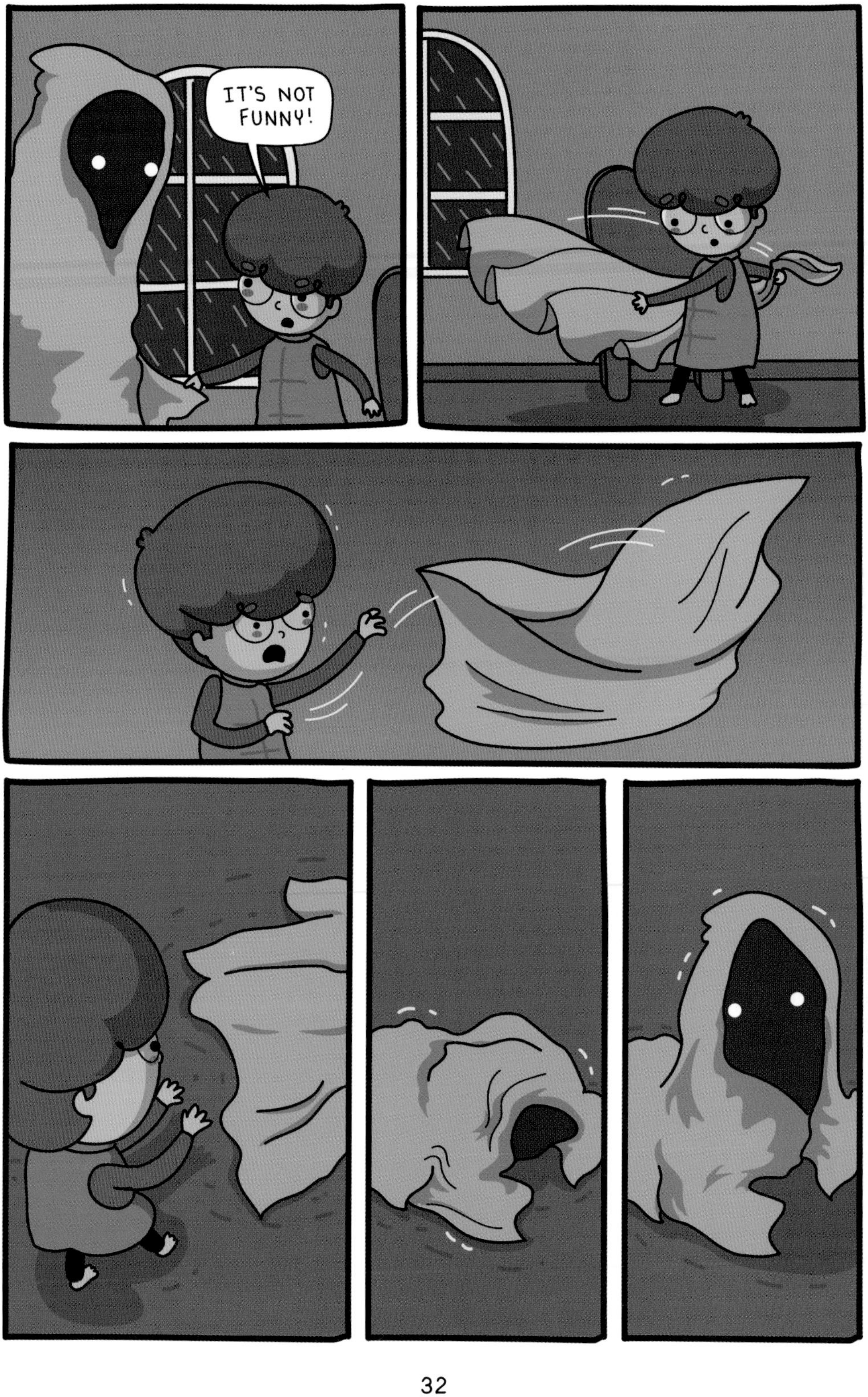
IT'S NOT FUNNY!

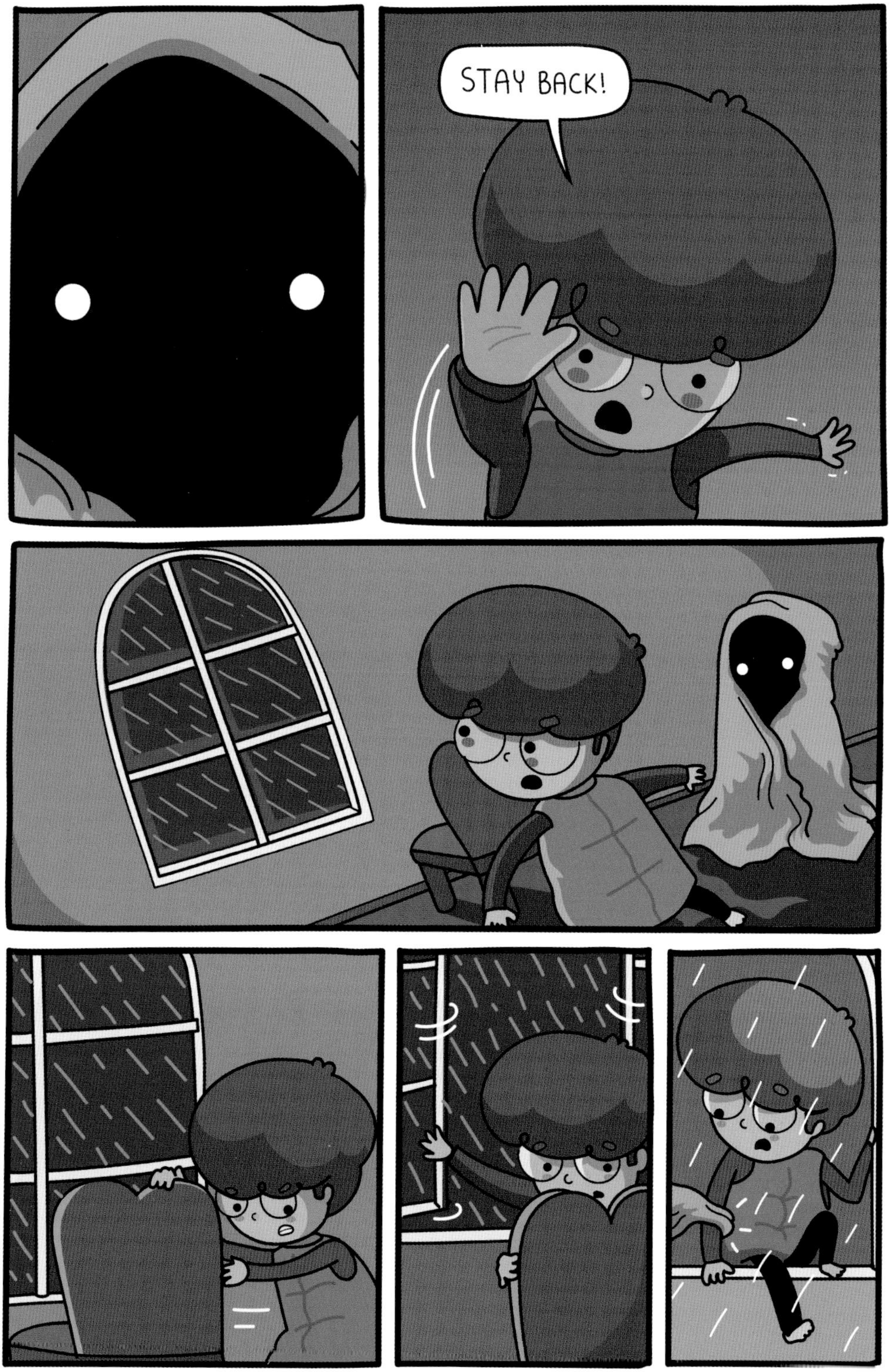
STAY BACK!

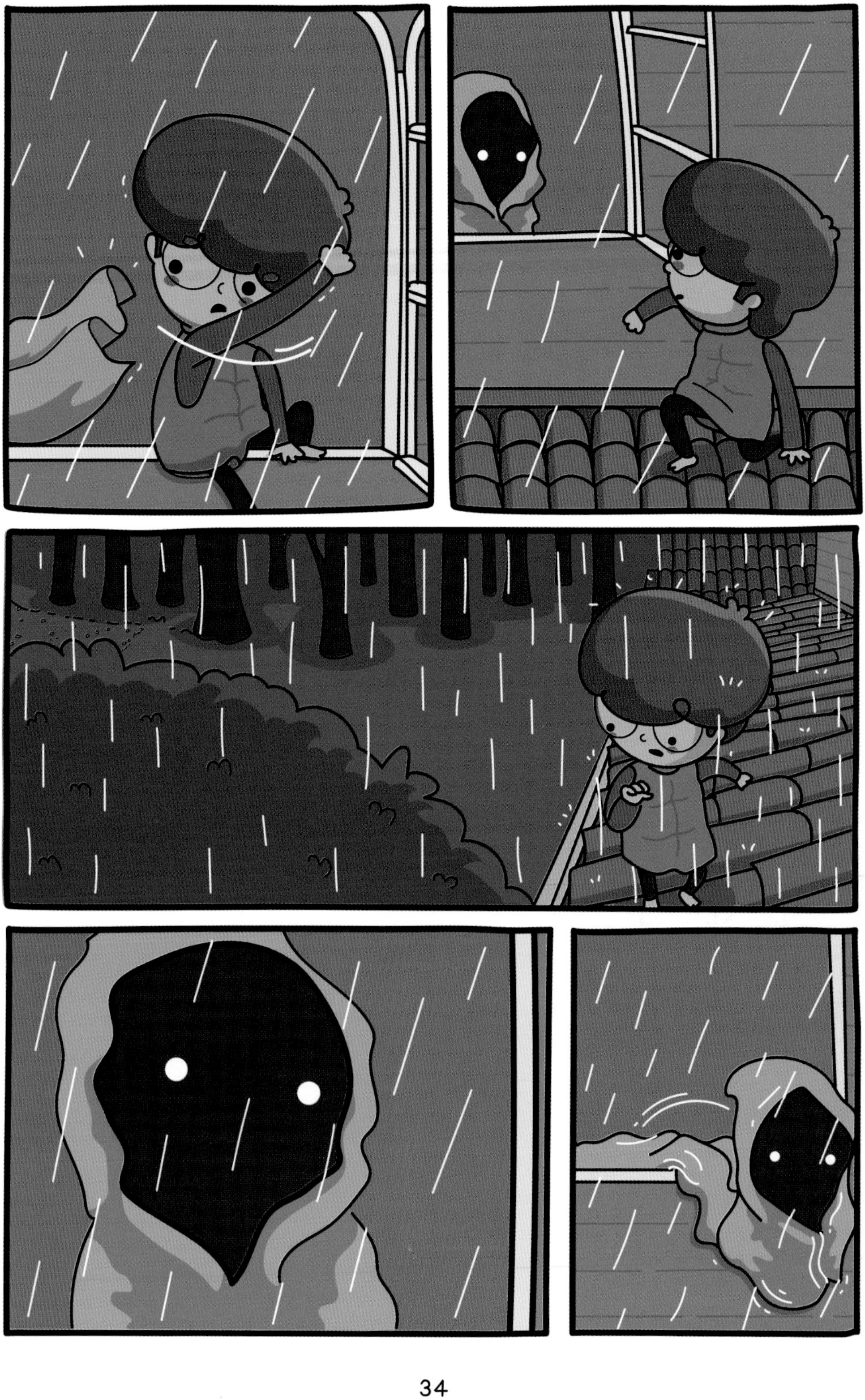

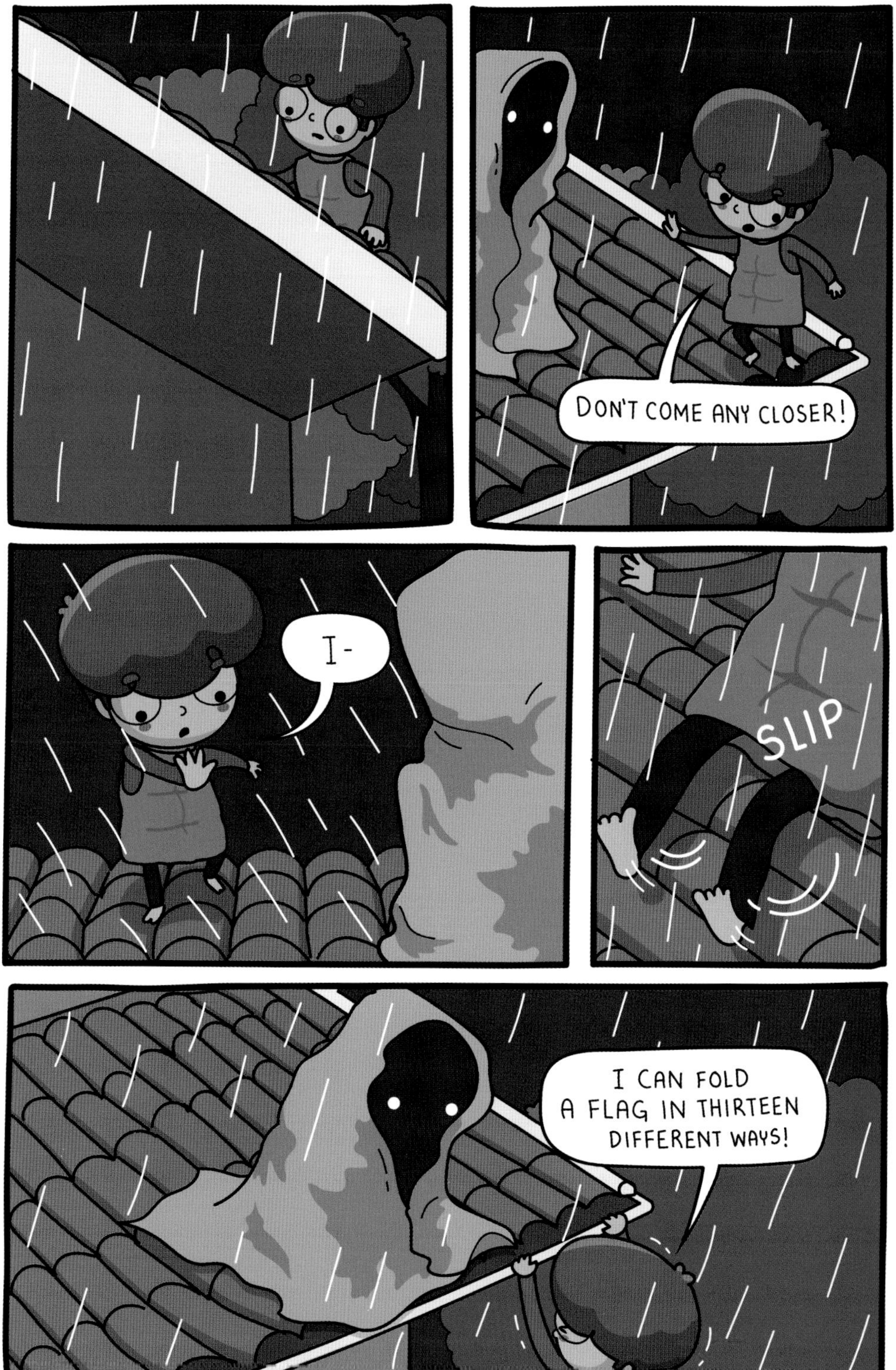
DON'T COME ANY CLOSER!
I-
SLIP
I CAN FOLD A FLAG IN THIRTEEN DIFFERENT WAYS!

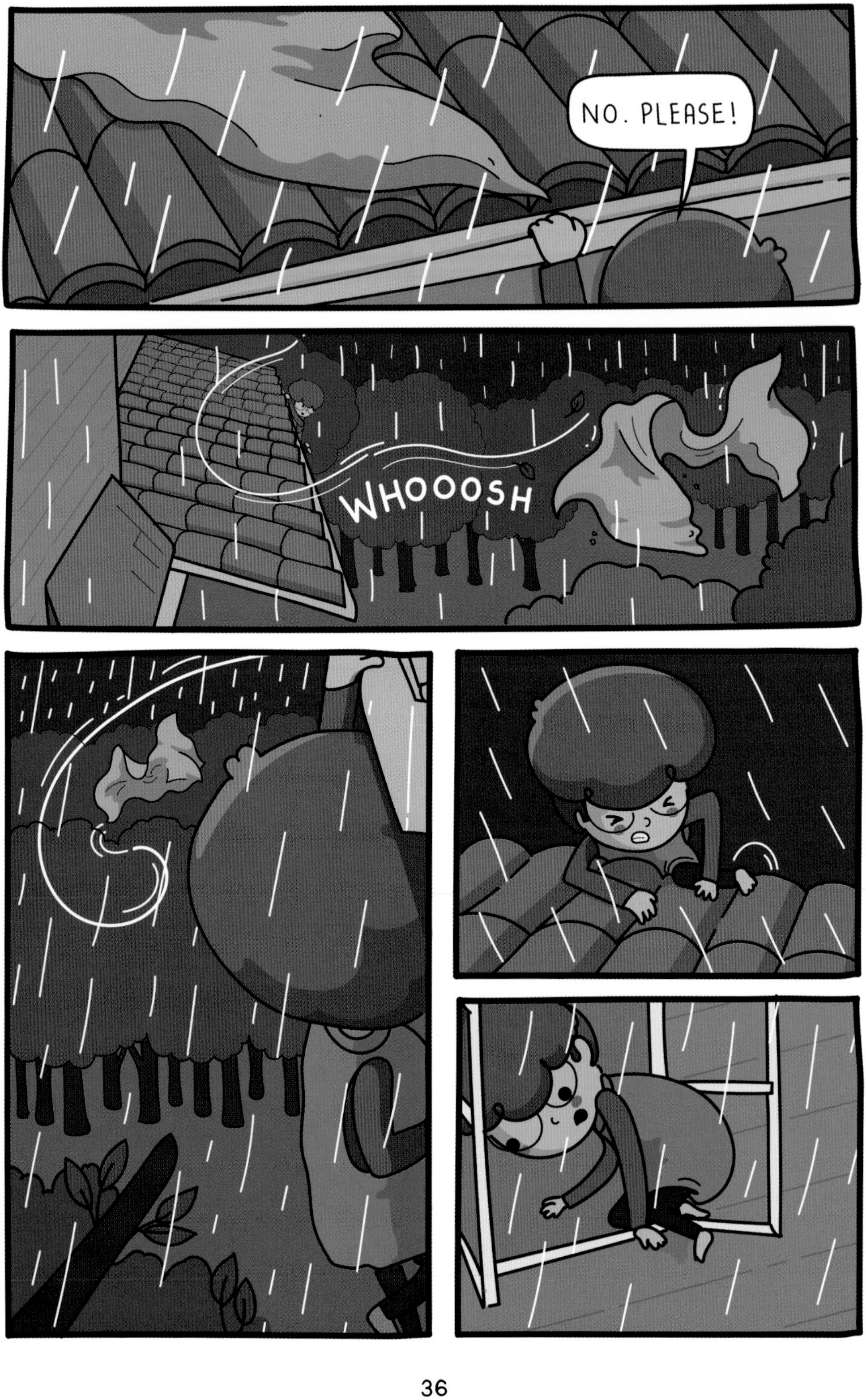
NO. PLEASE!
WHOOOSH

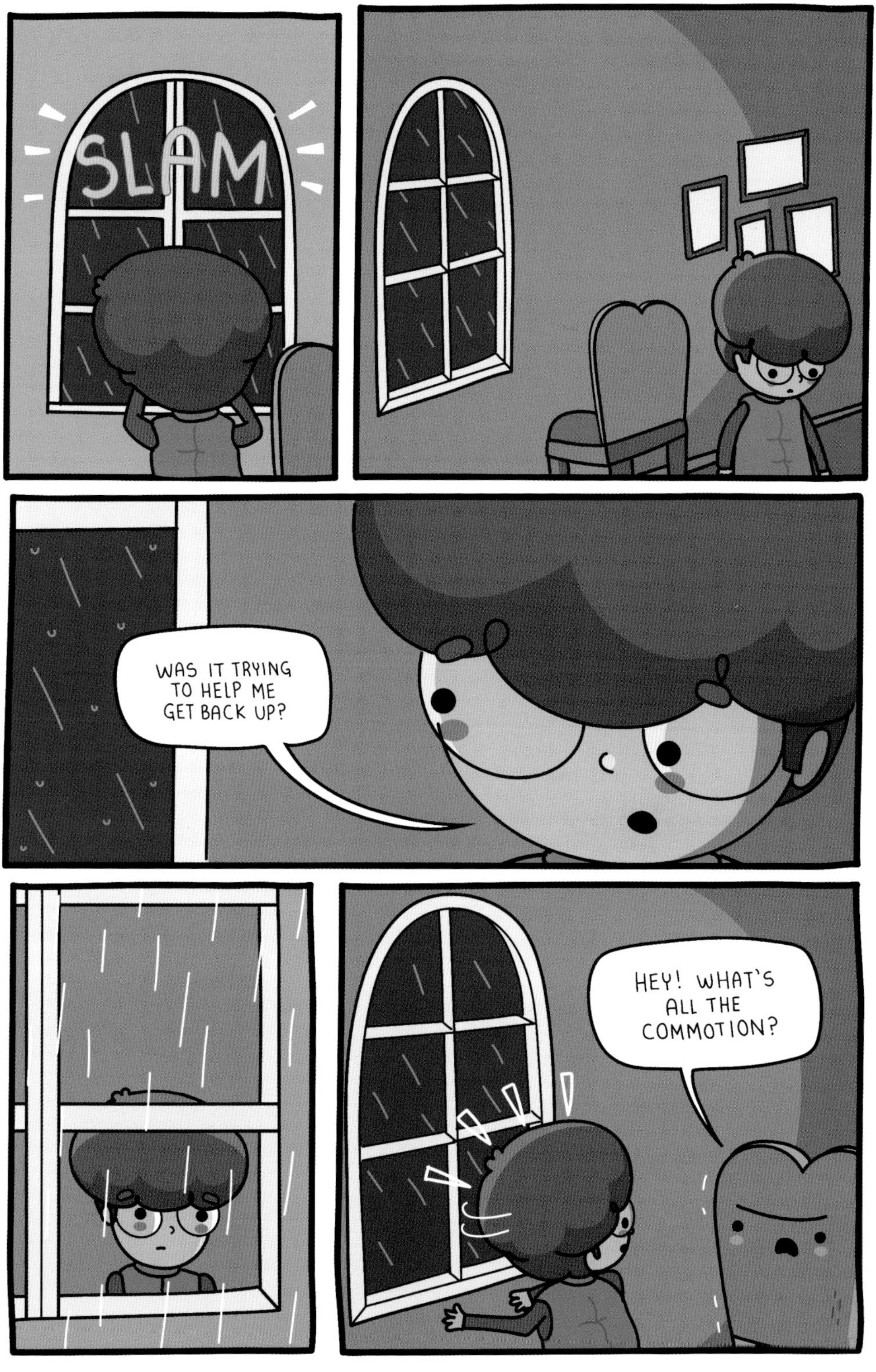
SLAM
WAS IT TRYING TO HELP ME GET BACK UP?
HEY! WHAT'S ALL THE COMMOTION?

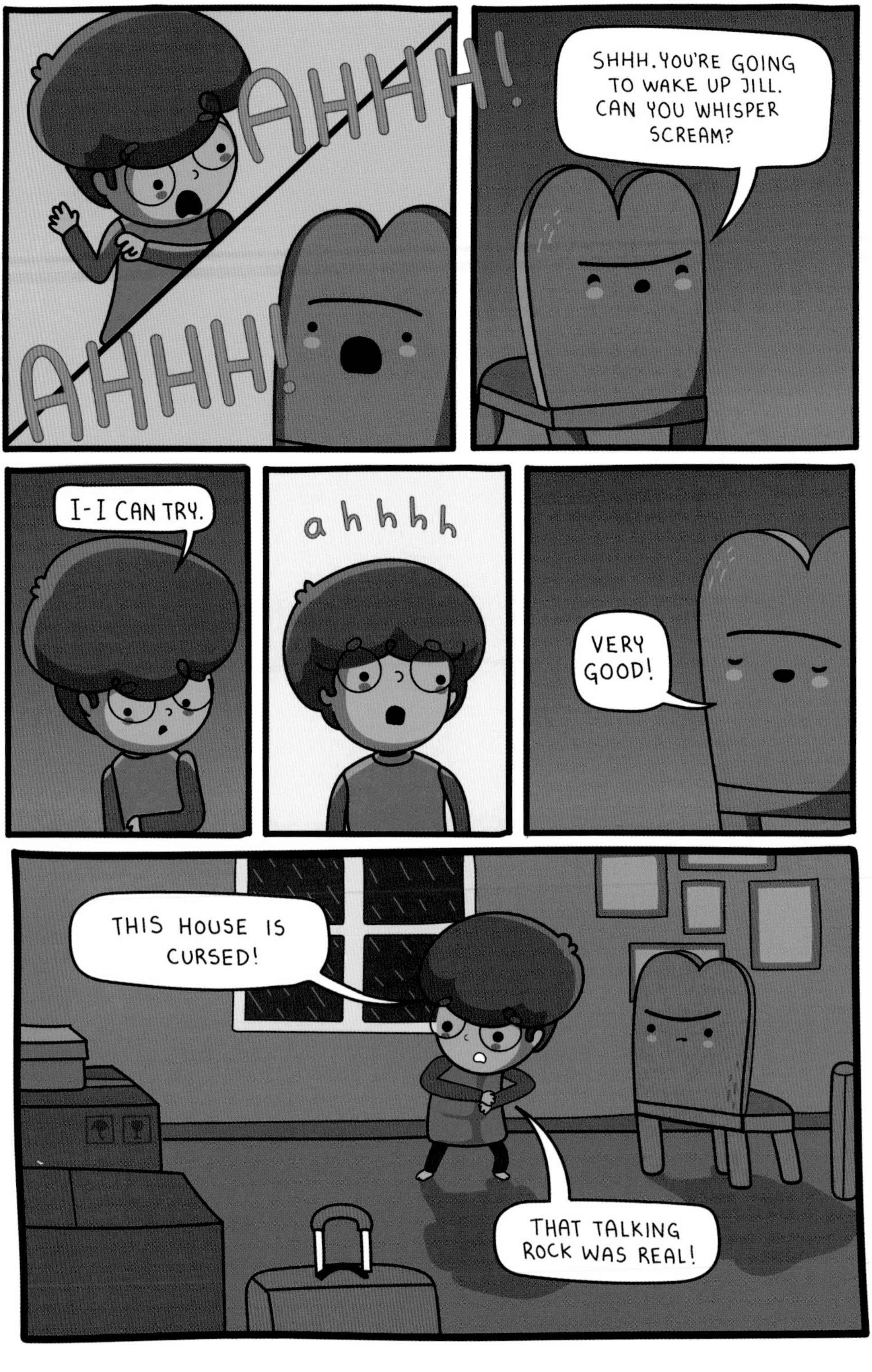
AHHHH!
AHHHH!
SHHH. YOU'RE GOING TO WAKE UP JILL. CAN YOU WHISPER SCREAM?
I-I CAN TRY.
a h h h h
VERY GOOD!
THIS HOUSE IS CURSED!
THAT TALKING ROCK WAS REAL!

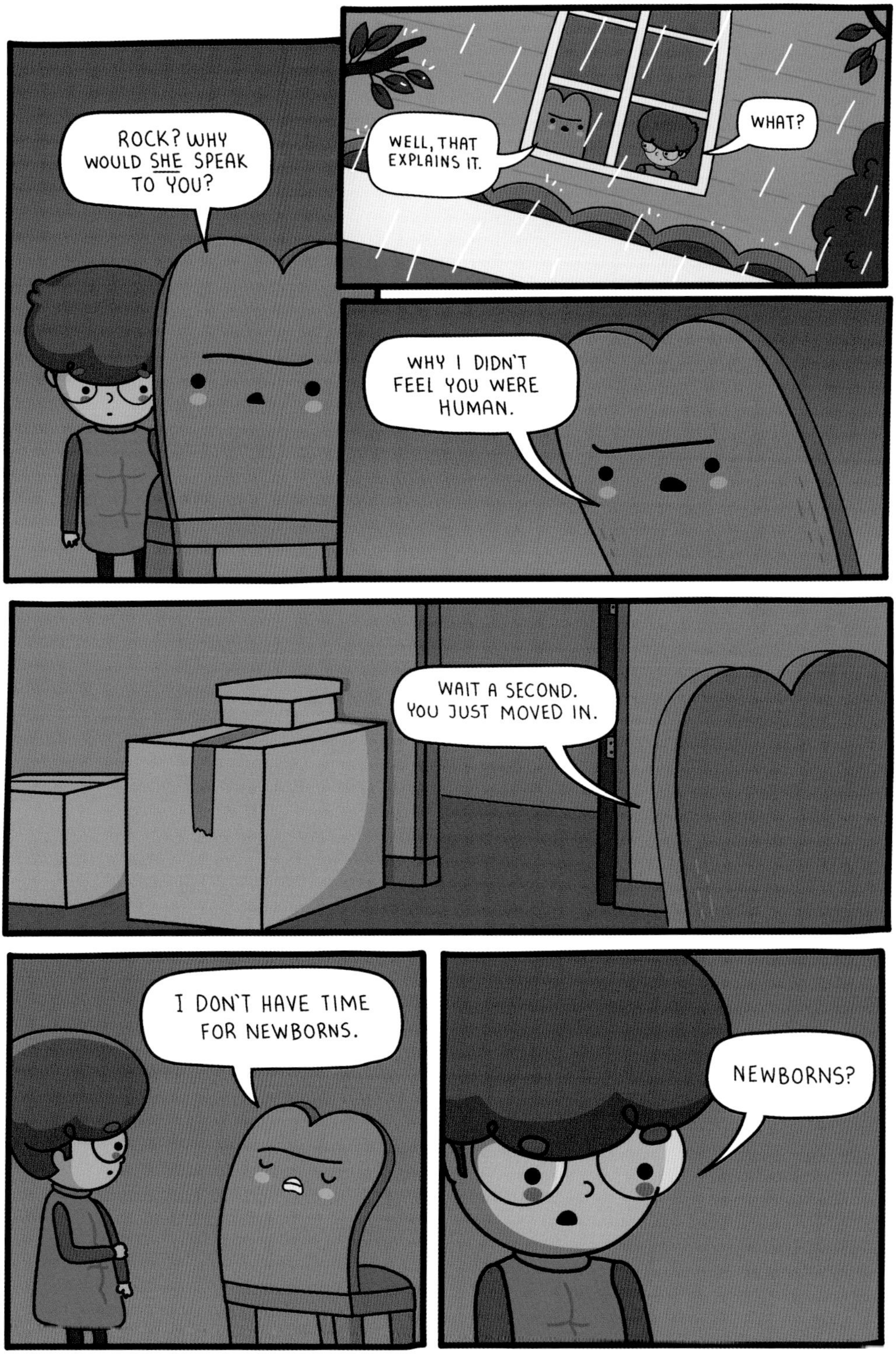
ROCK? WHY WOULD SHE SPEAK TO YOU?
WELL, THAT EXPLAINS IT.
WHAT?
WHY I DIDN'T FEEL YOU WERE HUMAN.
WAIT A SECOND. YOU JUST MOVED IN.
I DON'T HAVE TIME FOR NEWBORNS.
NEWBORNS?

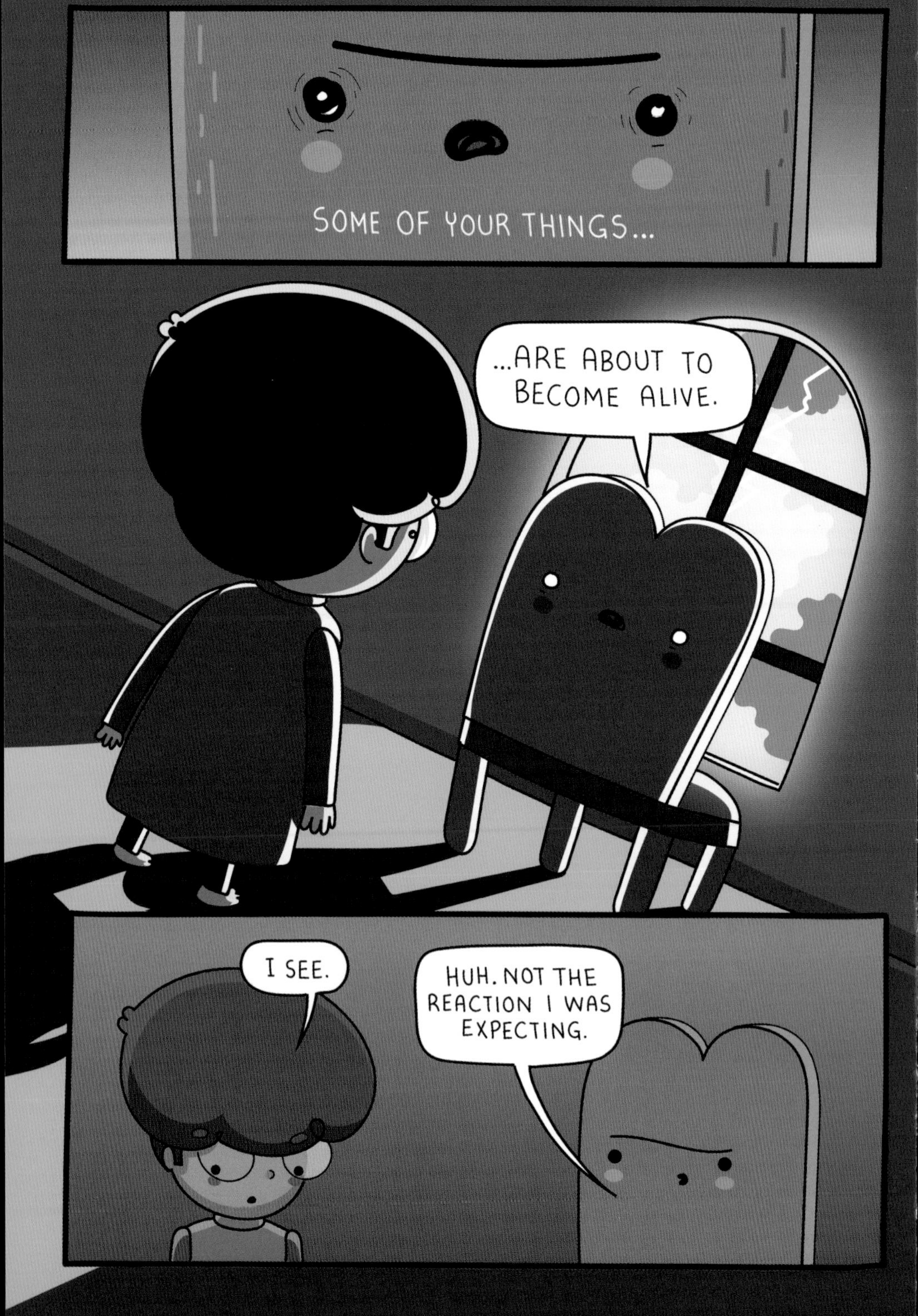
SOME OF YOUR THINGS...
...ARE ABOUT TO BECOME ALIVE.
I SEE.
HUH. NOT THE REACTION I WAS EXPECTING.

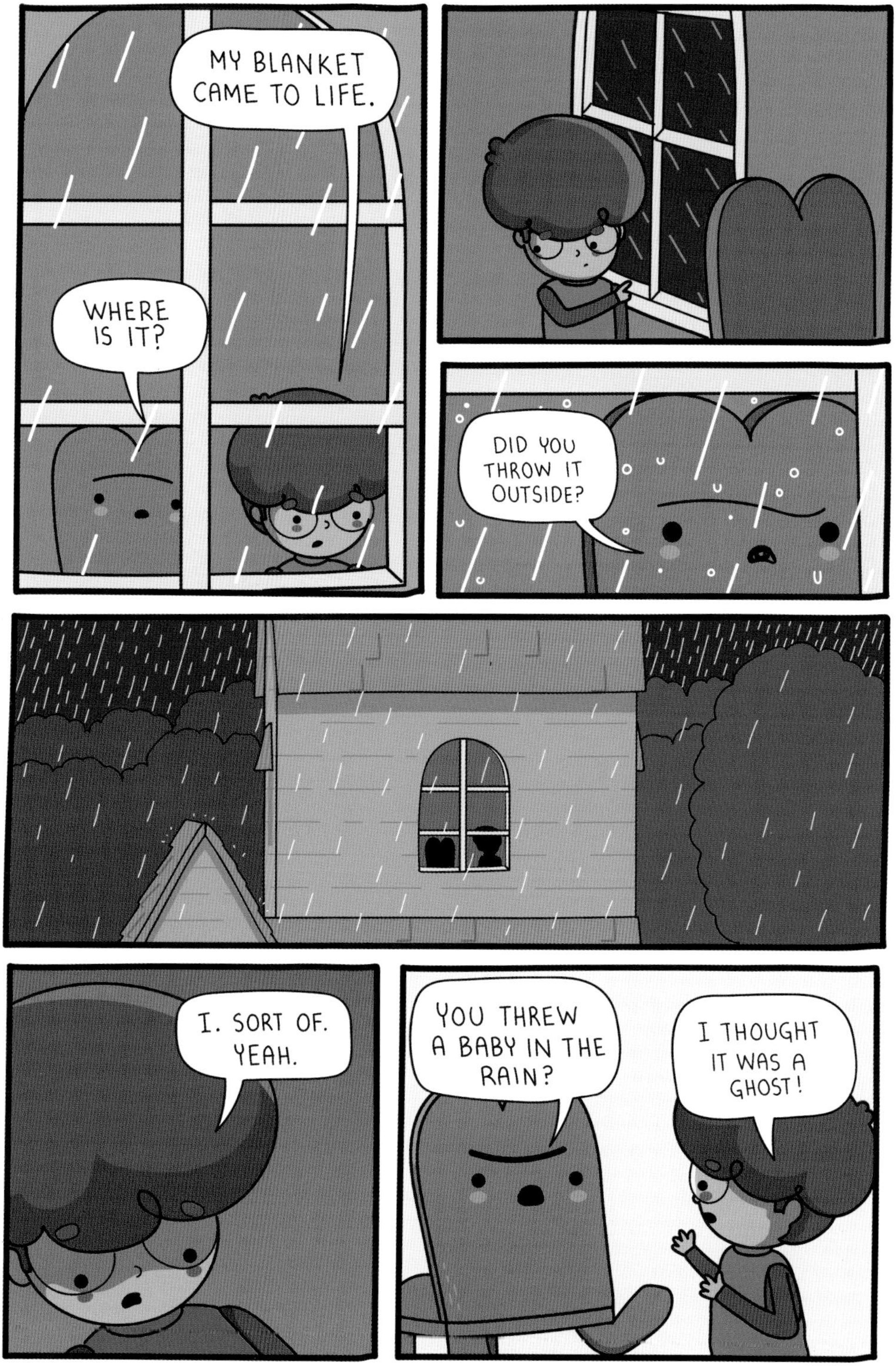
MY BLANKET CAME TO LIFE.
WHERE IS IT?
DID YOU THROW IT OUTSIDE?
I. SORT OF. YEAH.
YOU THREW A BABY IN THE RAIN?
I THOUGHT IT WAS A GHOST!

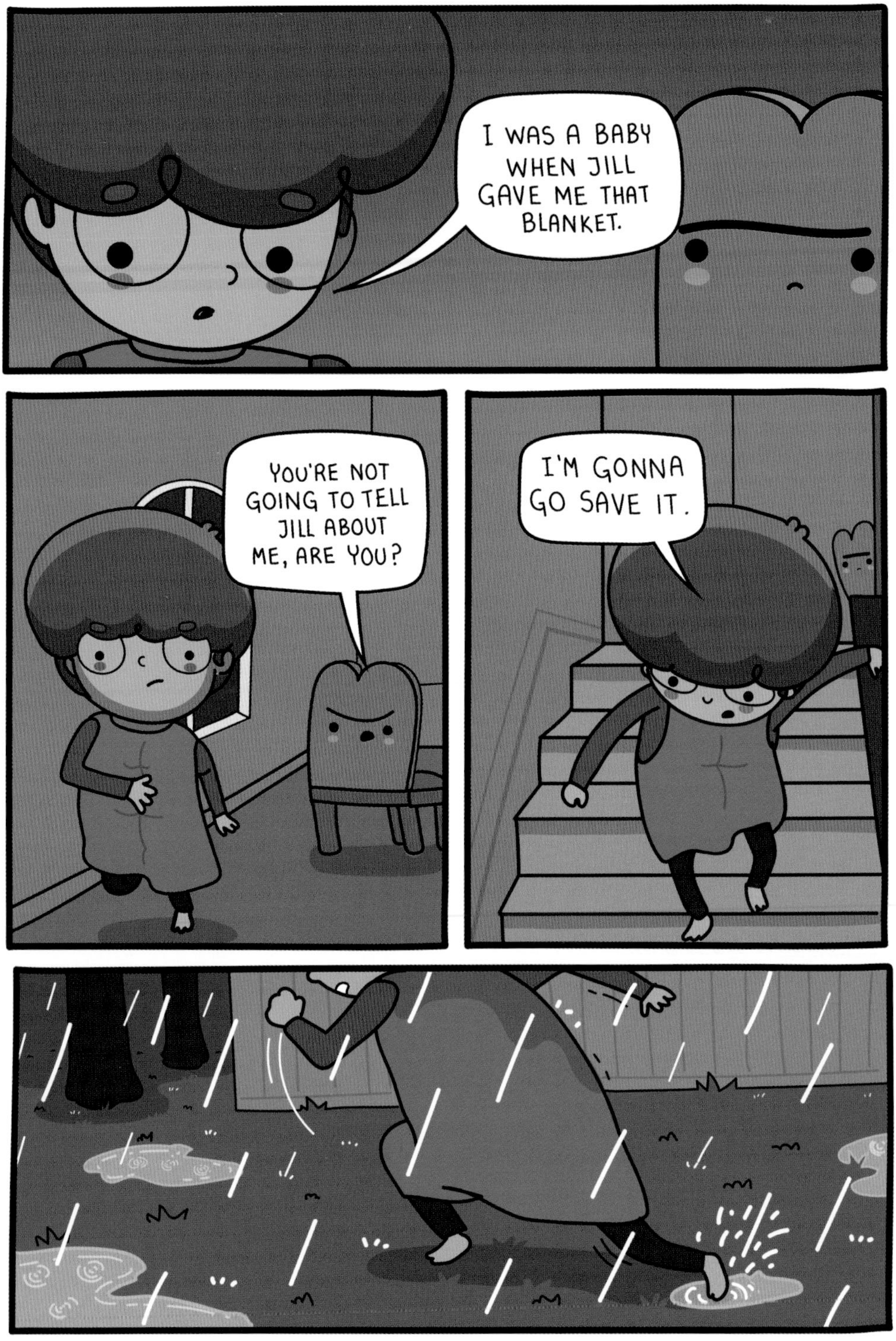
I WAS A BABY WHEN JILL GAVE ME THAT BLANKET.
YOU'RE NOT GOING TO TELL JILL ABOUT ME, ARE YOU?
I'M GONNA GO SAVE IT.

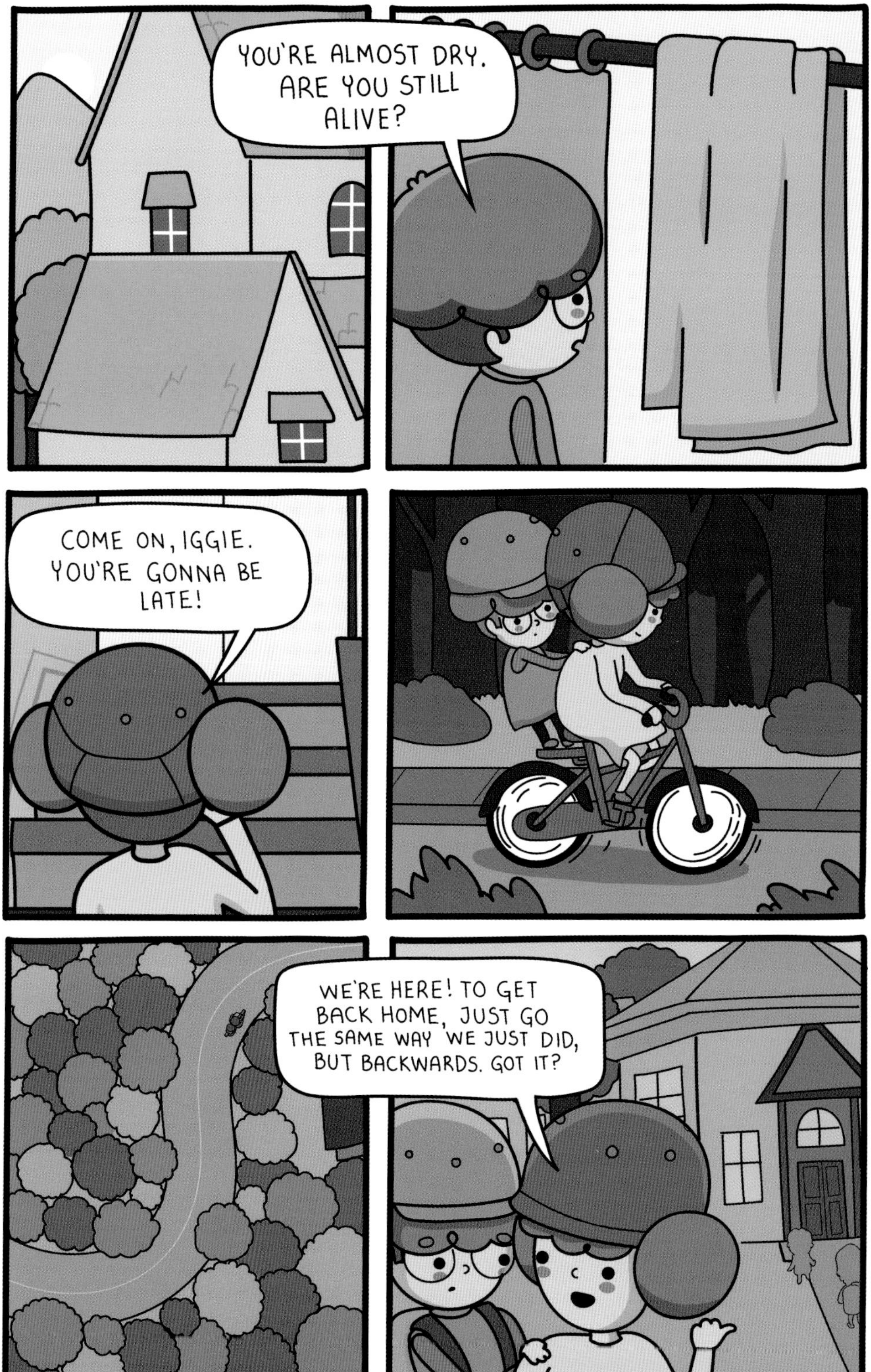
YOU'RE ALMOST DRY. ARE YOU STILL ALIVE?
COME ON, IGGIE. YOU'RE GONNA BE LATE!
WE'RE HERE! TO GET BACK HOME, JUST GO THE SAME WAY WE JUST DID, BUT BACKWARDS. GOT IT?

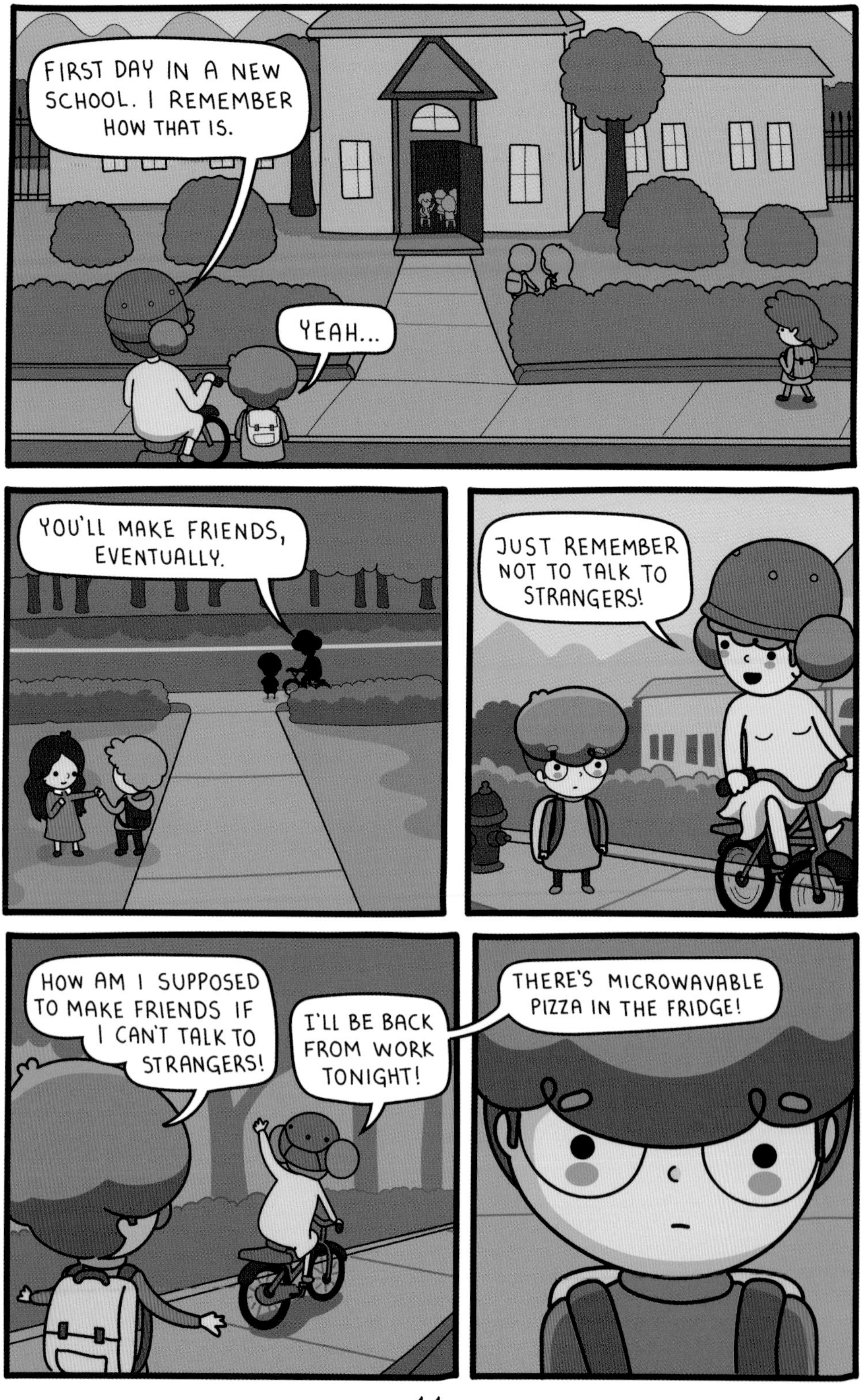
FIRST DAY IN A NEW SCHOOL. I REMEMBER HOW THAT IS.
YEAH...
YOU'LL MAKE FRIENDS, EVENTUALLY.
JUST REMEMBER NOT TO TALK TO STRANGERS!
HOW AM I SUPPOSED TO MAKE FRIENDS IF I CAN'T TALK TO STRANGERS!
I'LL BE BACK FROM WORK TONIGHT!
THERE'S MICROWAVABLE PIZZA IN THE FRIDGE!

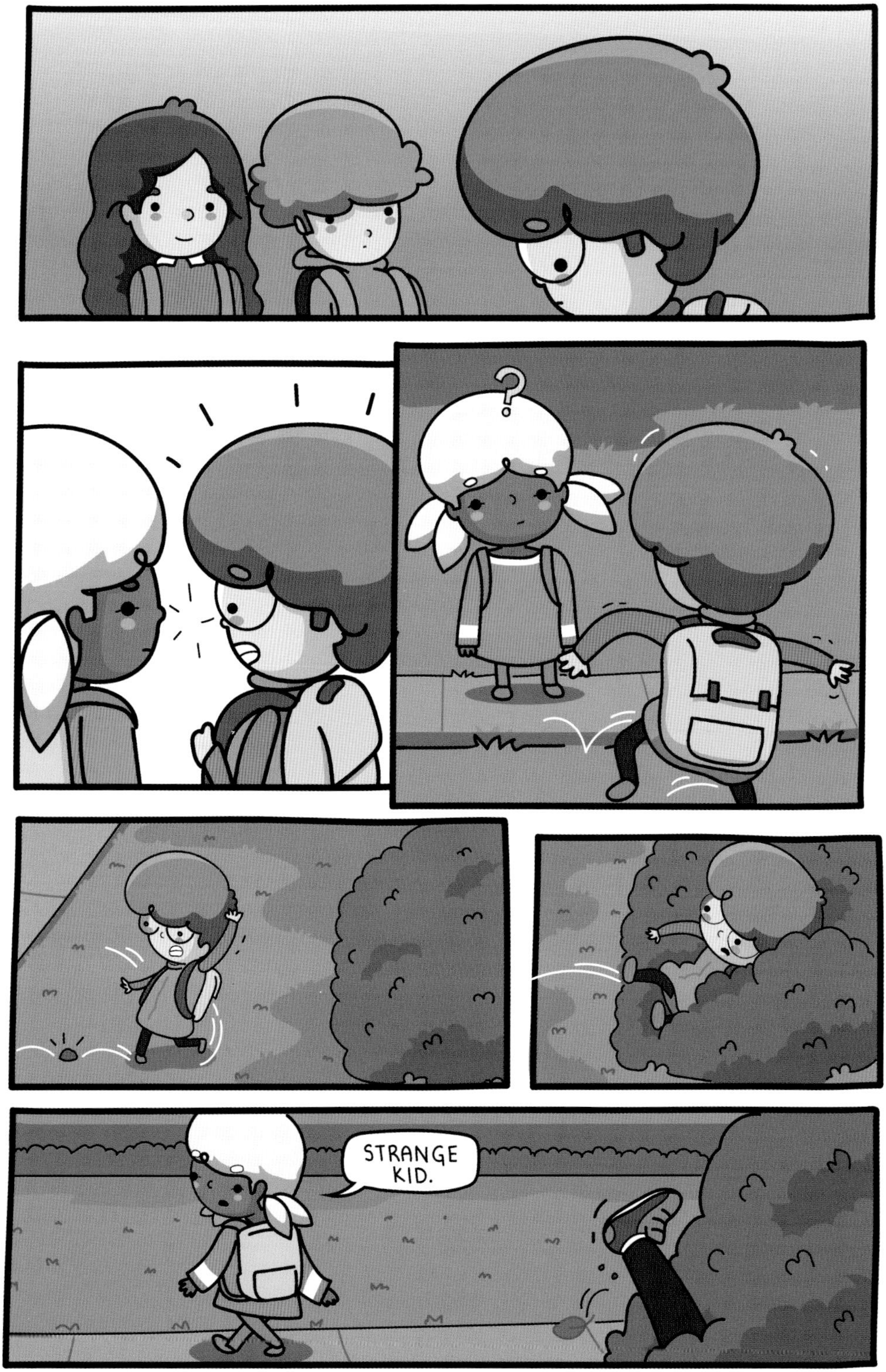
STRANGE KID.

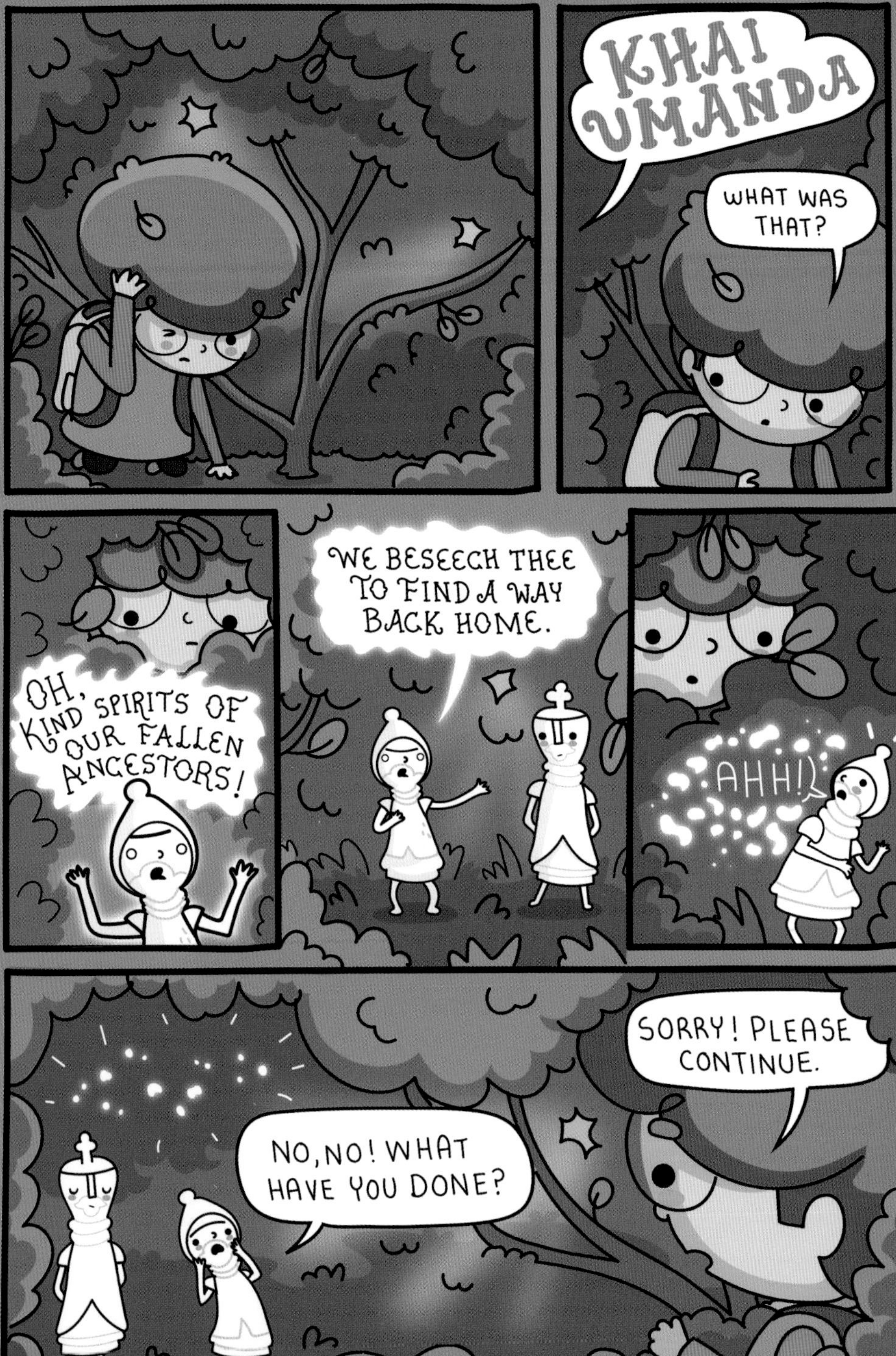
KHAI UMANDA
WHAT WAS THAT?
OH, KIND SPIRITS OF OUR FALLEN ANCESTORS!
WE BESEECH THEE TO FIND A WAY BACK HOME.
AHH!
SORRY! PLEASE CONTINUE.
NO, NO! WHAT HAVE YOU DONE?

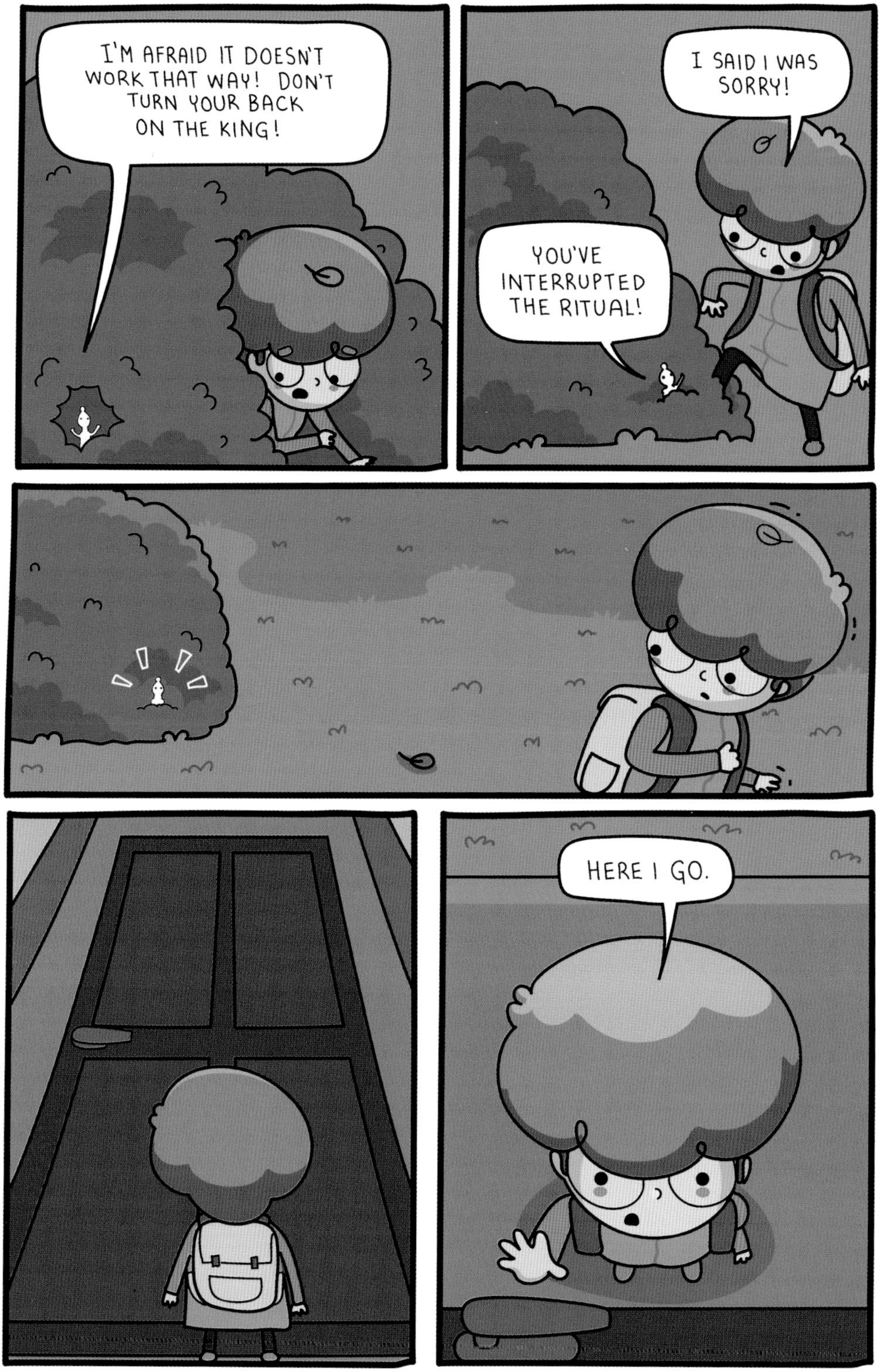
I'M AFRAID IT DOESN'T WORK THAT WAY! DON'T TURN YOUR BACK ON THE KING!
I SAID I WAS SORRY!
YOU'VE INTERRUPTED THE RITUAL!
HERE I GO.

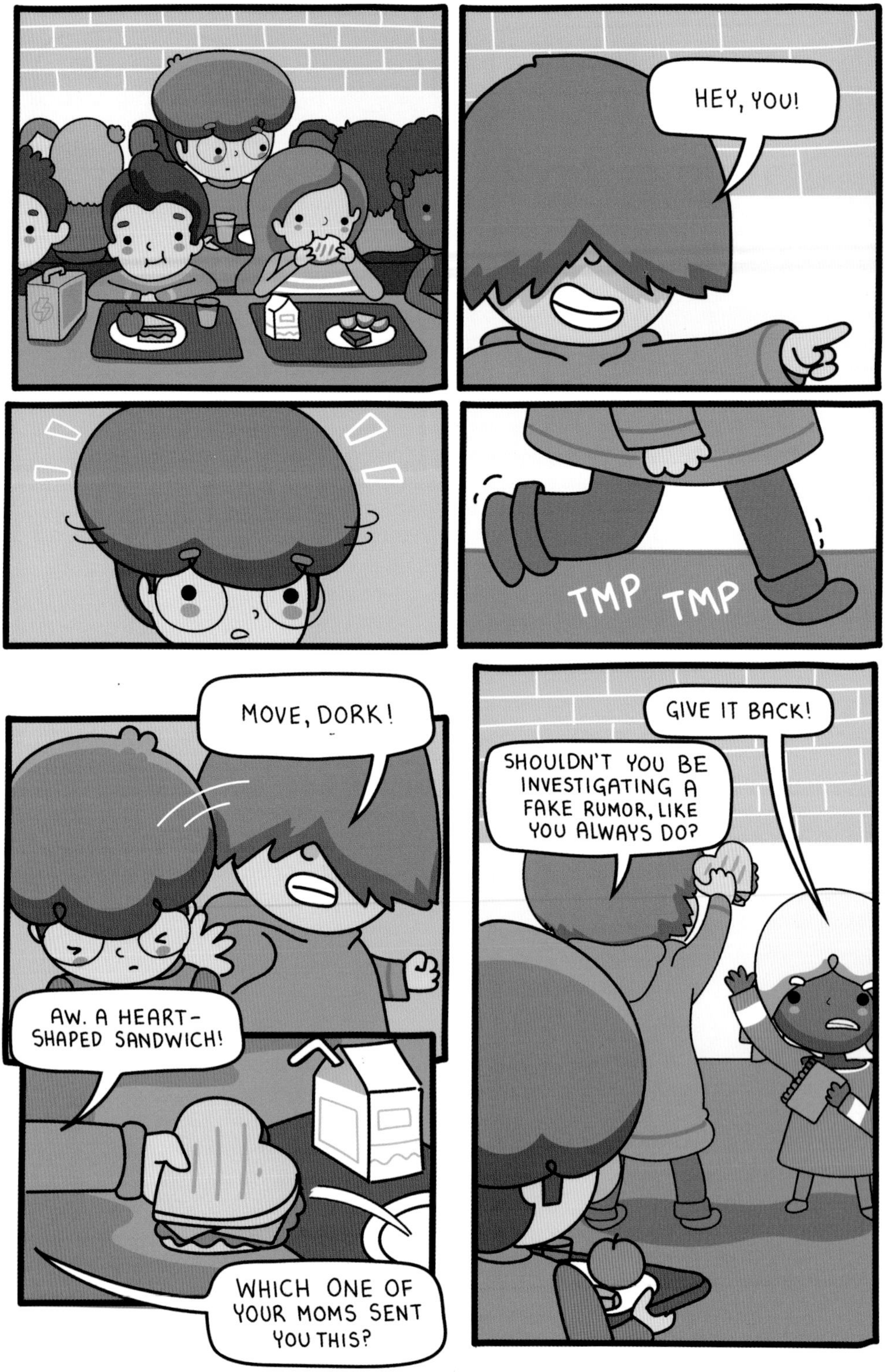
HEY, YOU!
TMP TMP
MOVE, DORK!
AW. A HEART-SHAPED SANDWICH!
WHICH ONE OF YOUR MOMS SENT YOU THIS?
GIVE IT BACK!
SHOULDN'T YOU BE INVESTIGATING A FAKE RUMOR, LIKE YOU ALWAYS DO?

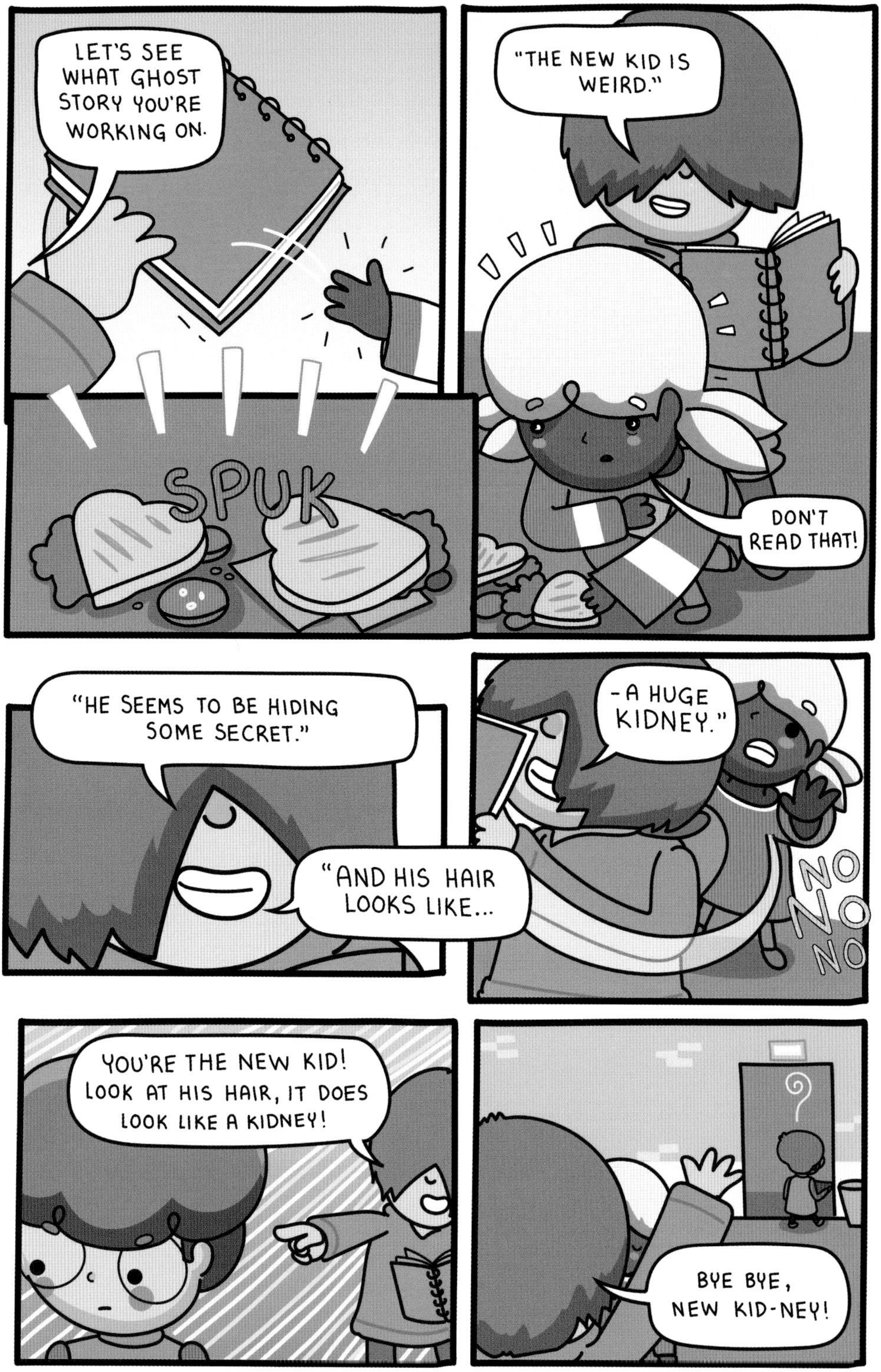
LET'S SEE WHAT GHOST STORY YOU'RE WORKING ON.
"THE NEW KID IS WEIRD."
SPUK
DON'T READ THAT!
"HE SEEMS TO BE HIDING SOME SECRET."
"AND HIS HAIR LOOKS LIKE...
-A HUGE KIDNEY."
NO NO NO
YOU'RE THE NEW KID! LOOK AT HIS HAIR, IT DOES LOOK LIKE A KIDNEY!
BYE BYE, NEW KID-NEY!

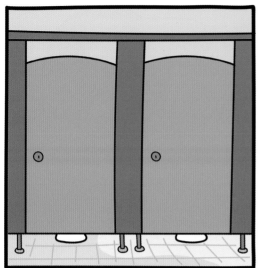

HOW DID YOU TWO GET IN HERE?

THIS PLACE IS NOT EXACTLY A FORTRESS.

THEY MUST UPGRADE THEIR DEFENSES.

...AND THEIR AIR FRESHENER.

WHAT DO YOU WANT FROM ME?

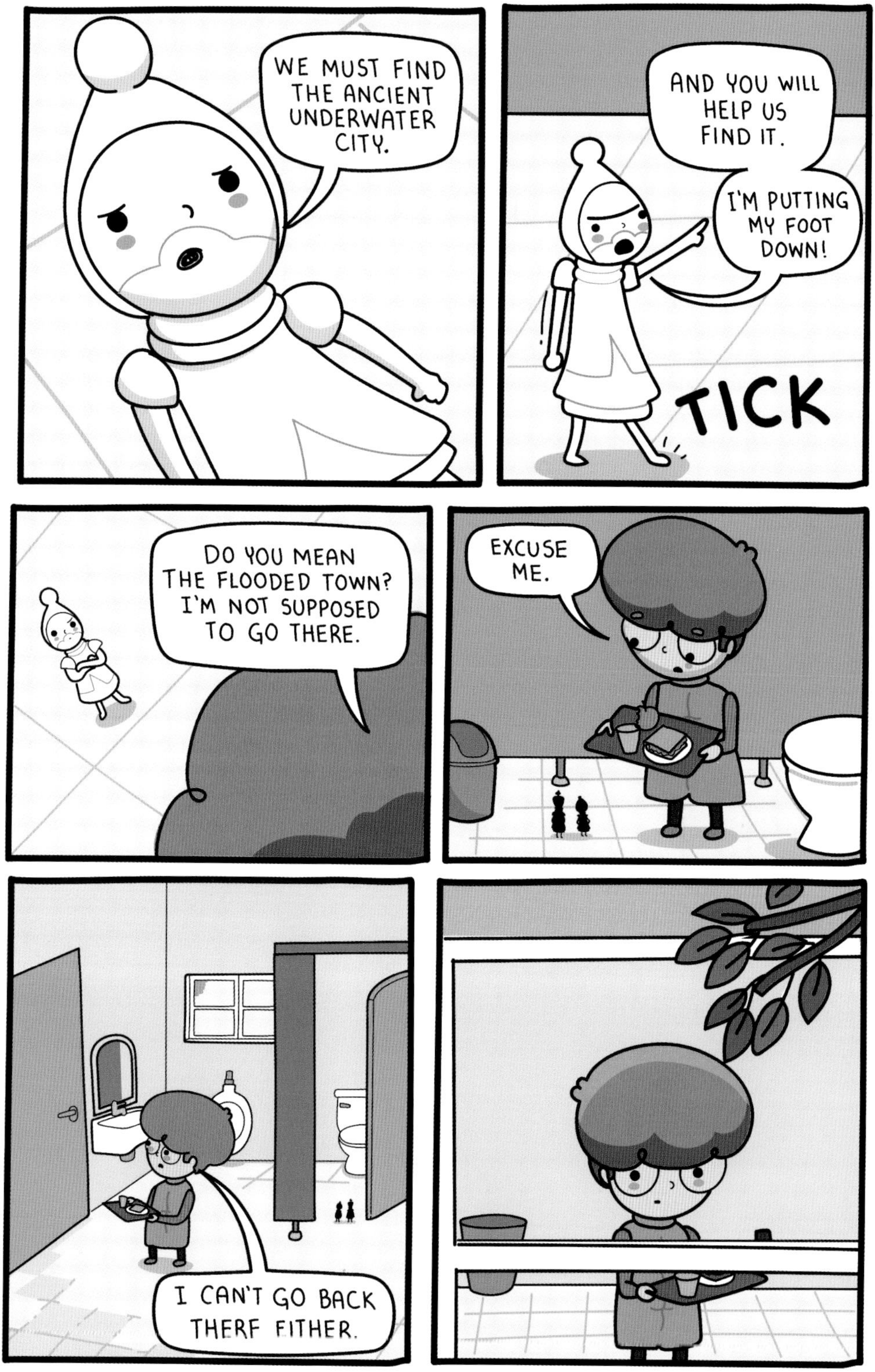
WE MUST FIND THE ANCIENT UNDERWATER CITY.
AND YOU WILL HELP US FIND IT.
I'M PUTTING MY FOOT DOWN!
TICK
DO YOU MEAN THE FLOODED TOWN? I'M NOT SUPPOSED TO GO THERE.
EXCUSE ME.
I CAN'T GO BACK THERE EITHER.

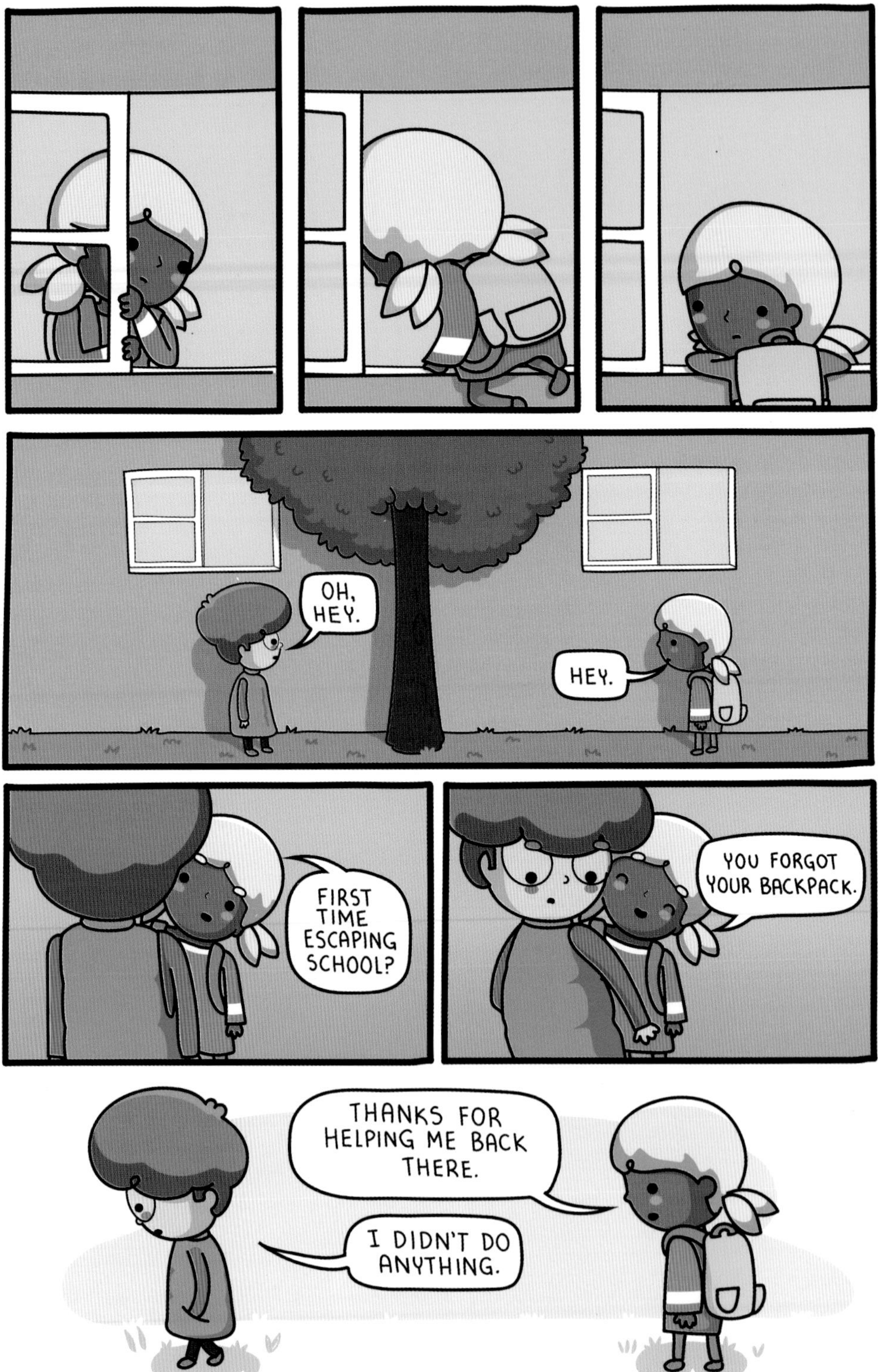
OH, HEY.
HEY.
FIRST TIME ESCAPING SCHOOL?
YOU FORGOT YOUR BACKPACK.
THANKS FOR HELPING ME BACK THERE.
I DIDN'T DO ANYTHING.

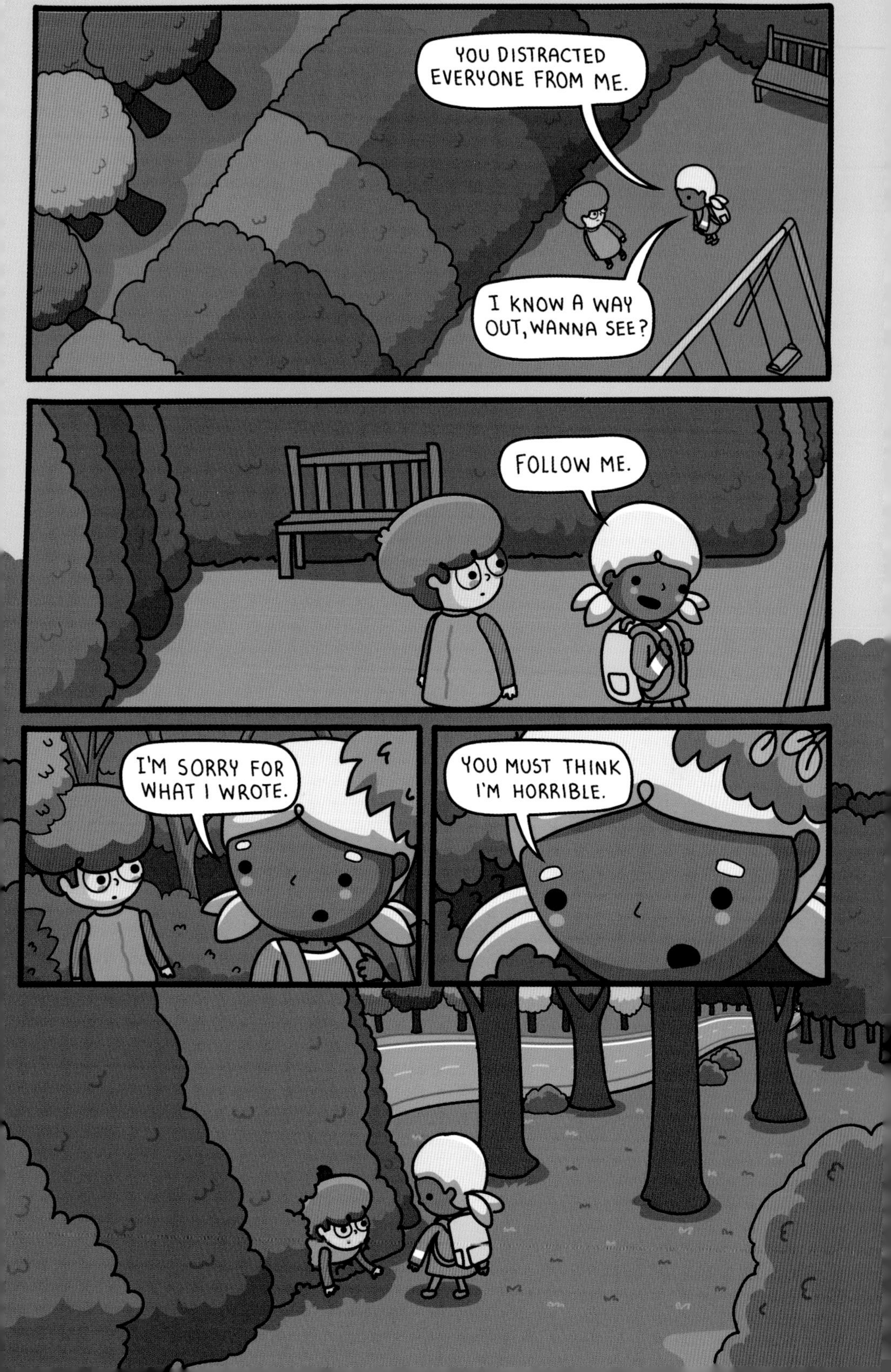
YOU DISTRACTED EVERYONE FROM ME.
I KNOW A WAY OUT, WANNA SEE?
FOLLOW ME.
I'M SORRY FOR WHAT I WROTE.
YOU MUST THINK I'M HORRIBLE.

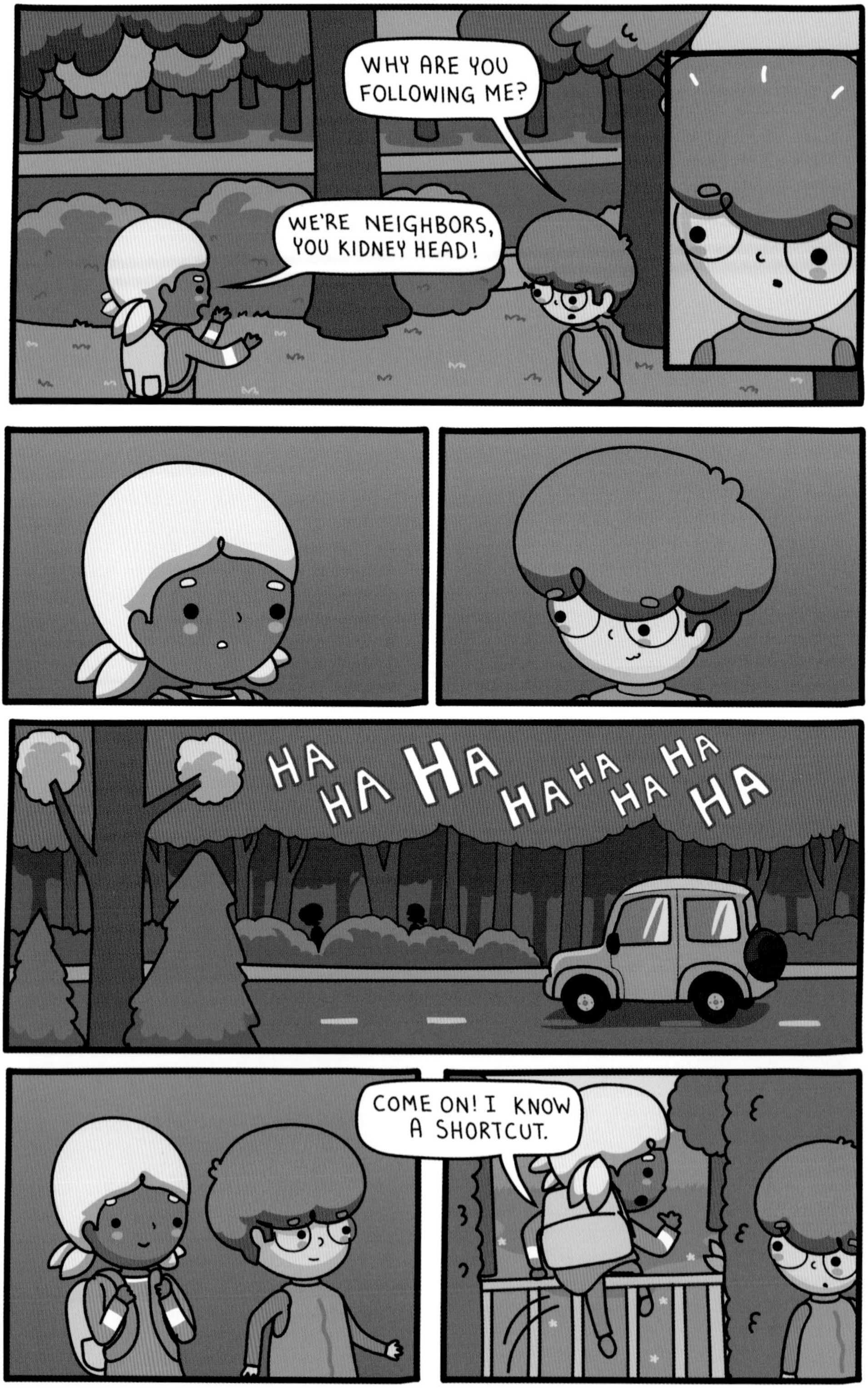
WHY ARE YOU FOLLOWING ME?
WE'RE NEIGHBORS, YOU KIDNEY HEAD!
HA HA HA HA HA HA HA HA HA HA
COME ON! I KNOW A SHORTCUT.

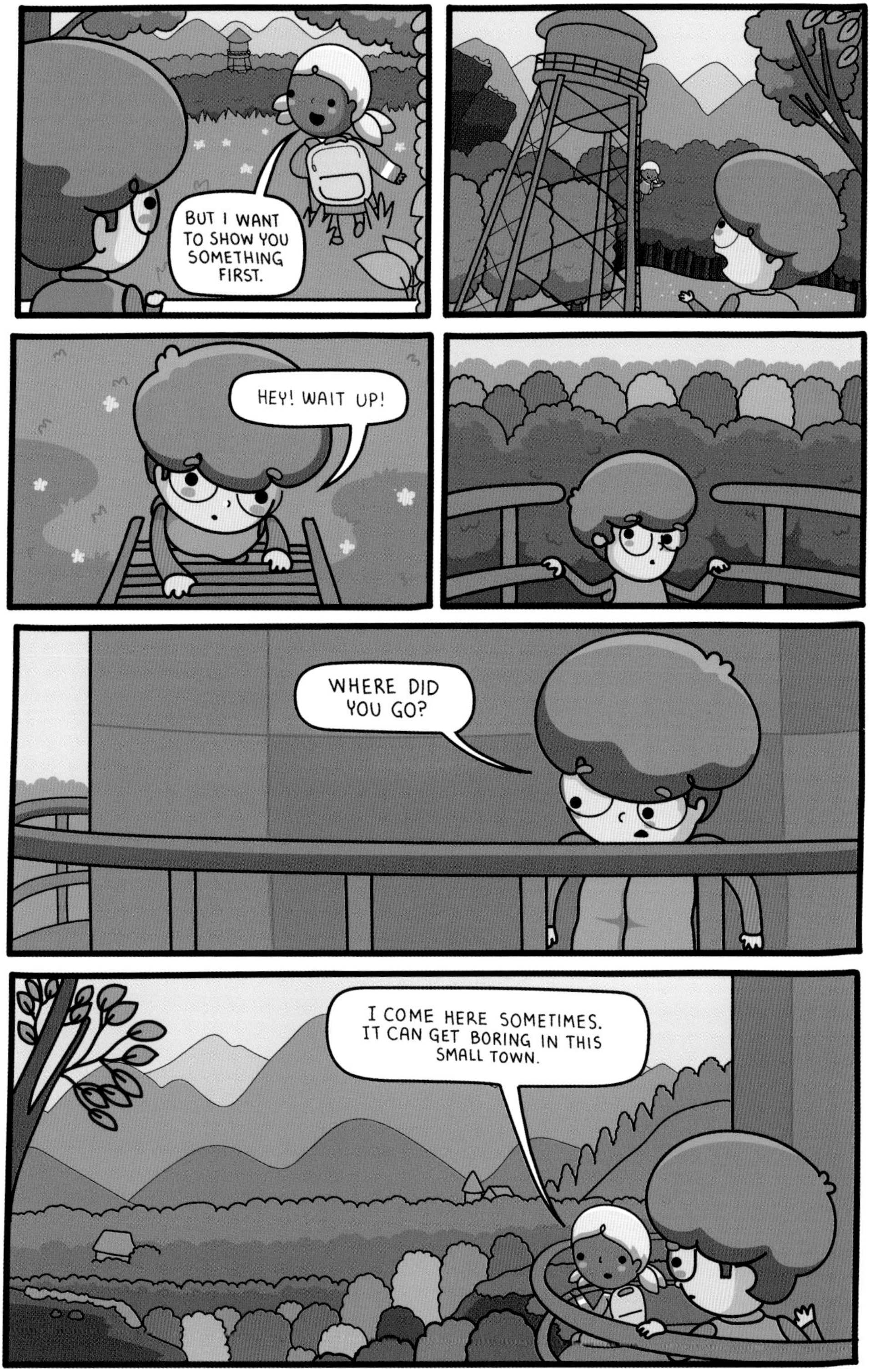
BUT I WANT TO SHOW YOU SOMETHING FIRST.
HEY! WAIT UP!
WHERE DID YOU GO?
I COME HERE SOMETIMES. IT CAN GET BORING IN THIS SMALL TOWN.

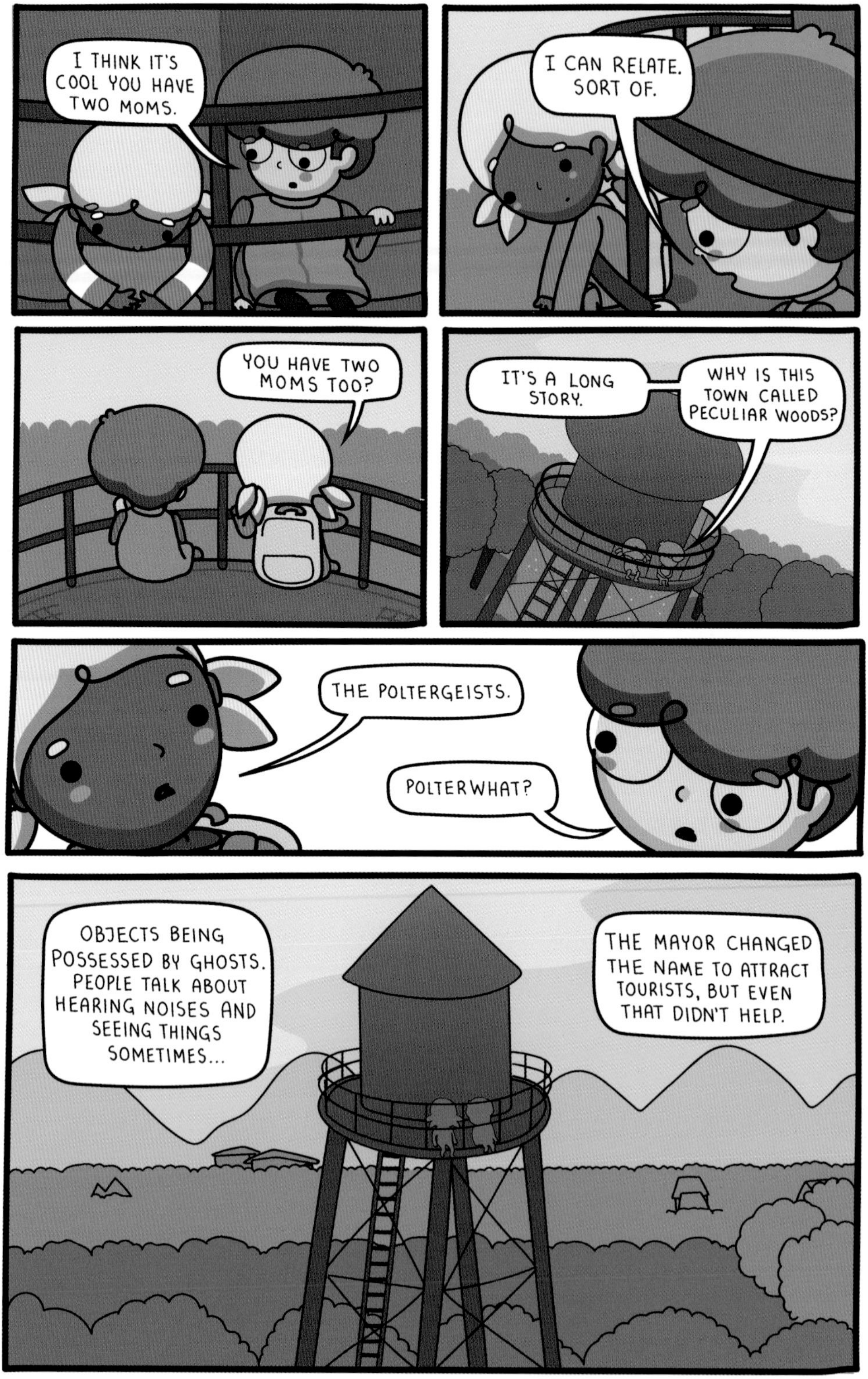
I THINK IT'S COOL YOU HAVE TWO MOMS.
I CAN RELATE. SORT OF.
YOU HAVE TWO MOMS TOO?
IT'S A LONG STORY.
WHY IS THIS TOWN CALLED PECULIAR WOODS?
THE POLTERGEISTS.
POLTERWHAT?
OBJECTS BEING POSSESSED BY GHOSTS. PEOPLE TALK ABOUT HEARING NOISES AND SEEING THINGS SOMETIMES...
THE MAYOR CHANGED THE NAME TO ATTRACT TOURISTS, BUT EVEN THAT DIDN'T HELP.

DO YOU BELIEVE THOSE GHOST STORIES?

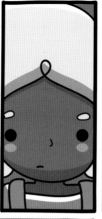

I ACTUALLY WISH THEY WERE REAL.

WHAT WOULD YOU DO IF YOU SAW AN OBJECT MOVING?

HAHA! NOTHING NEARLY AS EXCITING AS THAT WILL EVER HAPPEN IN THIS PLACE!

THAT'S WHY I LOVE TO COME HERE.

SOMETIMES I IMAGINE PEOPLE HAVING ADVENTURES SOMEWHERE OUT THERE. AND FOR A SECOND, THEY STOP AND SEE ME.

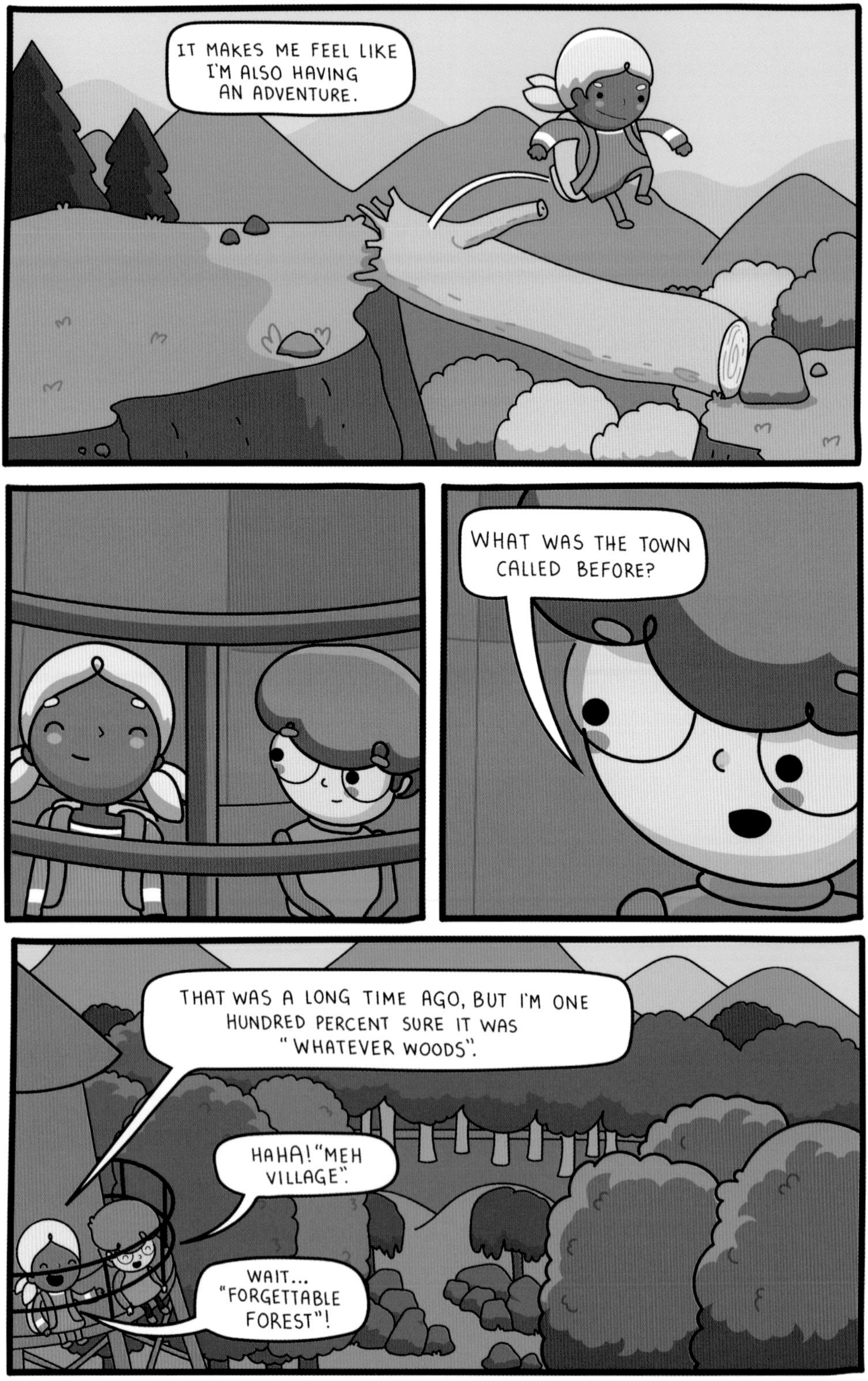
IT MAKES ME FEEL LIKE I'M ALSO HAVING AN ADVENTURE.
WHAT WAS THE TOWN CALLED BEFORE?
THAT WAS A LONG TIME AGO, BUT I'M ONE HUNDRED PERCENT SURE IT WAS "WHATEVER WOODS".
HAHA! "MEH VILLAGE".
WAIT... "FORGETTABLE FOREST"!

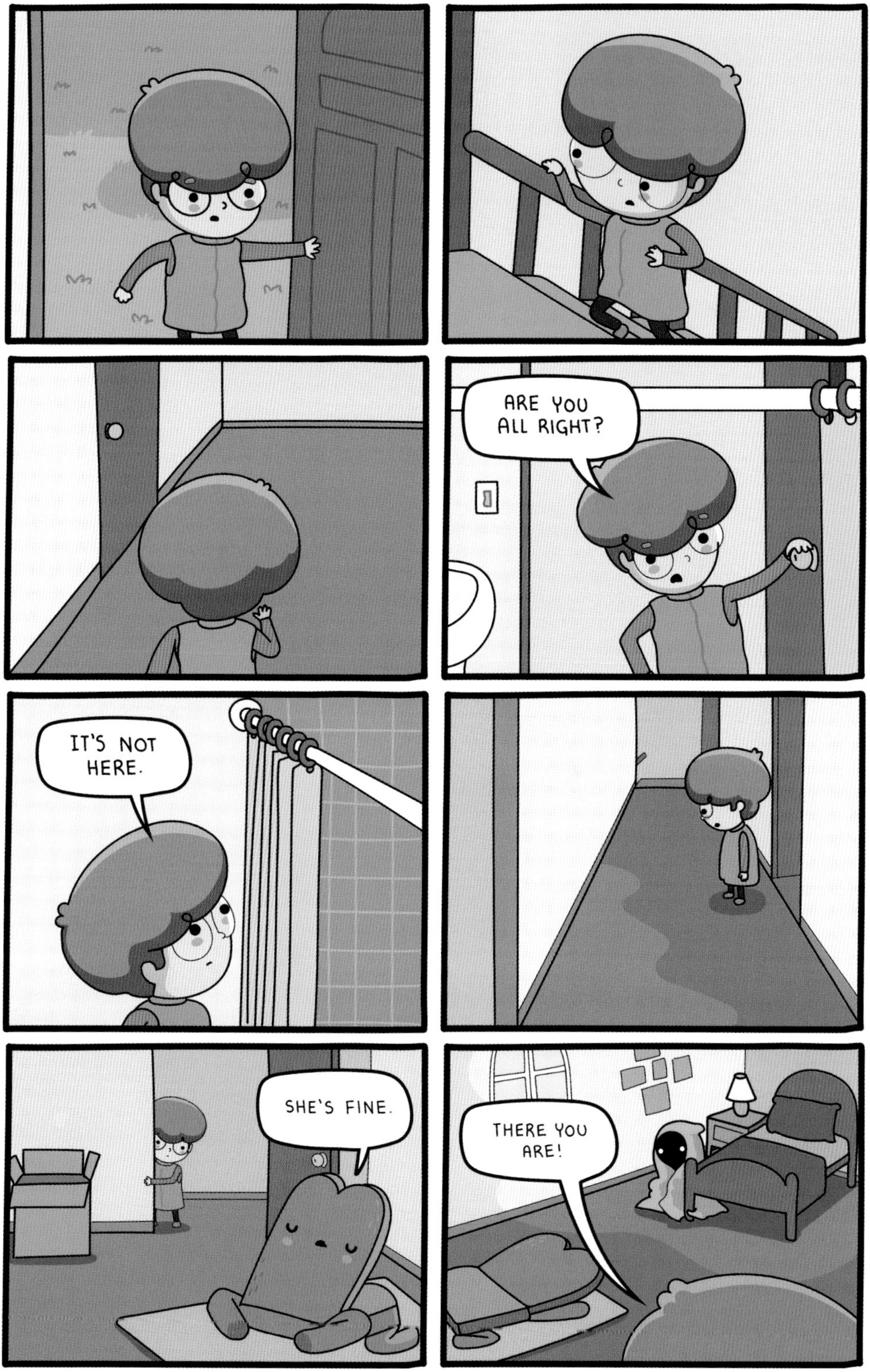
ARE YOU ALL RIGHT?
IT'S NOT HERE.
SHE'S FINE.
THERE YOU ARE!

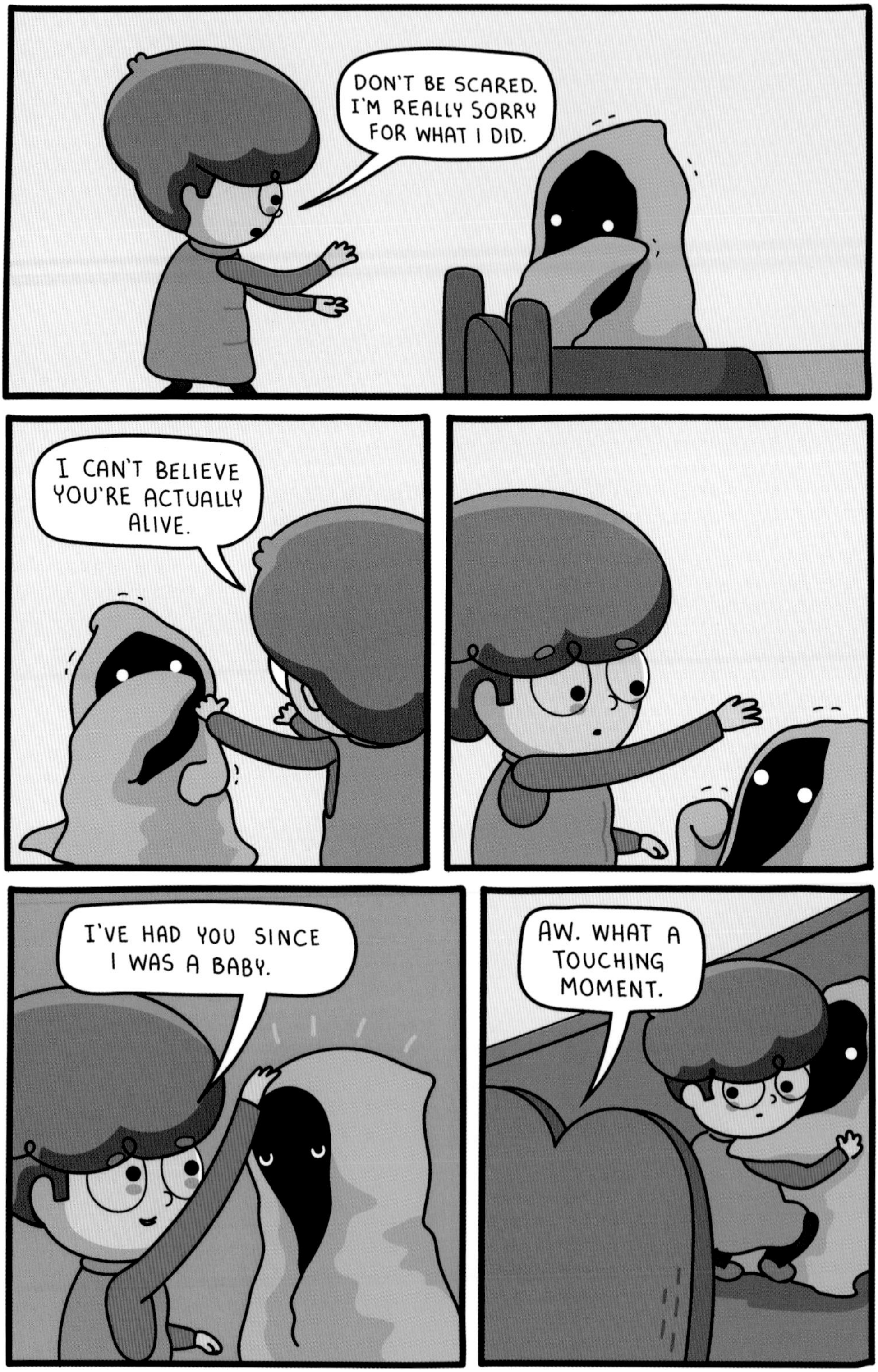
DON'T BE SCARED. I'M REALLY SORRY FOR WHAT I DID.
I CAN'T BELIEVE YOU'RE ACTUALLY ALIVE.
I'VE HAD YOU SINCE I WAS A BABY.
AW. WHAT A TOUCHING MOMENT.

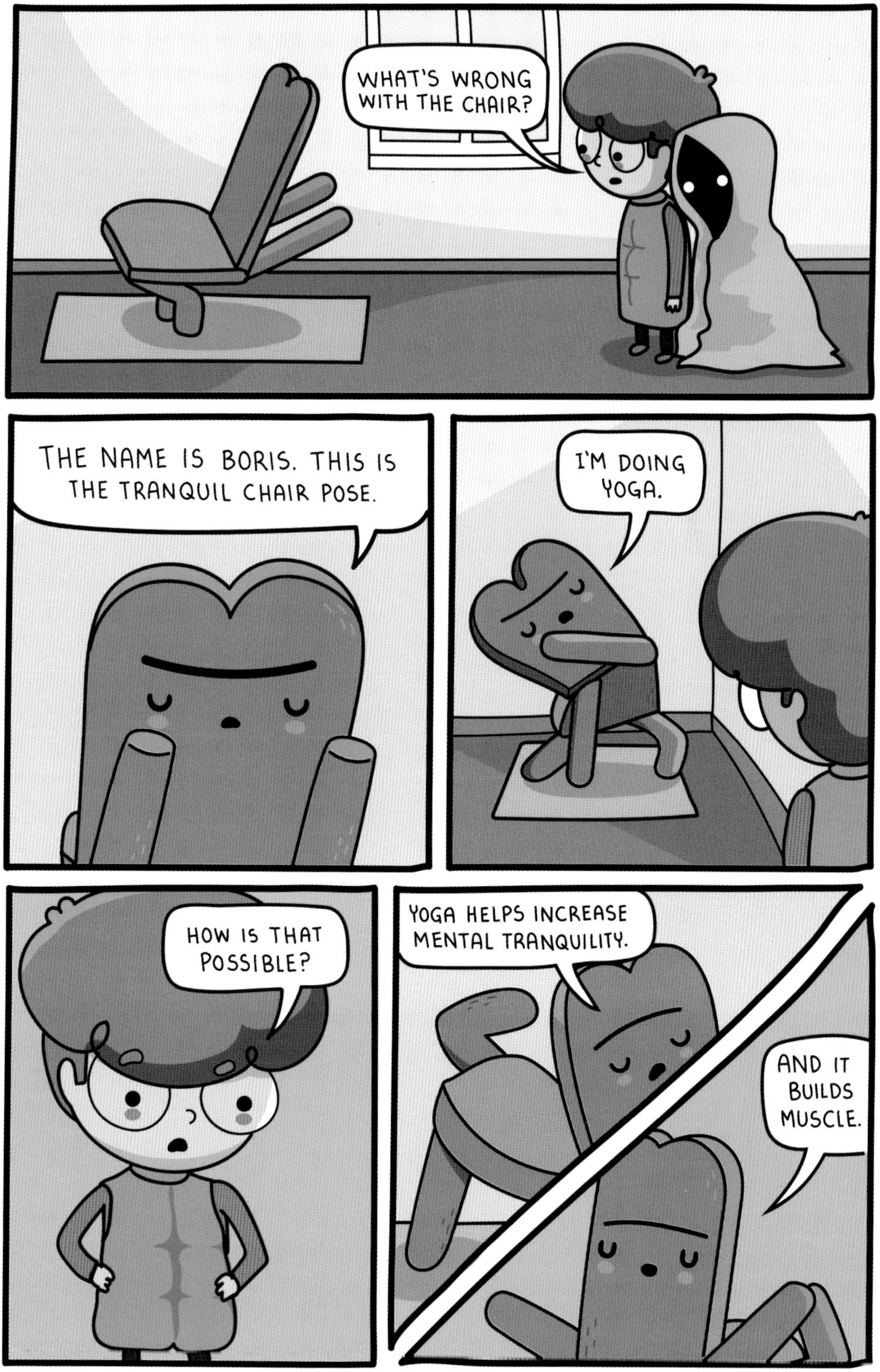
WHAT'S WRONG WITH THE CHAIR?
THE NAME IS BORIS. THIS IS THE TRANQUIL CHAIR POSE.
I'M DOING YOGA.
HOW IS THAT POSSIBLE?
YOGA HELPS INCREASE MENTAL TRANQUILITY.
AND IT BUILDS MUSCLE.

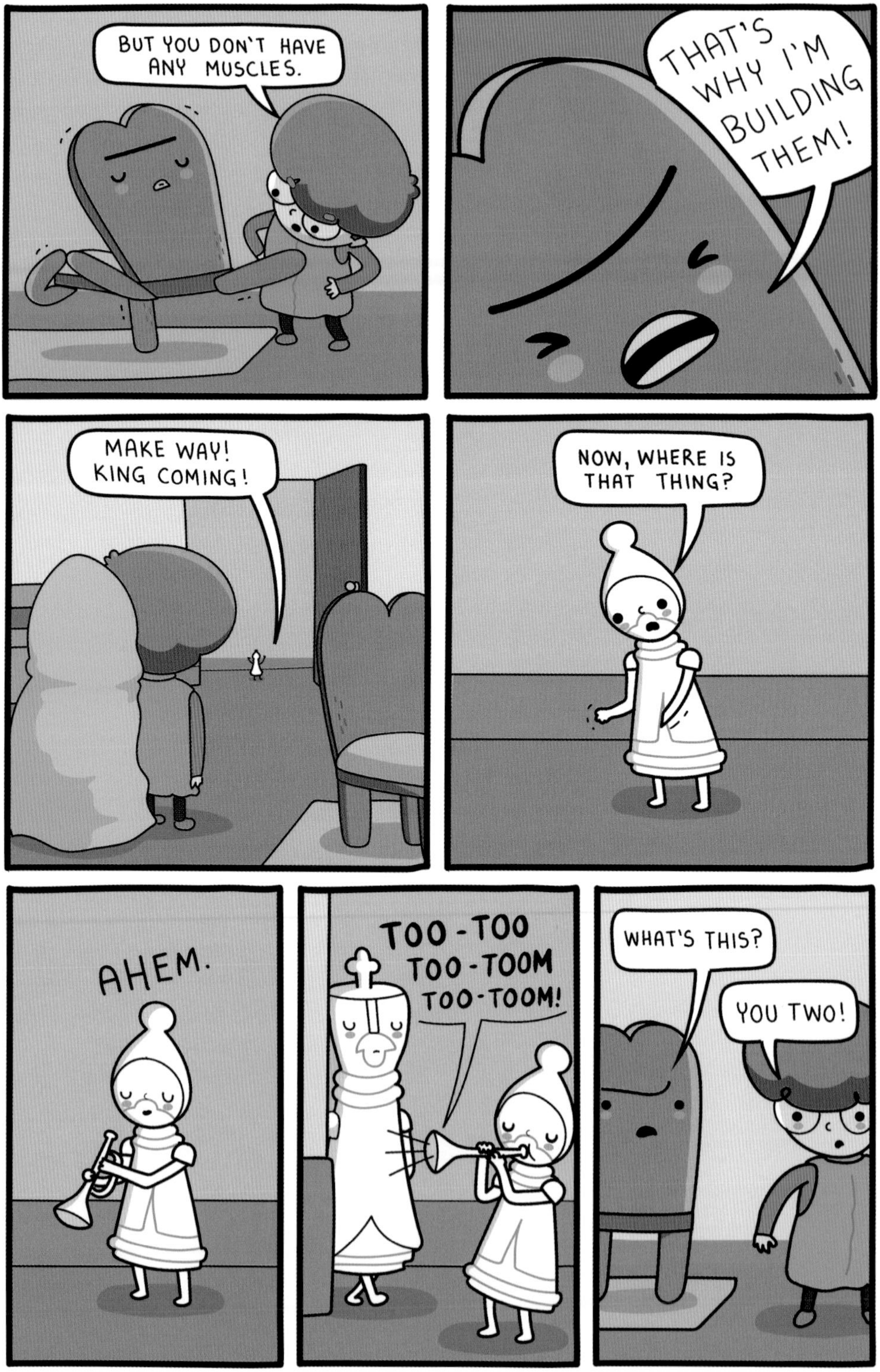
BUT YOU DON'T HAVE ANY MUSCLES.
THAT'S WHY I'M BUILDING THEM!
MAKE WAY! KING COMING!
NOW, WHERE IS THAT THING?
AHEM.
TOO-TOO TOO-TOOM TOO-TOOM!
WHAT'S THIS?
YOU TWO!

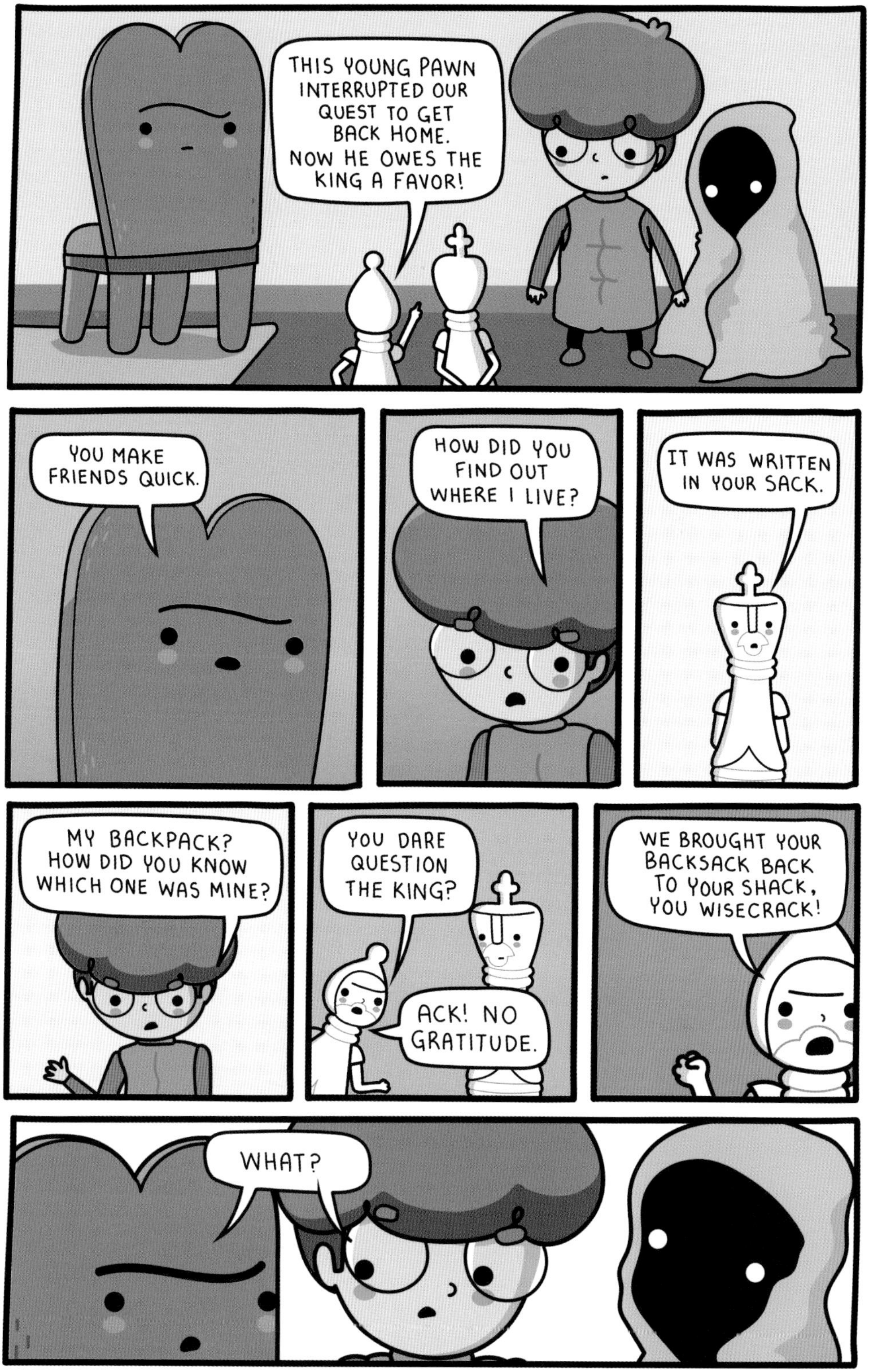
THIS YOUNG PAWN INTERRUPTED OUR QUEST TO GET BACK HOME. NOW HE OWES THE KING A FAVOR!
YOU MAKE FRIENDS QUICK.
HOW DID YOU FIND OUT WHERE I LIVE?
IT WAS WRITTEN IN YOUR SACK.
MY BACKPACK? HOW DID YOU KNOW WHICH ONE WAS MINE?
YOU DARE QUESTION THE KING?
ACK! NO GRATITUDE.
WE BROUGHT YOUR BACKSACK BACK TO YOUR SHACK, YOU WISECRACK!
WHAT?

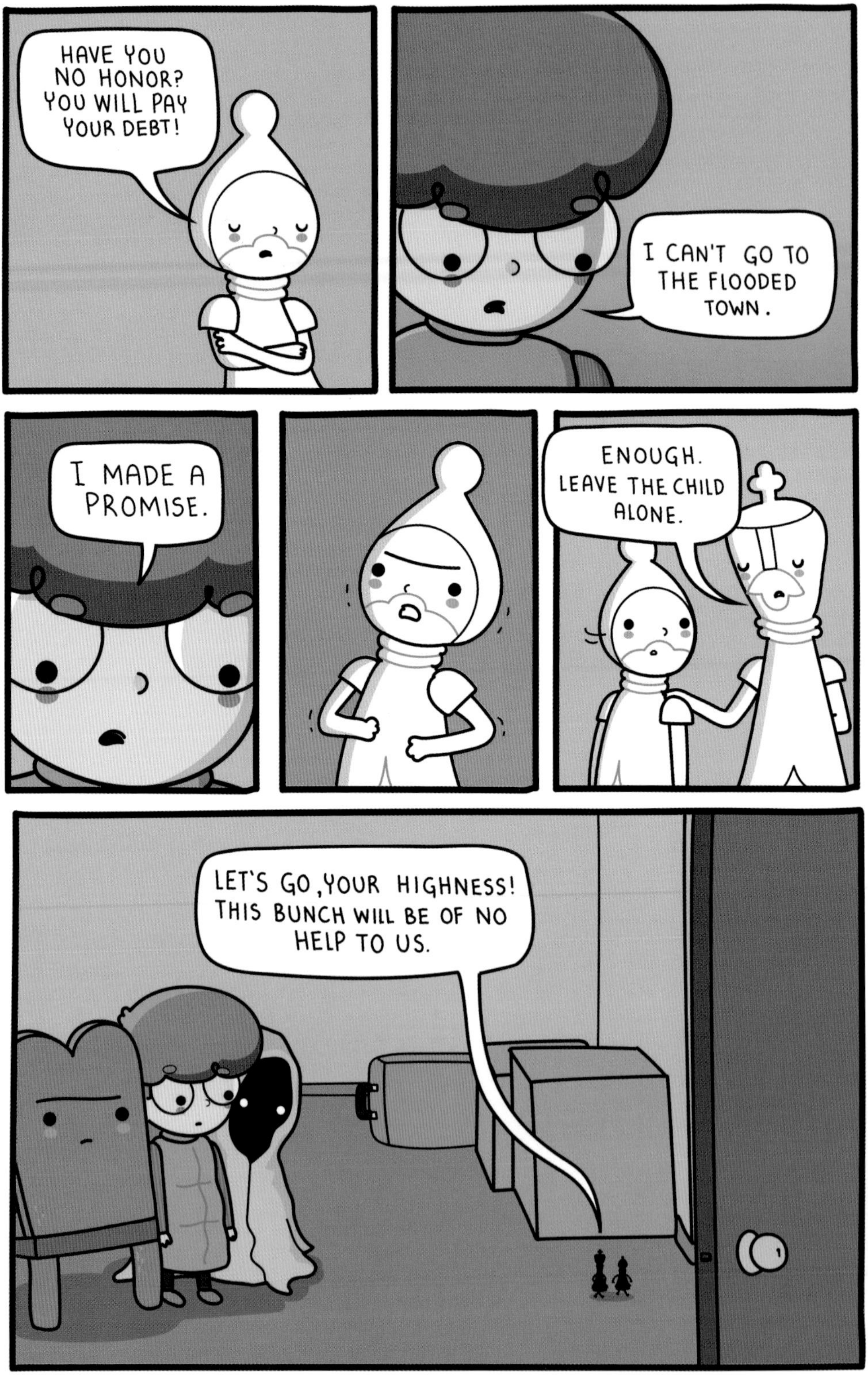
HAVE YOU NO HONOR? YOU WILL PAY YOUR DEBT!
I CAN'T GO TO THE FLOODED TOWN.
I MADE A PROMISE.
ENOUGH. LEAVE THE CHILD ALONE.
LET'S GO, YOUR HIGHNESS! THIS BUNCH WILL BE OF NO HELP TO US.

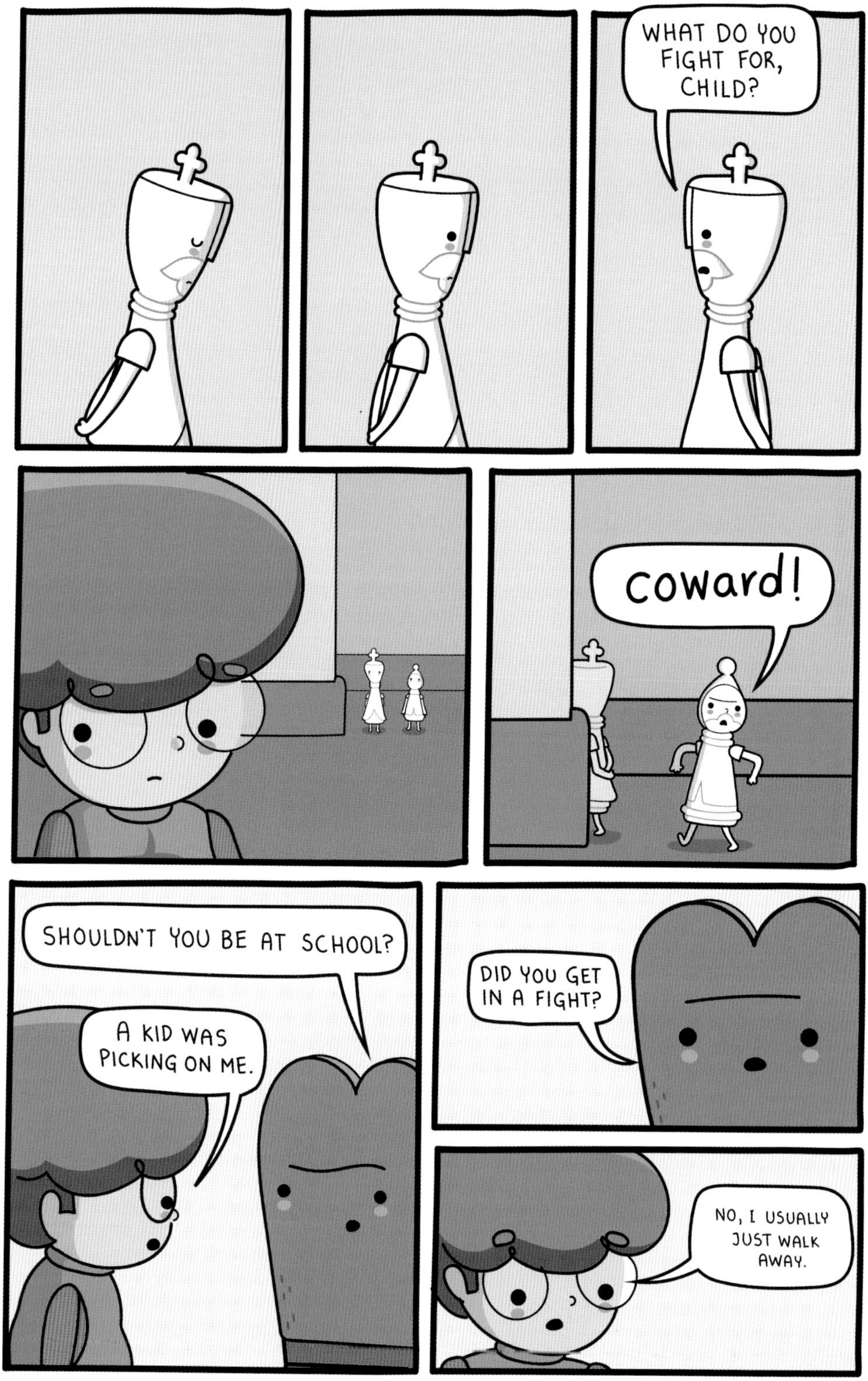
WHAT DO YOU FIGHT FOR, CHILD?
coward!
SHOULDN'T YOU BE AT SCHOOL?
A KID WAS PICKING ON ME.
DID YOU GET IN A FIGHT?
NO, I USUALLY JUST WALK AWAY.

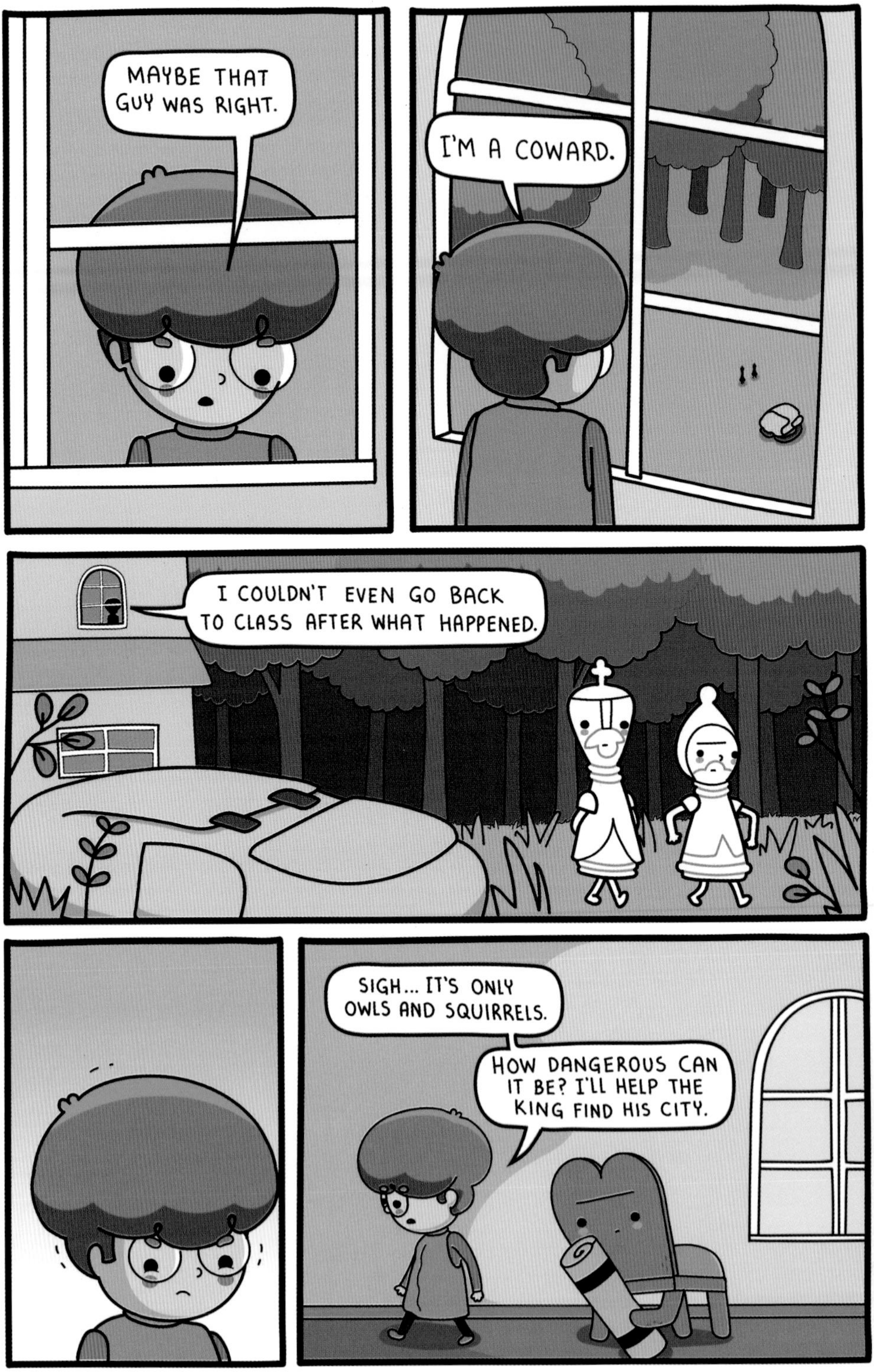
MAYBE THAT GUY WAS RIGHT.
I'M A COWARD.
I COULDN'T EVEN GO BACK TO CLASS AFTER WHAT HAPPENED.
SIGH... IT'S ONLY OWLS AND SQUIRRELS.
HOW DANGEROUS CAN IT BE? I'LL HELP THE KING FIND HIS CITY.

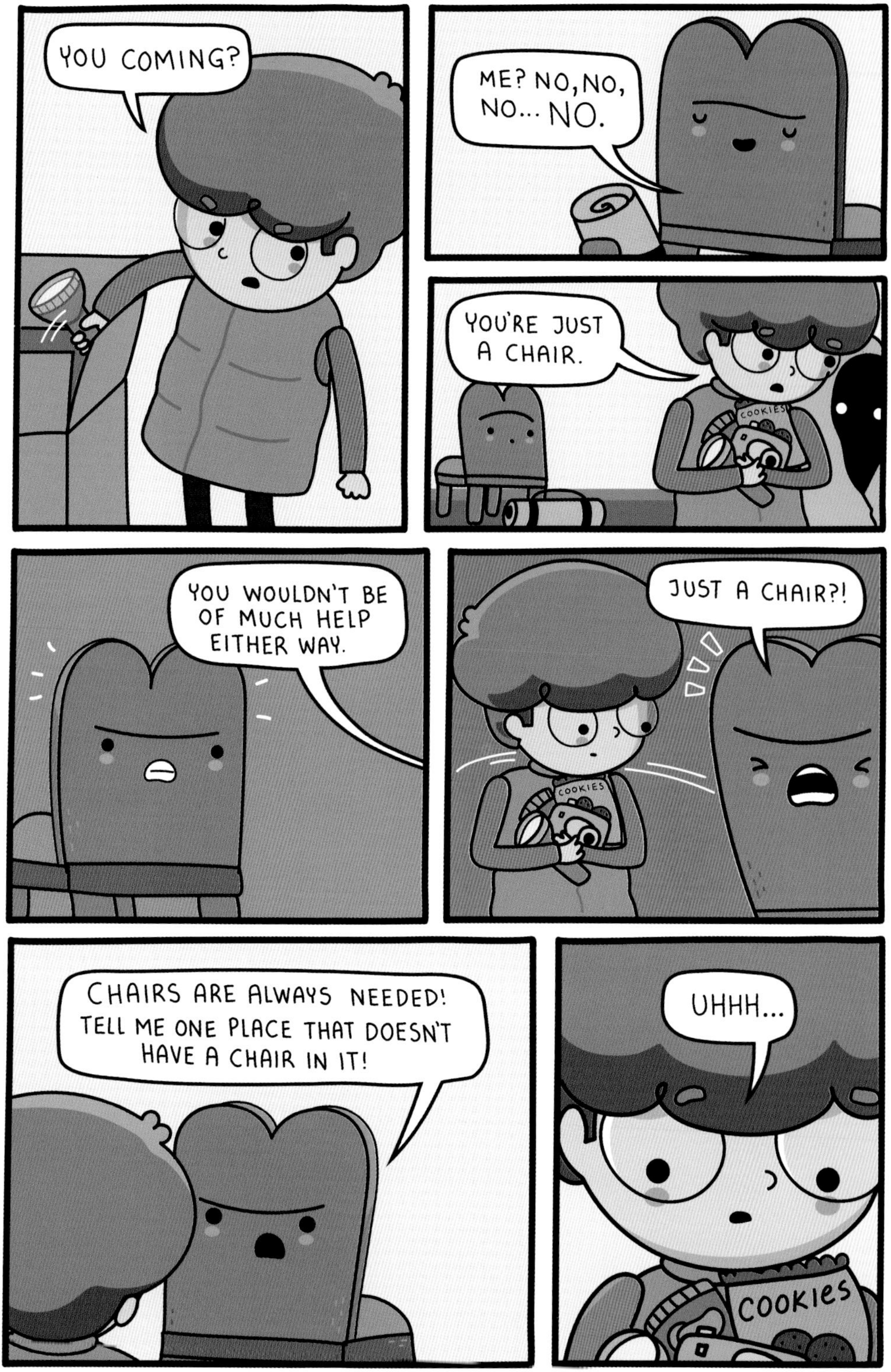
YOU COMING?
ME? NO, NO, NO... NO.
YOU'RE JUST A CHAIR.
COOKIES
YOU WOULDN'T BE OF MUCH HELP EITHER WAY.
JUST A CHAIR?!
COOKIES
CHAIRS ARE ALWAYS NEEDED! TELL ME ONE PLACE THAT DOESN'T HAVE A CHAIR IN IT!
UHHH...
COOKIES

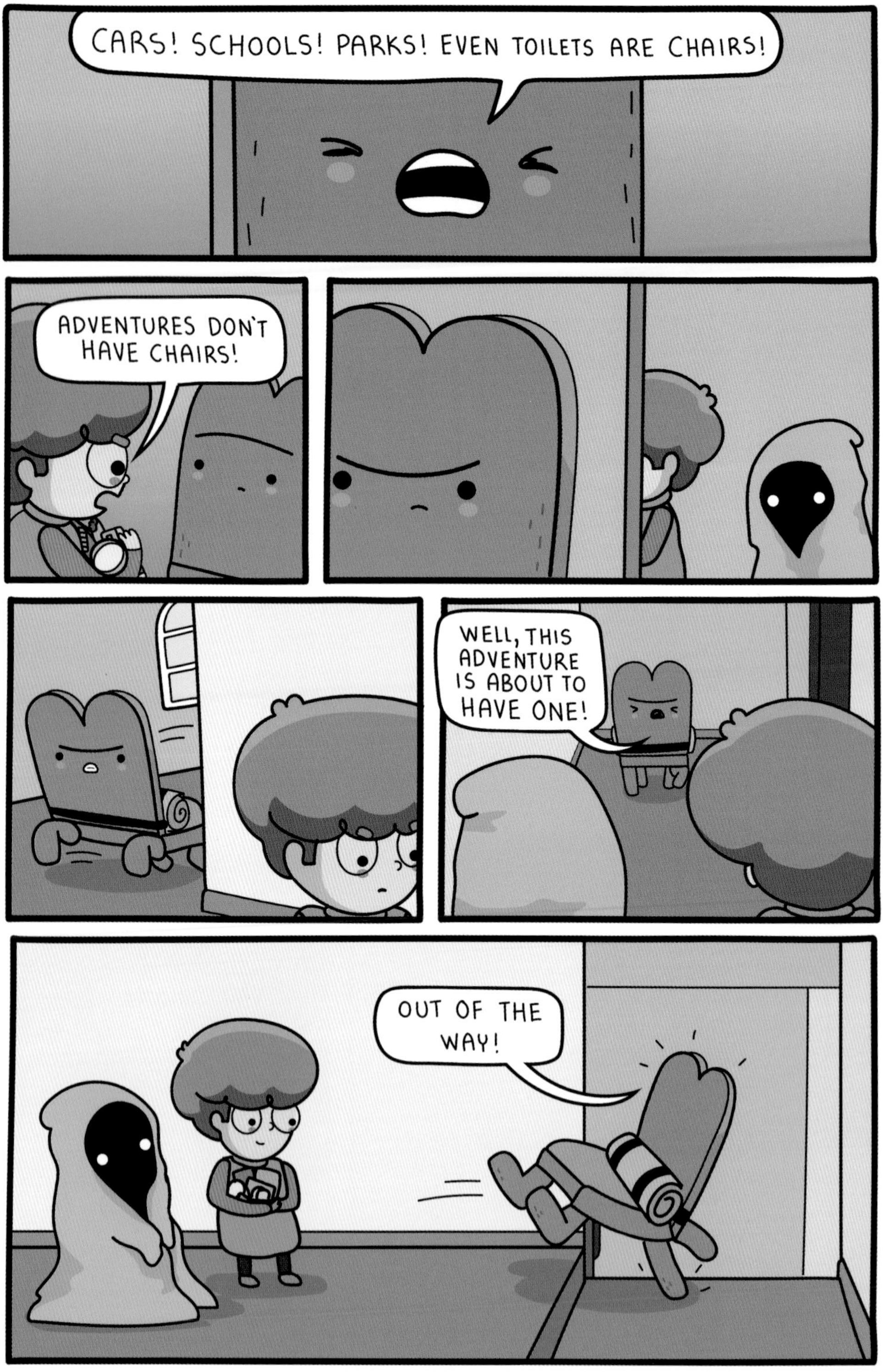
CARS! SCHOOLS! PARKS! EVEN TOILETS ARE CHAIRS!
ADVENTURES DON'T HAVE CHAIRS!
WELL, THIS ADVENTURE IS ABOUT TO HAVE ONE!
OUT OF THE WAY!

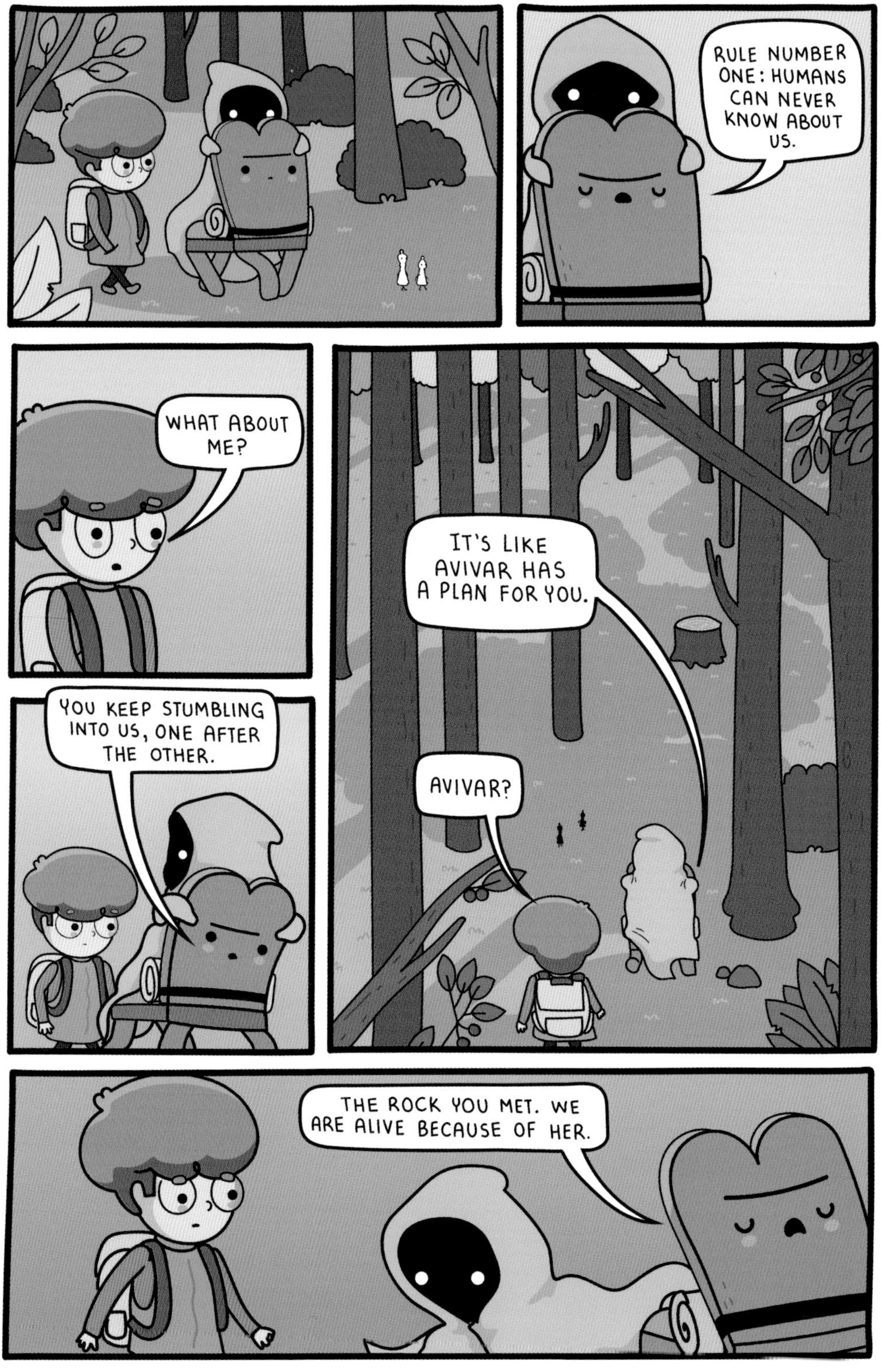
RULE NUMBER ONE: HUMANS CAN NEVER KNOW ABOUT US.
WHAT ABOUT ME?
YOU KEEP STUMBLING INTO US, ONE AFTER THE OTHER.
IT'S LIKE AVIVAR HAS A PLAN FOR YOU.
AVIVAR?
THE ROCK YOU MET. WE ARE ALIVE BECAUSE OF HER.

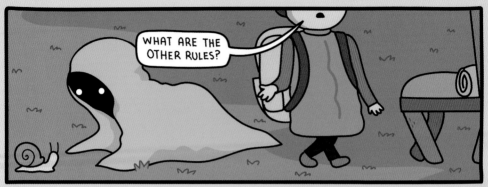

WHAT ARE THE OTHER RULES?

THAT'S PRETTY MUCH IT.

BUT, YOU SAID—

—IF I START WITH "RULE NUMBER ONE," PEOPLE PAY MORE ATTENTION TO ME.

I DON'T LIKE REPEATING MYSELF.

THIS IS SO EXCITING! WE ARE ON A QUEST!

THE SLOWEST QUEST IN THE HISTORY OF QUESTS.

CAN WE PICK UP THE PACE? MY LEGS AREN'T EVEN MOVING.

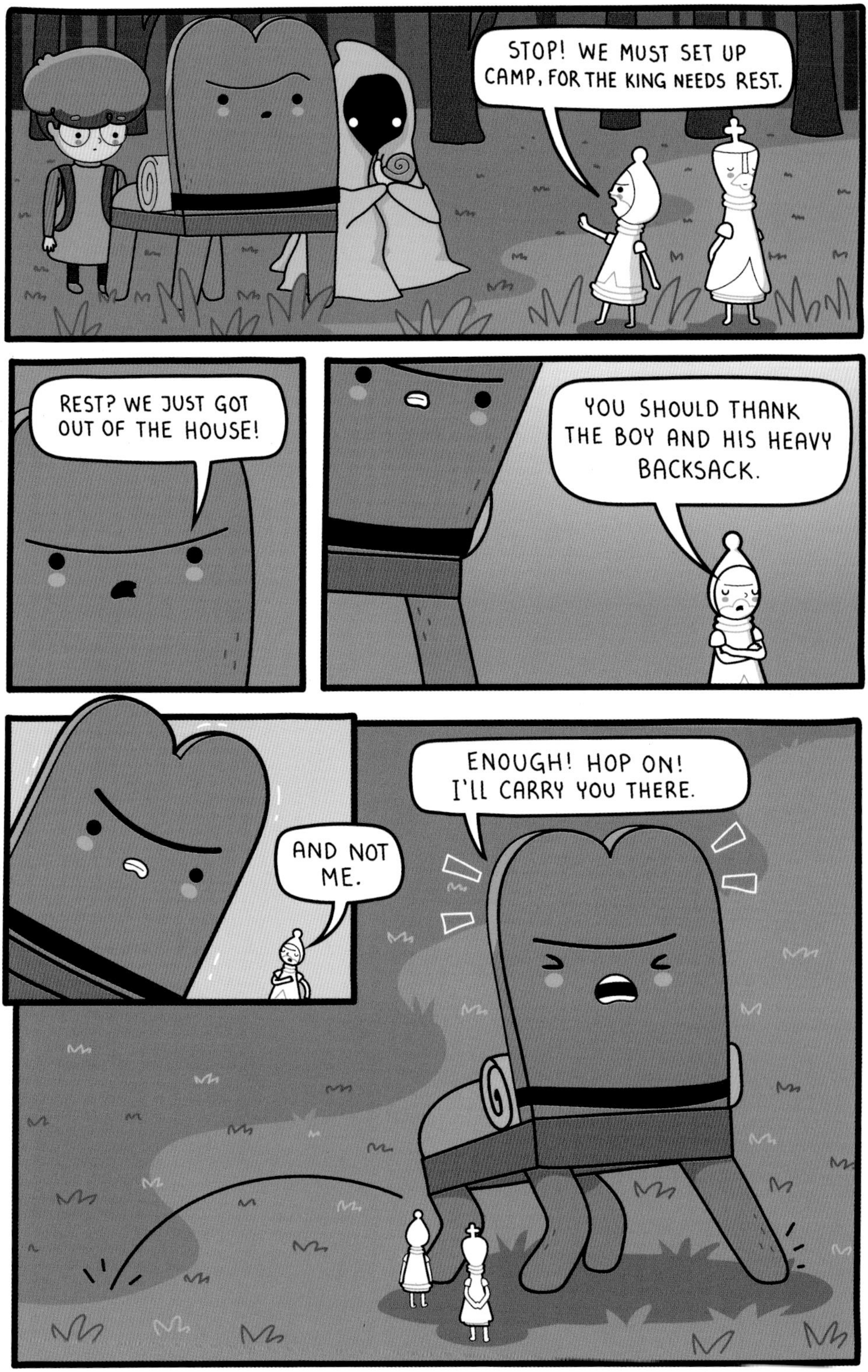
STOP! WE MUST SET UP CAMP, FOR THE KING NEEDS REST.
REST? WE JUST GOT OUT OF THE HOUSE!
YOU SHOULD THANK THE BOY AND HIS HEAVY BACKSACK.
AND NOT ME.
ENOUGH! HOP ON! I'LL CARRY YOU THERE.

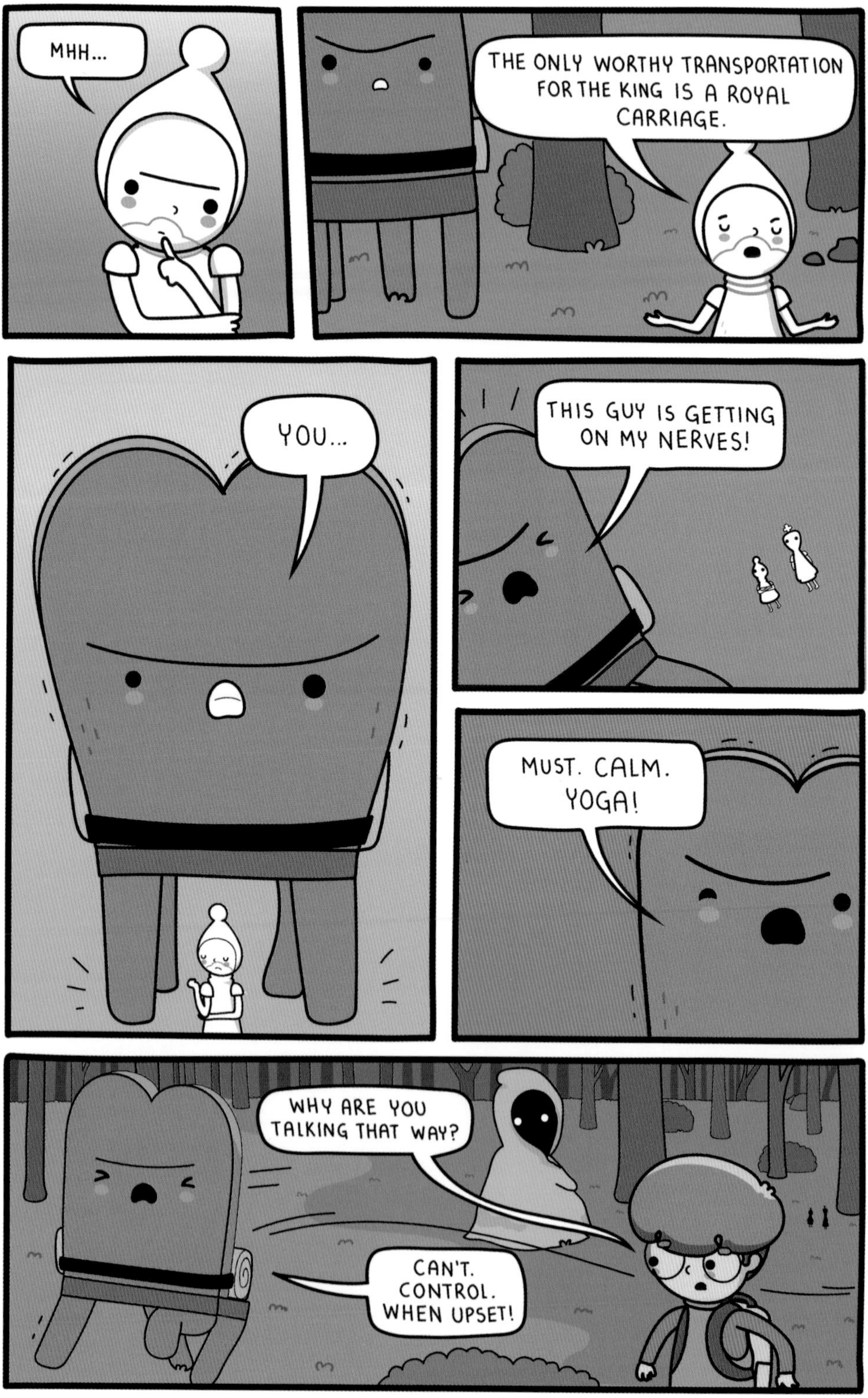
MHH...
THE ONLY WORTHY TRANSPORTATION FOR THE KING IS A ROYAL CARRIAGE.
YOU...
THIS GUY IS GETTING ON MY NERVES!
MUST. CALM. YOGA!
WHY ARE YOU TALKING THAT WAY?
CAN'T. CONTROL. WHEN UPSET!

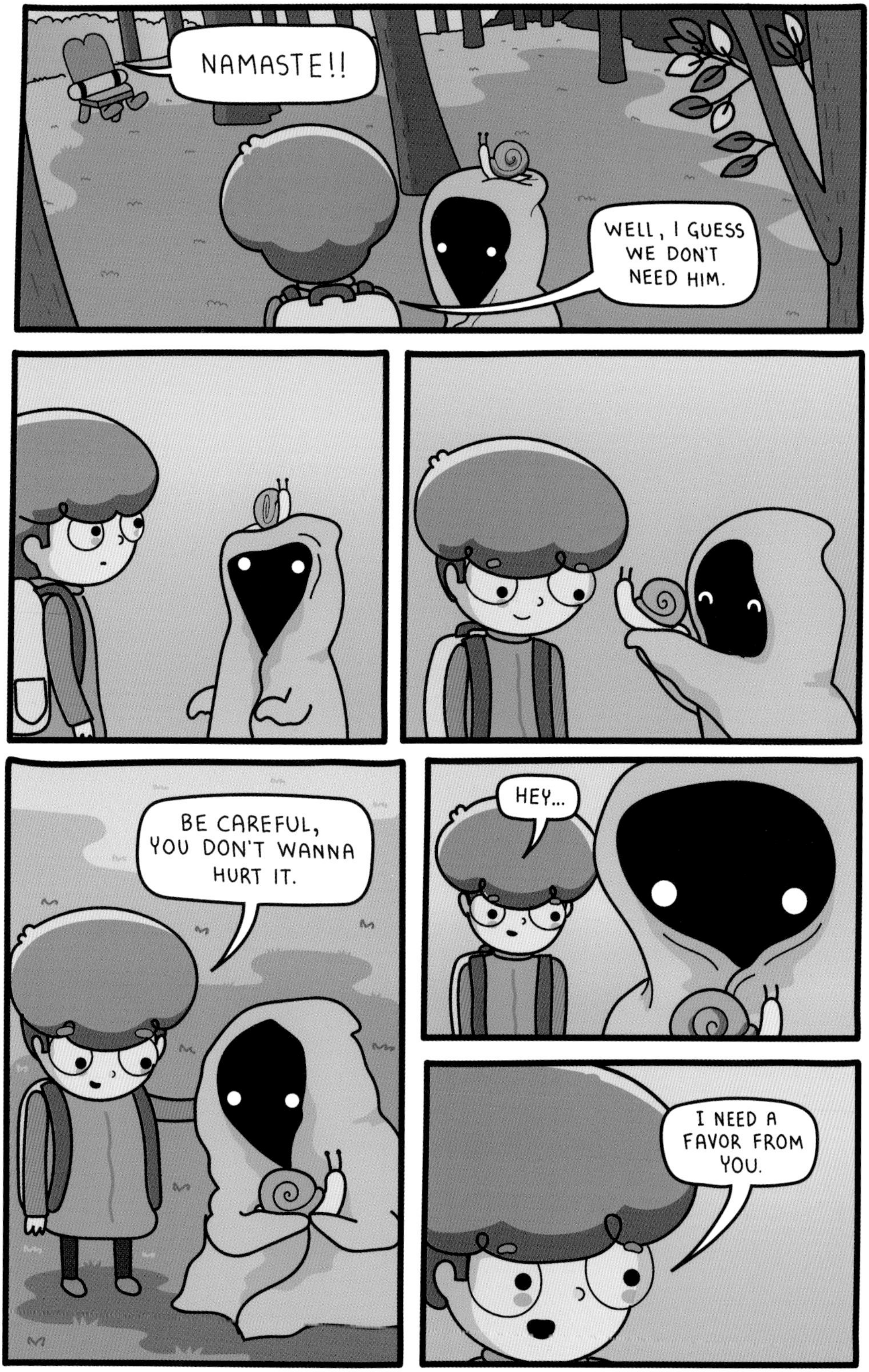
NAMASTE!!
WELL, I GUESS WE DON'T NEED HIM.
BE CAREFUL, YOU DON'T WANNA HURT IT.
HEY...
I NEED A FAVOR FROM YOU.

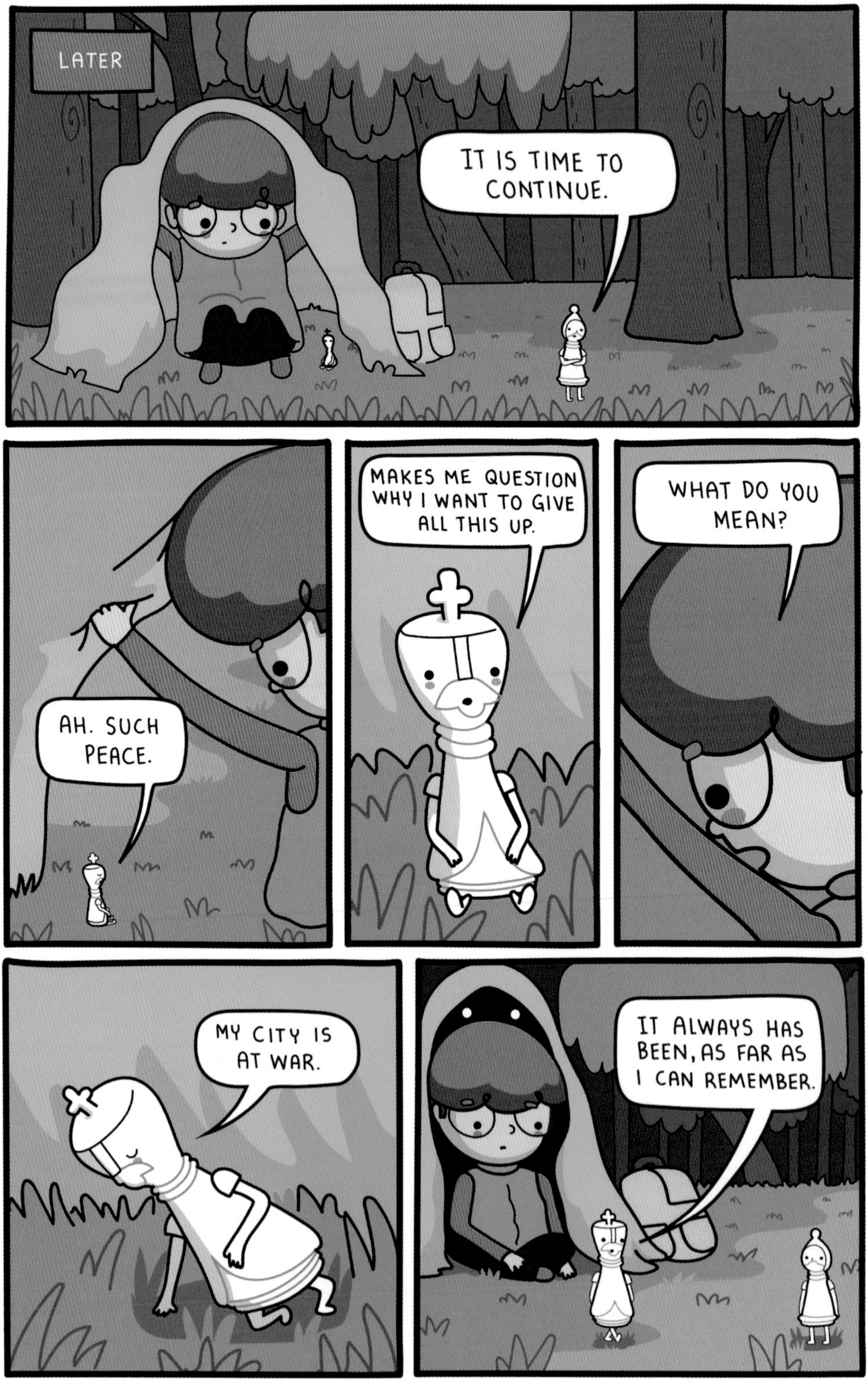
LATER
IT IS TIME TO CONTINUE.
AH. SUCH PEACE.
MAKES ME QUESTION WHY I WANT TO GIVE ALL THIS UP.
WHAT DO YOU MEAN?
MY CITY IS AT WAR.
IT ALWAYS HAS BEEN, AS FAR AS I CAN REMEMBER.

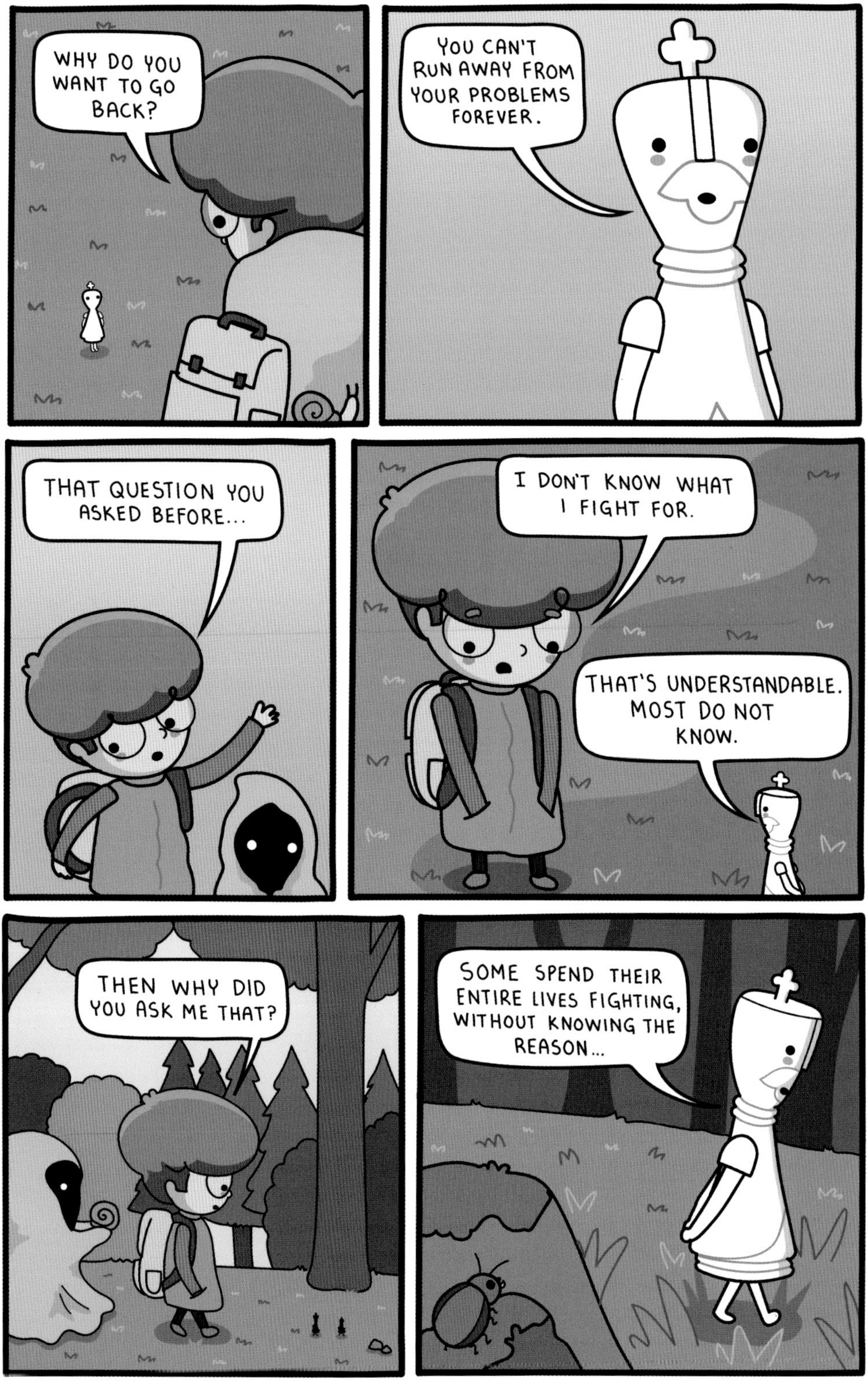
WHY DO YOU WANT TO GO BACK?
YOU CAN'T RUN AWAY FROM YOUR PROBLEMS FOREVER.
THAT QUESTION YOU ASKED BEFORE...
I DON'T KNOW WHAT I FIGHT FOR.
THAT'S UNDERSTANDABLE. MOST DO NOT KNOW.
THEN WHY DID YOU ASK ME THAT?
SOME SPEND THEIR ENTIRE LIVES FIGHTING, WITHOUT KNOWING THE REASON...

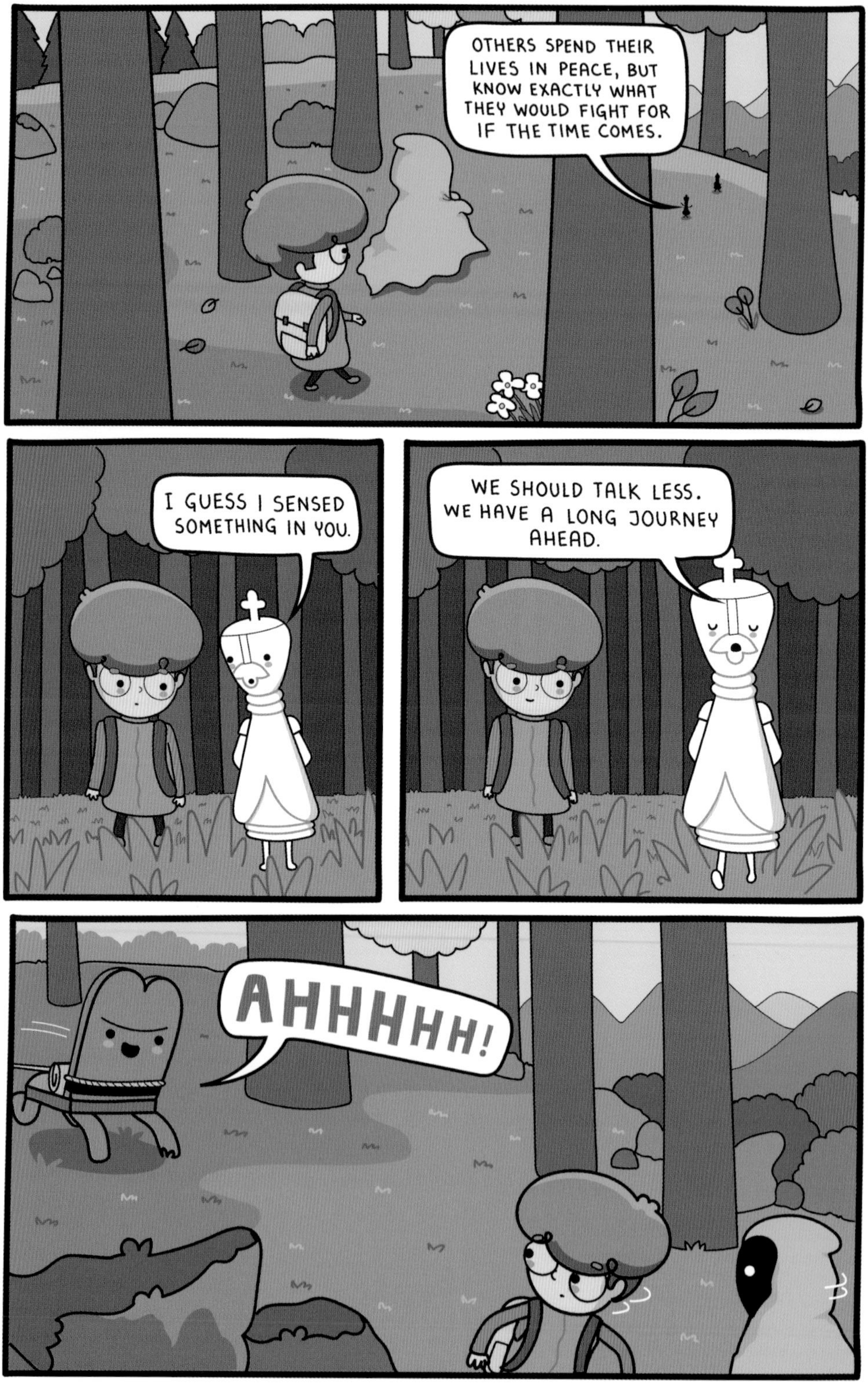
OTHERS SPEND THEIR LIVES IN PEACE, BUT KNOW EXACTLY WHAT THEY WOULD FIGHT FOR IF THE TIME COMES.
I GUESS I SENSED SOMETHING IN YOU.
WE SHOULD TALK LESS. WE HAVE A LONG JOURNEY AHEAD.
AHHHHH!

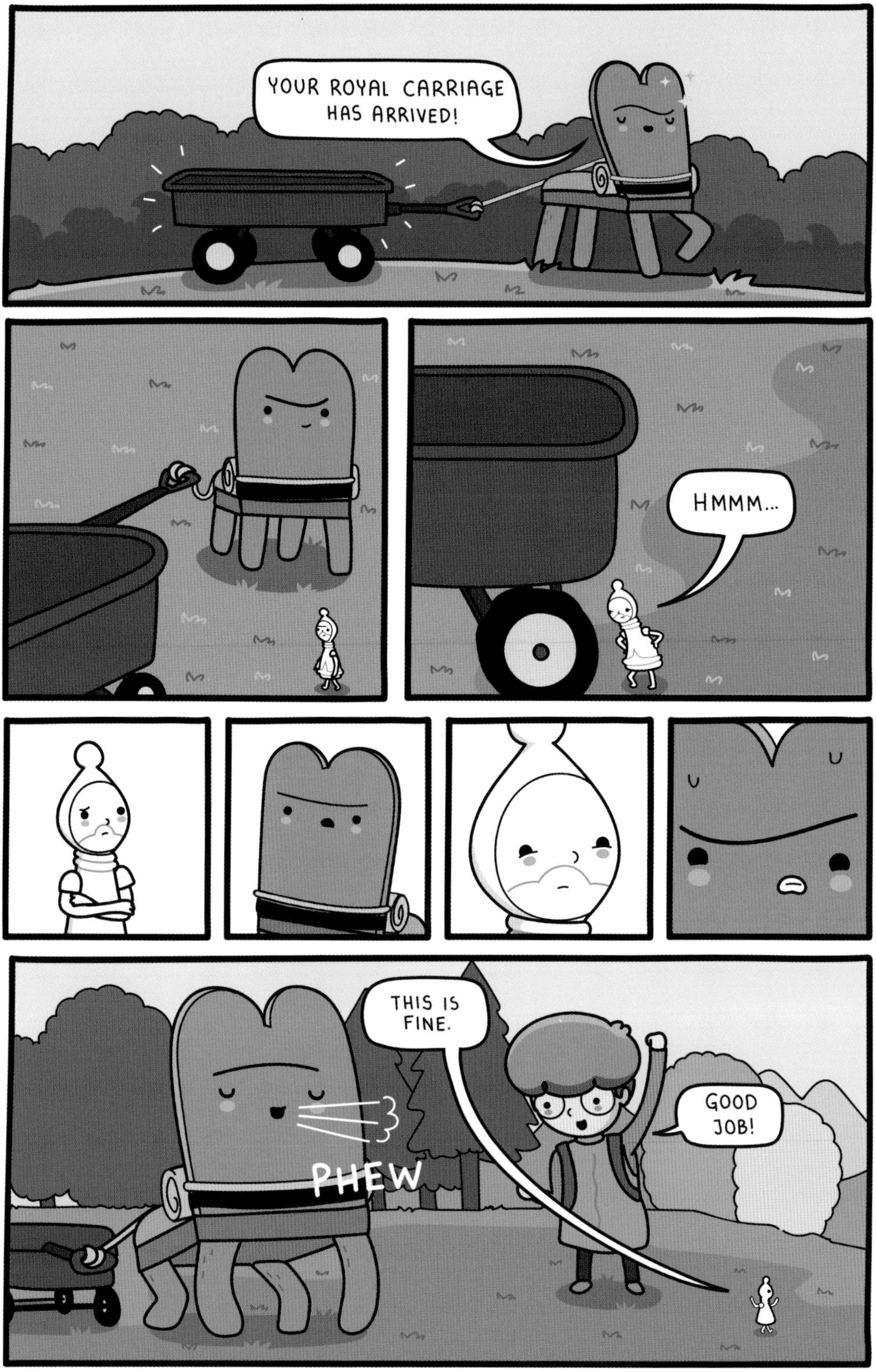
YOUR ROYAL CARRIAGE HAS ARRIVED!
HMMM...
THIS IS FINE.
PHEW
GOOD JOB!

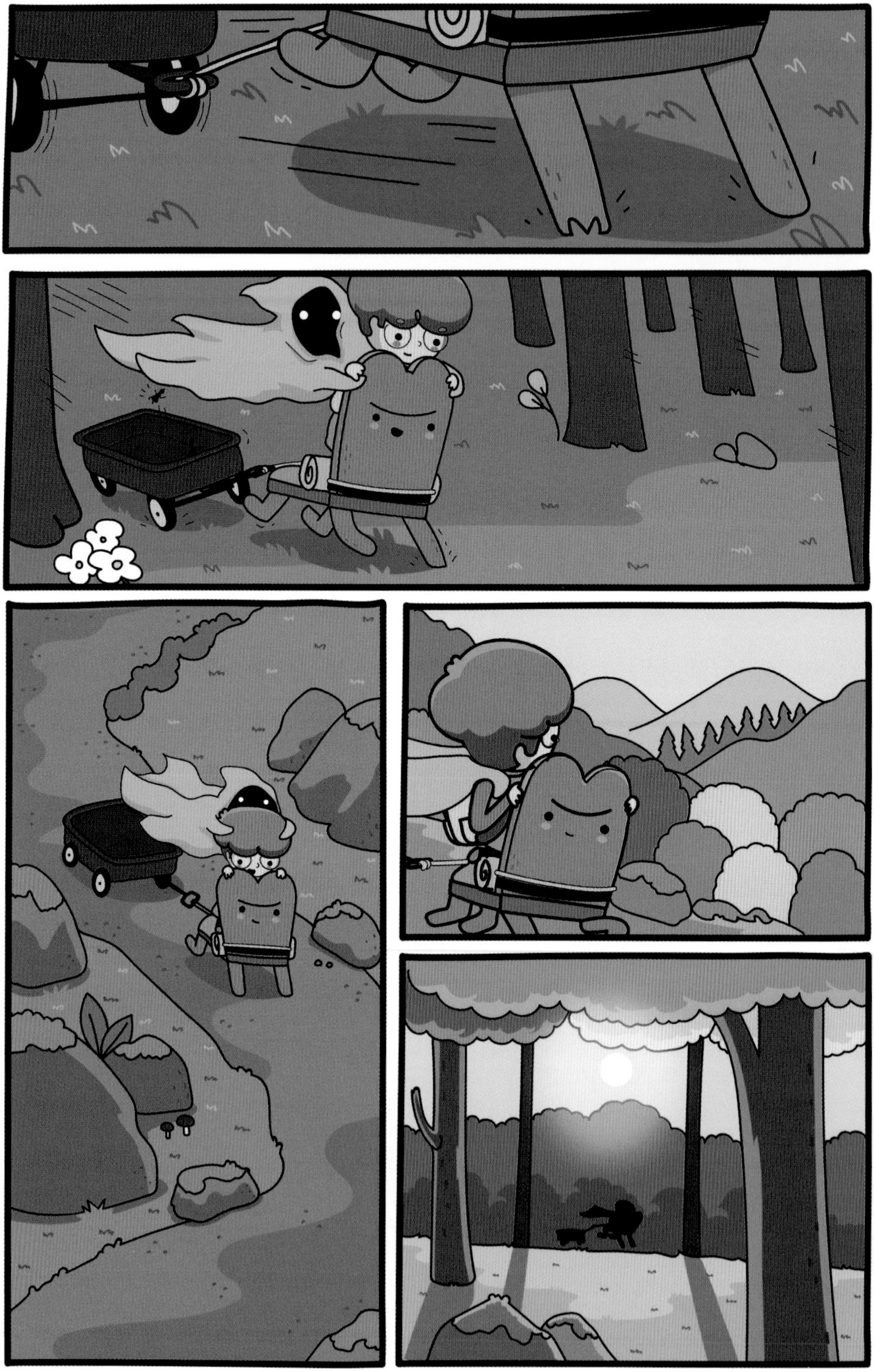

WHY DID YOU STOP?

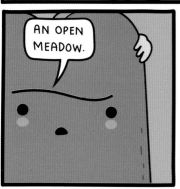

AN OPEN MEADOW.

WE COULD BE SEEN BY HUMANS.

THOSE HORSES.

IF WE RUN AMONG THEM, MAYBE WE CAN GET THERE UNSEEN. CAN YOU DO IT?

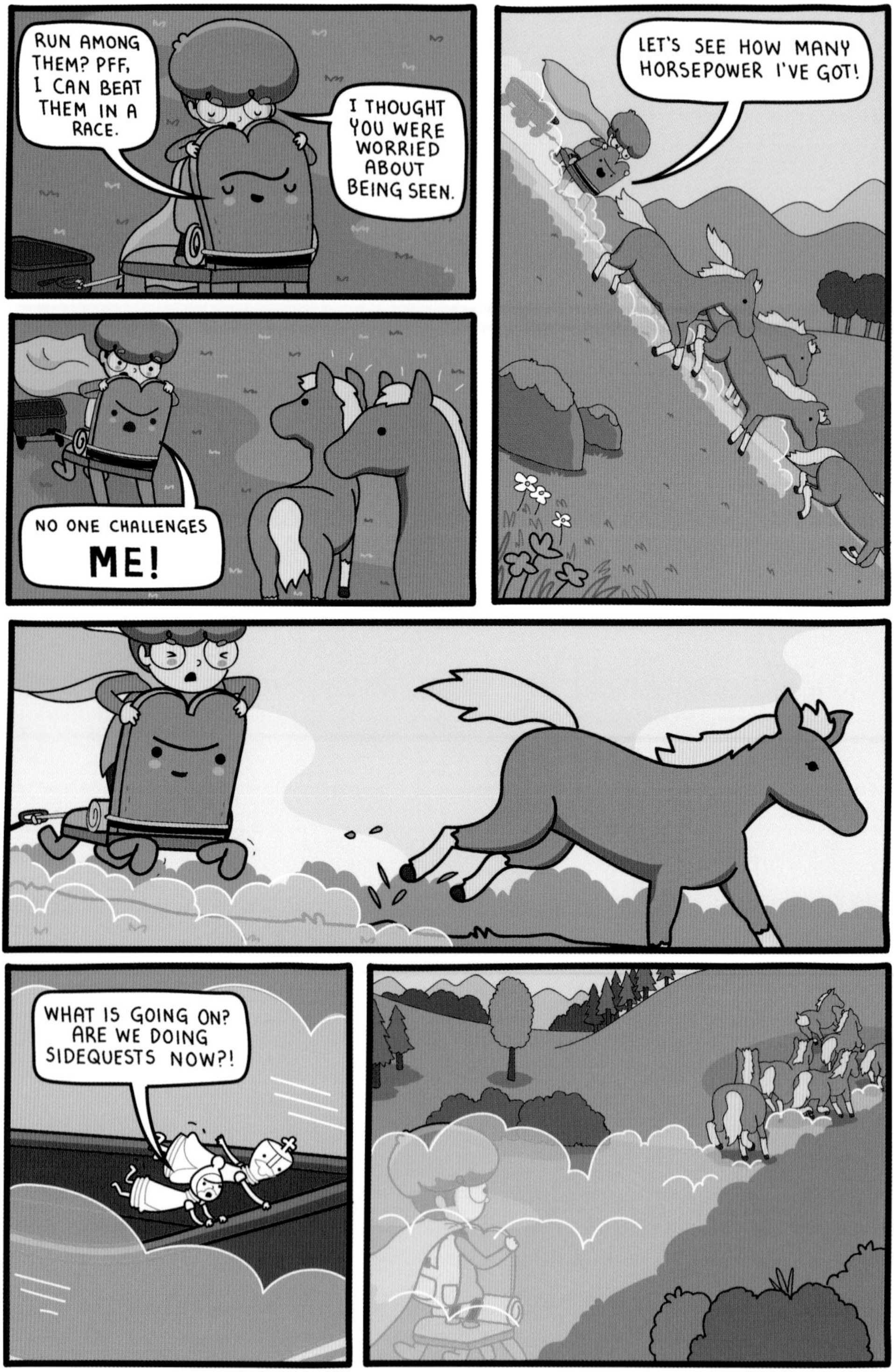
RUN AMONG THEM? PFF, I CAN BEAT THEM IN A RACE.
I THOUGHT YOU WERE WORRIED ABOUT BEING SEEN.
NO ONE CHALLENGES ME!
LET'S SEE HOW MANY HORSEPOWER I'VE GOT!
WHAT IS GOING ON? ARE WE DOING SIDEQUESTS NOW?!

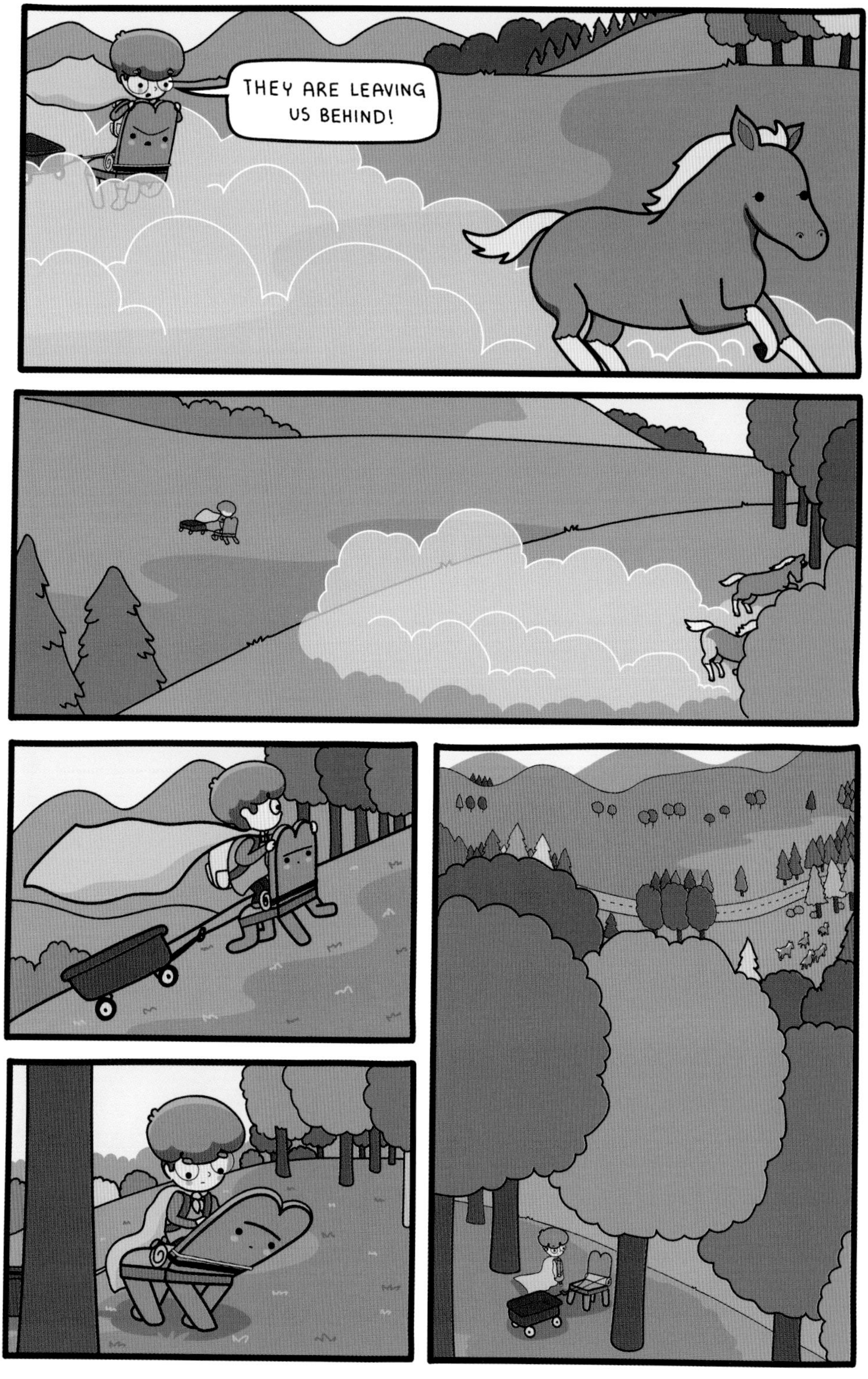
THEY ARE LEAVING US BEHIND!

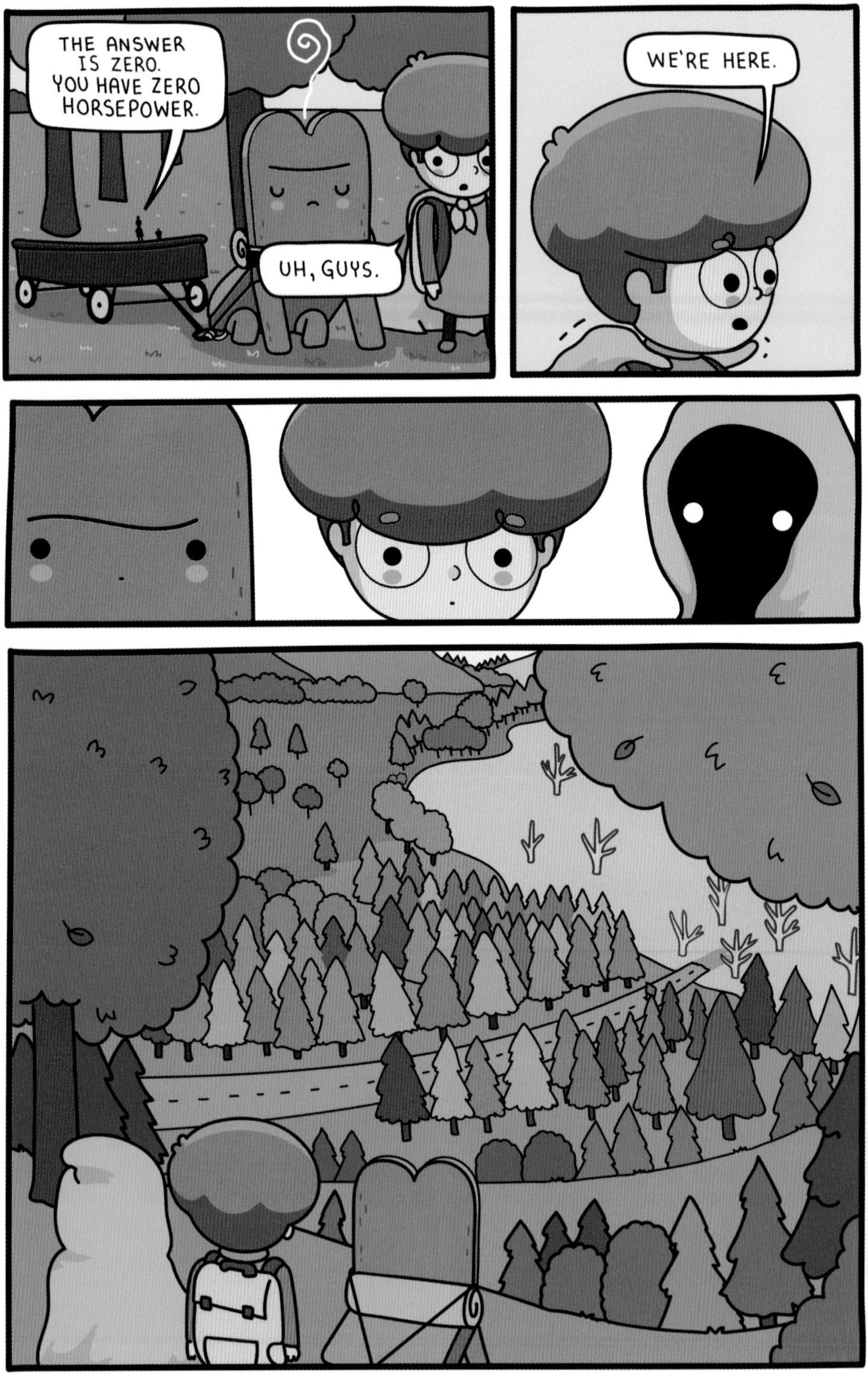
THE ANSWER IS ZERO. YOU HAVE ZERO HORSEPOWER.
UH, GUYS.
WE'RE HERE.

ARE YOU OK?

I'M PERFECT.

JILL WILL BE SO MAD IF SHE FINDS OUT I SKIPPED SCHOOL FOR THIS.

SHE WON'T BE BACK BEFORE THE SUN SETS.

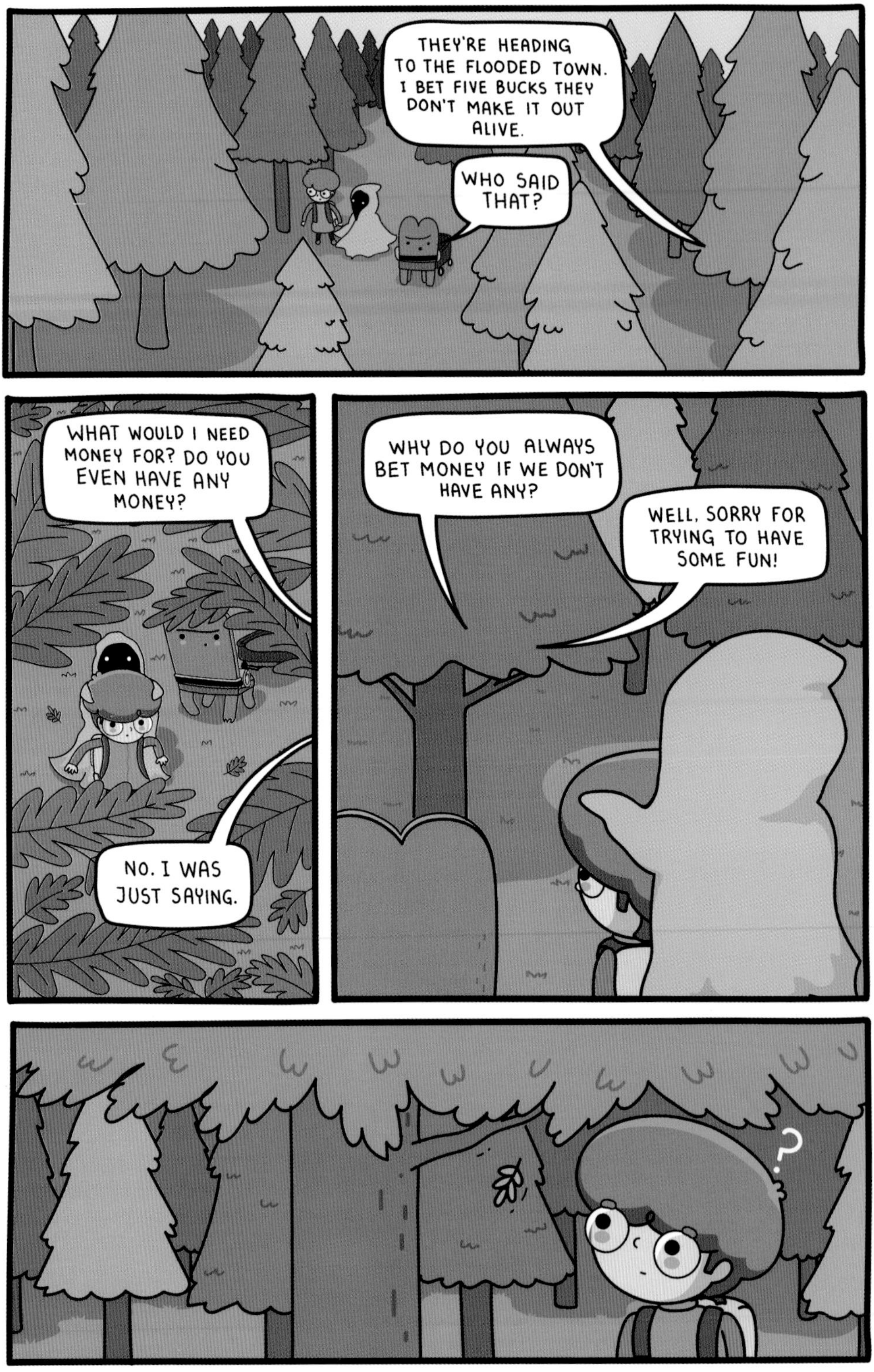
THEY'RE HEADING TO THE FLOODED TOWN. I BET FIVE BUCKS THEY DON'T MAKE IT OUT ALIVE.
WHO SAID THAT?
WHAT WOULD I NEED MONEY FOR? DO YOU EVEN HAVE ANY MONEY?
NO. I WAS JUST SAYING.
WHY DO YOU ALWAYS BET MONEY IF WE DON'T HAVE ANY?
WELL, SORRY FOR TRYING TO HAVE SOME FUN!
?

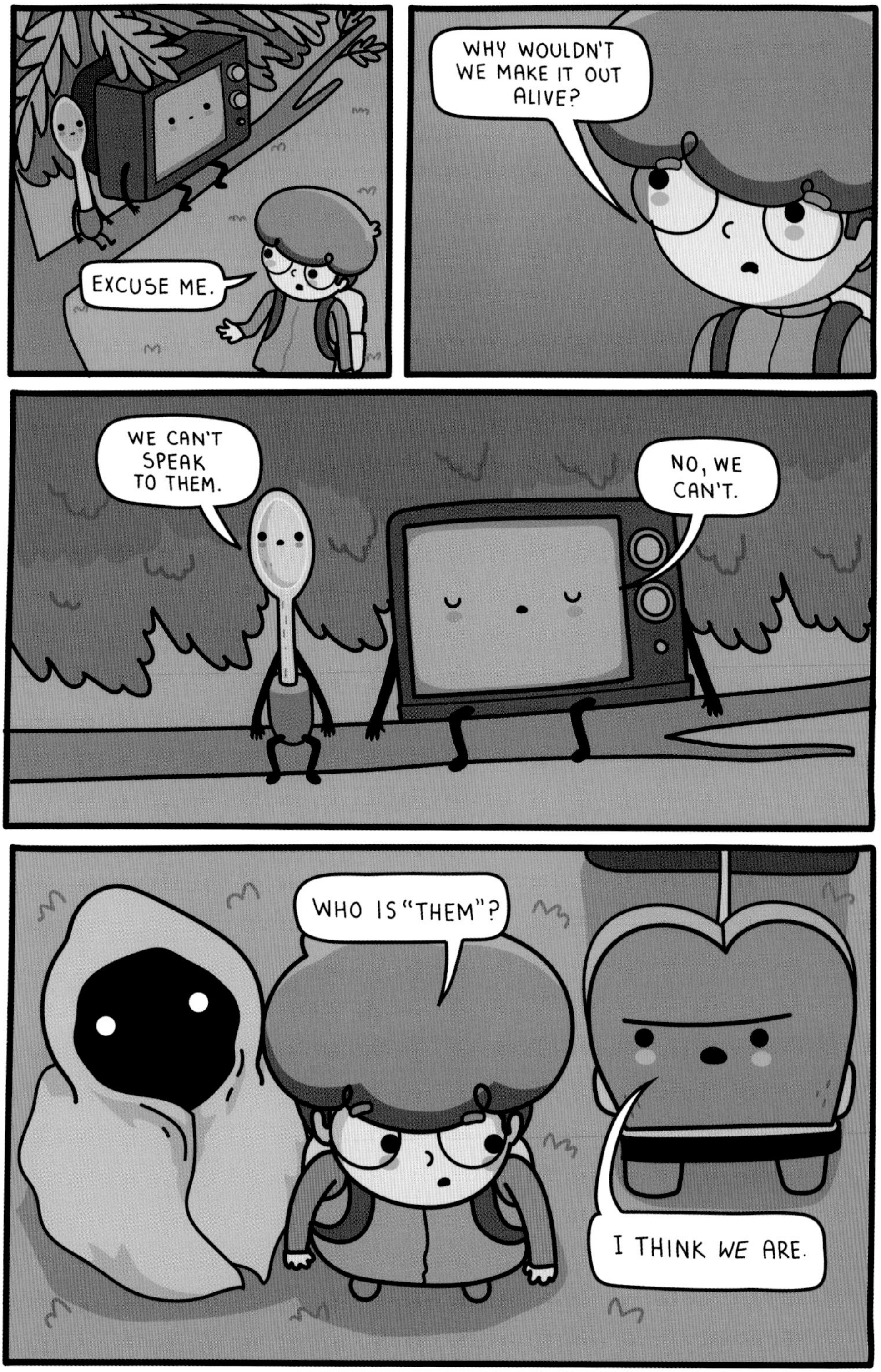
EXCUSE ME.
WHY WOULDN'T WE MAKE IT OUT ALIVE?
WE CAN'T SPEAK TO THEM.
NO, WE CAN'T.
WHO IS "THEM"?
I THINK WE ARE.

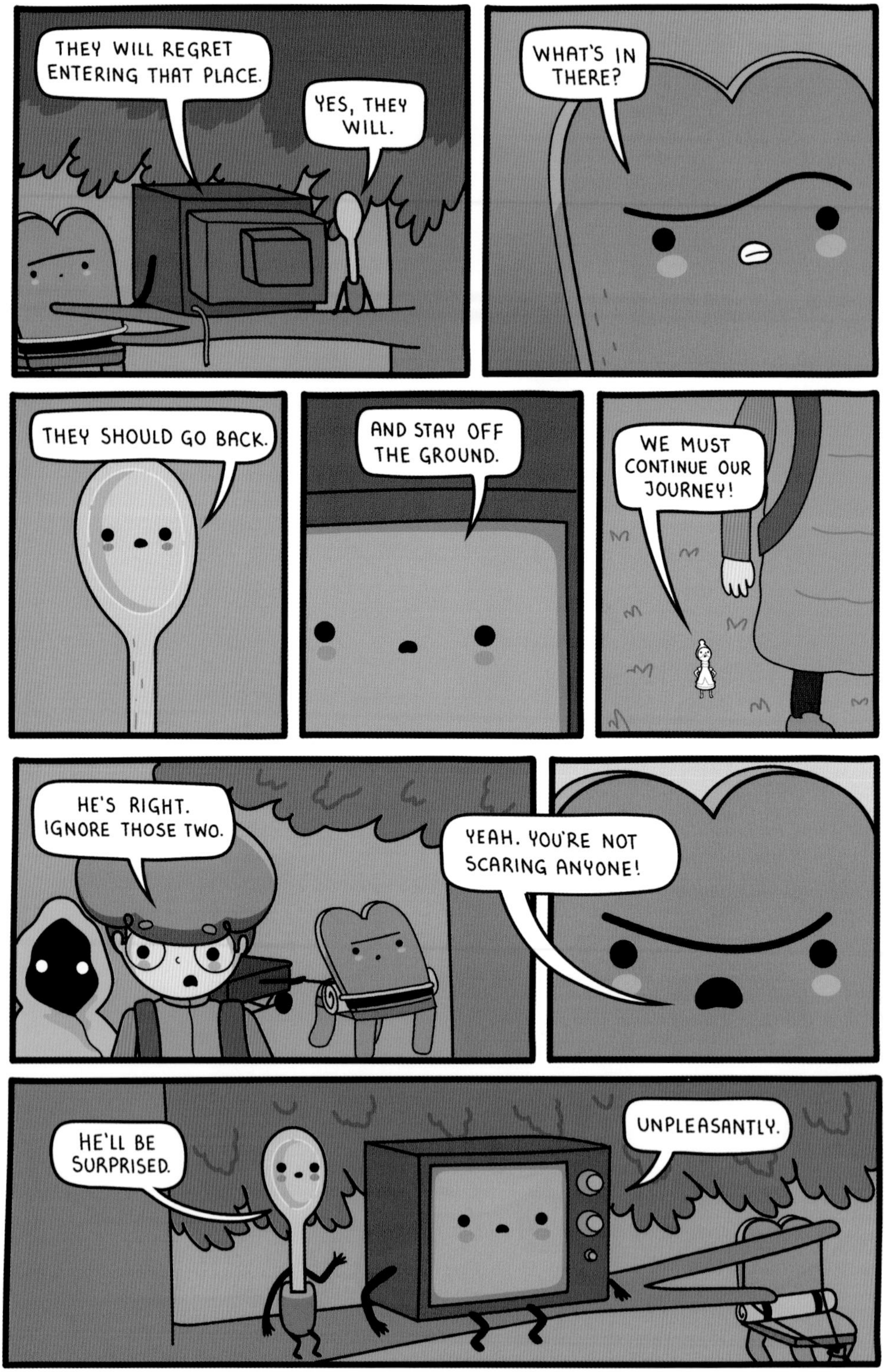
THEY WILL REGRET ENTERING THAT PLACE.
YES, THEY WILL.
WHAT'S IN THERE?
THEY SHOULD GO BACK.
AND STAY OFF THE GROUND.
WE MUST CONTINUE OUR JOURNEY!
HE'S RIGHT. IGNORE THOSE TWO.
YEAH. YOU'RE NOT SCARING ANYONE!
HE'LL BE SURPRISED.
UNPLEASANTLY.

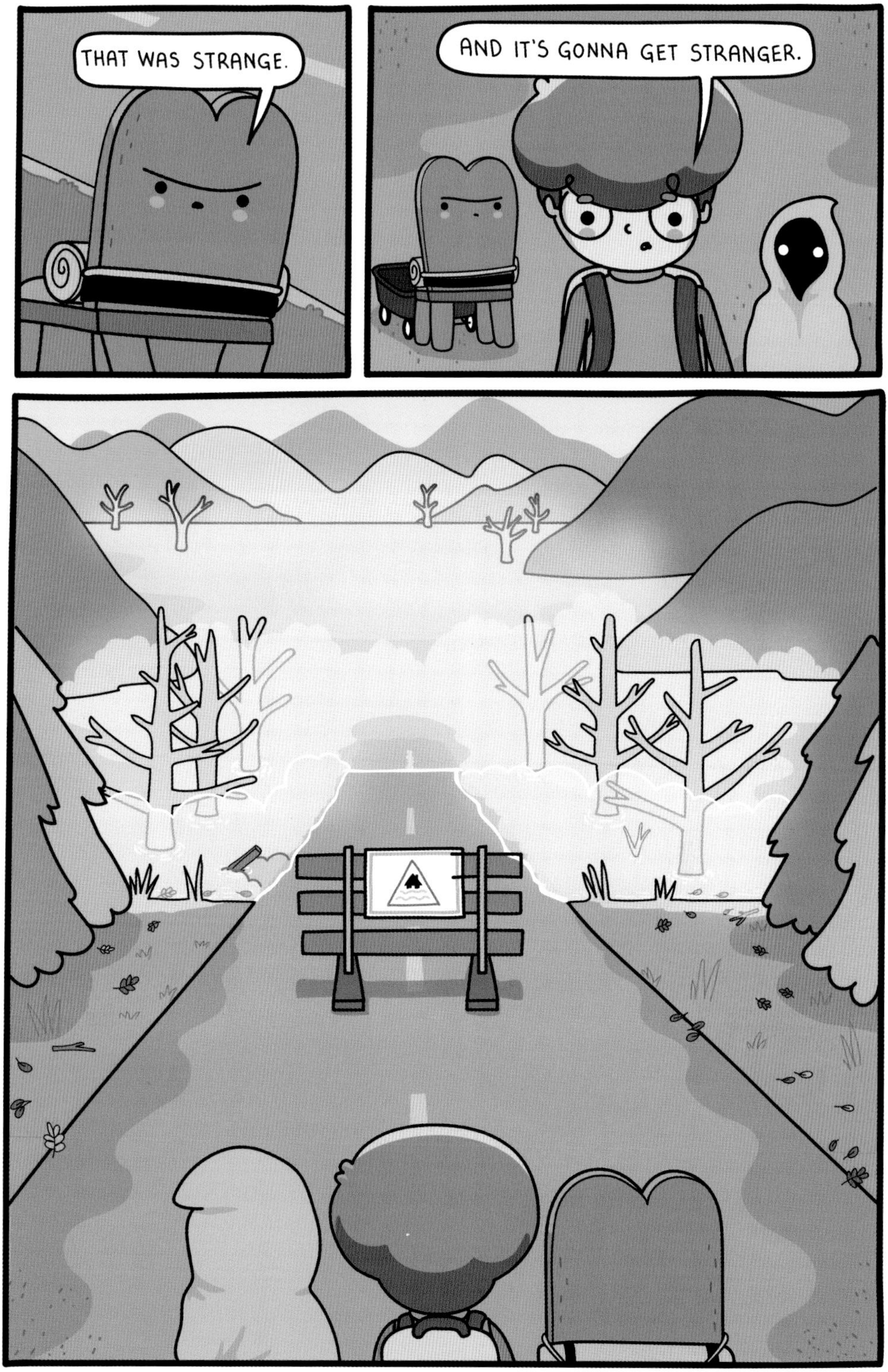
THAT WAS STRANGE.
AND IT'S GONNA GET STRANGER.

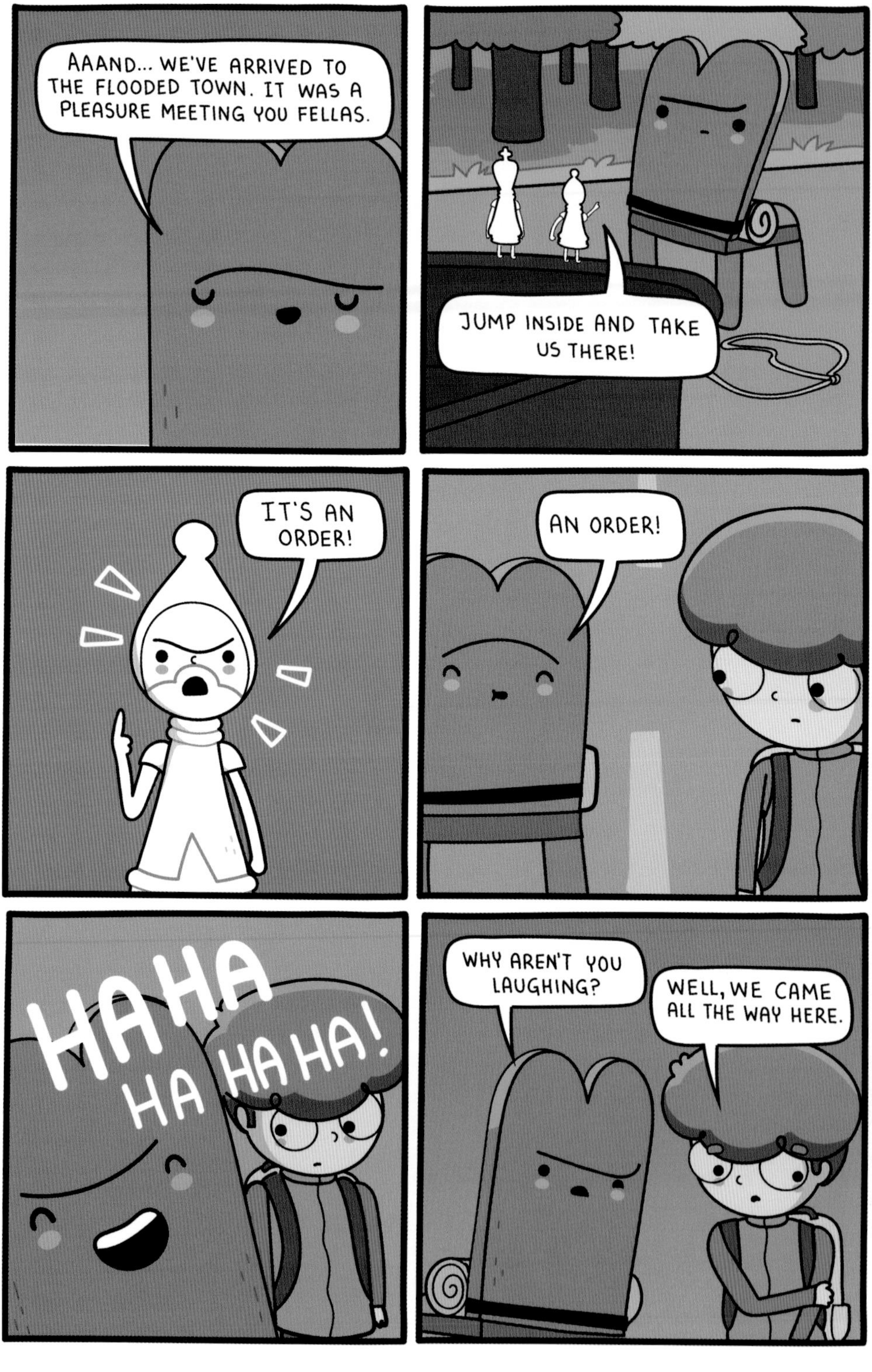
AAAND... WE'VE ARRIVED TO THE FLOODED TOWN. IT WAS A PLEASURE MEETING YOU FELLAS.
JUMP INSIDE AND TAKE US THERE!
IT'S AN ORDER!
AN ORDER!
HAHA HA HAHA!
WHY AREN'T YOU LAUGHING?
WELL, WE CAME ALL THE WAY HERE.

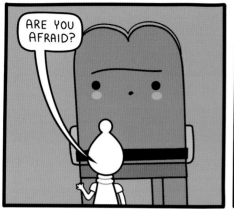

ARE YOU AFRAID?

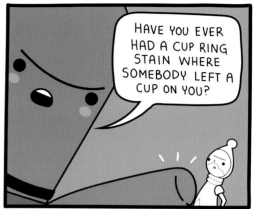

HAVE YOU EVER HAD A CUP RING STAIN WHERE SOMEBODY LEFT A CUP ON YOU?

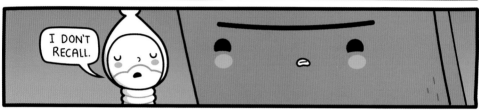

I DON'T RECALL.

PICTURE THAT TIMES A THOUSAND. I CAN'T GET WET!

PLUS, YOU HEARD THOSE TWO BACK THERE ...

WE WON'T GET OUT ALIVE FROM THERE!

FIND US A SHIP, THEN!

EVEN IF I FIND THE PERFECT BOAT FOR YOU, IT WON'T BE ROYAL ENOUGH FOR YOUR PRECIOUS KING!

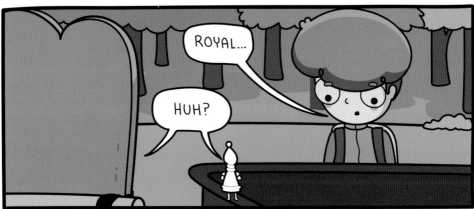

ROYAL...

HUH?

DO YOU THINK THIS FLOATS?

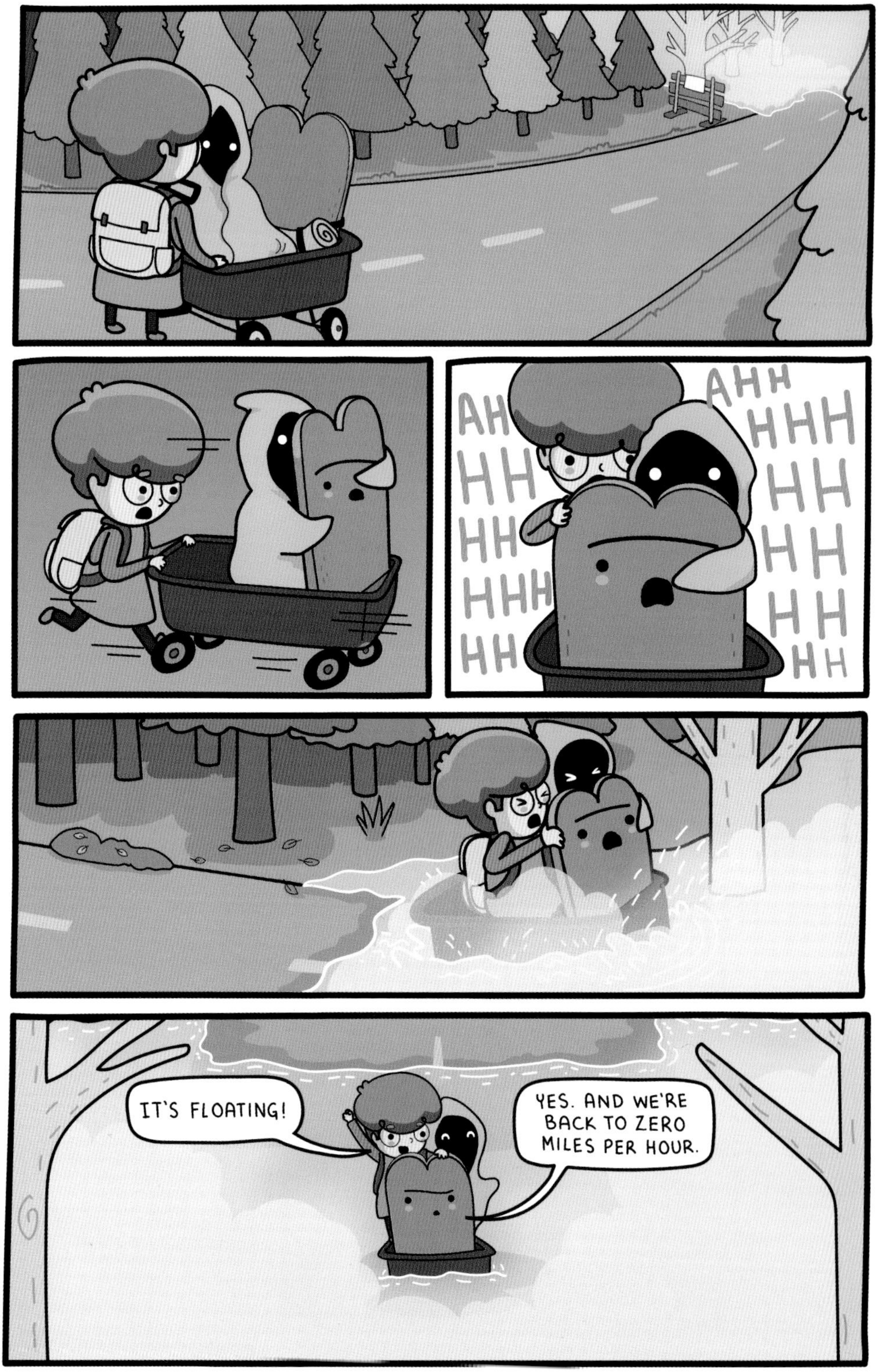
AHHHHHHHHHH
AHHHHHHHHHHHHHH
IT'S FLOATING!
YES. AND WE'RE BACK TO ZERO MILES PER HOUR.

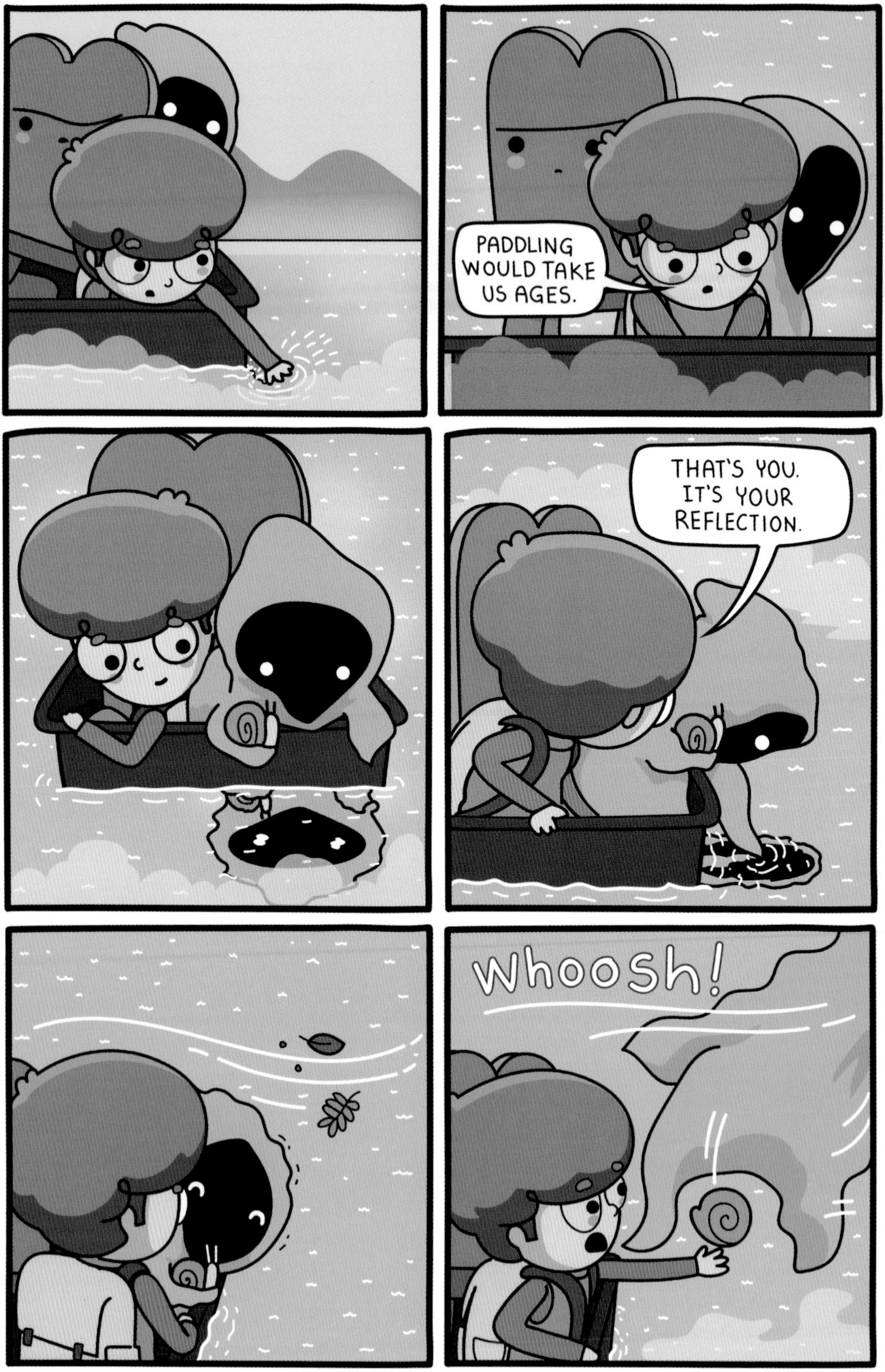
PADDLING WOULD TAKE US AGES.
THAT'S YOU. IT'S YOUR REFLECTION.
Whoosh!

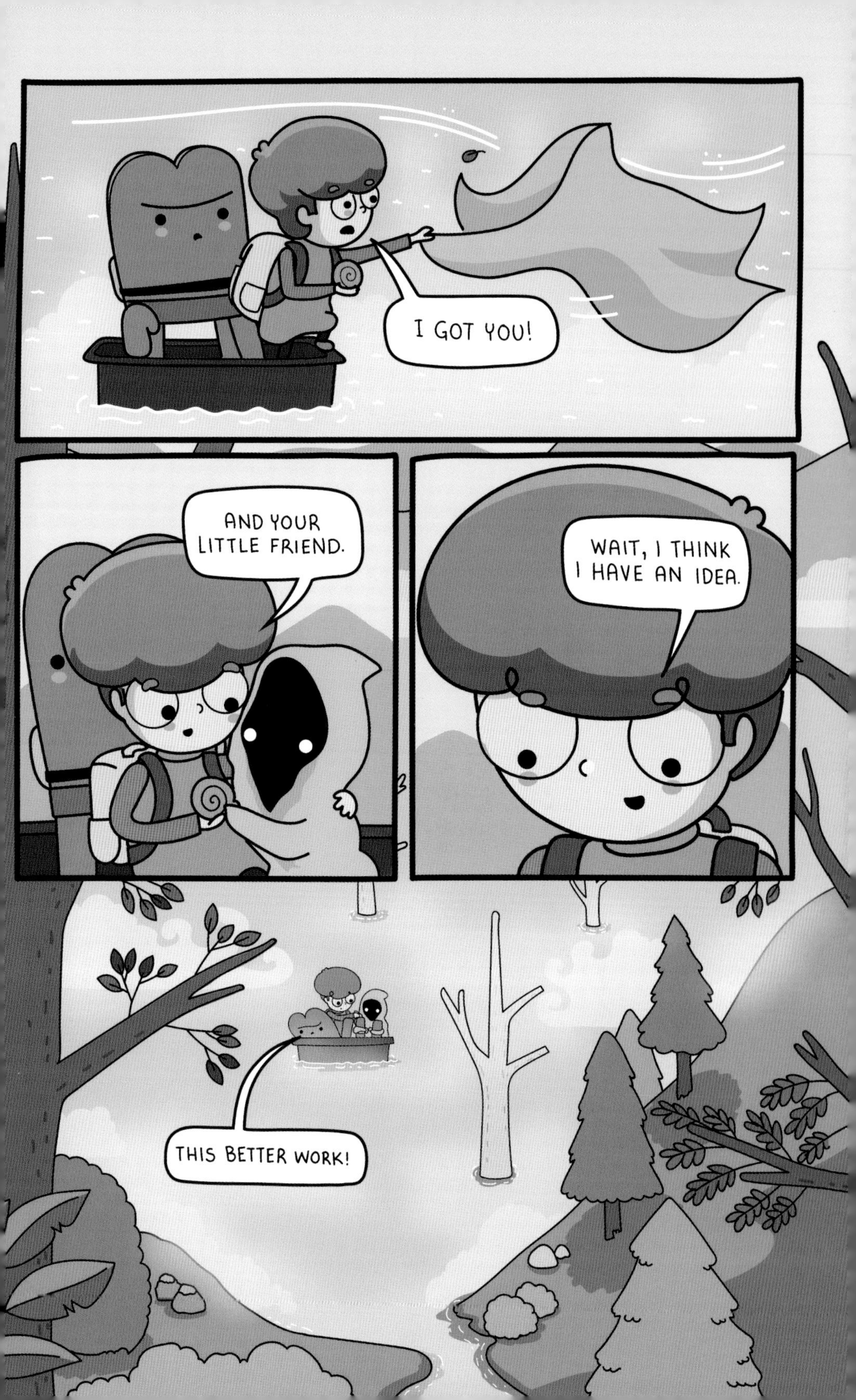
I GOT YOU!
AND YOUR LITTLE FRIEND.
WAIT, I THINK I HAVE AN IDEA.
THIS BETTER WORK!

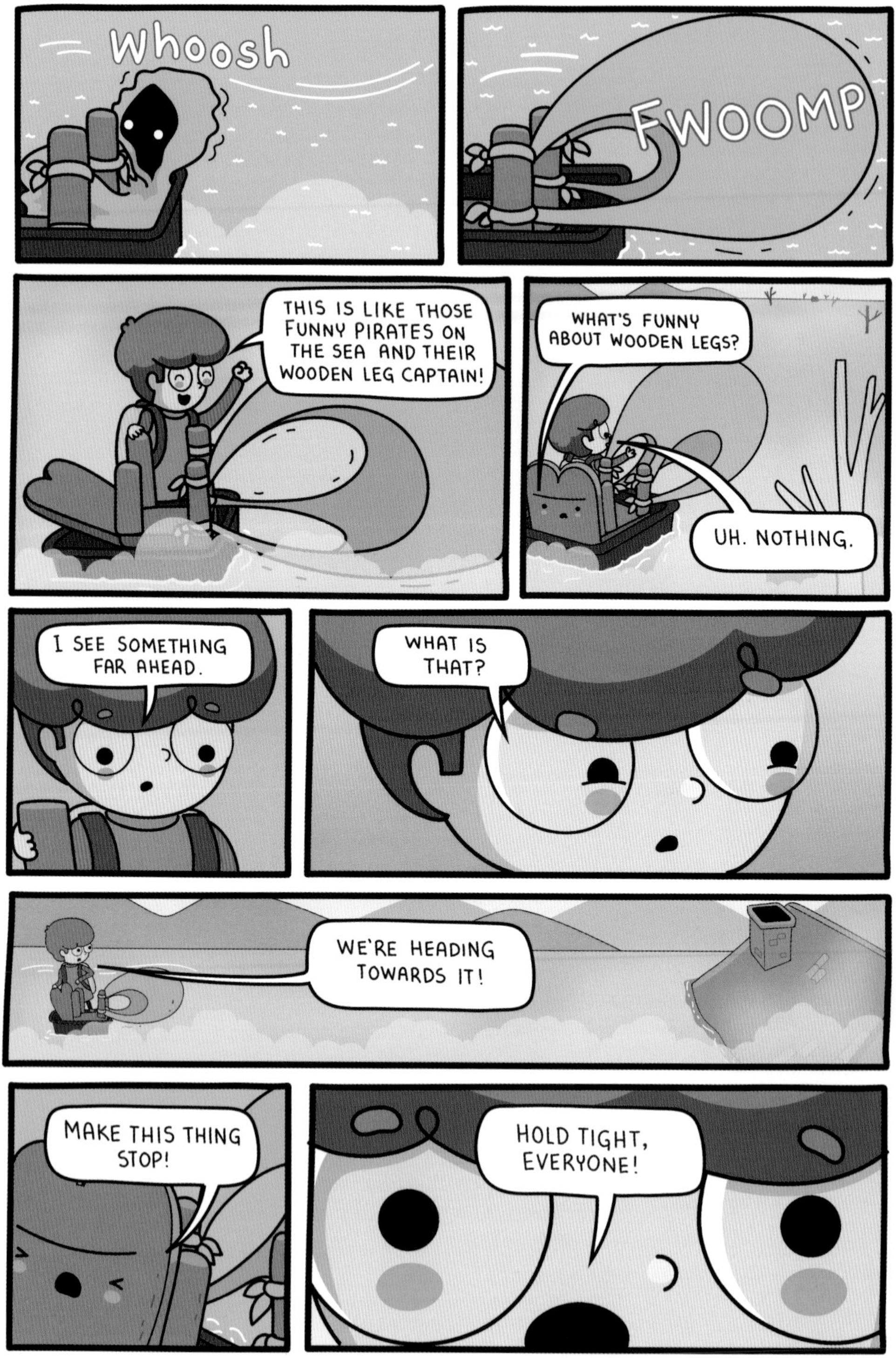
Whoosh
FWOOMP
THIS IS LIKE THOSE FUNNY PIRATES ON THE SEA AND THEIR WOODEN LEG CAPTAIN!
WHAT'S FUNNY ABOUT WOODEN LEGS?
UH. NOTHING.
I SEE SOMETHING FAR AHEAD.
WHAT IS THAT?
WE'RE HEADING TOWARDS IT!
MAKE THIS THING STOP!
HOLD TIGHT, EVERYONE!

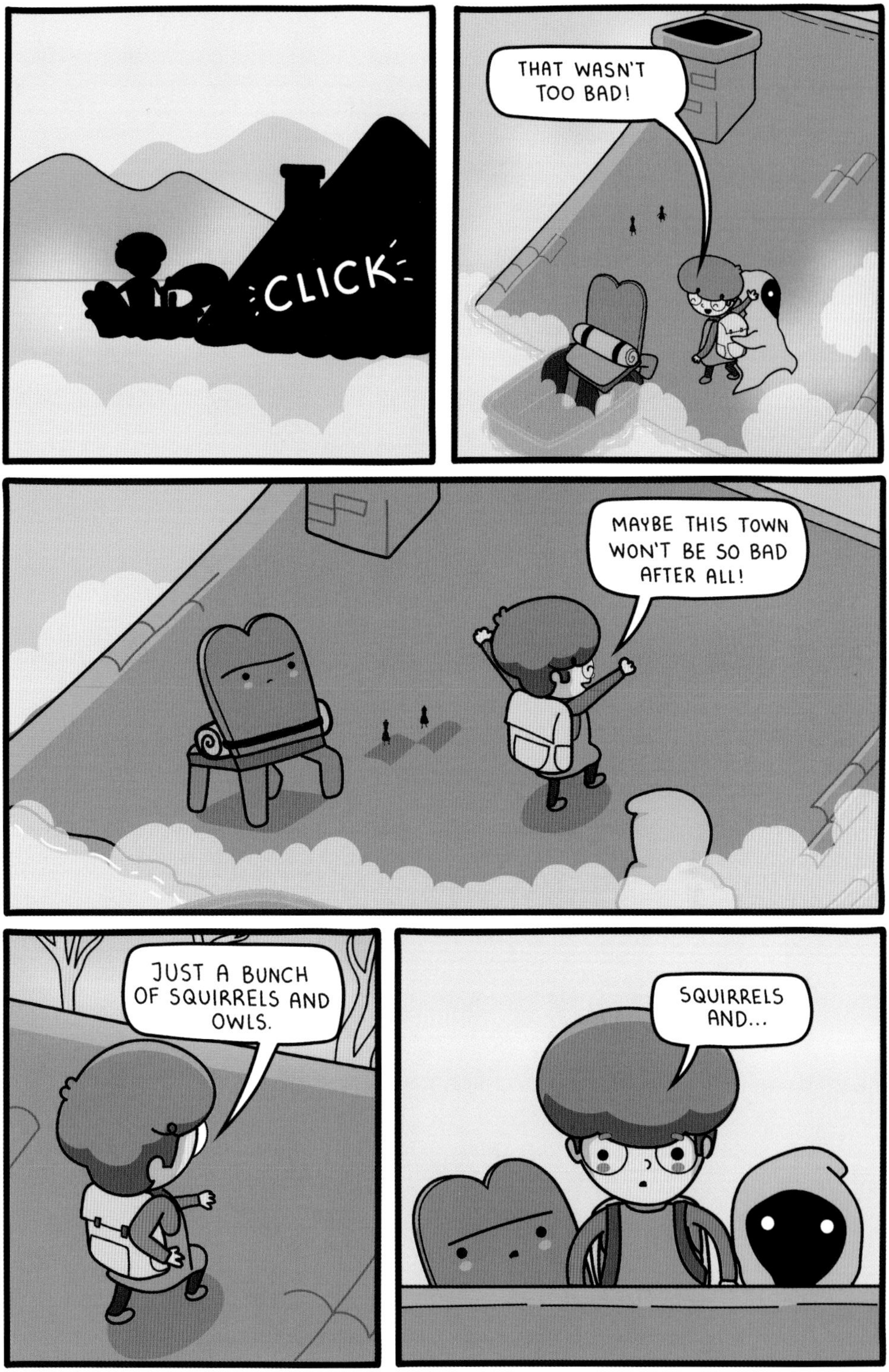
CLICK
THAT WASN'T TOO BAD!
MAYBE THIS TOWN WON'T BE SO BAD AFTER ALL!
JUST A BUNCH OF SQUIRRELS AND OWLS.
SQUIRRELS AND...

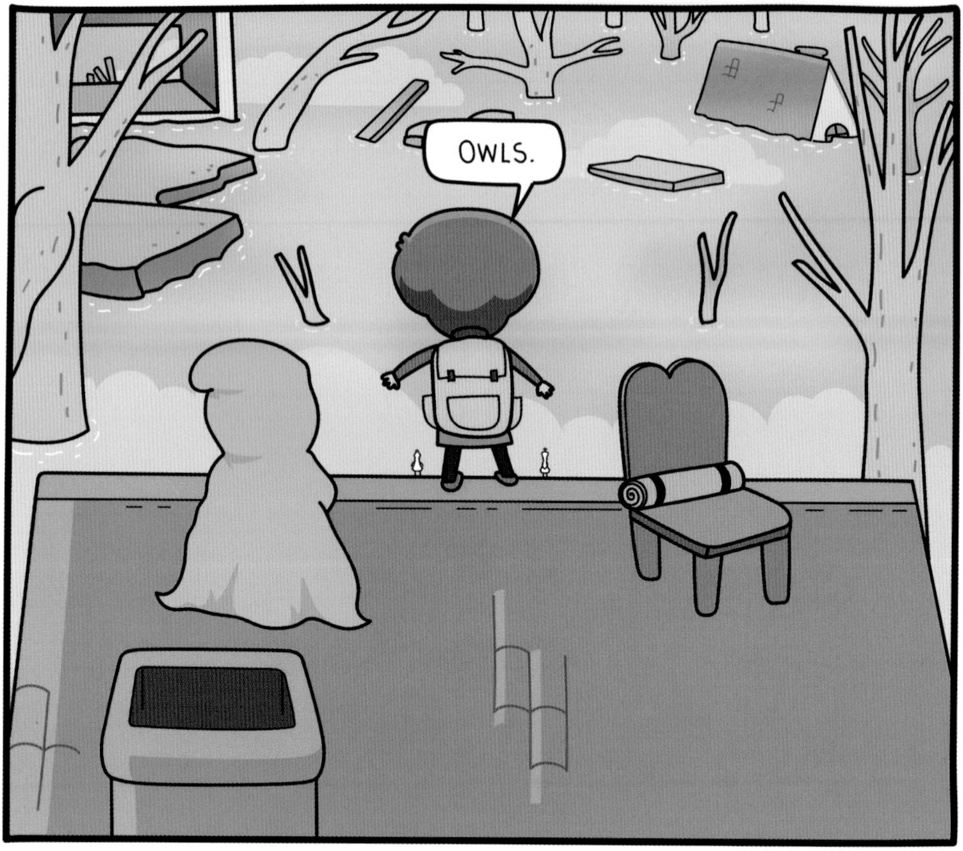
OWLS.

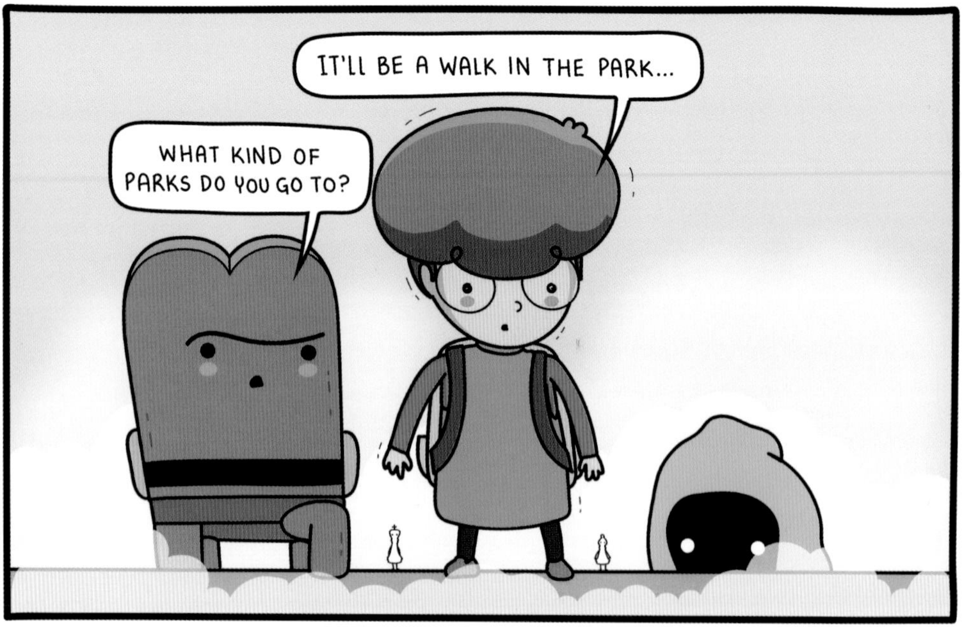
IT'LL BE A WALK IN THE PARK...
WHAT KIND OF PARKS DO YOU GO TO?

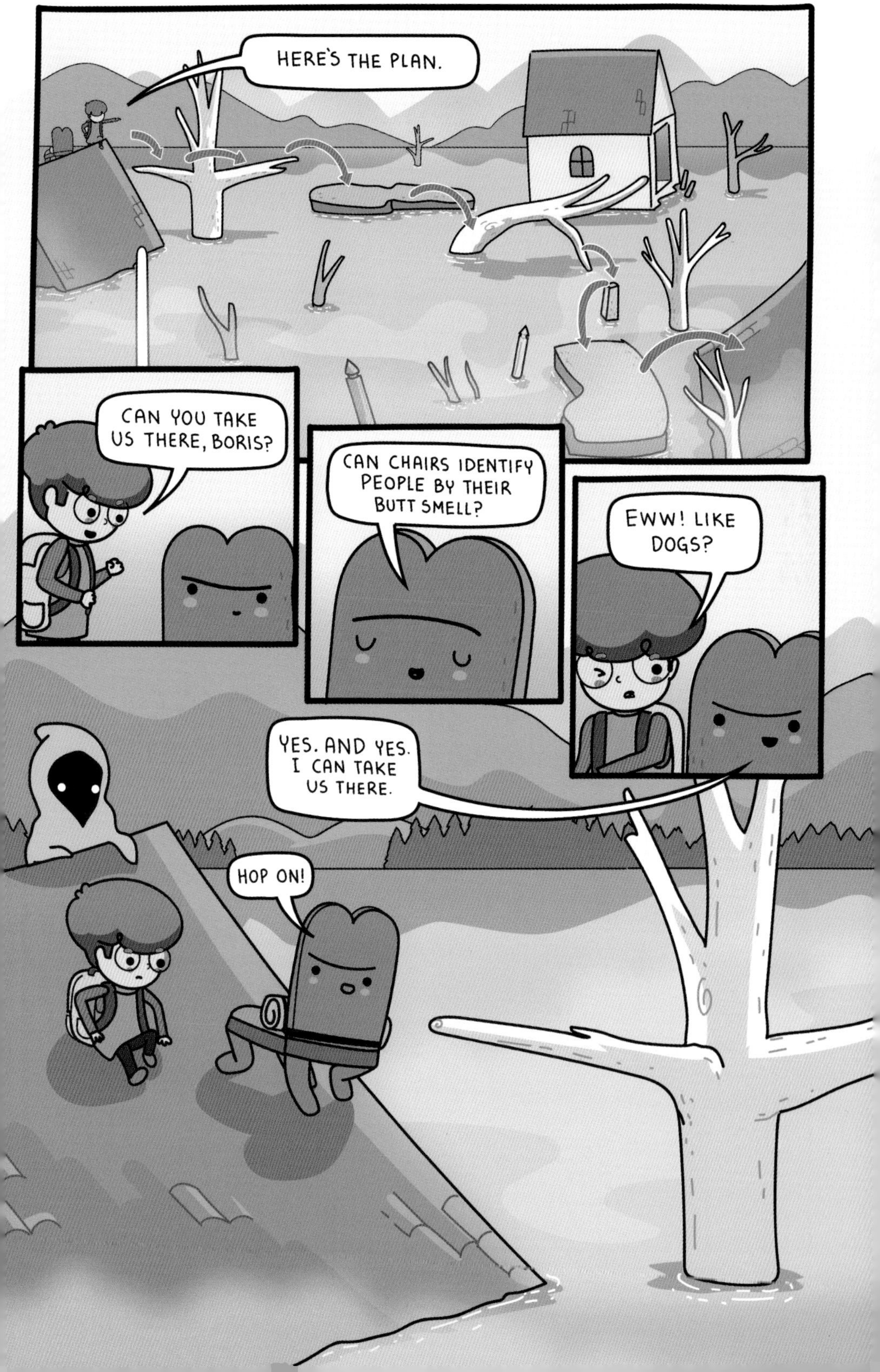
HERE'S THE PLAN.
CAN YOU TAKE US THERE, BORIS?
CAN CHAIRS IDENTIFY PEOPLE BY THEIR BUTT SMELL?
EWW! LIKE DOGS?
YES. AND YES. I CAN TAKE US THERE.
HOP ON!

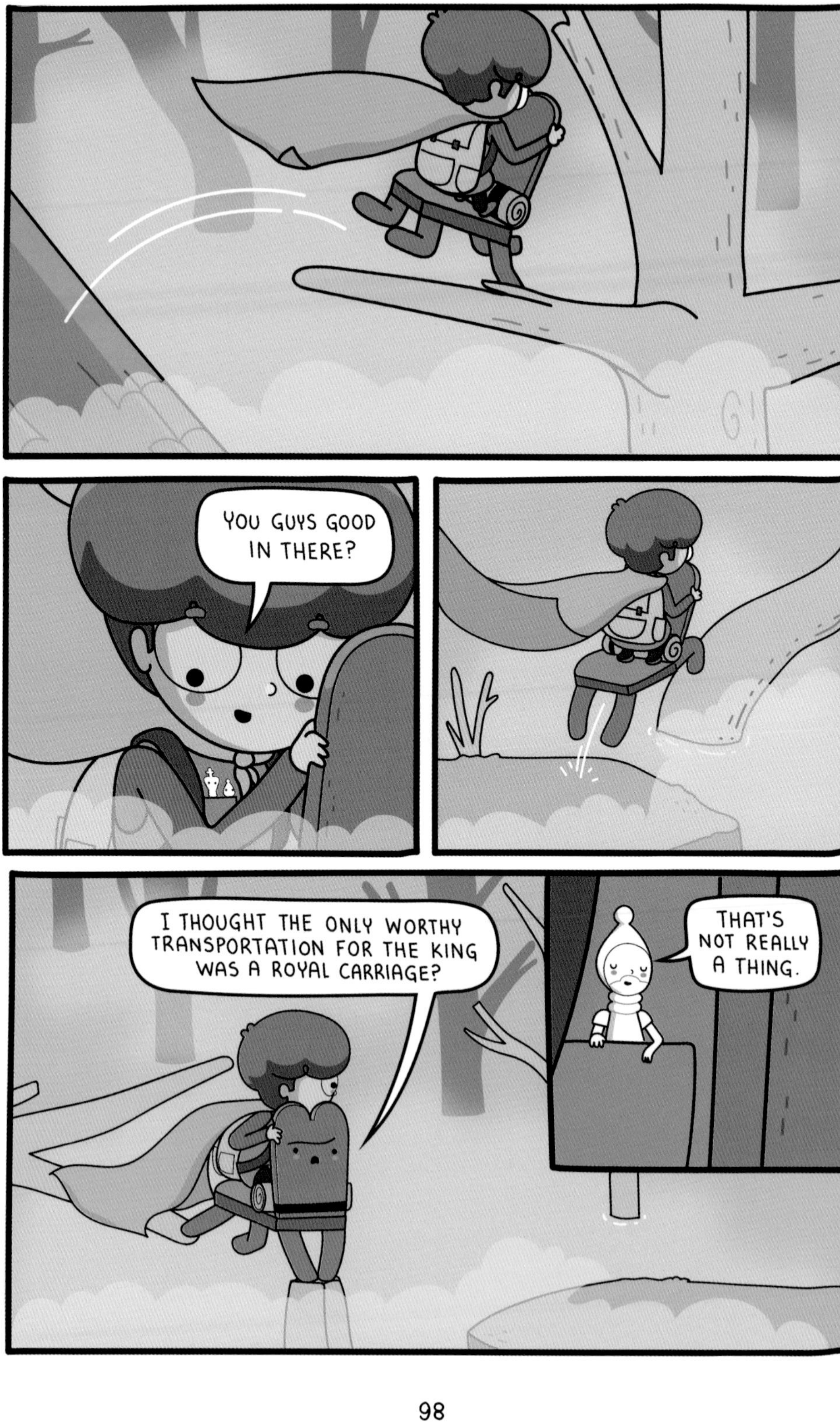
YOU GUYS GOOD IN THERE?
I THOUGHT THE ONLY WORTHY TRANSPORTATION FOR THE KING WAS A ROYAL CARRIAGE?
THAT'S NOT REALLY A THING.

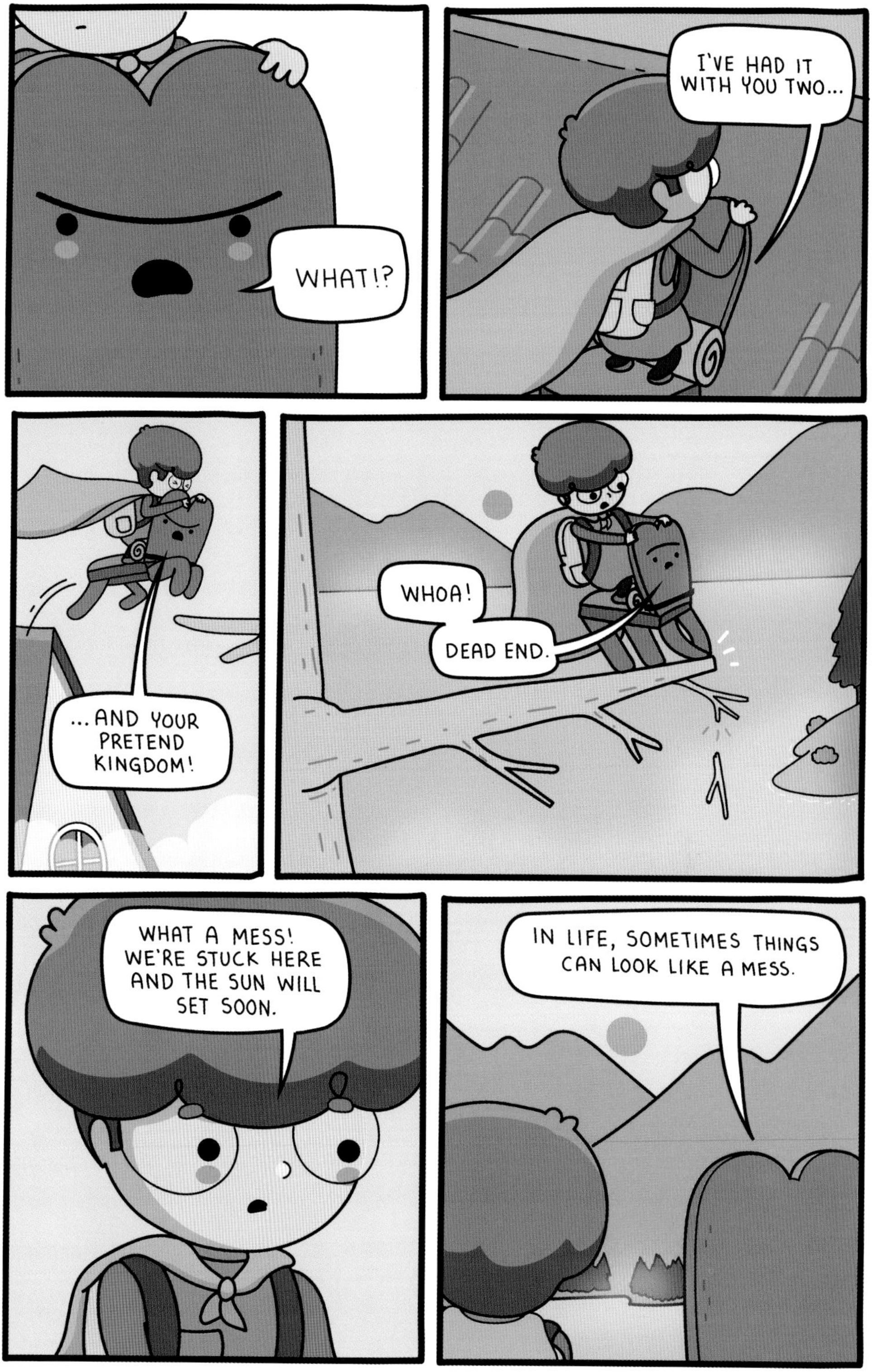
WHAT!?
I'VE HAD IT WITH YOU TWO...
...AND YOUR PRETEND KINGDOM!
WHOA!
DEAD END.
WHAT A MESS! WE'RE STUCK HERE AND THE SUN WILL SET SOON.
IN LIFE, SOMETIMES THINGS CAN LOOK LIKE A MESS.

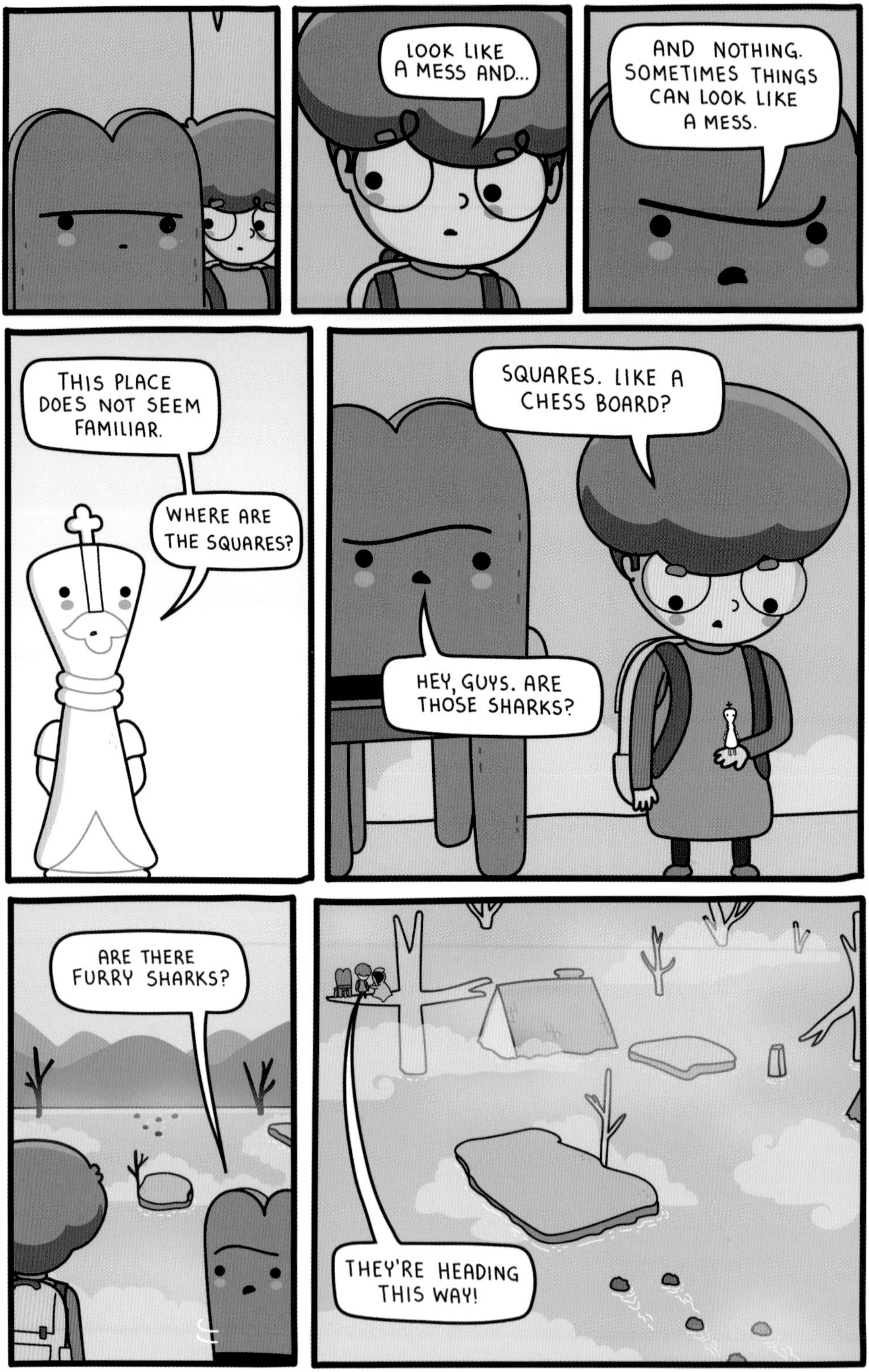
LOOK LIKE A MESS AND...
AND NOTHING. SOMETIMES THINGS CAN LOOK LIKE A MESS.
THIS PLACE DOES NOT SEEM FAMILIAR.
WHERE ARE THE SQUARES?
SQUARES. LIKE A CHESS BOARD?
HEY, GUYS. ARE THOSE SHARKS?
ARE THERE FURRY SHARKS?
THEY'RE HEADING THIS WAY!

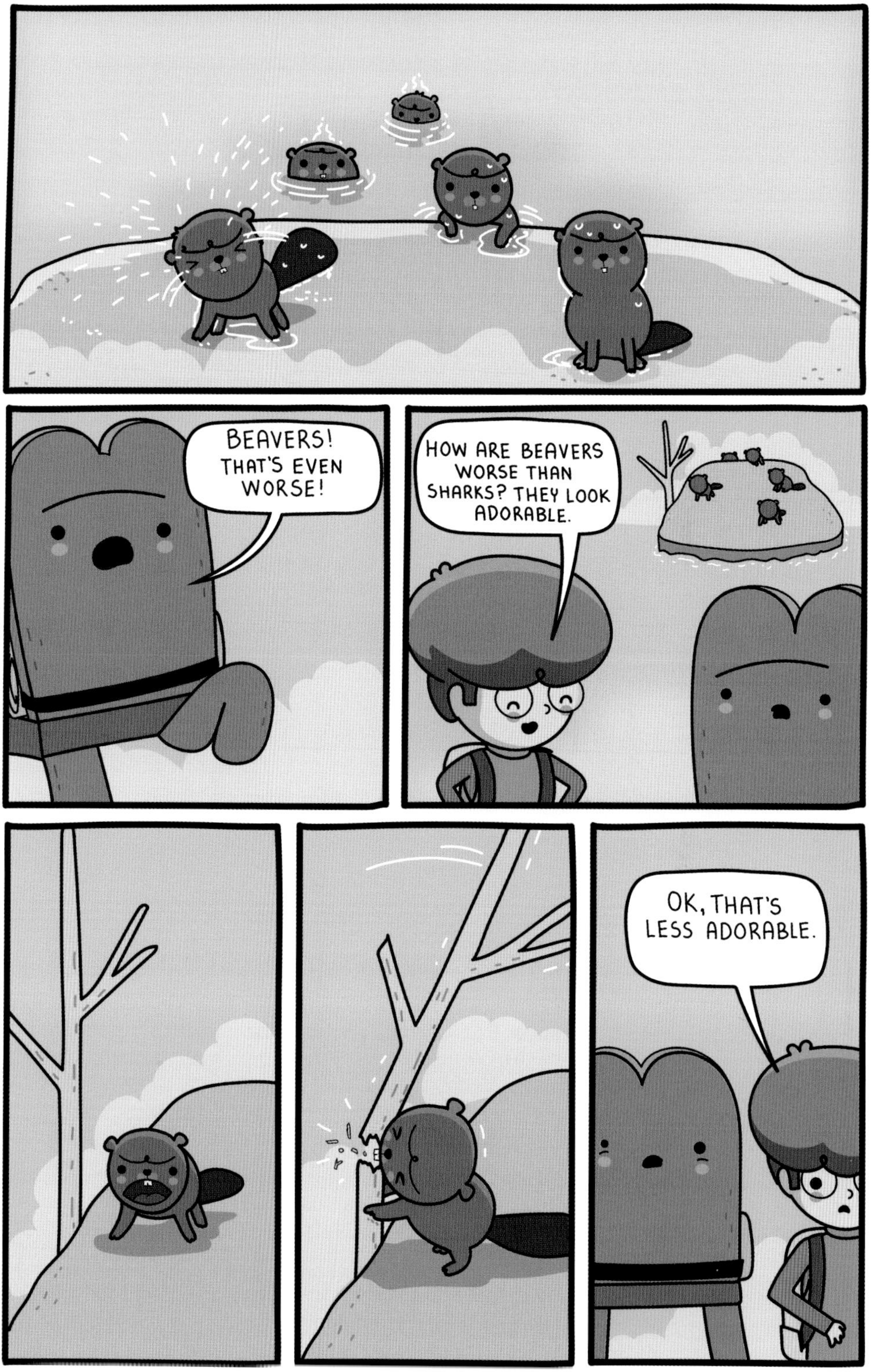
BEAVERS! THAT'S EVEN WORSE!
HOW ARE BEAVERS WORSE THAN SHARKS? THEY LOOK ADORABLE.
OK, THAT'S LESS ADORABLE.

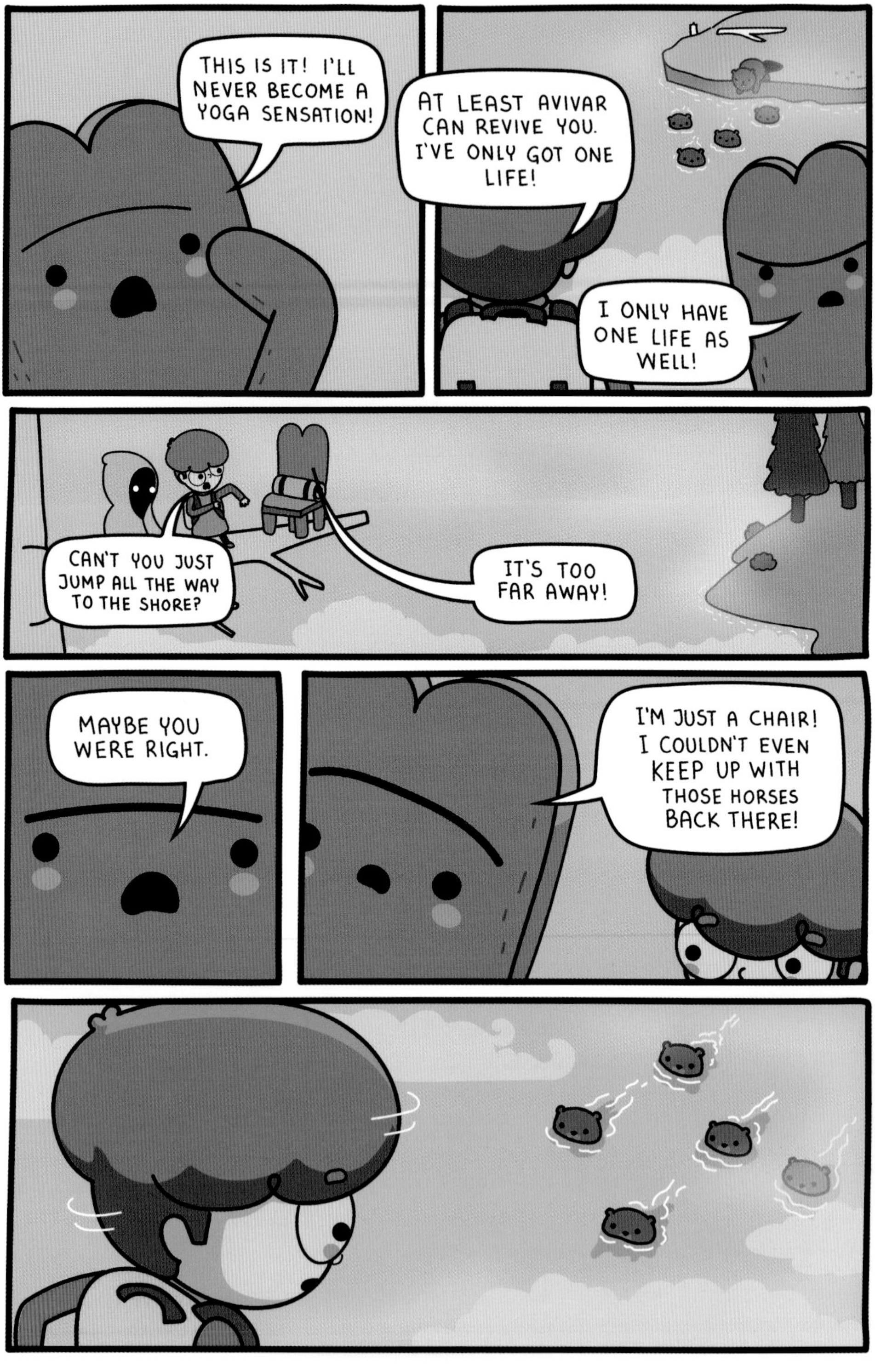
THIS IS IT! I'LL NEVER BECOME A YOGA SENSATION!
AT LEAST AVIVAR CAN REVIVE YOU. I'VE ONLY GOT ONE LIFE!
I ONLY HAVE ONE LIFE AS WELL!
CAN'T YOU JUST JUMP ALL THE WAY TO THE SHORE?
IT'S TOO FAR AWAY!
MAYBE YOU WERE RIGHT.
I'M JUST A CHAIR! I COULDN'T EVEN KEEP UP WITH THOSE HORSES BACK THERE!

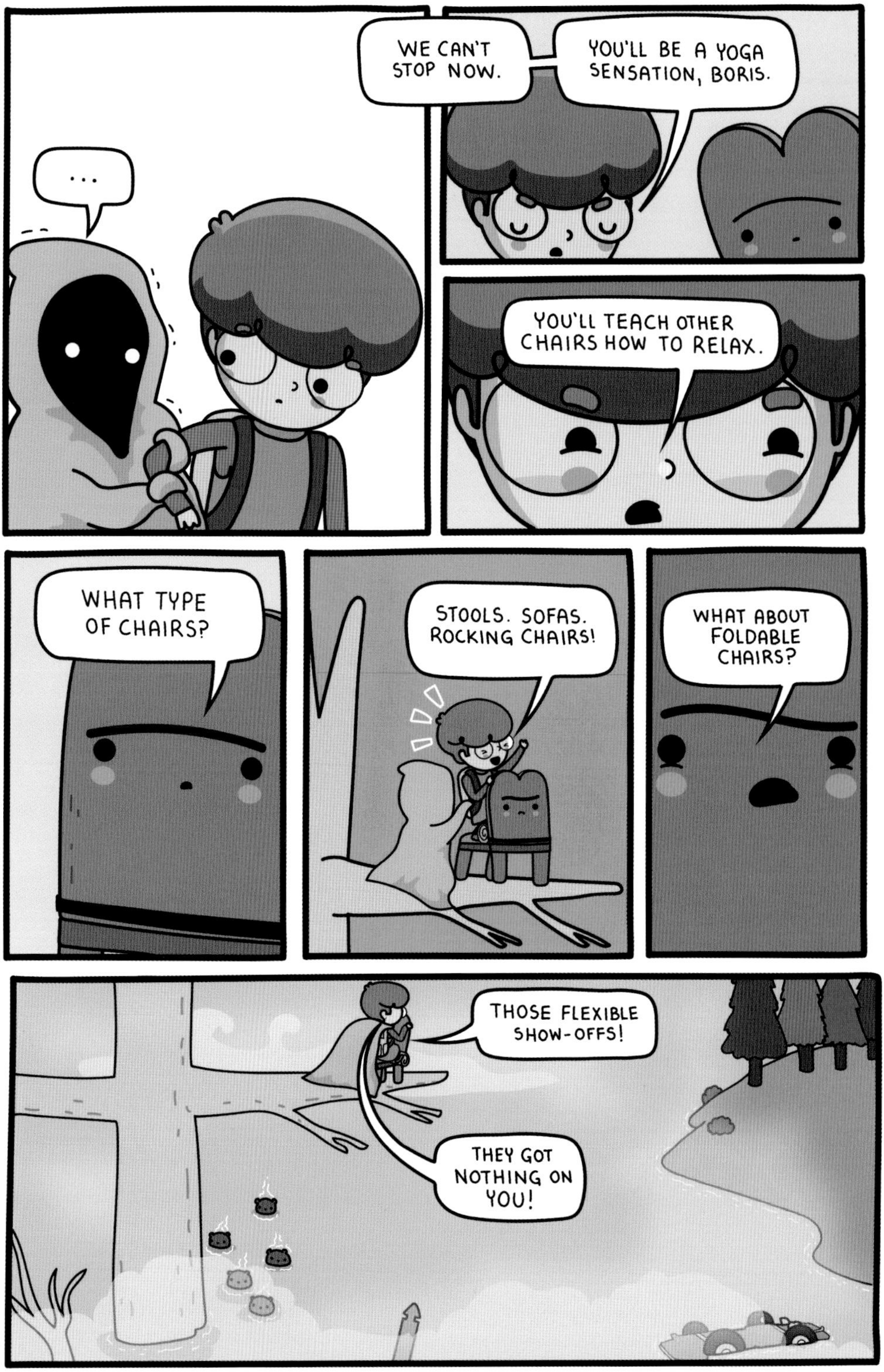
...
WE CAN'T STOP NOW.
YOU'LL BE A YOGA SENSATION, BORIS.
YOU'LL TEACH OTHER CHAIRS HOW TO RELAX.
WHAT TYPE OF CHAIRS?
STOOLS. SOFAS. ROCKING CHAIRS!
WHAT ABOUT FOLDABLE CHAIRS?
THOSE FLEXIBLE SHOW-OFFS!
THEY GOT NOTHING ON YOU!

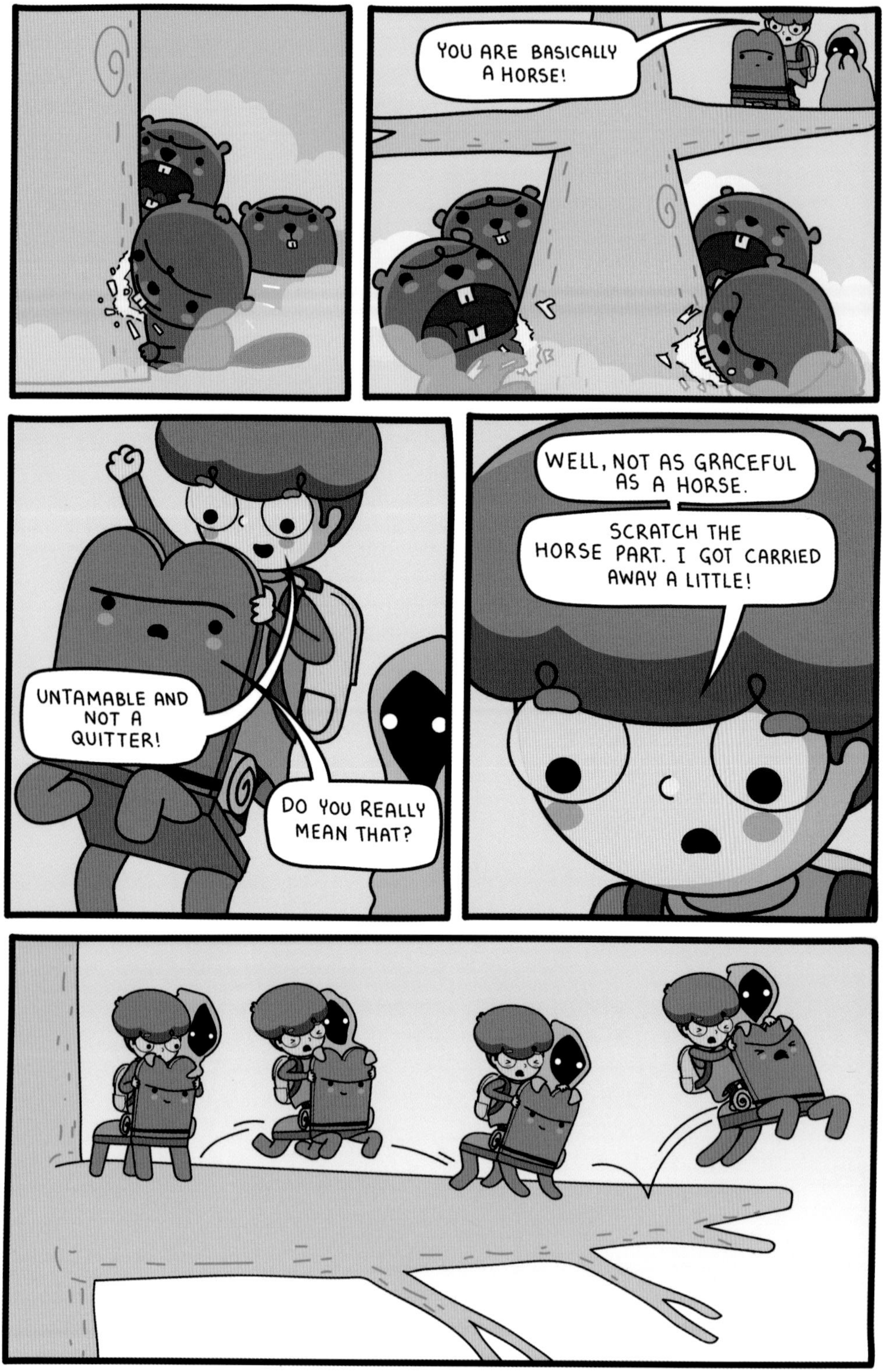
YOU ARE BASICALLY A HORSE!
UNTAMABLE AND NOT A QUITTER!
DO YOU REALLY MEAN THAT?
WELL, NOT AS GRACEFUL AS A HORSE.
SCRATCH THE HORSE PART. I GOT CARRIED AWAY A LITTLE!

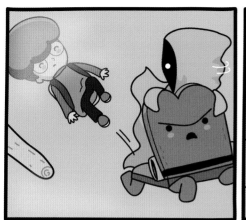

WHAT HAVE YOU DONE?

YOU ARE SACRIFICING YOURSELF FOR US? I WON'T FORGET THIS!

I'LL THANK YOU IN ALL MY YOGA VIDEOS.

I'M NOT SACRIFICING MYSELF!

IS IGGIE SPELLED WITH ONE OR TWO G'S?

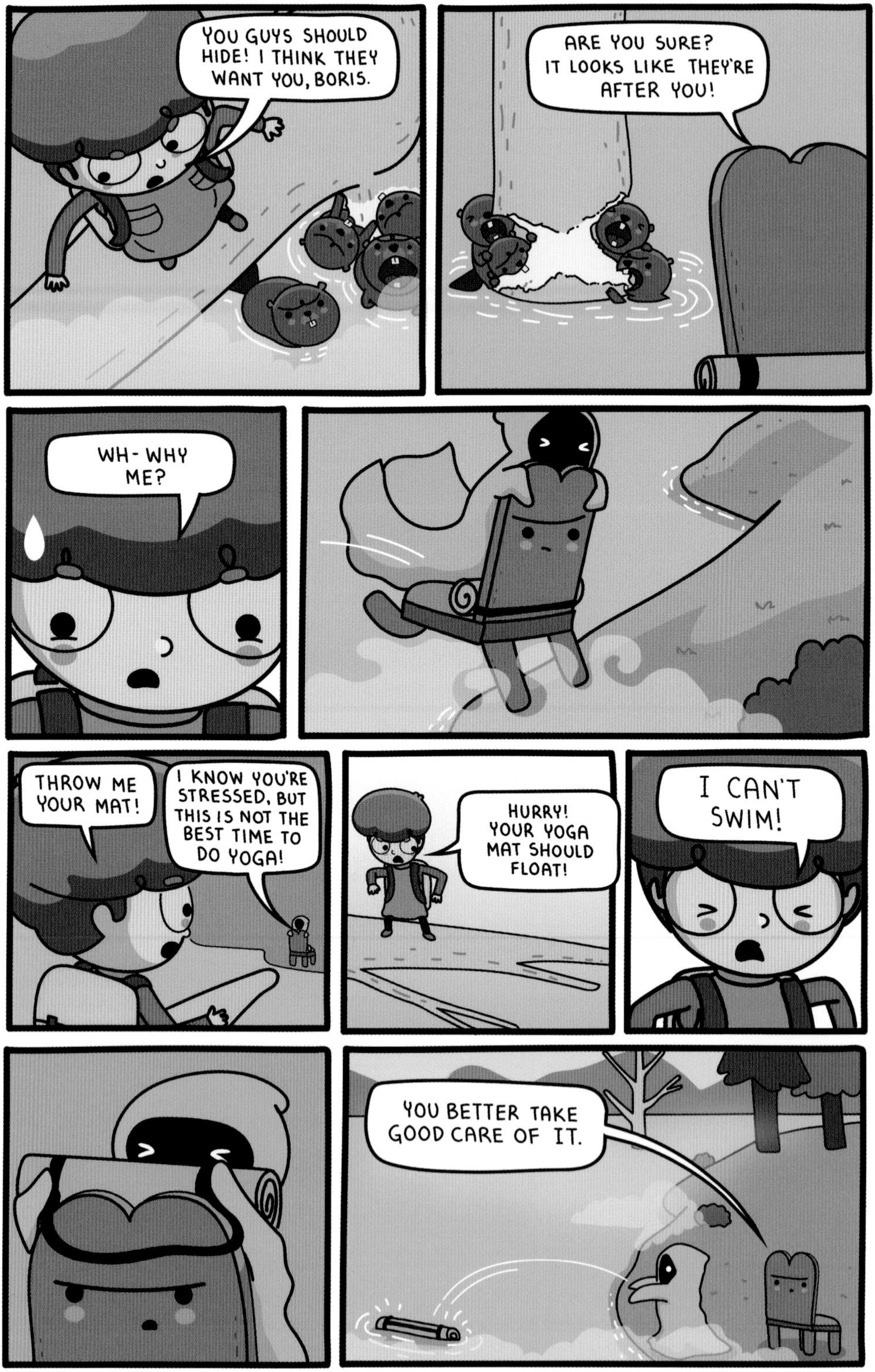
YOU GUYS SHOULD HIDE! I THINK THEY WANT YOU, BORIS.
ARE YOU SURE? IT LOOKS LIKE THEY'RE AFTER YOU!
WH- WHY ME?
THROW ME YOUR MAT!
I KNOW YOU'RE STRESSED, BUT THIS IS NOT THE BEST TIME TO DO YOGA!
HURRY! YOUR YOGA MAT SHOULD FLOAT!
I CAN'T SWIM!
YOU BETTER TAKE GOOD CARE OF IT.

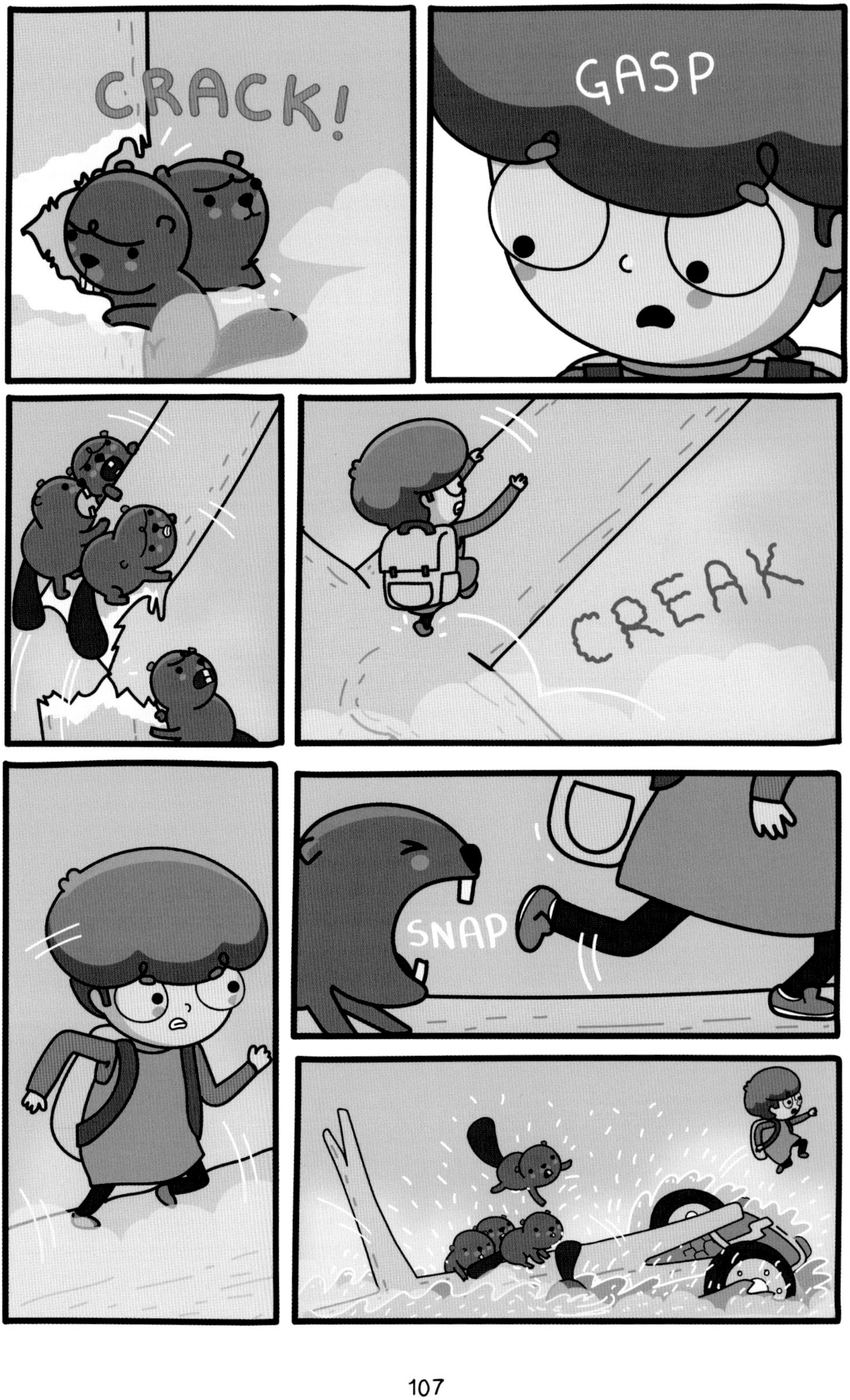
CRACK!
GASP
CREAK
SNAP

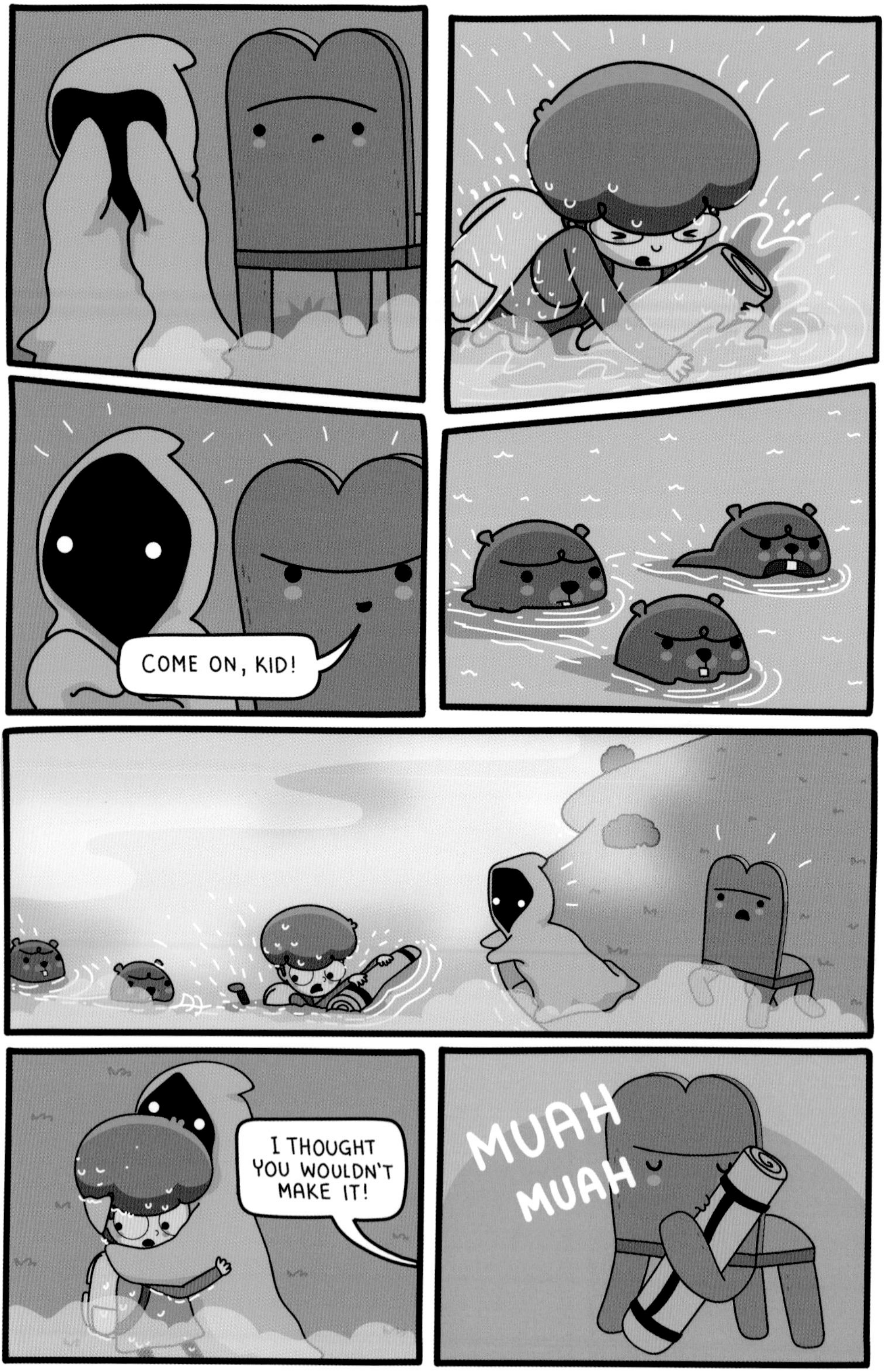
COME ON, KID!
I THOUGHT YOU WOULDN'T MAKE IT!
MUAH
MUAH

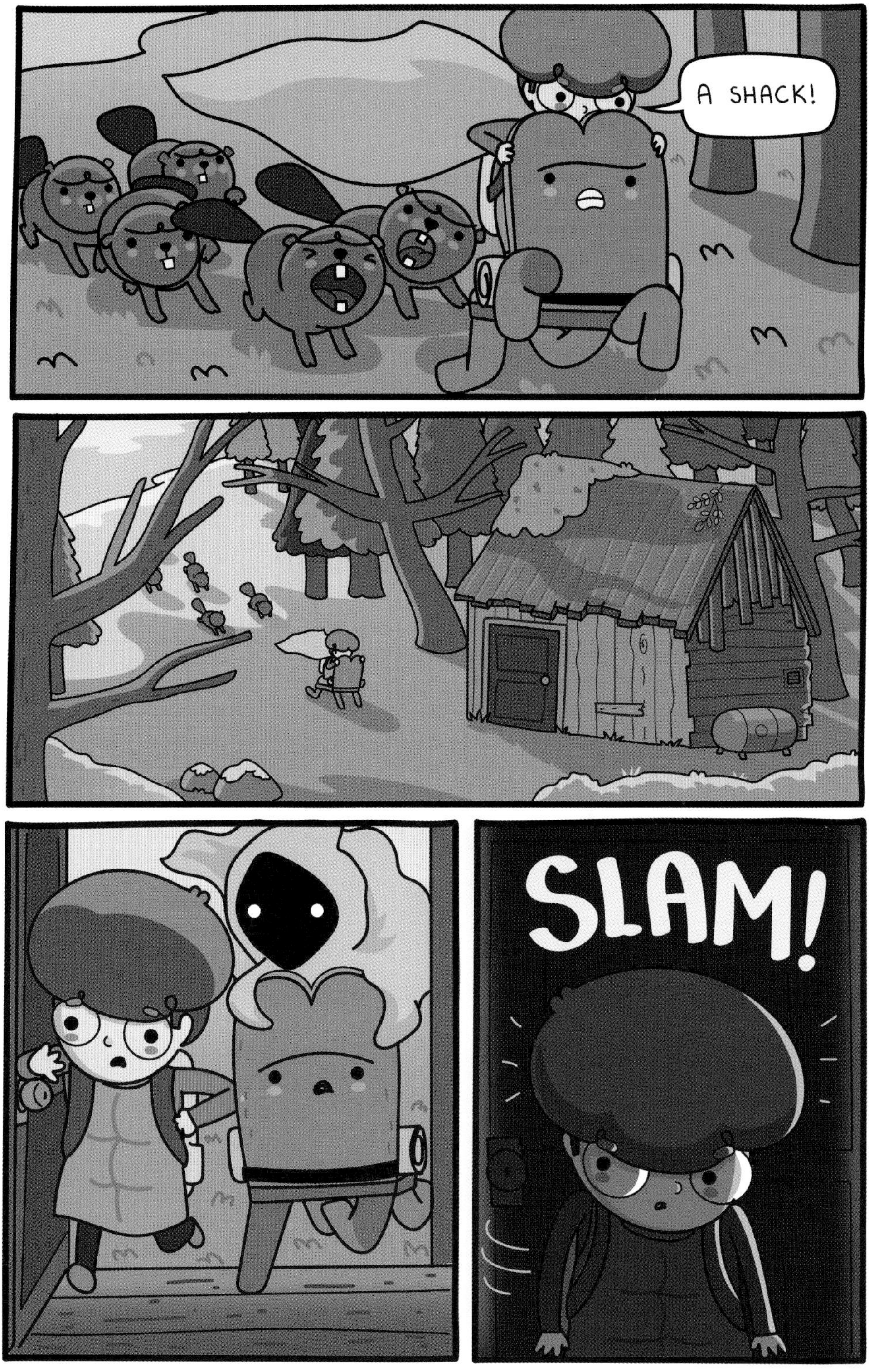
A SHACK!
SLAM!

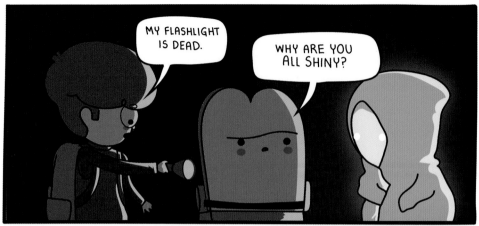

MY FLASHLIGHT IS DEAD.

WHY ARE YOU ALL SHINY?

I HATE TO BEAR BAD NEWS.

WHAT COULD BE WORSE THAN THIS?

WE'RE HIDING FROM BEAVERS.

...IN A SHACK MADE OF WOOD!

WHAT'S NEXT, KID? ARE YOU GOING TO JUMP ROPE USING SNAKES?!

HEY, IT GLOWS!

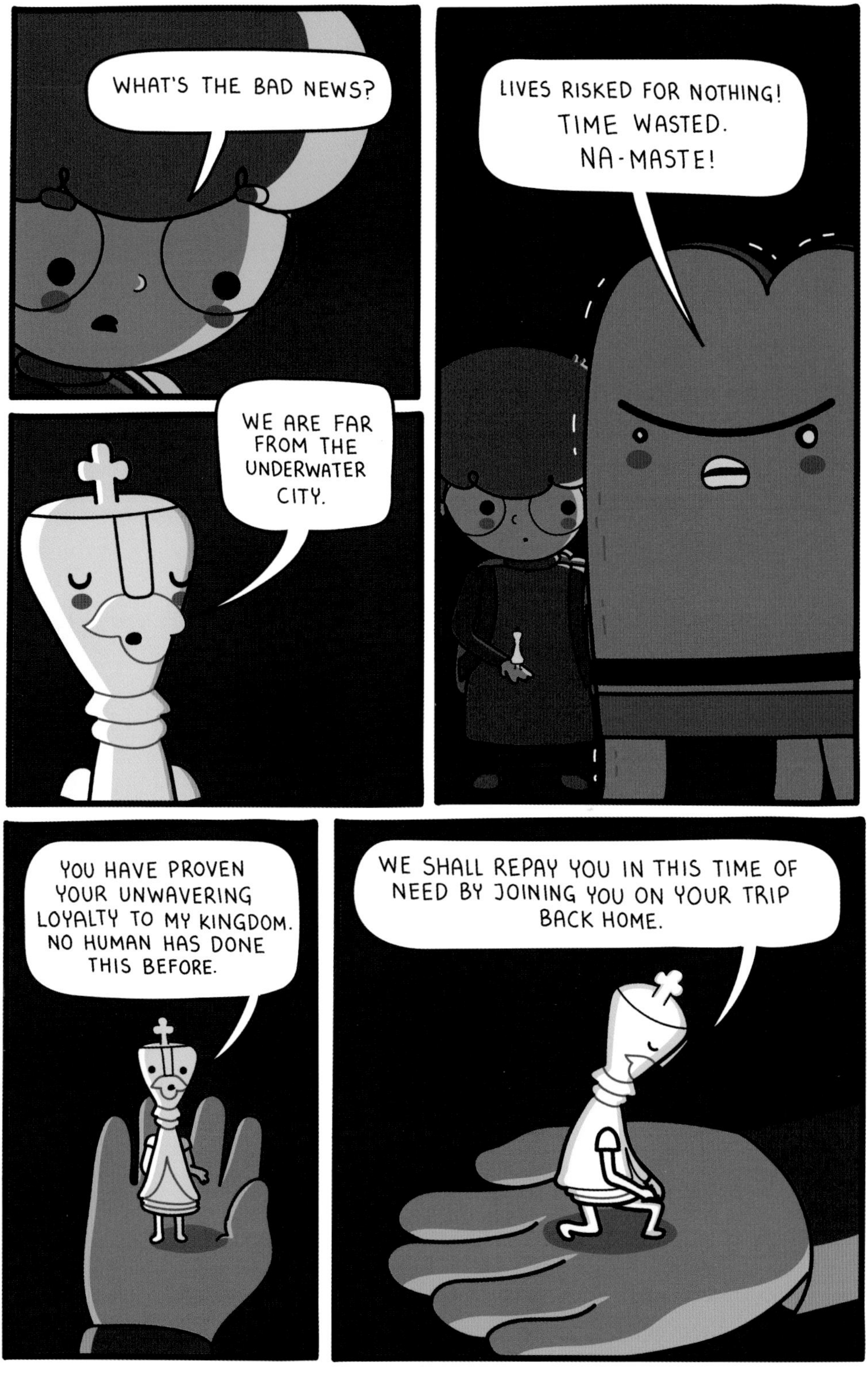
WHAT'S THE BAD NEWS?
LIVES RISKED FOR NOTHING! TIME WASTED. NA-MASTE!
WE ARE FAR FROM THE UNDERWATER CITY.
YOU HAVE PROVEN YOUR UNWAVERING LOYALTY TO MY KINGDOM. NO HUMAN HAS DONE THIS BEFORE.
WE SHALL REPAY YOU IN THIS TIME OF NEED BY JOINING YOU ON YOUR TRIP BACK HOME.

HOW ARE WE SUPPOSED TO GO BACK? THOSE GUYS ARE STILL OUT THERE!

BUBBLES?

POP

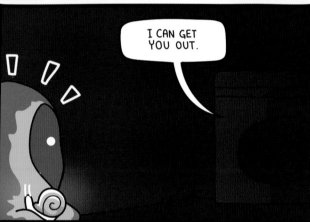

I CAN GET YOU OUT.

WHO SAID THAT?

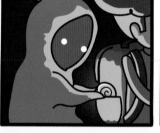

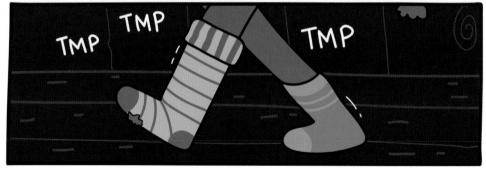

TMP TMP TMP

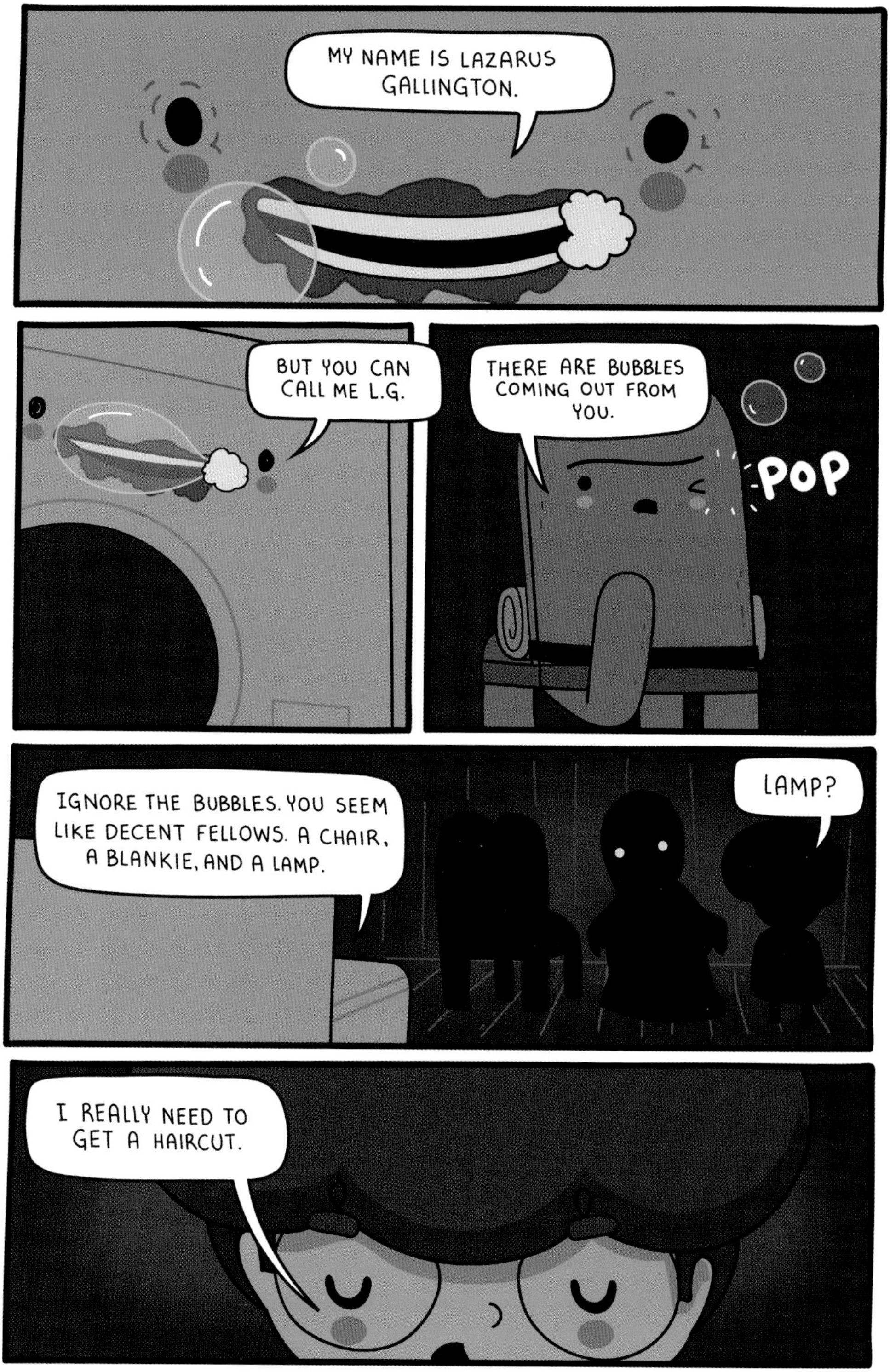
MY NAME IS LAZARUS GALLINGTON.
BUT YOU CAN CALL ME L.G.
THERE ARE BUBBLES COMING OUT FROM YOU.
POP
IGNORE THE BUBBLES. YOU SEEM LIKE DECENT FELLOWS. A CHAIR, A BLANKIE, AND A LAMP.
LAMP?
I REALLY NEED TO GET A HAIRCUT.

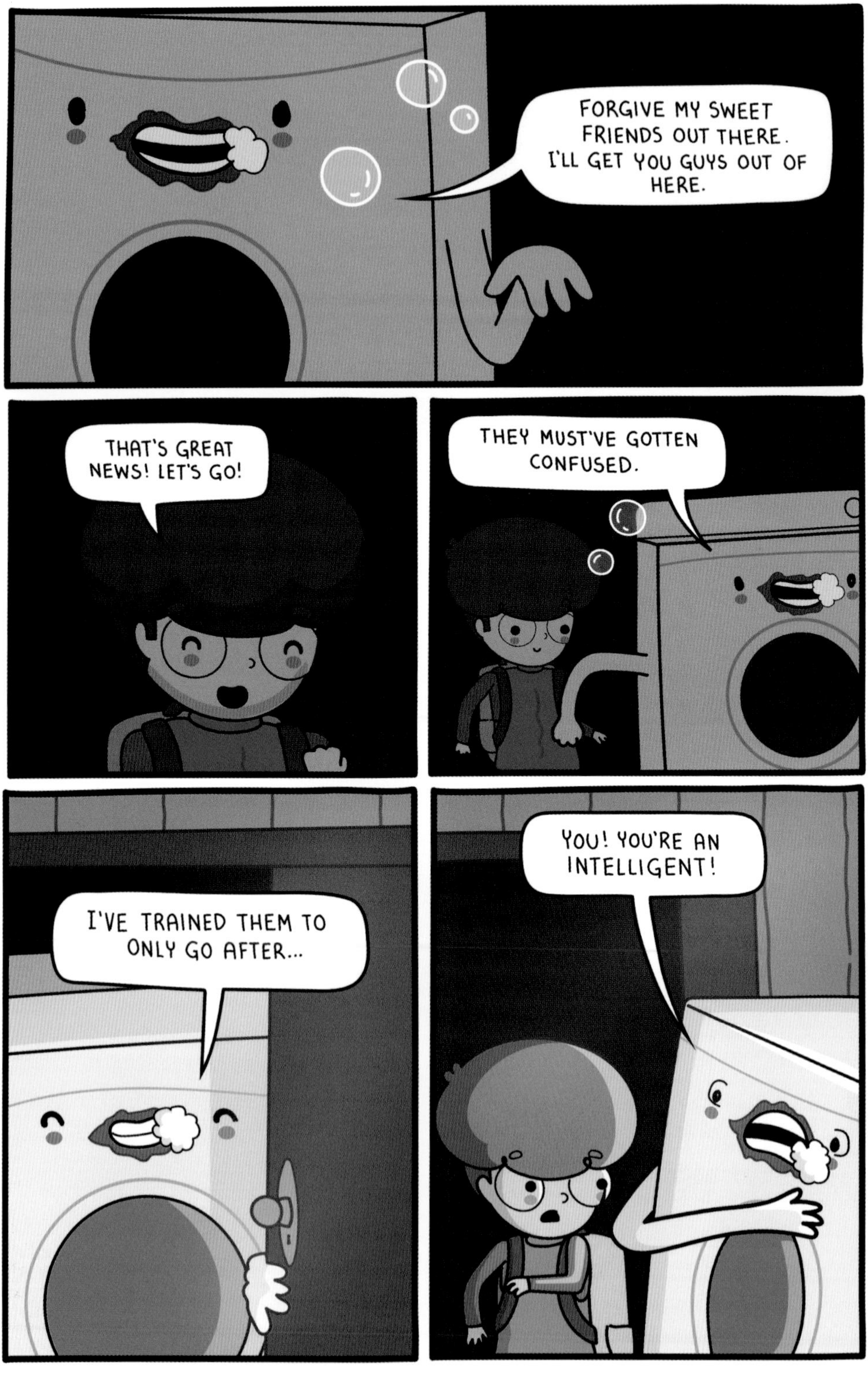
FORGIVE MY SWEET FRIENDS OUT THERE. I'LL GET YOU GUYS OUT OF HERE.
THAT'S GREAT NEWS! LET'S GO!
THEY MUST'VE GOTTEN CONFUSED.
I'VE TRAINED THEM TO ONLY GO AFTER...
YOU! YOU'RE AN INTELLIGENT!

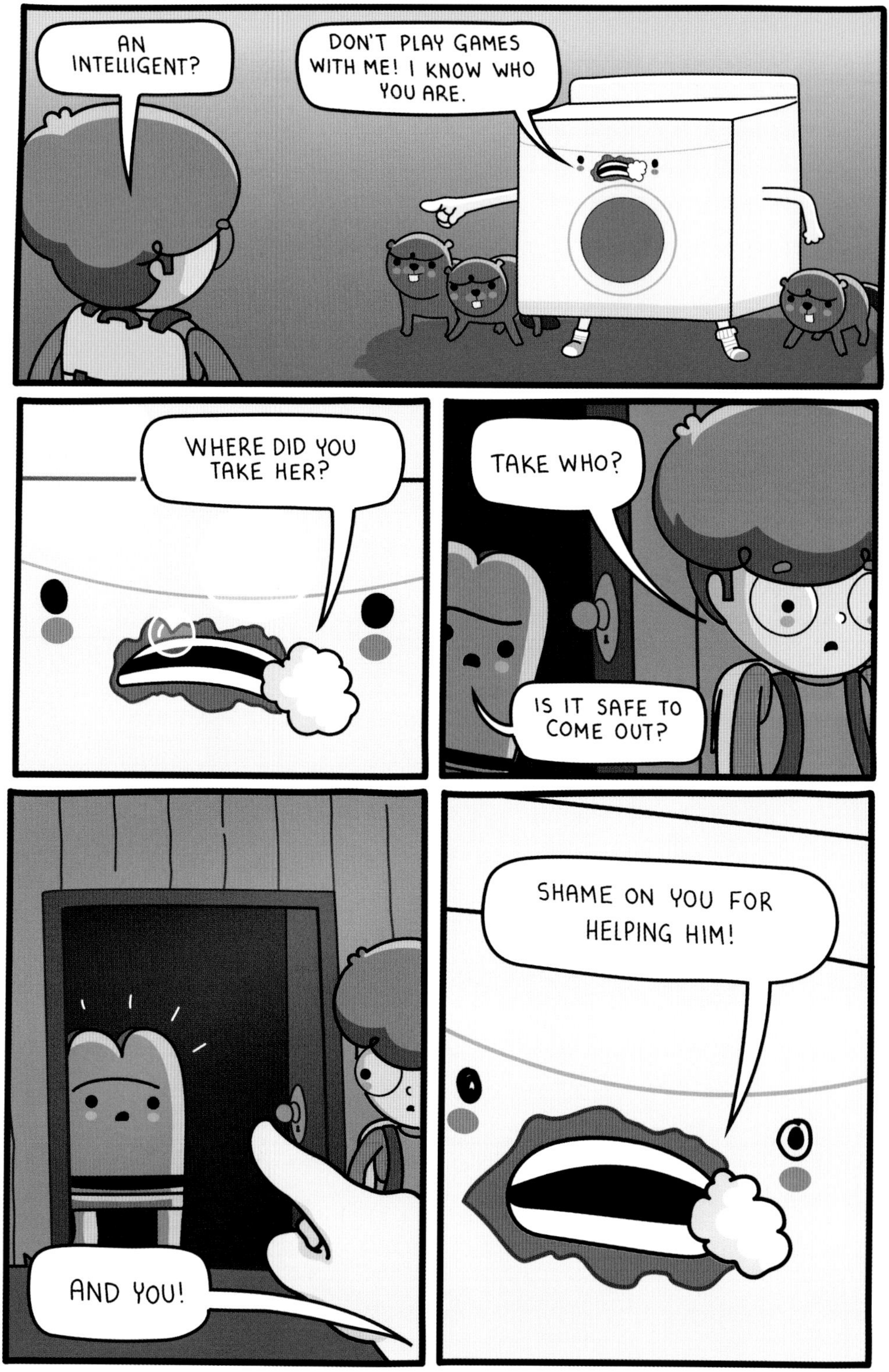
AN INTELLIGENT?
DON'T PLAY GAMES WITH ME! I KNOW WHO YOU ARE.
WHERE DID YOU TAKE HER?
TAKE WHO?
IS IT SAFE TO COME OUT?
AND YOU!
SHAME ON YOU FOR HELPING HIM!

YOU REALLY DO MAKE FRIENDS FAST, DON'T YOU?

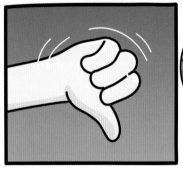

WHY IS HE TURNING BACK?

HUH?
DID HE REALLY JUMP IN THERE? WHAT IS WRONG WITH HIM?

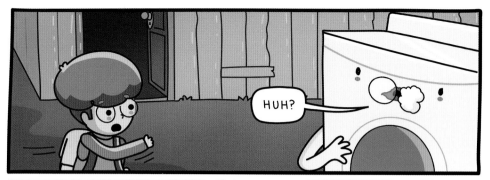

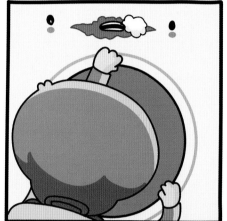

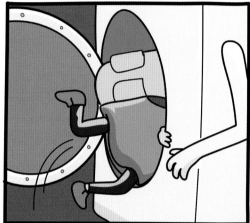

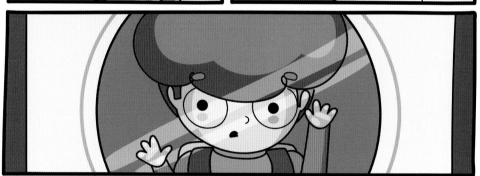

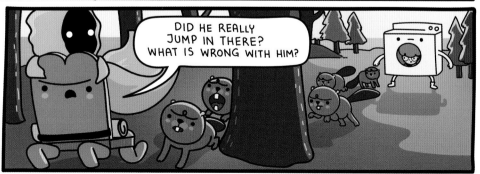

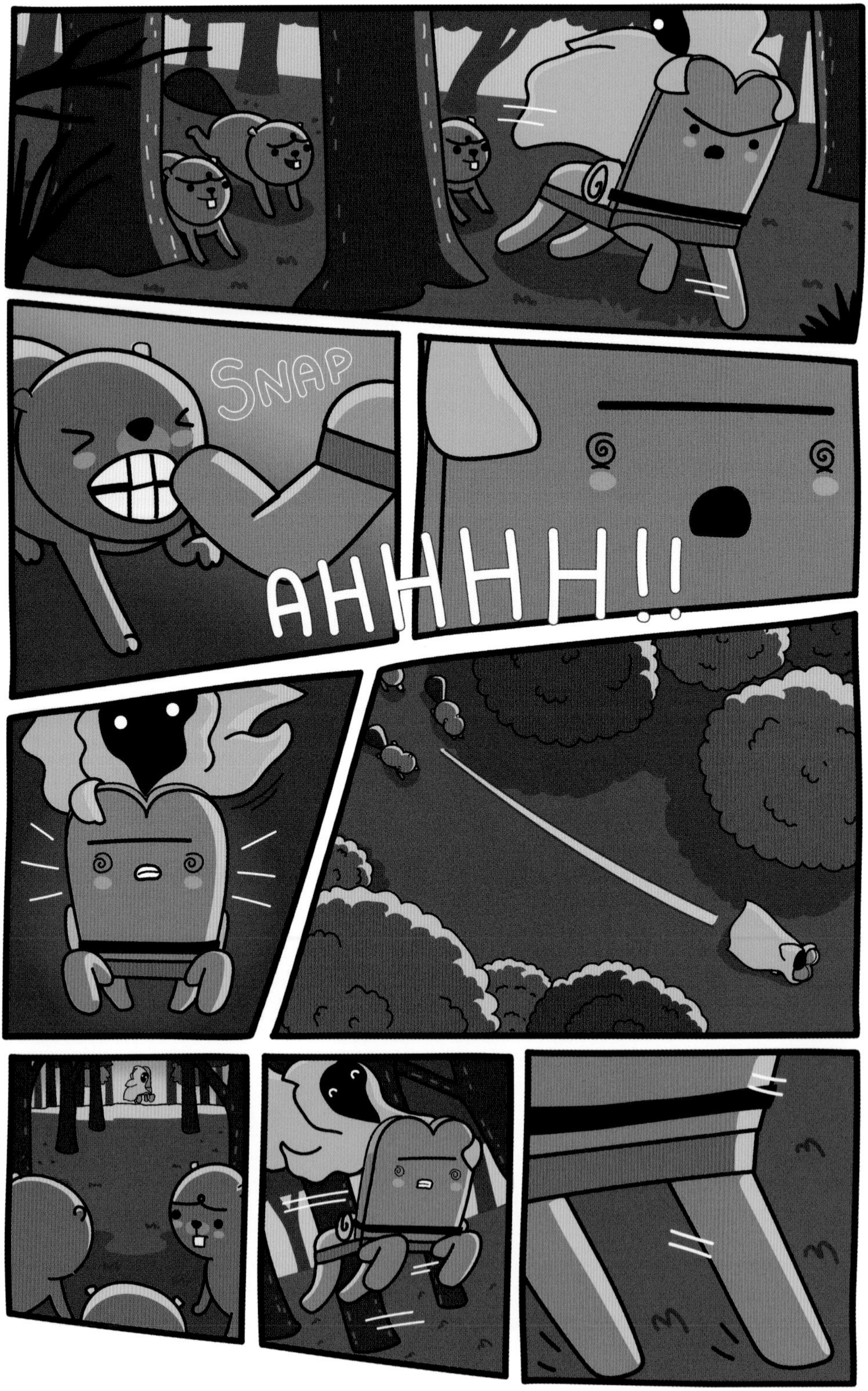
SNAP
AHHHH!!

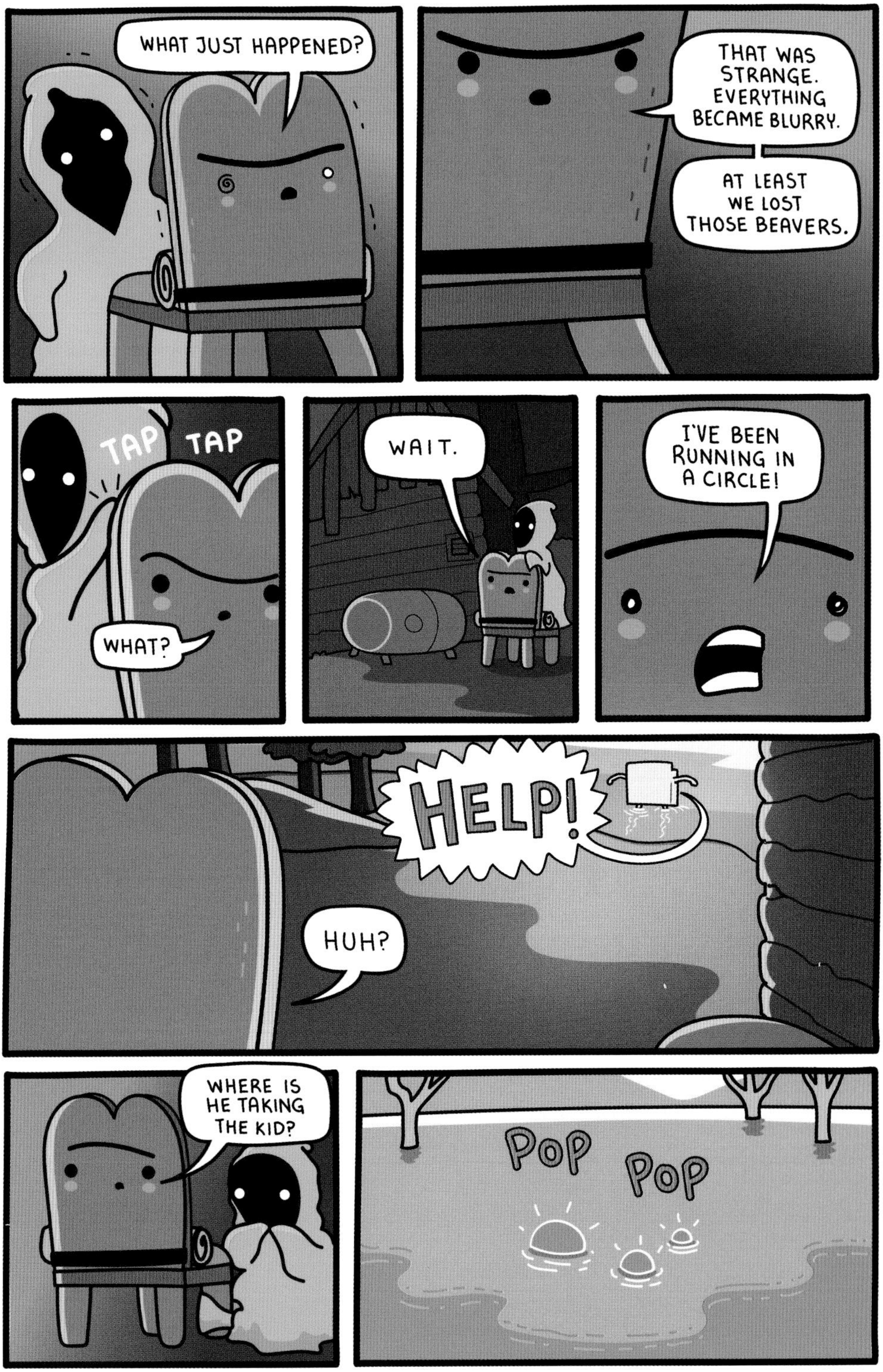
WHAT JUST HAPPENED?
THAT WAS STRANGE. EVERYTHING BECAME BLURRY.
AT LEAST WE LOST THOSE BEAVERS.
TAP TAP
WHAT?
WAIT.
I'VE BEEN RUNNING IN A CIRCLE!
HELP!
HUH?
WHERE IS HE TAKING THE KID?
POP POP

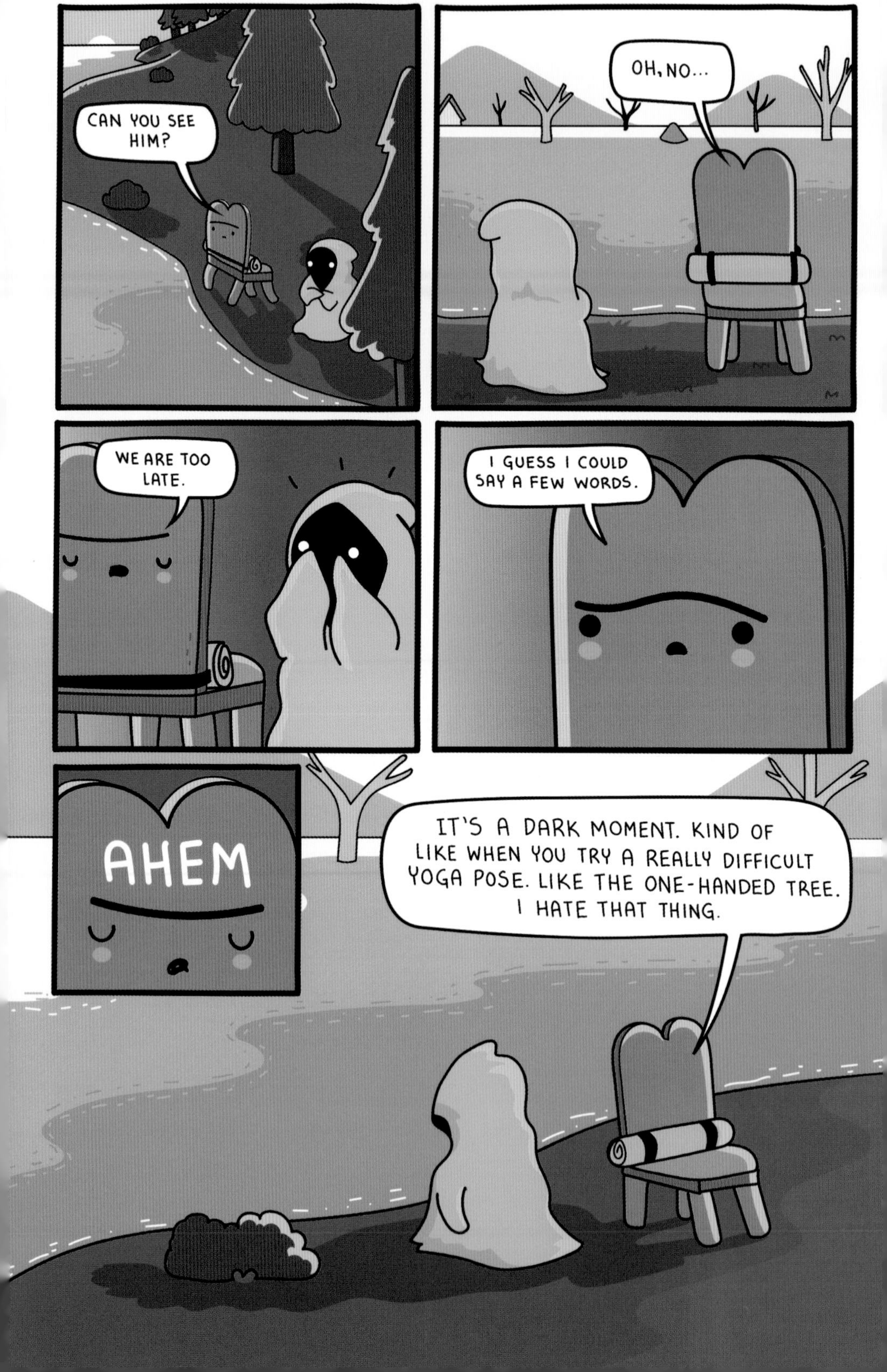
CAN YOU SEE HIM?
OH, NO...
WE ARE TOO LATE.
I GUESS I COULD SAY A FEW WORDS.
AHEM
IT'S A DARK MOMENT. KIND OF LIKE WHEN YOU TRY A REALLY DIFFICULT YOGA POSE. LIKE THE ONE-HANDED TREE. I HATE THAT THING.

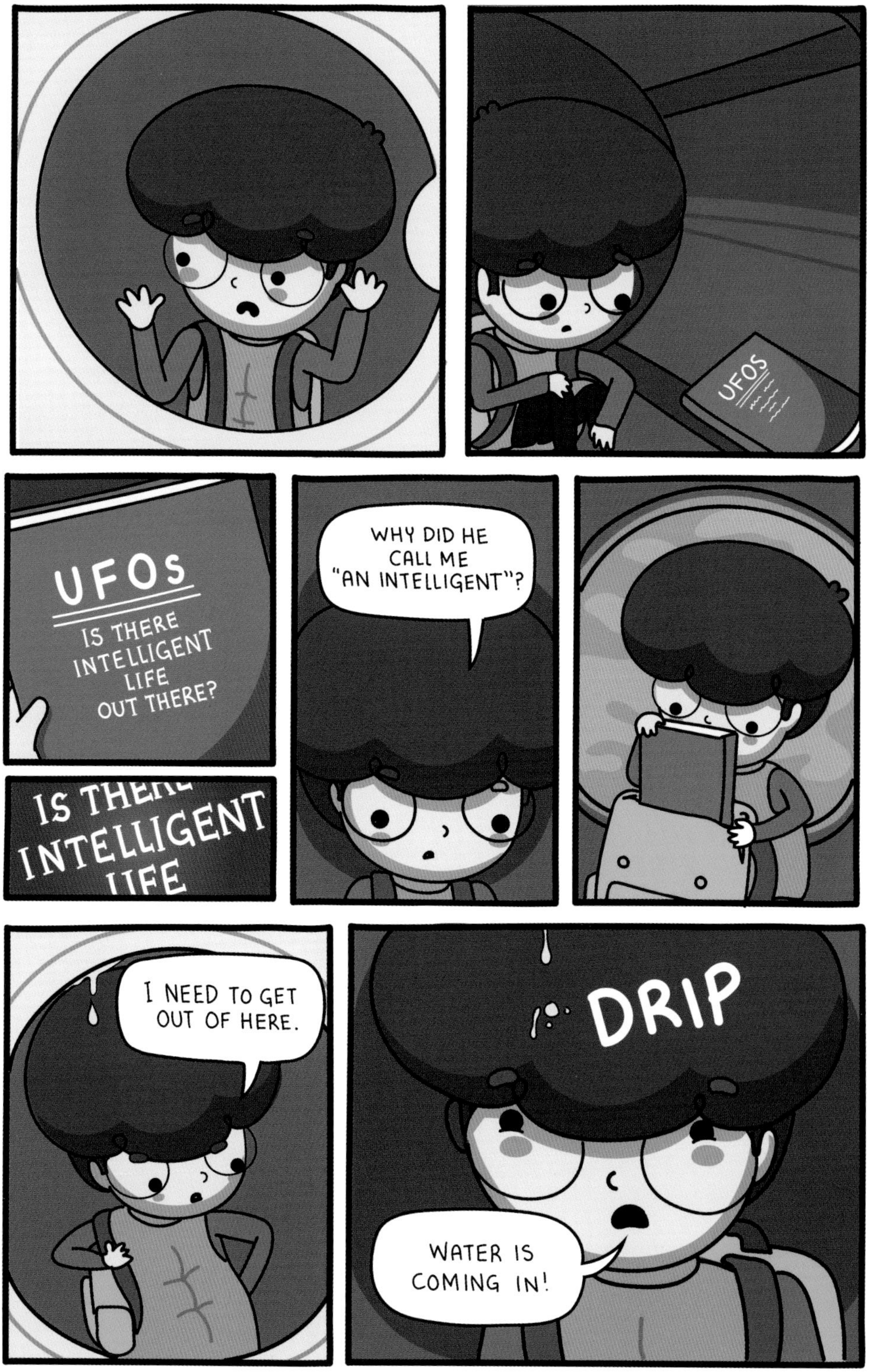
UFOs
UFOs
IS THERE INTELLIGENT LIFE OUT THERE?
IS THERE INTELLIGENT LIFE
WHY DID HE CALL ME "AN INTELLIGENT"?
I NEED TO GET OUT OF HERE.
DRIP
WATER IS COMING IN!

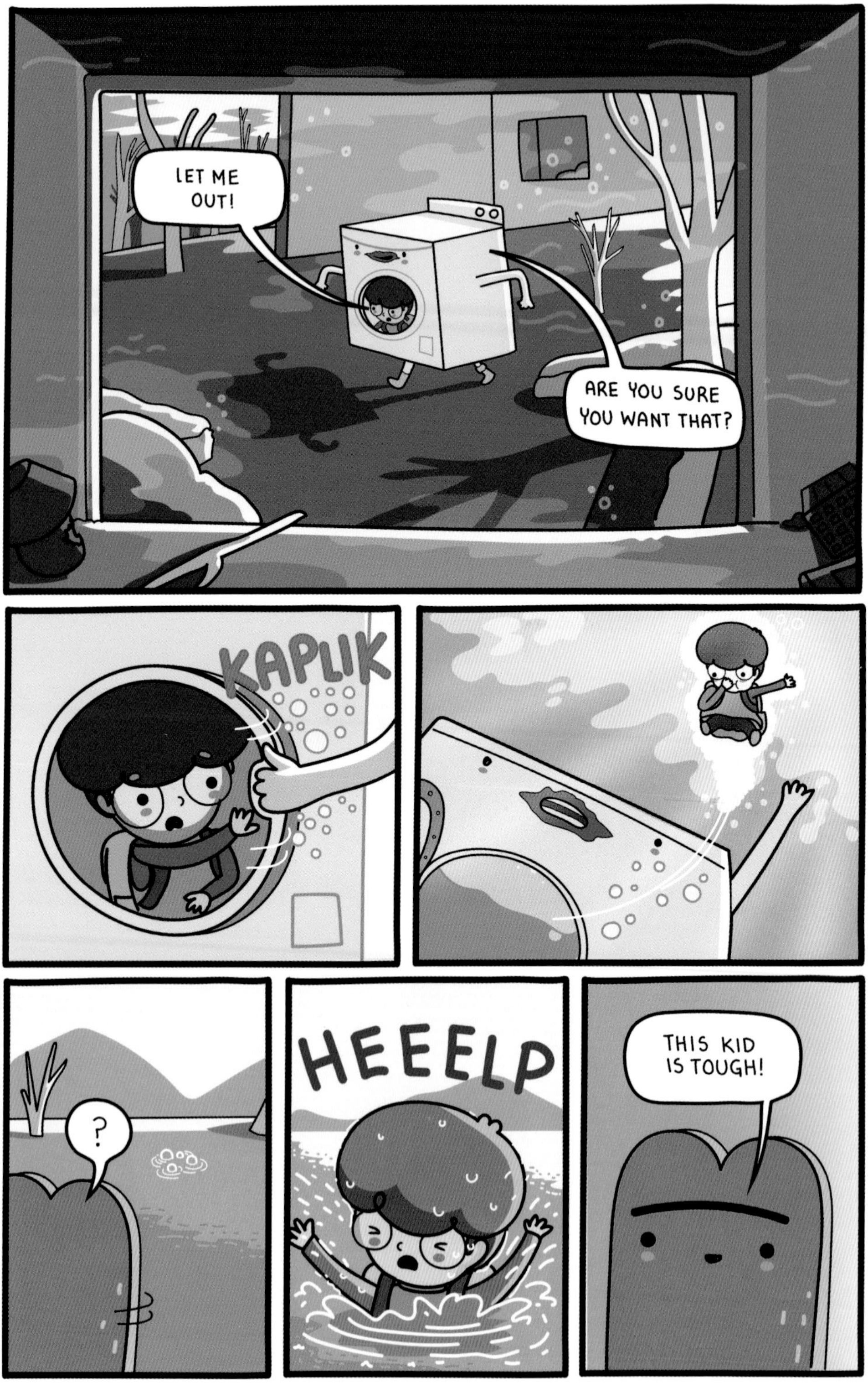
LET ME OUT!
ARE YOU SURE YOU WANT THAT?
KAPLIK
?
HEEELP
THIS KID IS TOUGH!

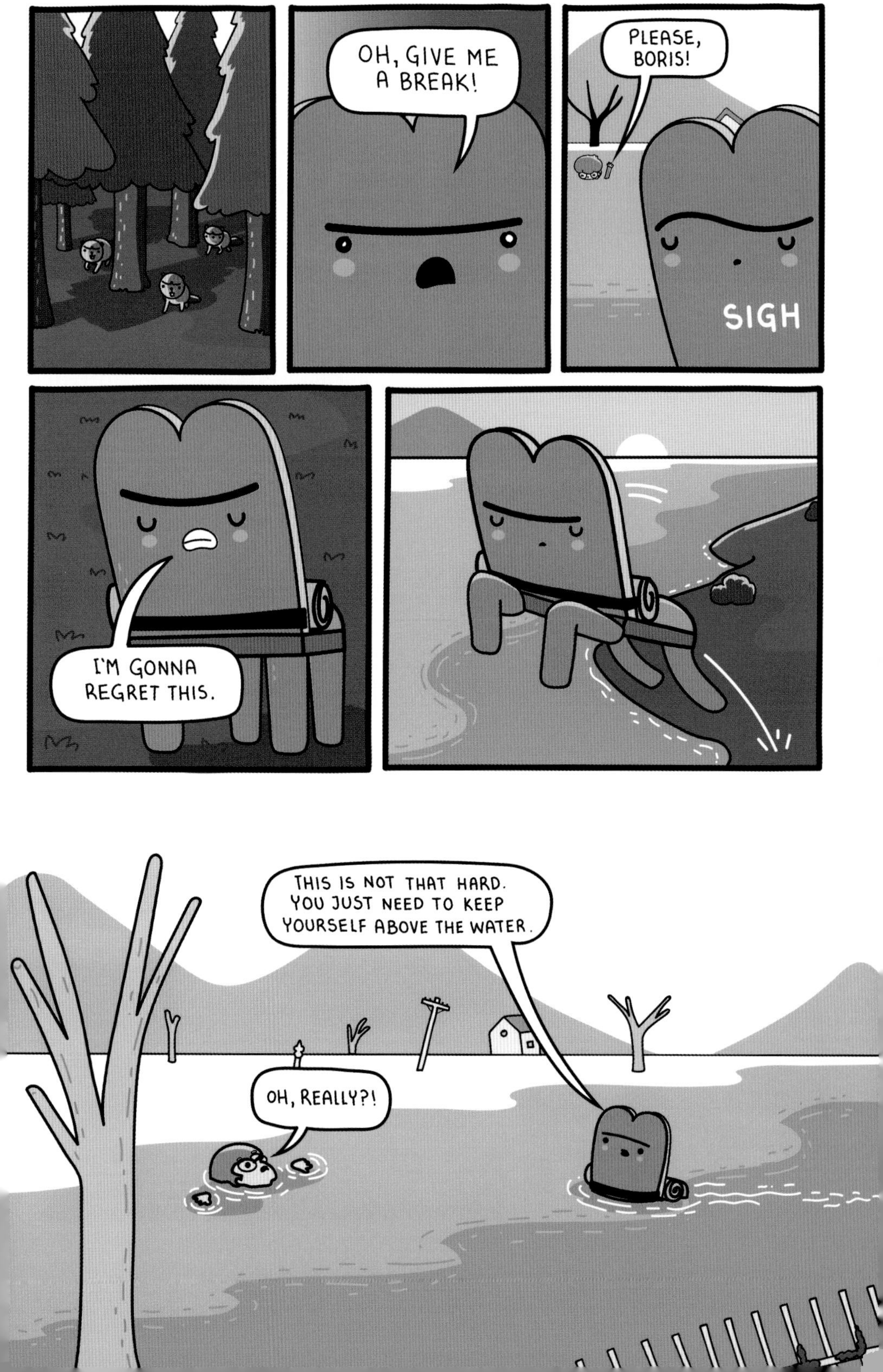
OH, GIVE ME A BREAK!
PLEASE, BORIS!
SIGH
I'M GONNA REGRET THIS.
THIS IS NOT THAT HARD. YOU JUST NEED TO KEEP YOURSELF ABOVE THE WATER.
OH, REALLY?!

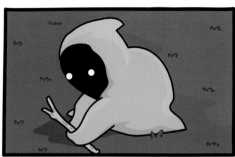

YOU JUMPED IN THE WATER FOR ME!

HURRY! THEY'RE GAINING ON US!

ARE YOU ALL RIGHT? YOUR EYES LOOK WEIRD.

I DON'T KNOW. IT'S THE SAME FEELING I HAD BACK THERE!

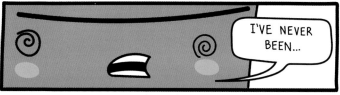

I'VE NEVER BEEN...

...SO SCARED!

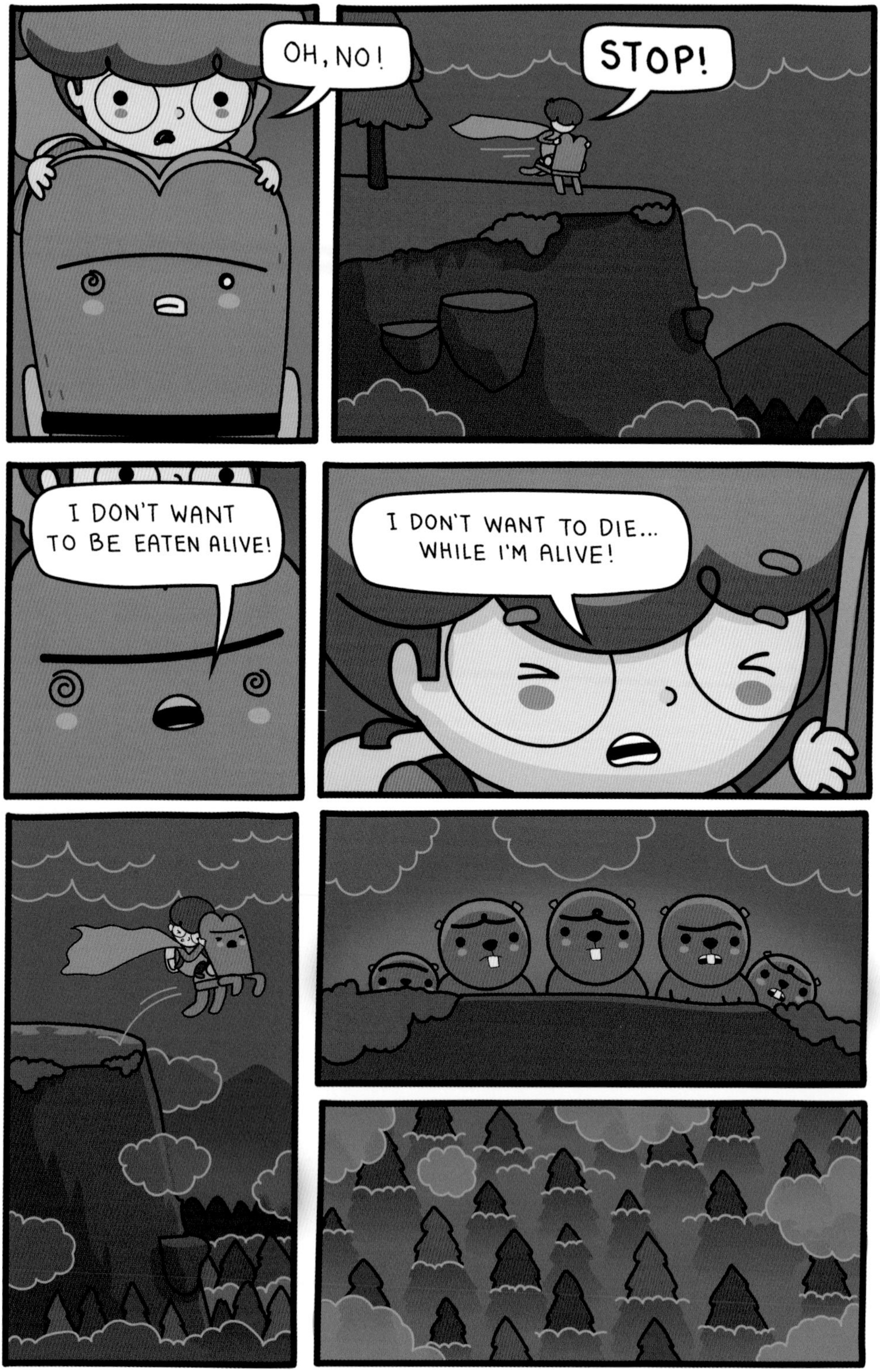
OH, NO!
STOP!
I DON'T WANT TO BE EATEN ALIVE!
I DON'T WANT TO DIE... WHILE I'M ALIVE!

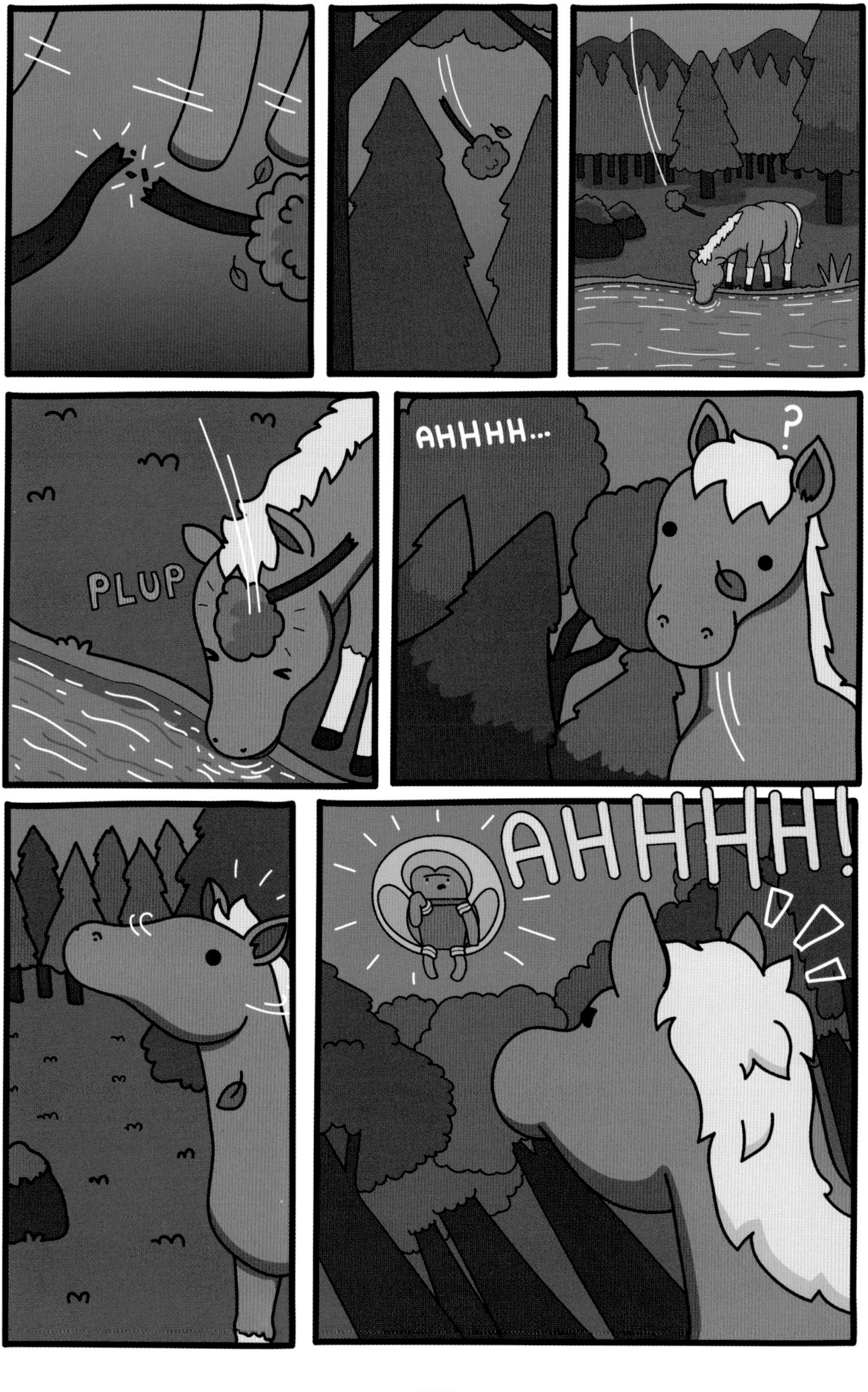
PLUP
AHHHH...
?
AHHHH!

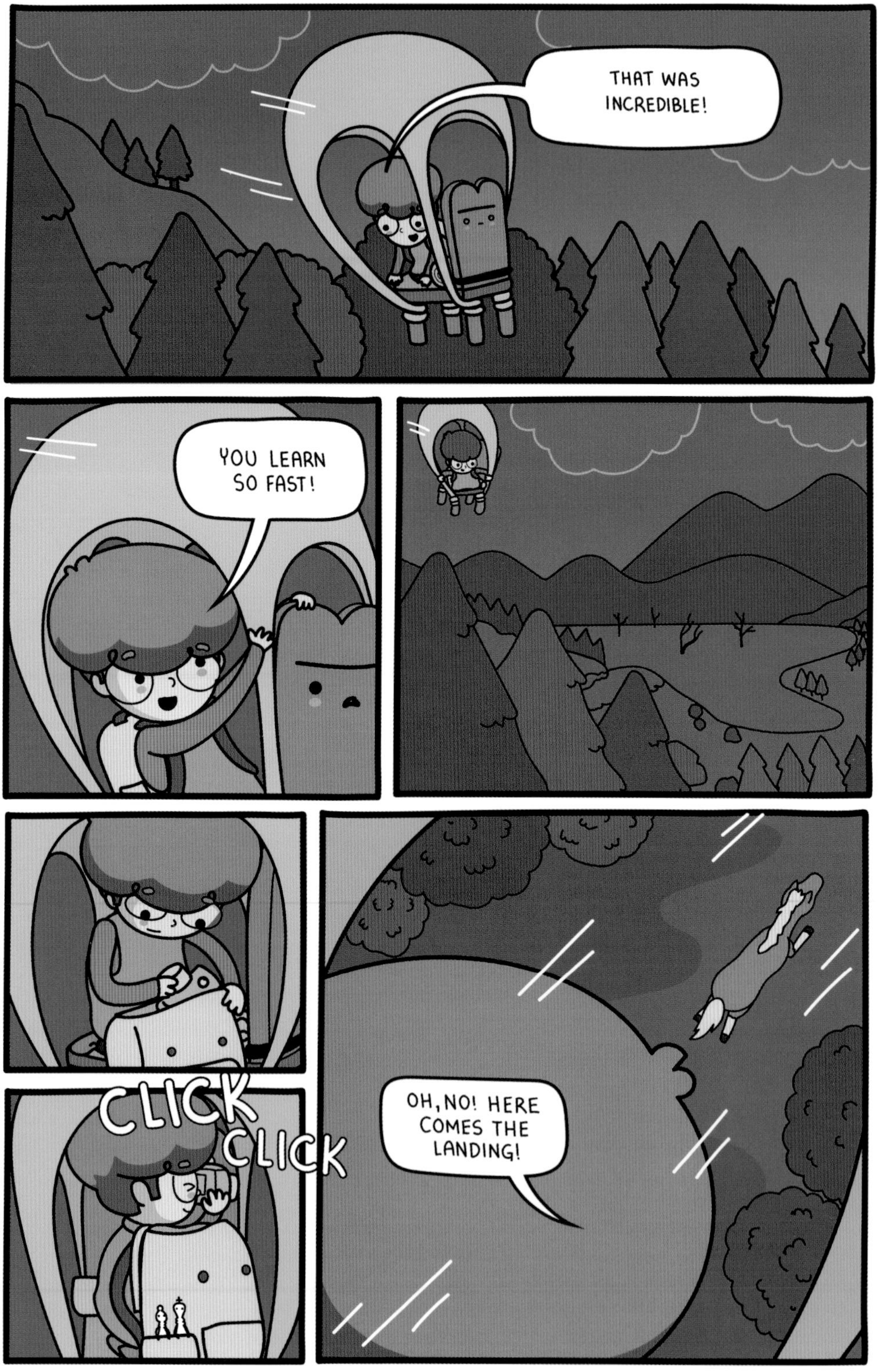
THAT WAS INCREDIBLE!
YOU LEARN SO FAST!
CLICK
CLICK
OH, NO! HERE COMES THE LANDING!

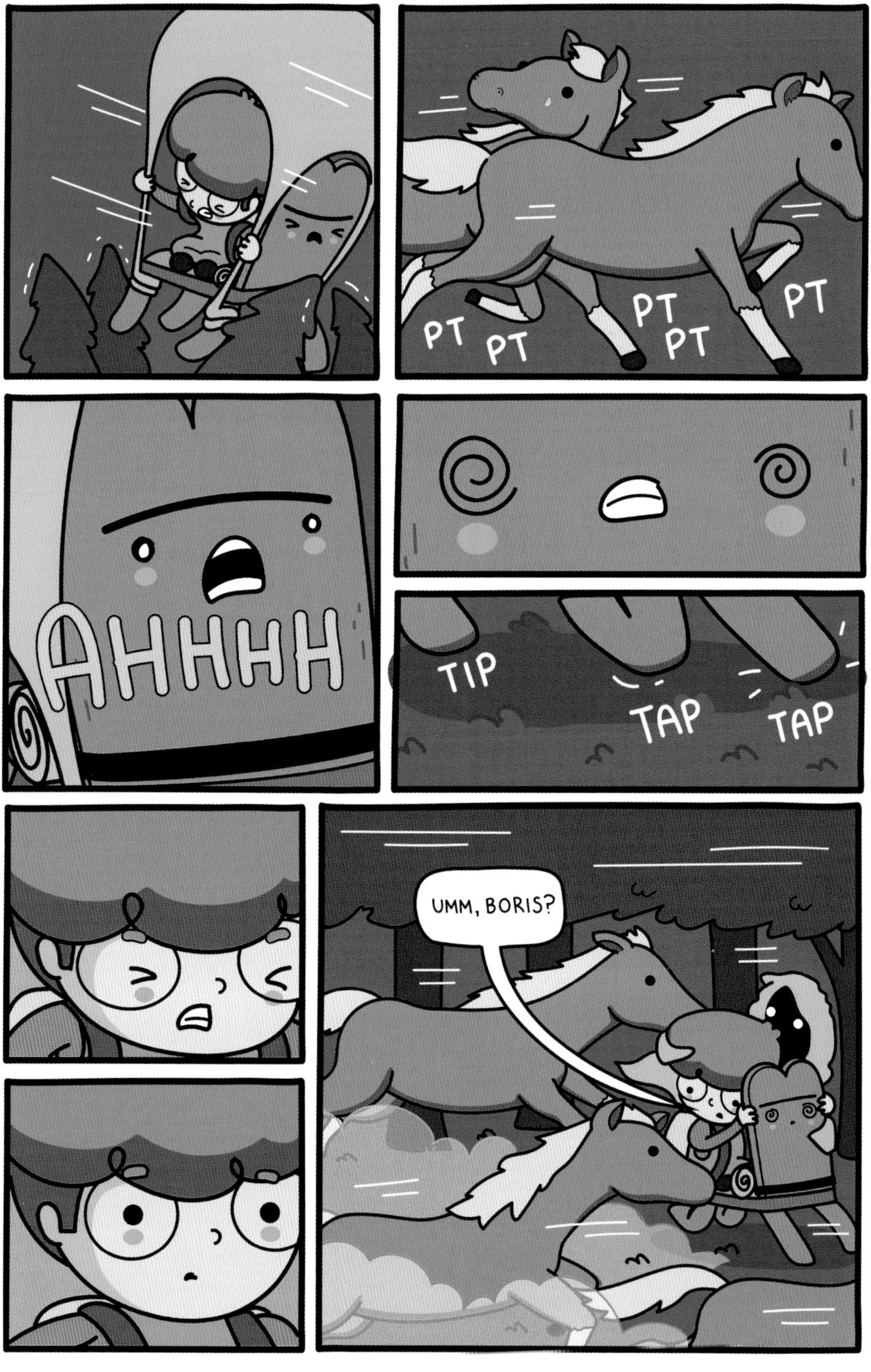
PT PT PT PT PT
AHHHH
TIP TAP TAP
UMM, BORIS?

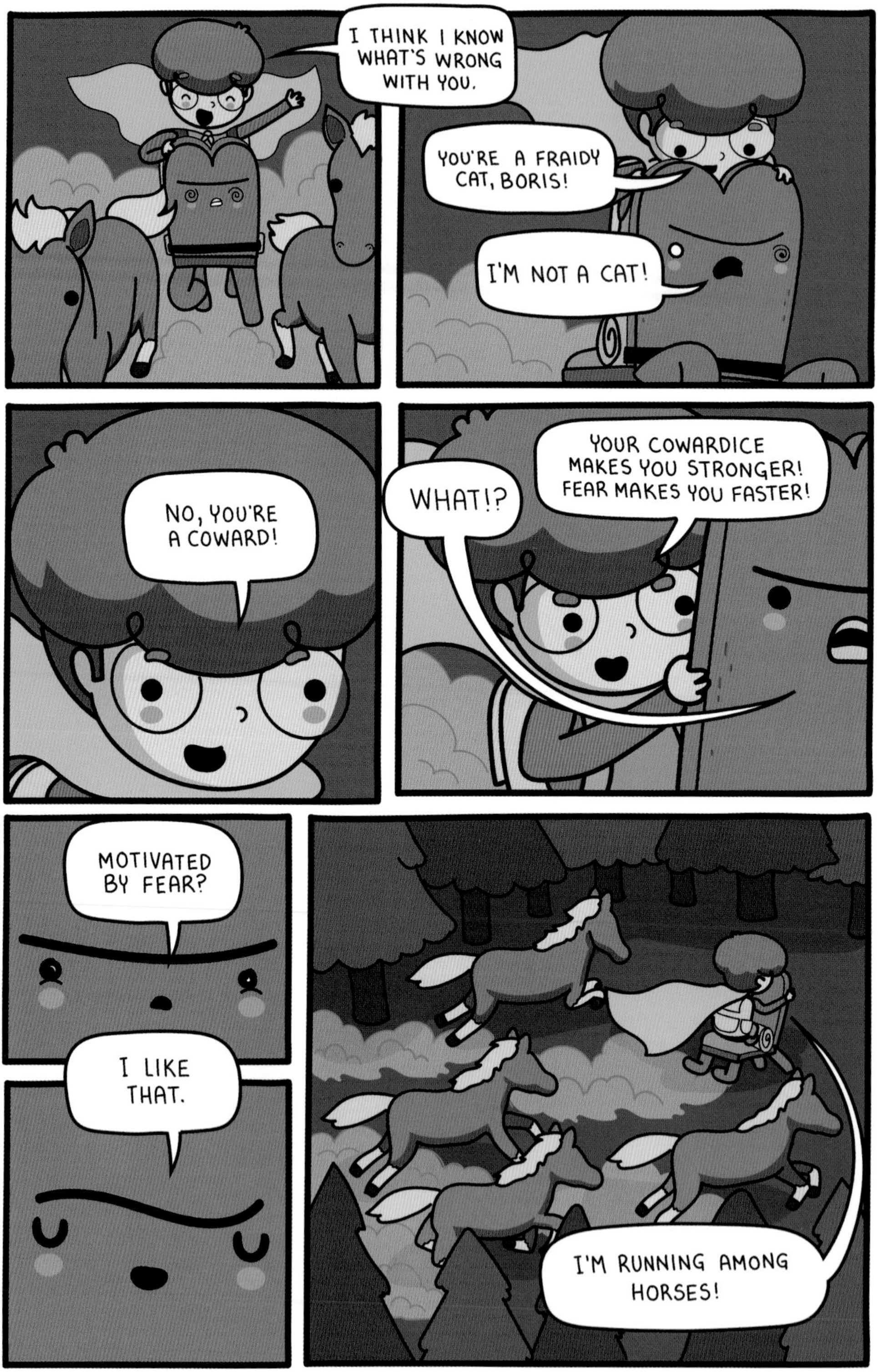
I THINK I KNOW WHAT'S WRONG WITH YOU.
YOU'RE A FRAIDY CAT, BORIS!
I'M NOT A CAT!
NO, YOU'RE A COWARD!
WHAT!?
YOUR COWARDICE MAKES YOU STRONGER! FEAR MAKES YOU FASTER!
MOTIVATED BY FEAR?
I LIKE THAT.
I'M RUNNING AMONG HORSES!

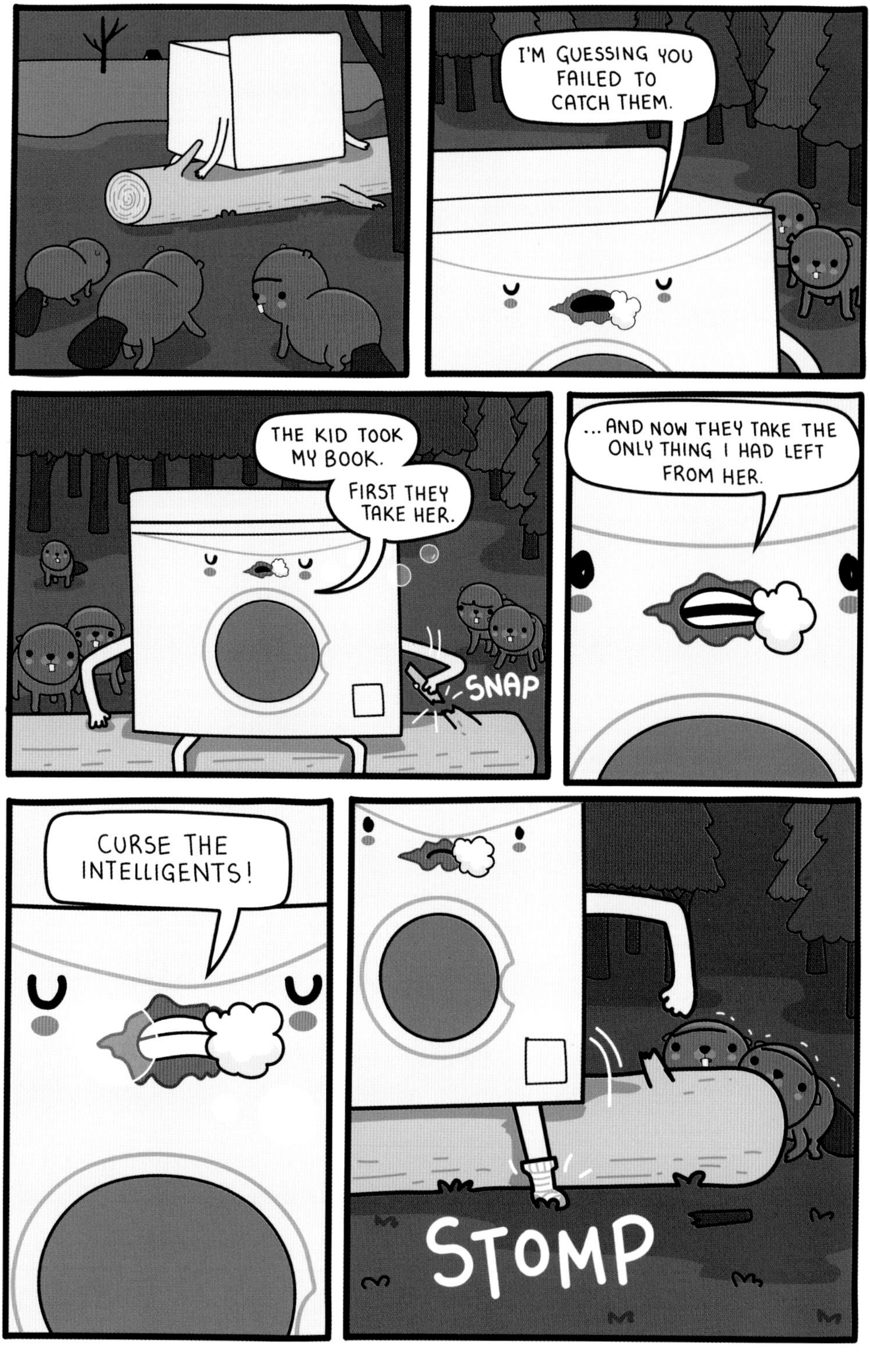
I'M GUESSING YOU FAILED TO CATCH THEM.
THE KID TOOK MY BOOK.
FIRST THEY TAKE HER.
SNAP
...AND NOW THEY TAKE THE ONLY THING I HAD LEFT FROM HER.
CURSE THE INTELLIGENTS!
STOMP

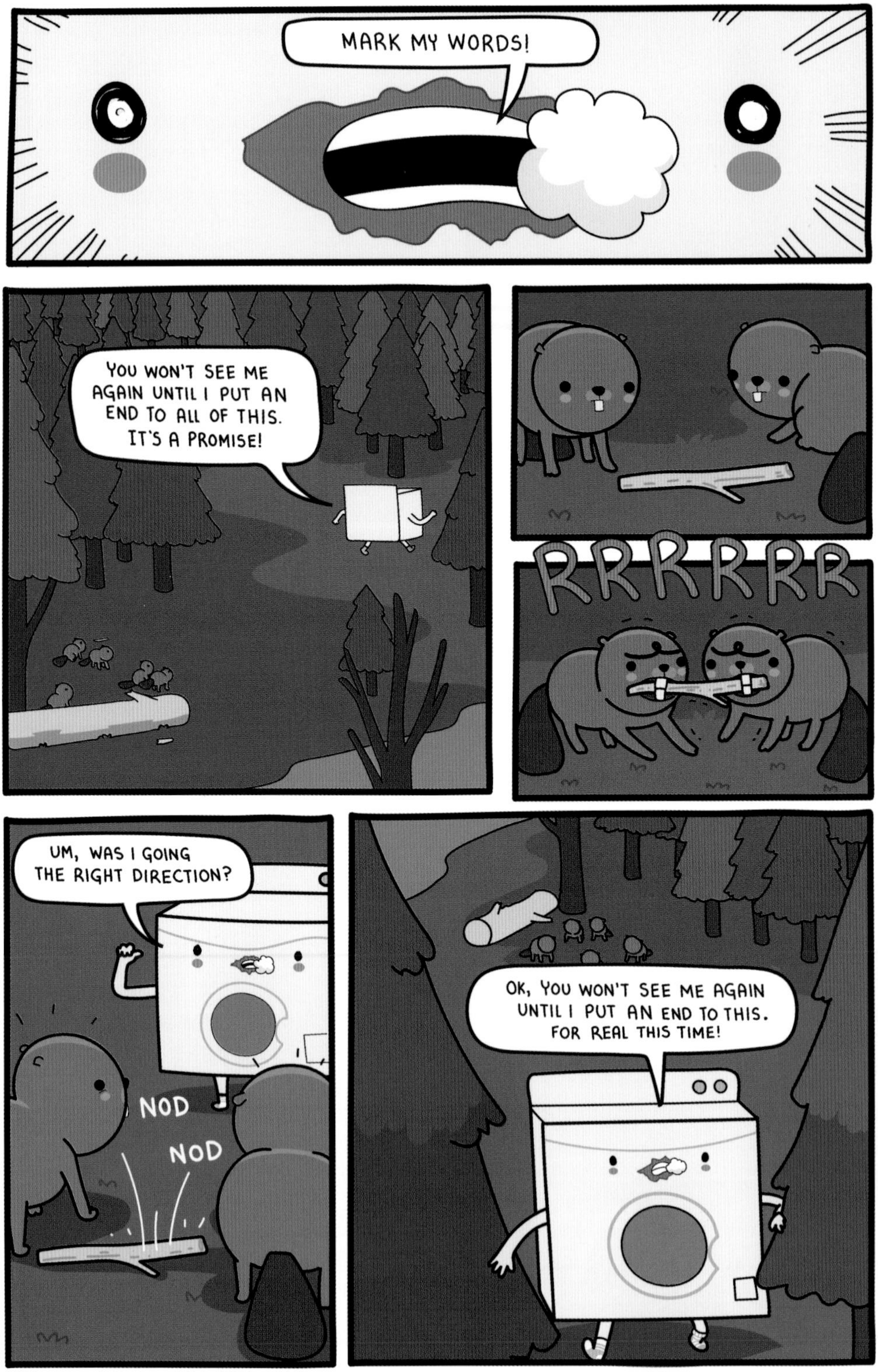
MARK MY WORDS!
YOU WON'T SEE ME AGAIN UNTIL I PUT AN END TO ALL OF THIS. IT'S A PROMISE!
RRRRRR
UM, WAS I GOING THE RIGHT DIRECTION?
NOD
NOD
OK, YOU WON'T SEE ME AGAIN UNTIL I PUT AN END TO THIS. FOR REAL THIS TIME!

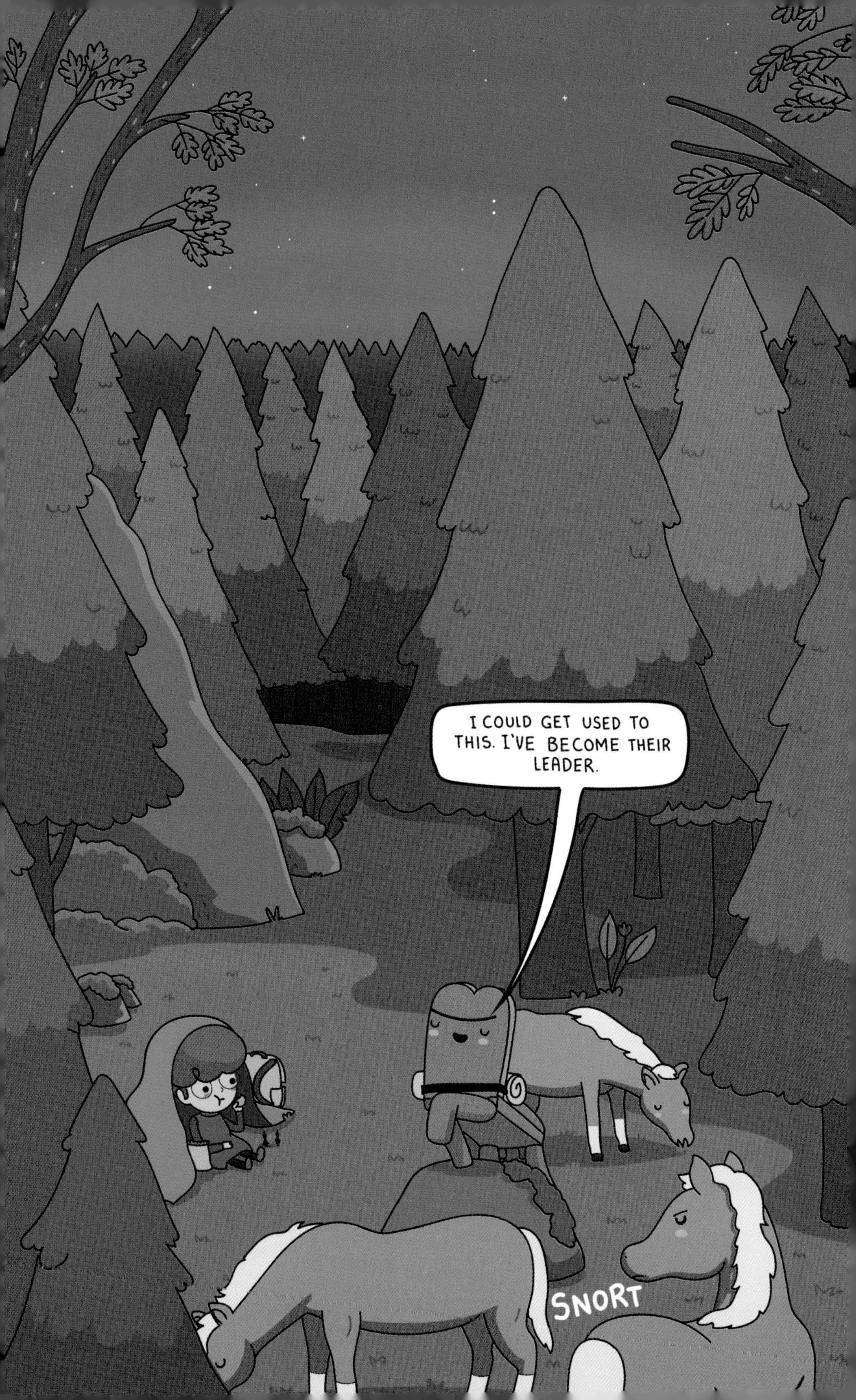
I COULD GET USED TO THIS. I'VE BECOME THEIR LEADER.
SNORT

WHAT IF WE DON'T FIND OUR WAY BACK HOME?

IS THAT REALLY WHAT'S BOTHERING YOU?

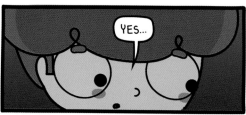

YES...

WELL...

IS IT REALLY YOUR HOME IF YOU HAVE NO FRIENDS? IF EVERYONE'S A STRANGER AND NO ONE KNOWS YOUR NAME?

THAT'S A TOUGH QUESTION.

CAN YOU BELIEVE HE'S THE CLOSEST THING I HAVE TO A FRIEND?

MOVE ALONG! KING CAMPING HERE!

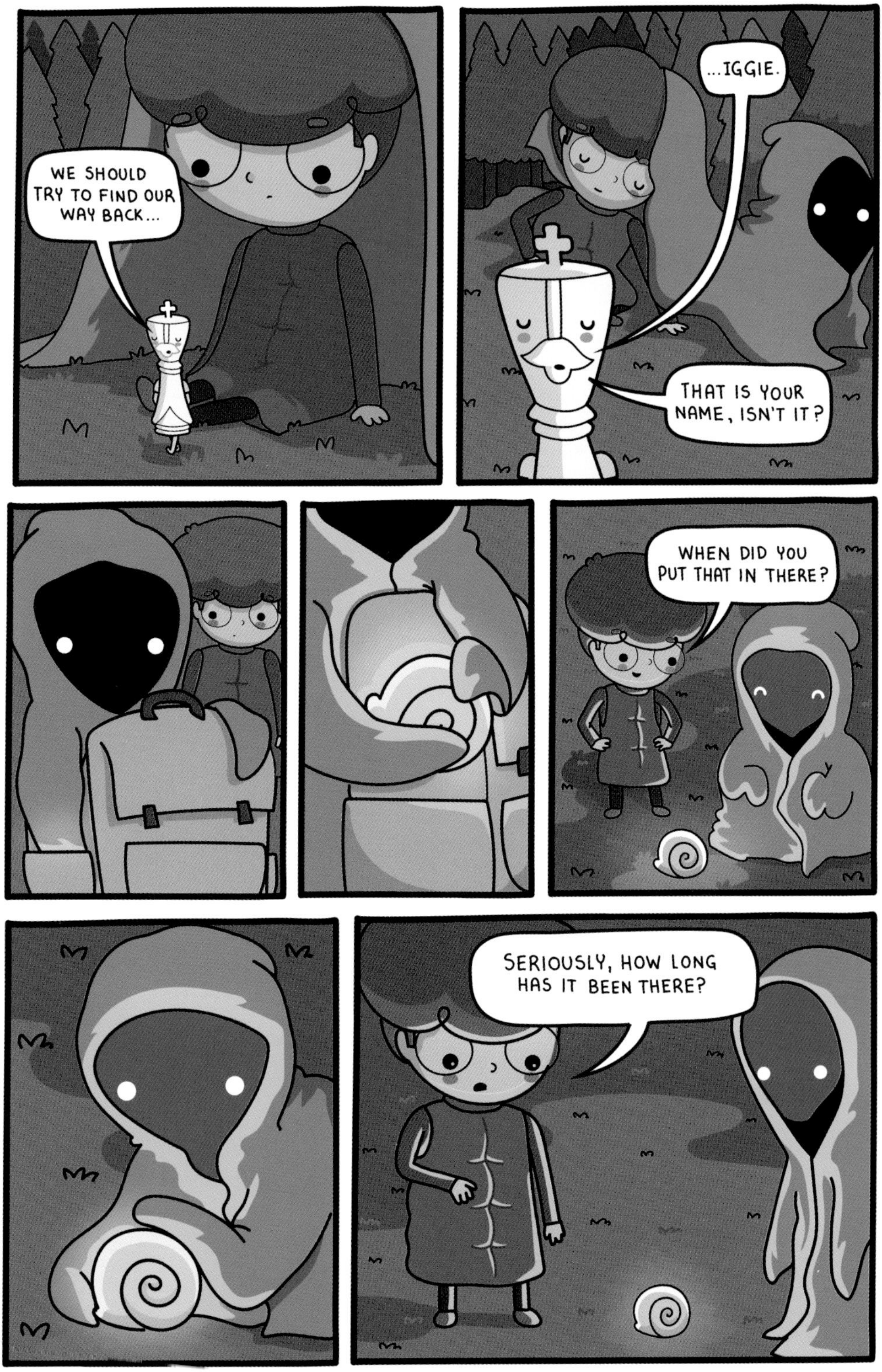
WE SHOULD TRY TO FIND OUR WAY BACK...
...IGGIE.
THAT IS YOUR NAME, ISN'T IT?
WHEN DID YOU PUT THAT IN THERE?
SERIOUSLY, HOW LONG HAS IT BEEN THERE?

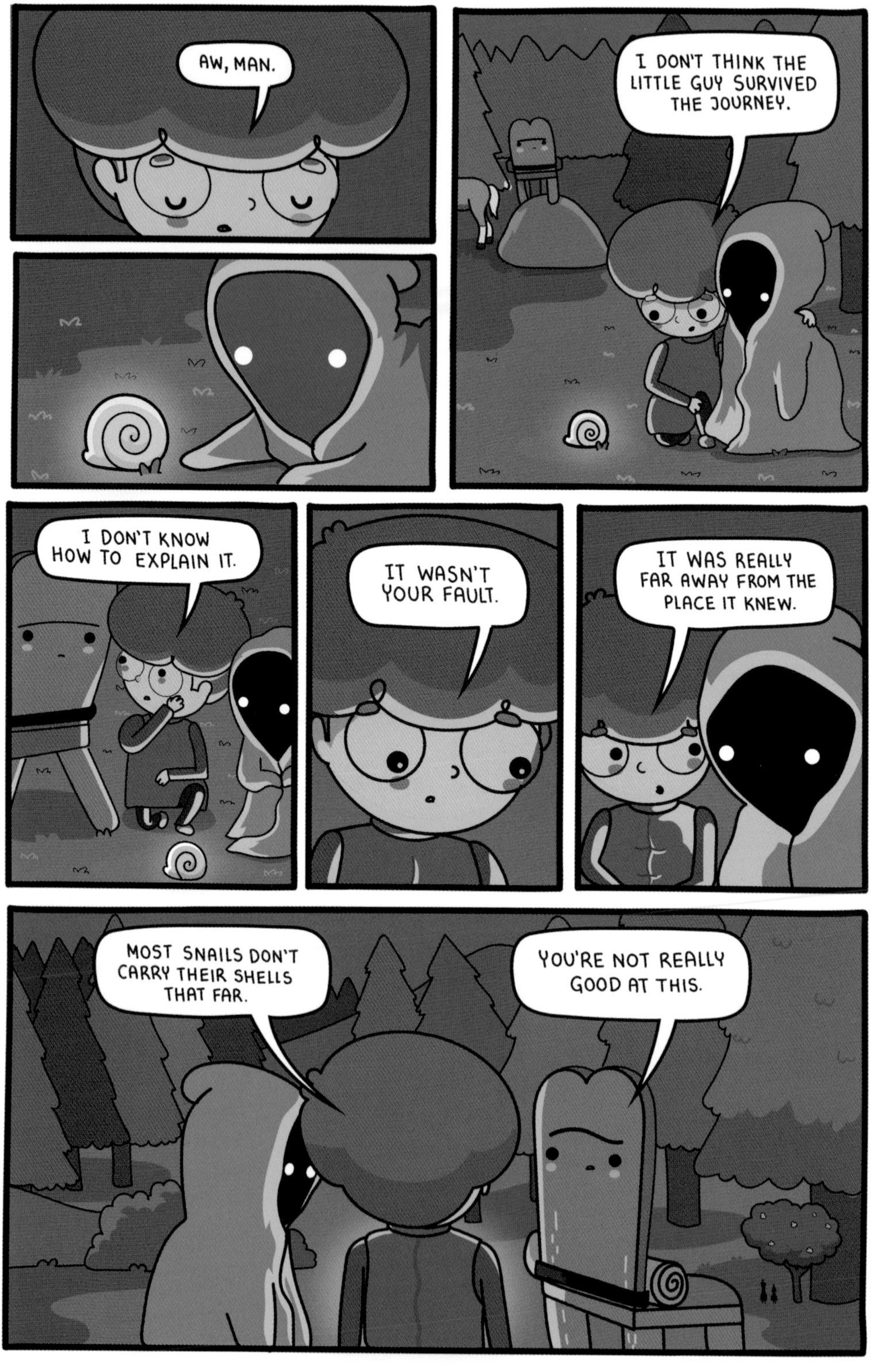
AW, MAN.
I DON'T THINK THE LITTLE GUY SURVIVED THE JOURNEY.
I DON'T KNOW HOW TO EXPLAIN IT.
IT WASN'T YOUR FAULT.
IT WAS REALLY FAR AWAY FROM THE PLACE IT KNEW.
MOST SNAILS DON'T CARRY THEIR SHELLS THAT FAR.
YOU'RE NOT REALLY GOOD AT THIS.

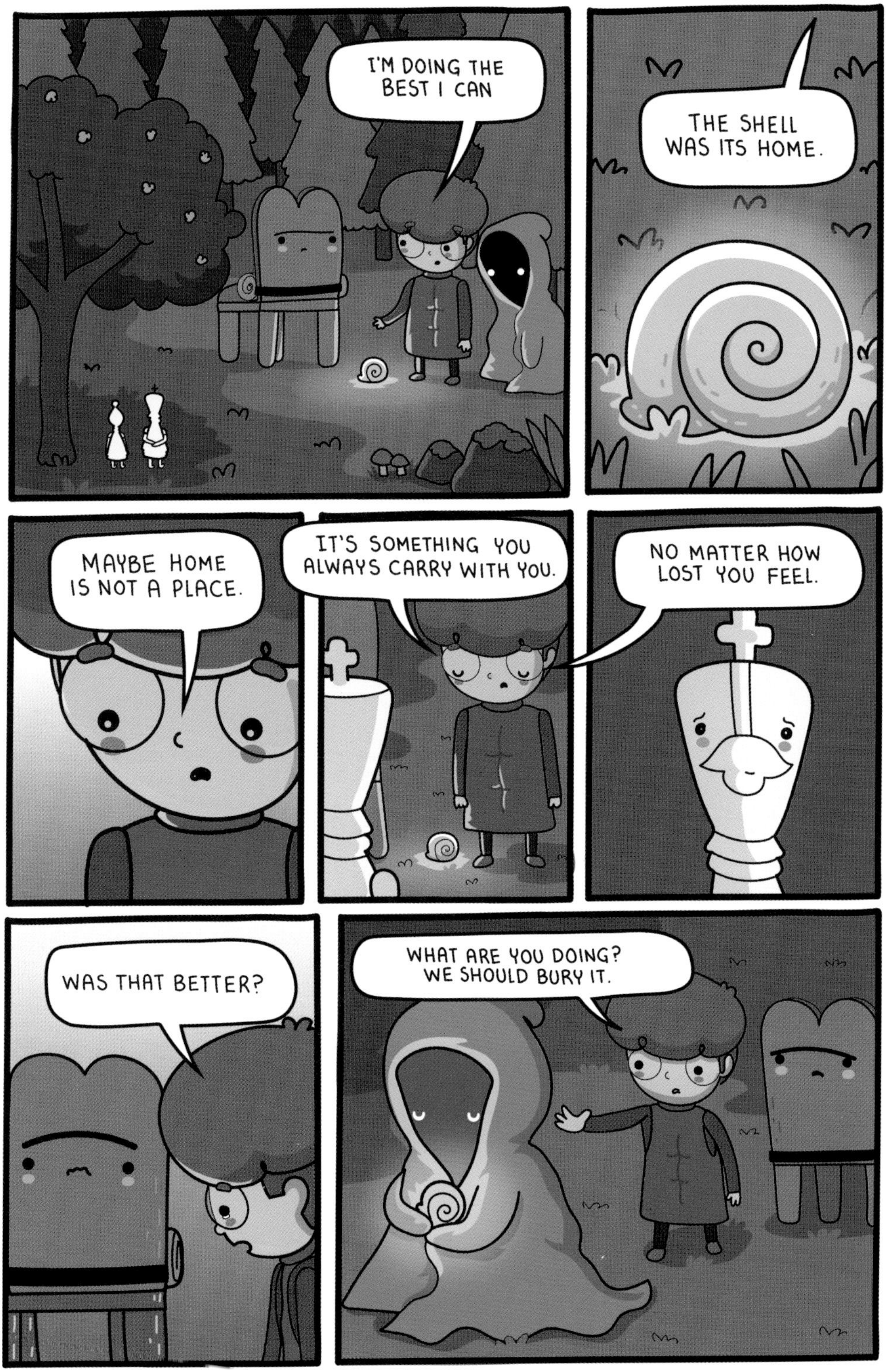
I'M DOING THE BEST I CAN
THE SHELL WAS ITS HOME.
MAYBE HOME IS NOT A PLACE.
IT'S SOMETHING YOU ALWAYS CARRY WITH YOU.
NO MATTER HOW LOST YOU FEEL.
WAS THAT BETTER?
WHAT ARE YOU DOING? WE SHOULD BURY IT.

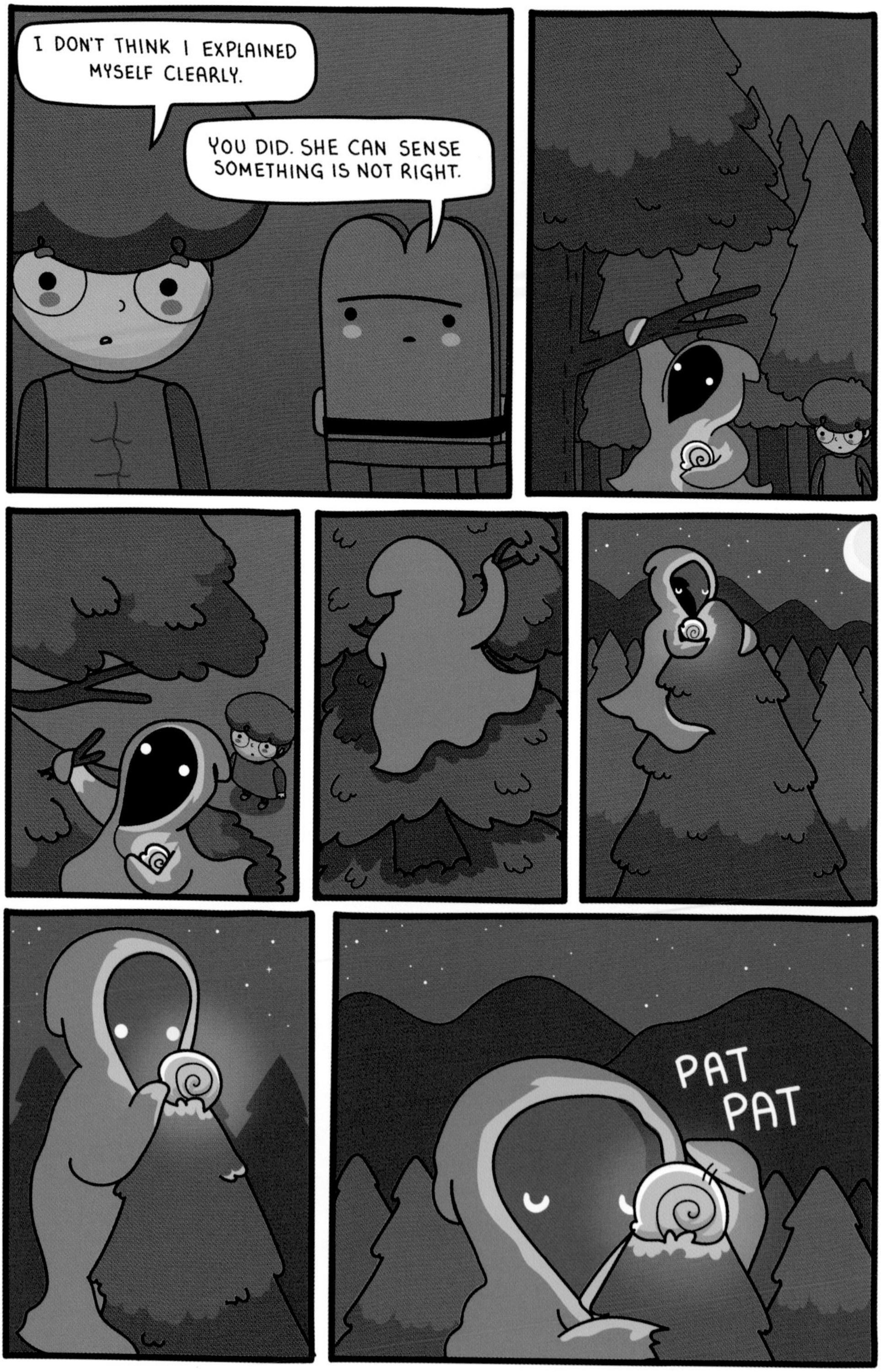
I DON'T THINK I EXPLAINED MYSELF CLEARLY.
YOU DID. SHE CAN SENSE SOMETHING IS NOT RIGHT.
PAT PAT

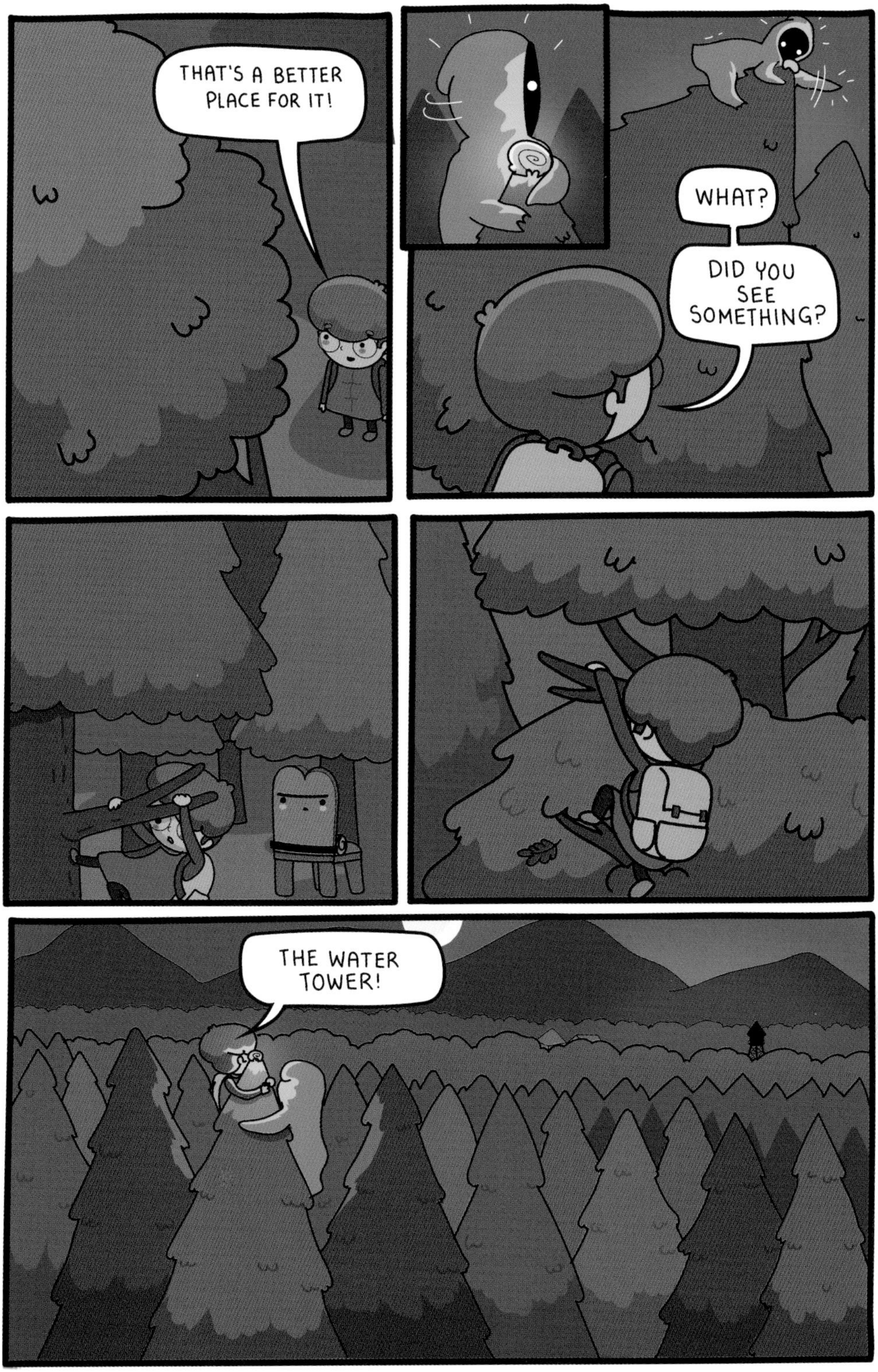
THAT'S A BETTER PLACE FOR IT!
WHAT?
DID YOU SEE SOMETHING?
THE WATER TOWER!

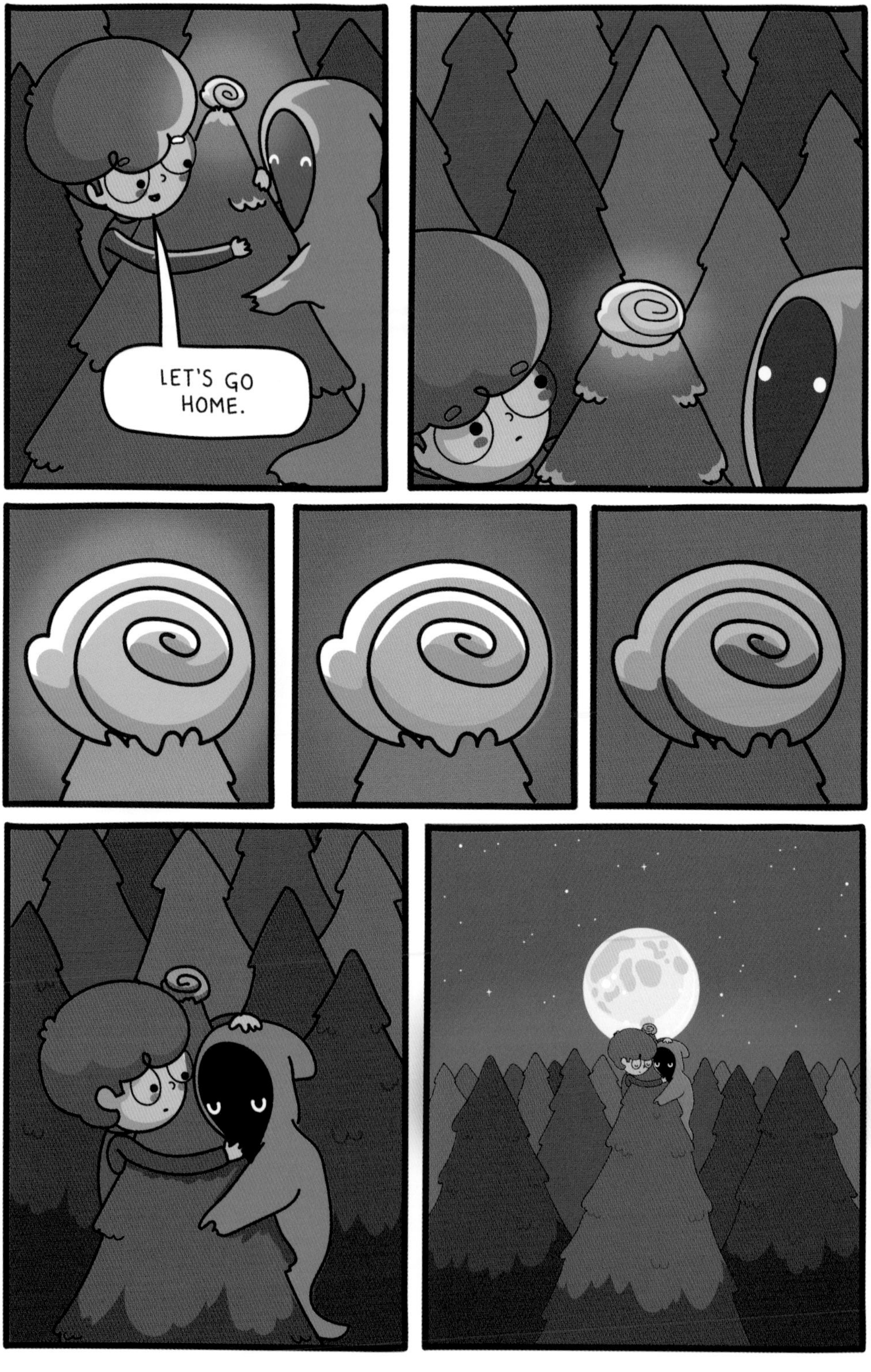
LET'S GO HOME.

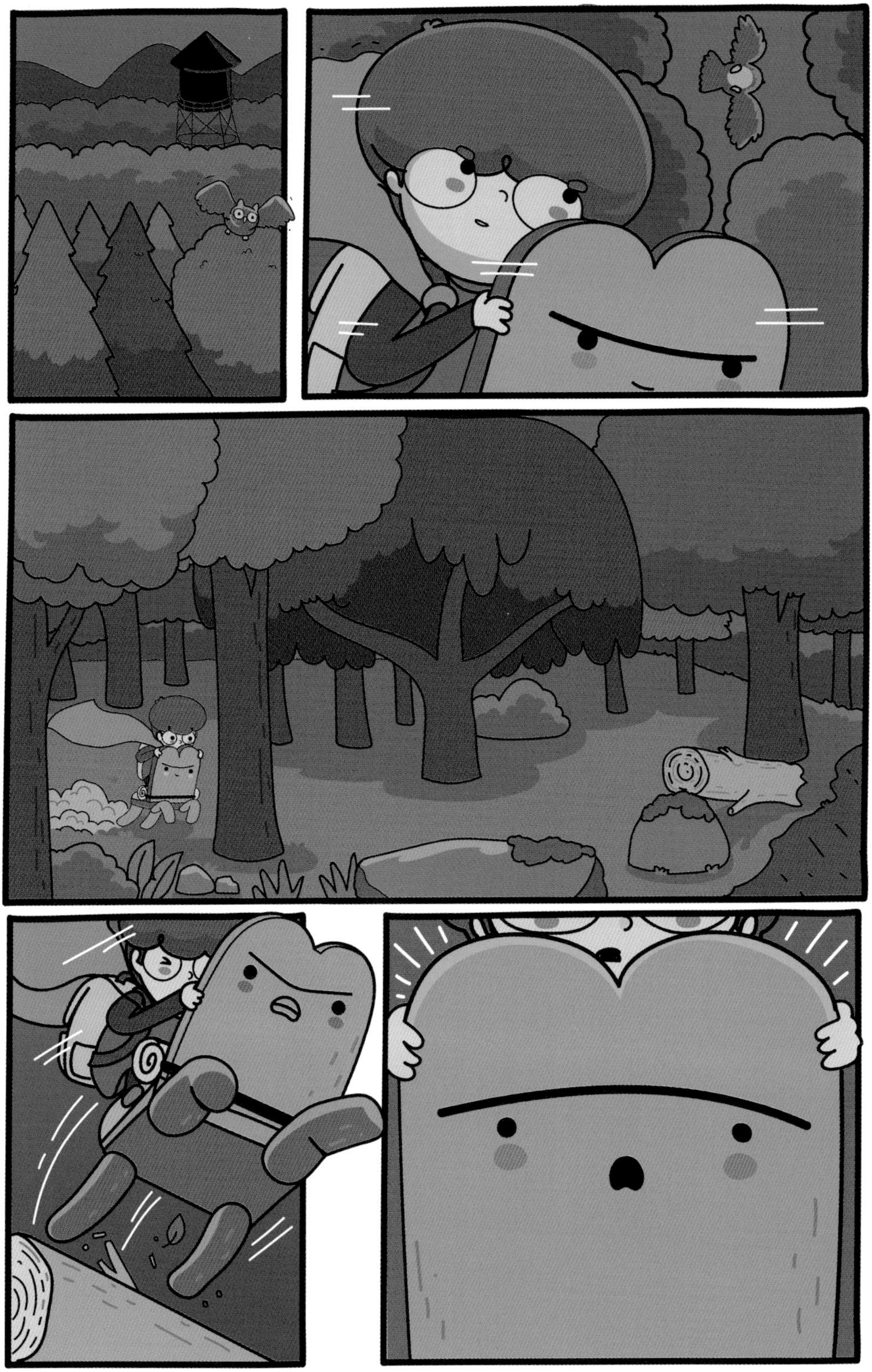

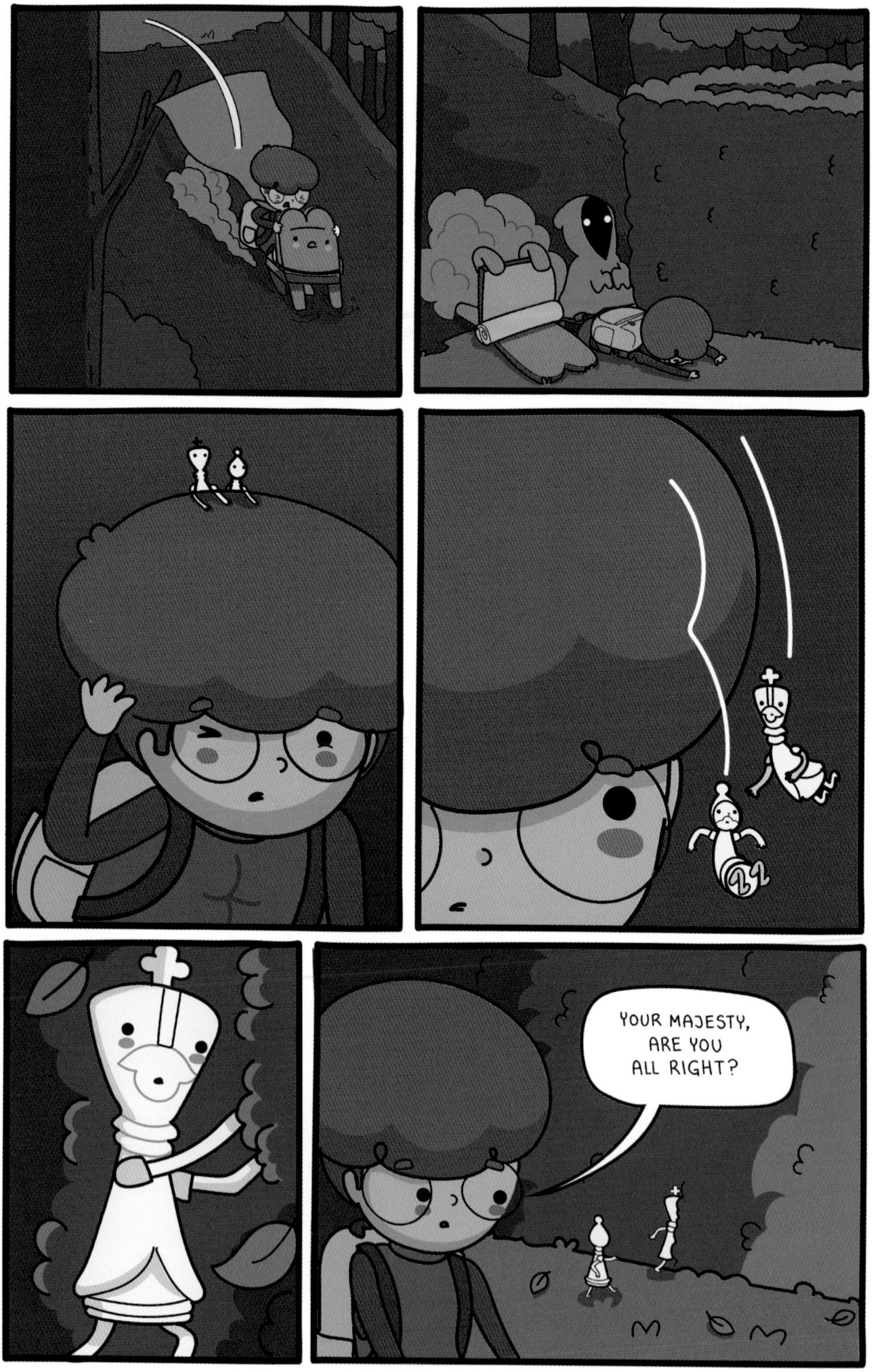
YOUR MAJESTY,
ARE YOU
ALL RIGHT?

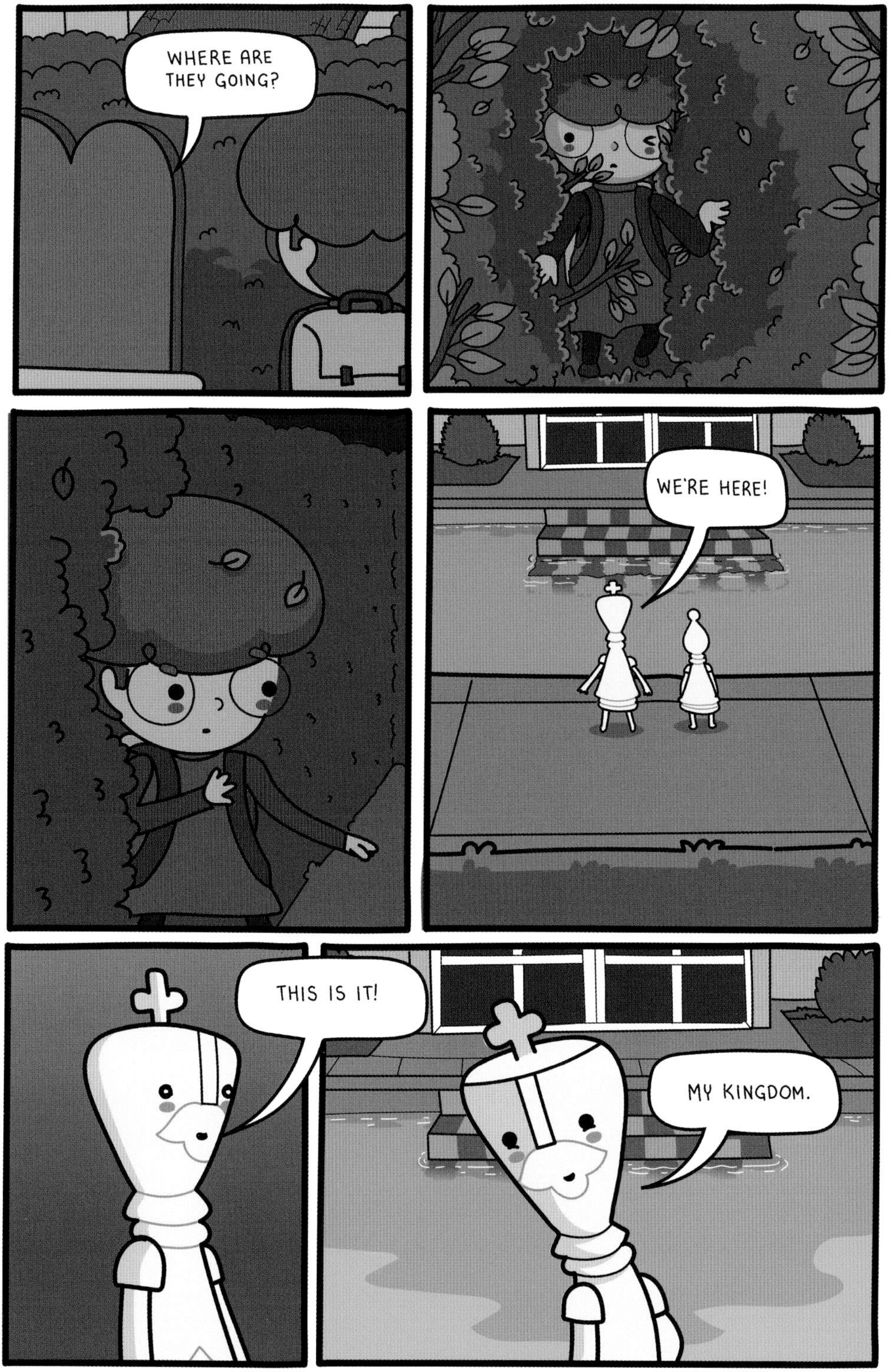
WHERE ARE THEY GOING?
WE'RE HERE!
THIS IS IT!
MY KINGDOM.

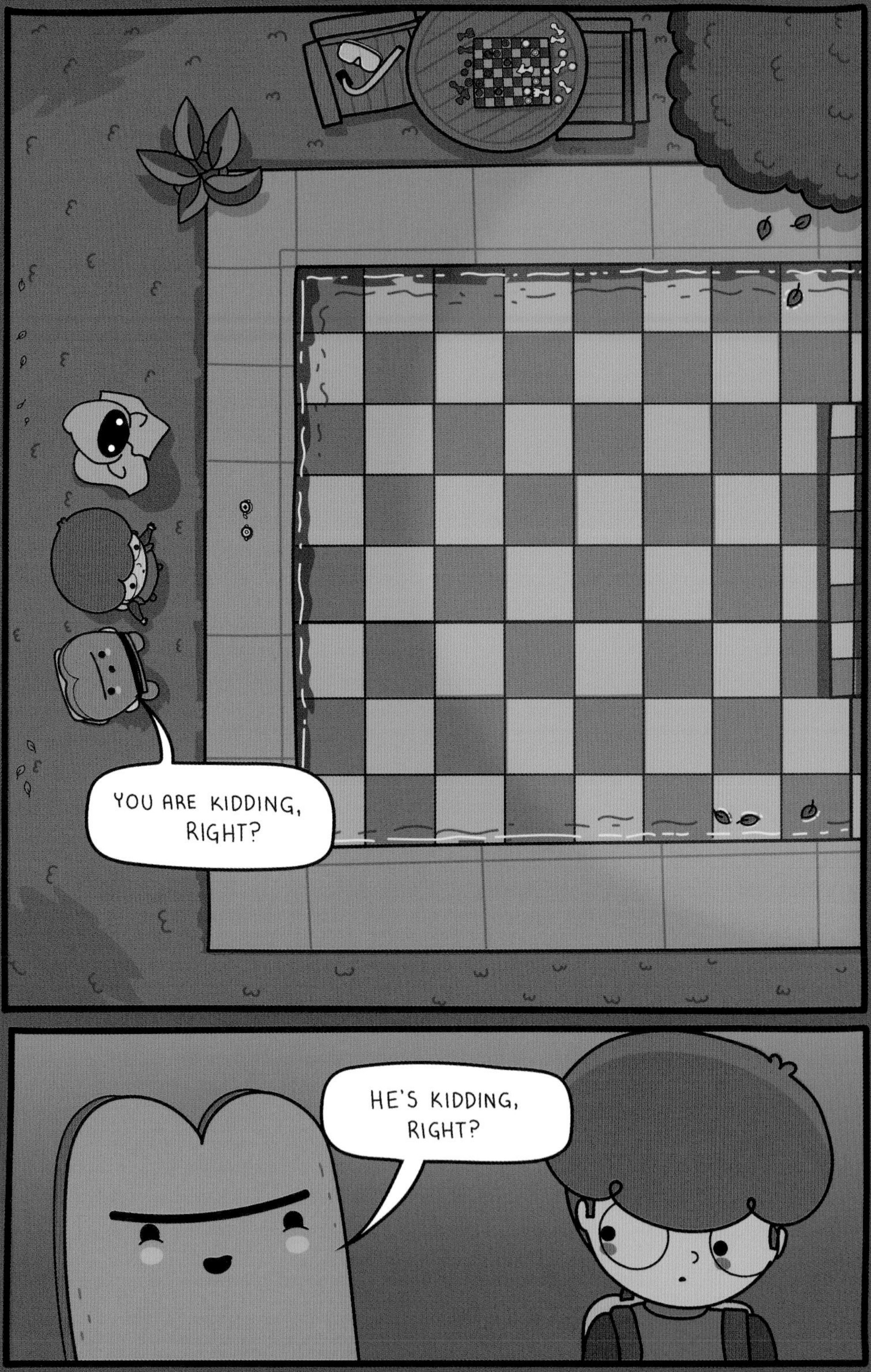
YOU ARE KIDDING, RIGHT?
HE'S KIDDING, RIGHT?

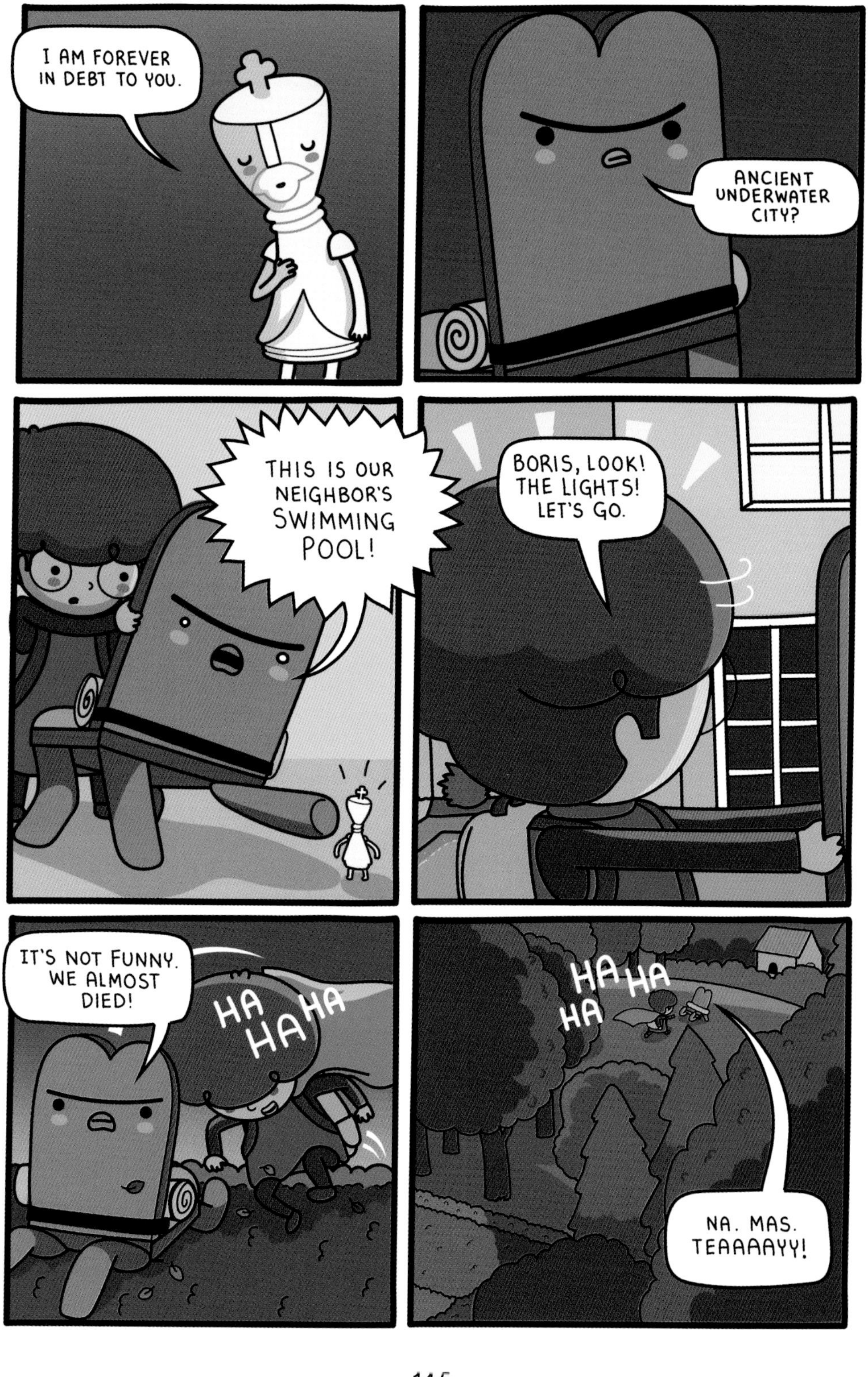
I AM FOREVER IN DEBT TO YOU.
ANCIENT UNDERWATER CITY?
THIS IS OUR NEIGHBOR'S SWIMMING POOL!
BORIS, LOOK! THE LIGHTS! LET'S GO.
IT'S NOT FUNNY. WE ALMOST DIED!
HA HA HA
HA HA HA
NA. MAS. TEAAAAYY!

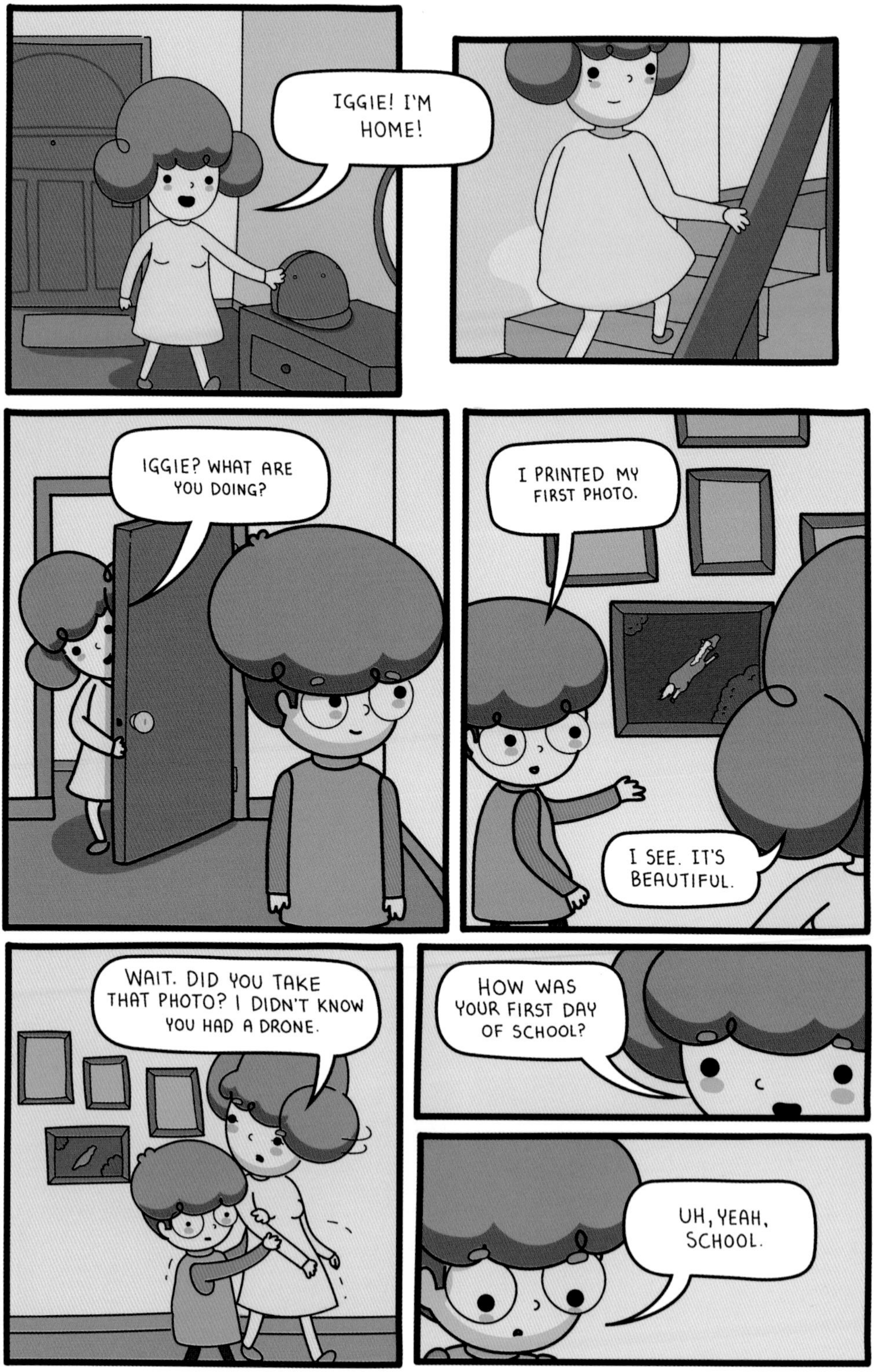
IGGIE! I'M HOME!
IGGIE? WHAT ARE YOU DOING?
I PRINTED MY FIRST PHOTO.
I SEE. IT'S BEAUTIFUL.
WAIT. DID YOU TAKE THAT PHOTO? I DIDN'T KNOW YOU HAD A DRONE.
HOW WAS YOUR FIRST DAY OF SCHOOL?
UH, YEAH, SCHOOL.

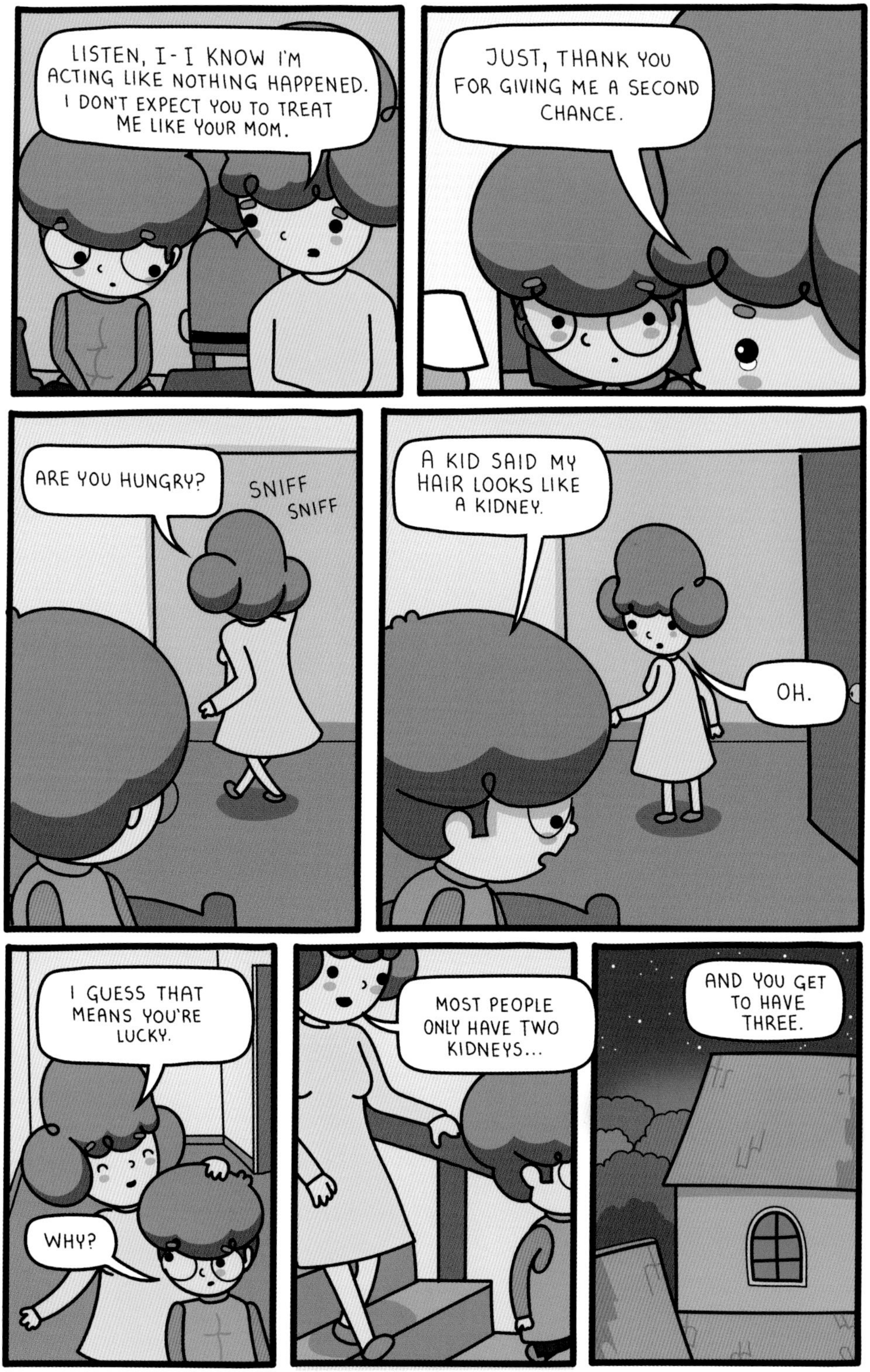
LISTEN, I-I KNOW I'M ACTING LIKE NOTHING HAPPENED. I DON'T EXPECT YOU TO TREAT ME LIKE YOUR MOM.
JUST, THANK YOU FOR GIVING ME A SECOND CHANCE.
ARE YOU HUNGRY?
SNIFF SNIFF
A KID SAID MY HAIR LOOKS LIKE A KIDNEY.
OH.
I GUESS THAT MEANS YOU'RE LUCKY.
WHY?
MOST PEOPLE ONLY HAVE TWO KIDNEYS...
AND YOU GET TO HAVE THREE.

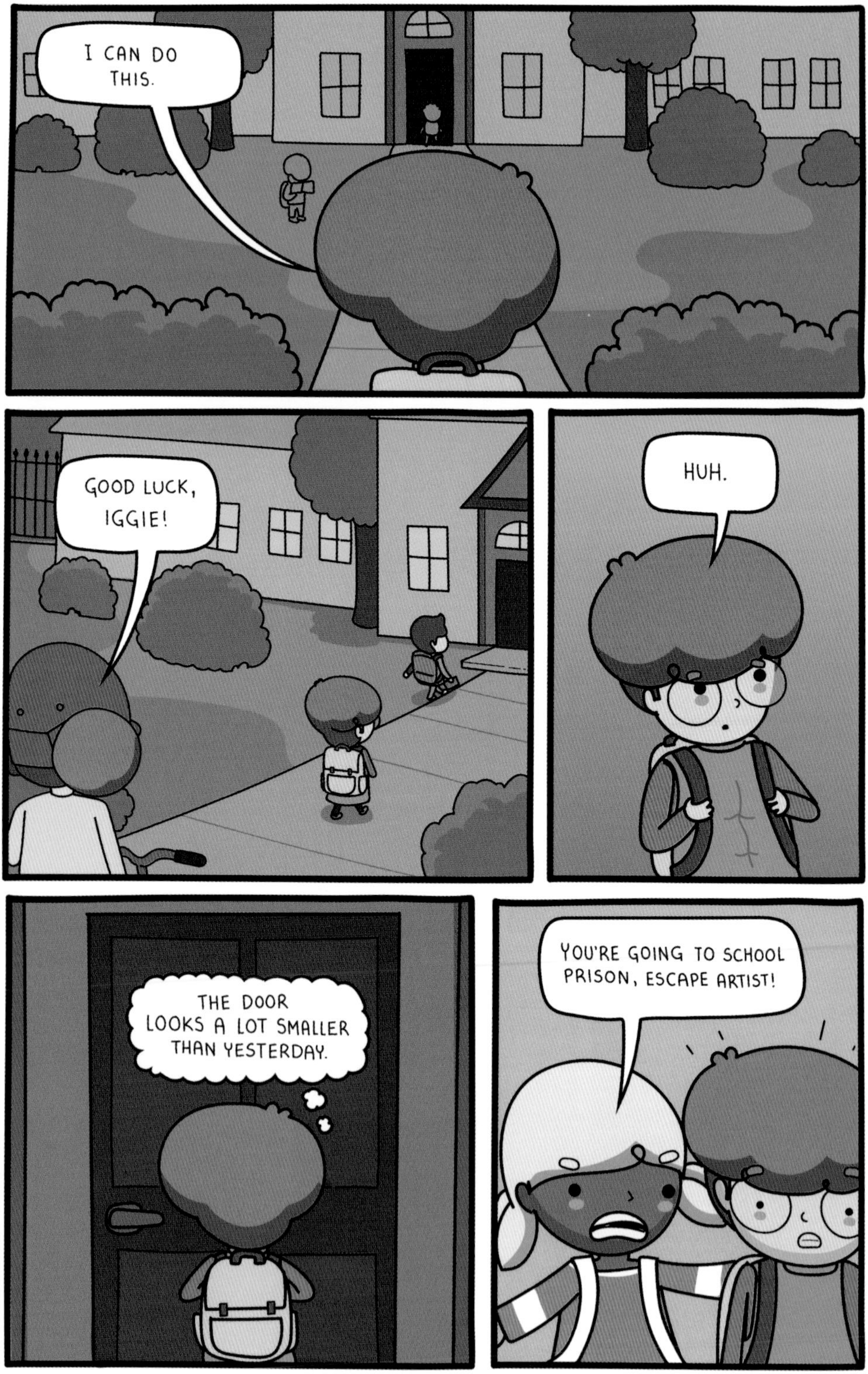
I CAN DO THIS.
GOOD LUCK, IGGIE!
HUH.
THE DOOR LOOKS A LOT SMALLER THAN YESTERDAY.
YOU'RE GOING TO SCHOOL PRISON, ESCAPE ARTIST!

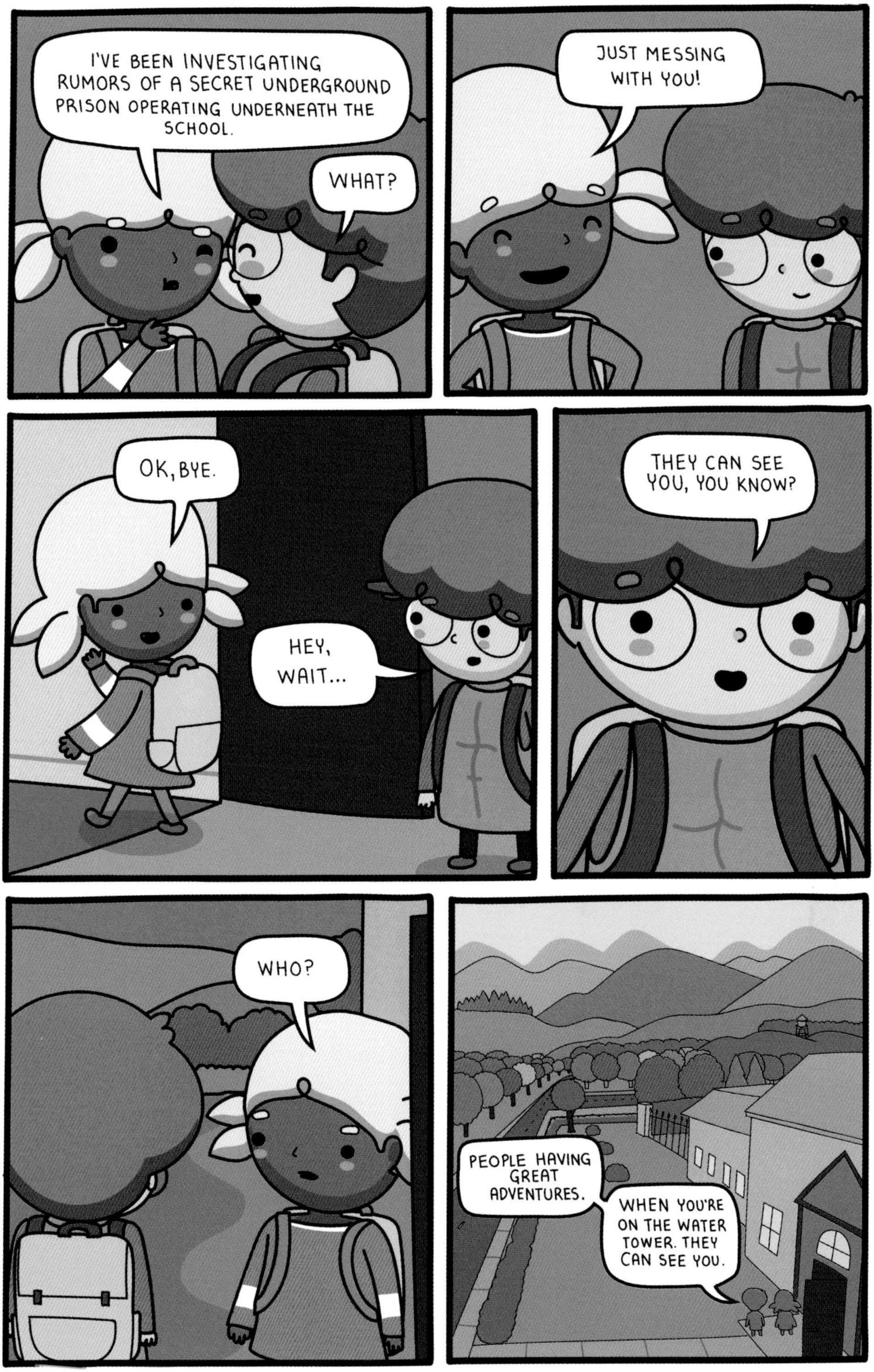
I'VE BEEN INVESTIGATING RUMORS OF A SECRET UNDERGROUND PRISON OPERATING UNDERNEATH THE SCHOOL.
WHAT?
JUST MESSING WITH YOU!
OK, BYE.
HEY, WAIT...
THEY CAN SEE YOU, YOU KNOW?
WHO?
PEOPLE HAVING GREAT ADVENTURES.
WHEN YOU'RE ON THE WATER TOWER. THEY CAN SEE YOU.

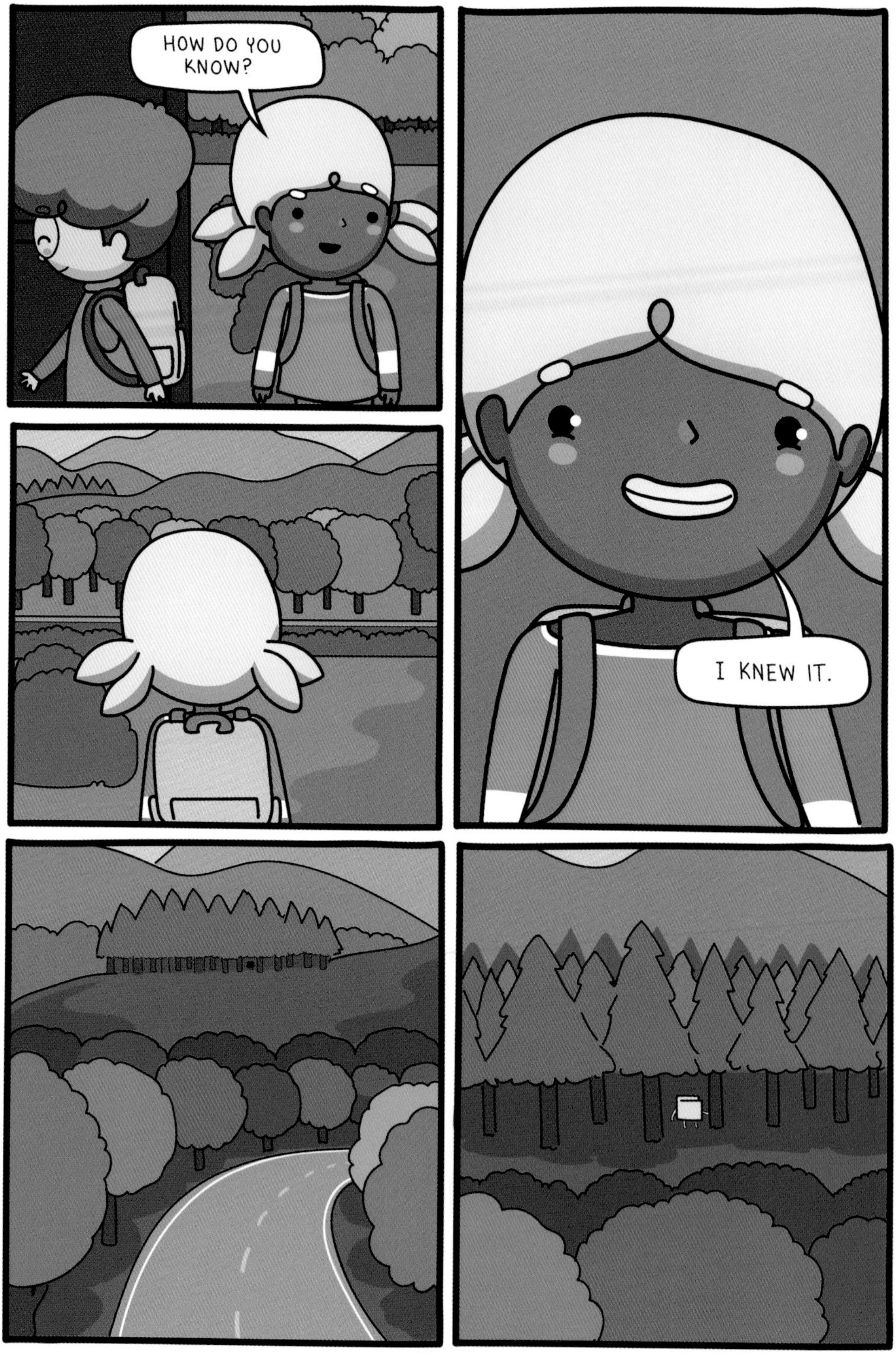
HOW DO YOU KNOW?
I KNEW IT.

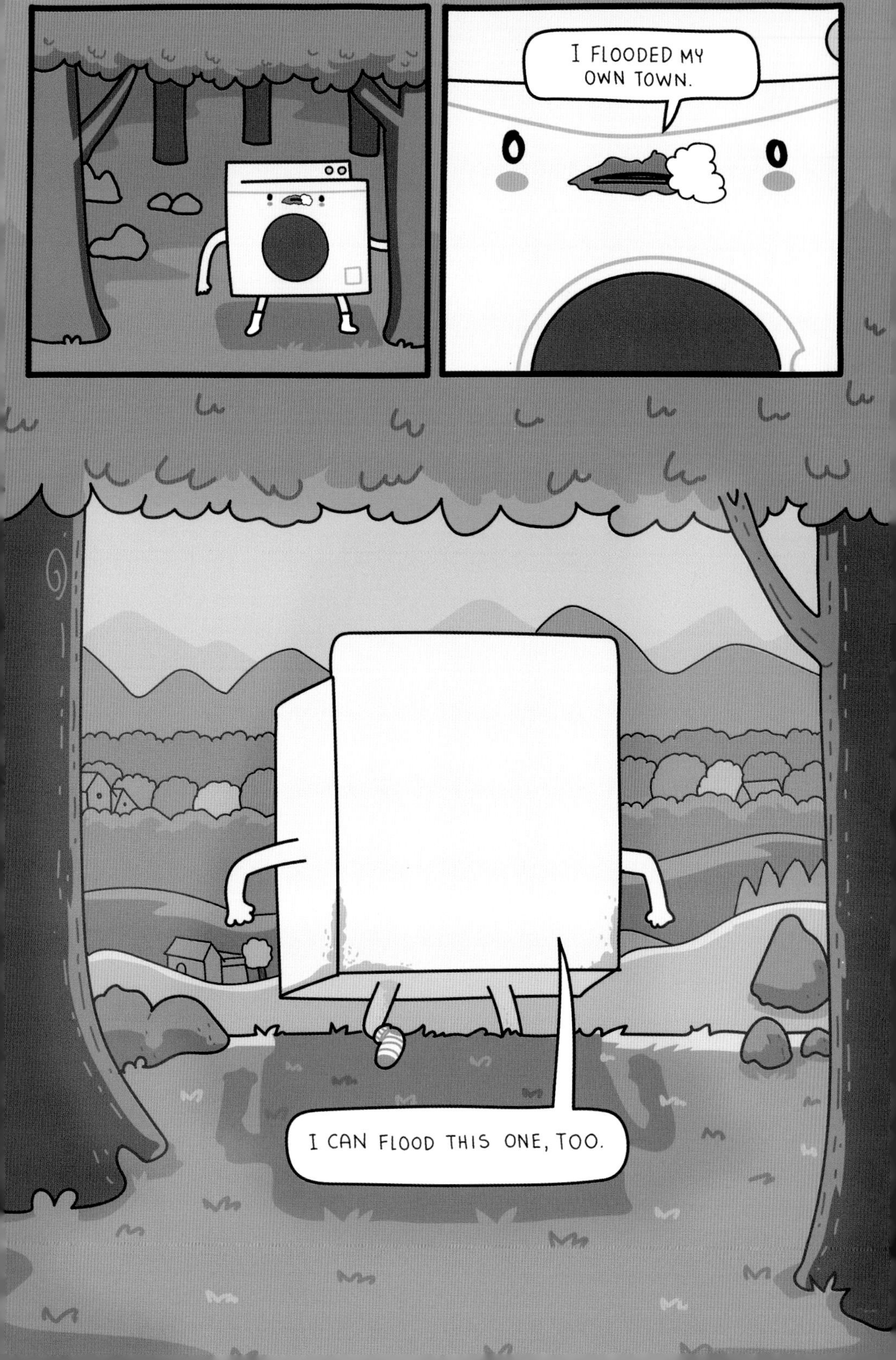
I FLOODED MY OWN TOWN.
I CAN FLOOD THIS ONE, TOO.

TO BE CONTINUED...

∾ ACKNOWLEDGMENTS ∾

To my wife, Viviana, who is still by my side even after my nonstop talking about this project for months. Your unconditional love and advice have helped me through this process more than anyone can imagine.

To my two kids, who constantly inspire me and my characters.

To my editor, Lucas Wetzel, whose hundreds of razor-sharp notes were exactly what I needed to organize my thoughts. And all the people at Andrews McMeel Pulishing who were involved in *Peculiar Woods*, making this book possible and giving me their valuable feedback.

To Oscar Colmenares, his assistance coloring pages and the insightful suggestions made it possible to finish the book on schedule.

To Kathleen Ortiz, for being the amazing agent who never doubts my work and always fuels my crazy ideas.

To my readers: This book exists because of you. Please never stop sharing, caring, and showing love.

And last but not least, I would like to express great thanks for the support and warmth over the years to my chair and blanket.

About the Author

Andrés J. Colmenares is a Colombian self-taught illustrator and the creator of *Wawawiwa Comics*, which he describes as being like a "visual hug" for his millions of readers around the world. He lives in Bogota, Colombia, with his wife, Viviana Navas, and their two children.

Andrews McMeel Publishing
a division of Andrews McMeel Universal
1130 Walnut Street, Kansas City, Missouri 64106

23 24 25 26 27 TEN 10 9 8 7 6 5 4 3 2 1

Paperback ISBN: 978-1-5248-7929-7
Hardback ISBN: 978-1-5248-8491-8

Library of Congress Control Number: 2022947525

Editor: Lucas Wetzel
Art Directors: Tiffany Meairs and Lynn Stoecklein
Production Editor: Julie Railsback
Production Manager: Tamara Haus

www.andrewsmcmeel.com

Made by:
1010 Printing International, Ltd.
Address and place of production:
1010 Avenue, Xia Nan Industrial District,
Yuan Zhou Town, Bo Luo County, Hui Zhou City,
Guang Dong Province 516123, China
1st Printing—12/26/2022

Look for these books!

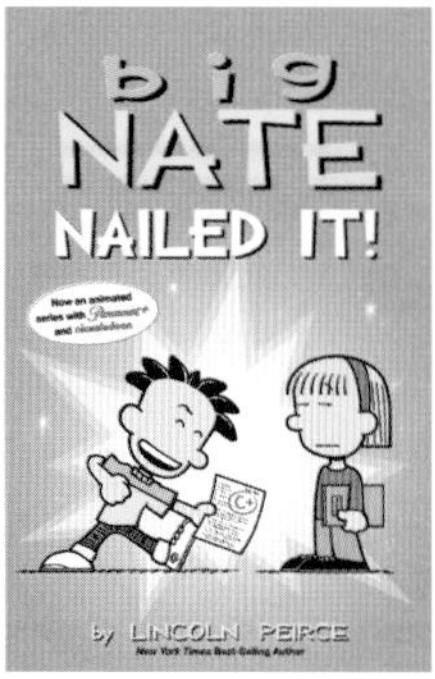
big
NATE
NAILED IT!
by LINCOLN PEIRCE

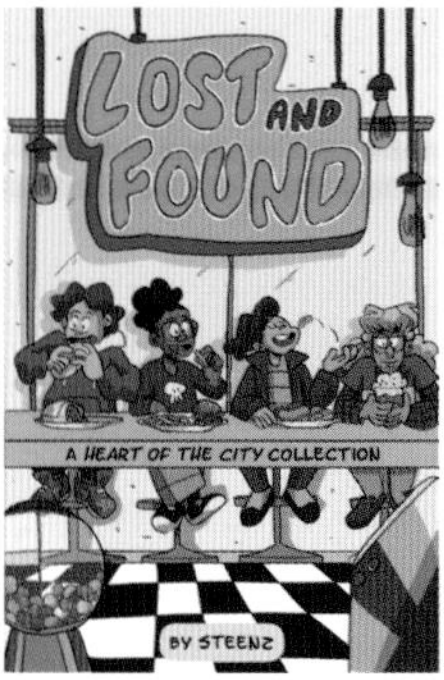
LOST AND FOUND
A HEART OF THE CITY COLLECTION
BY STEENZ

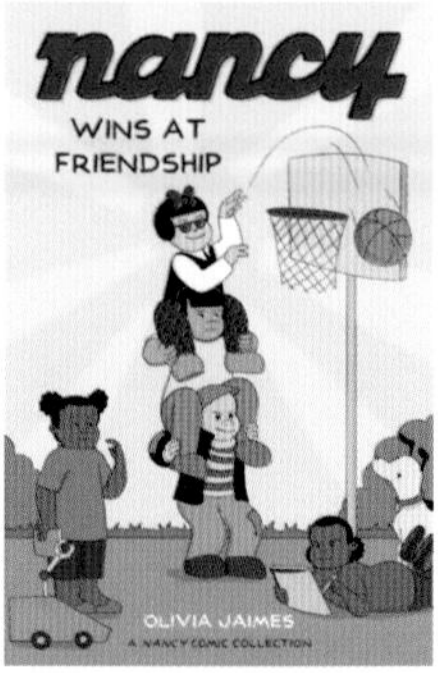
nancy
WINS AT FRIENDSHIP
OLIVIA JAIMES

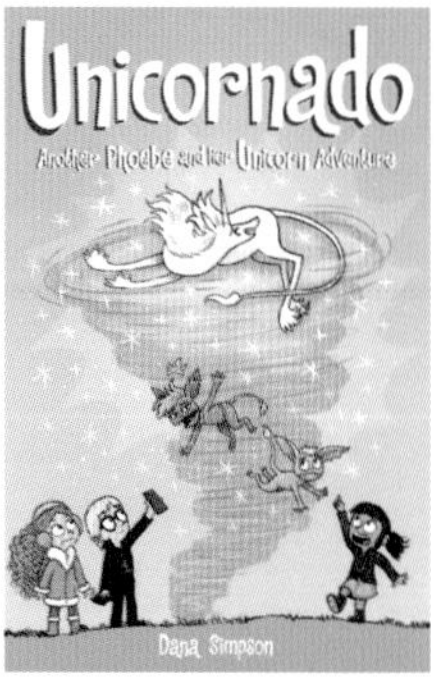
Unicornado
Another Phoebe and her Unicorn Adventure
Dana Simpson

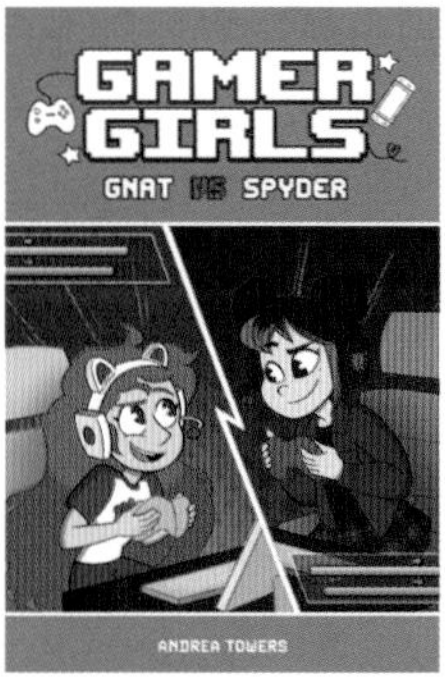
GAMER GIRLS
GNAT VS SPYDER
ANDREA TOWERS

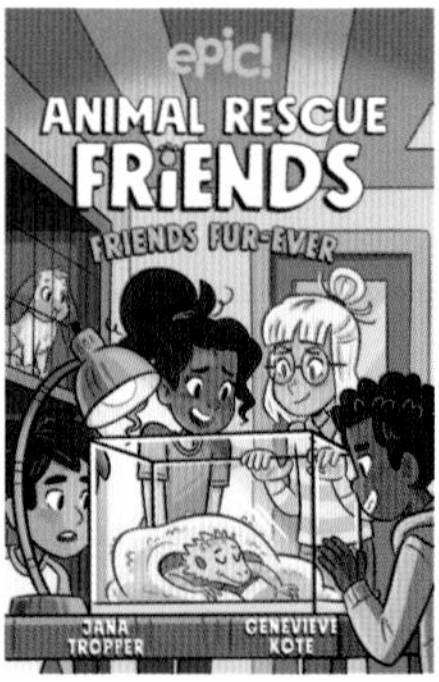
epic!
ANIMAL RESCUE FRIENDS
FRIENDS FUR-EVER
JANA TROPPER
GENEVIEVE KOTE

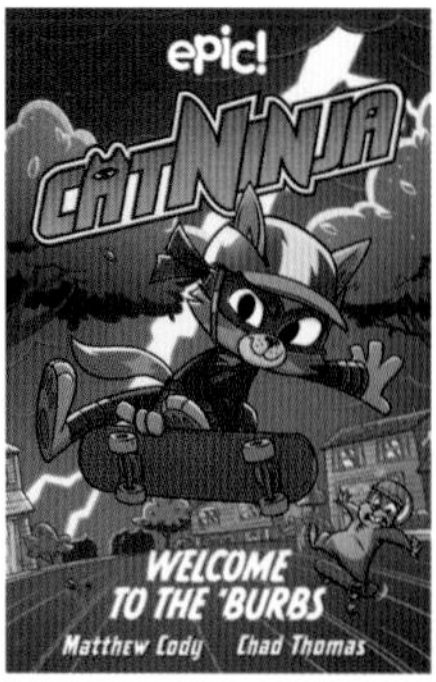
epic!
CAT NINJA
WELCOME TO THE 'BURBS
Matthew Cody
Chad Thomas

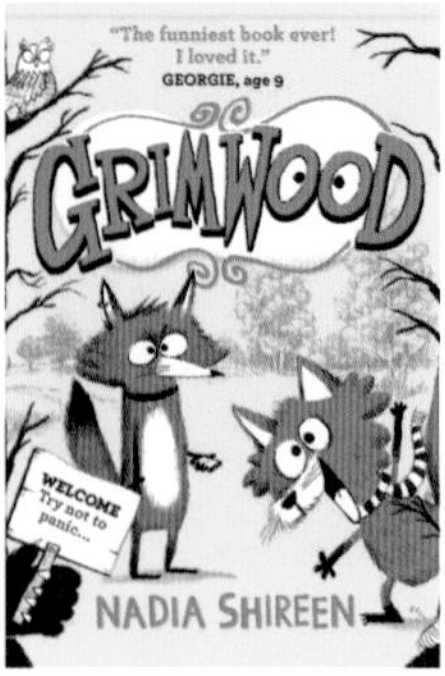
"The funniest book ever! I loved it."
GEORGIE, age 9
GRIMWOOD
WELCOME
Try not to panic...
NADIA SHIREEN

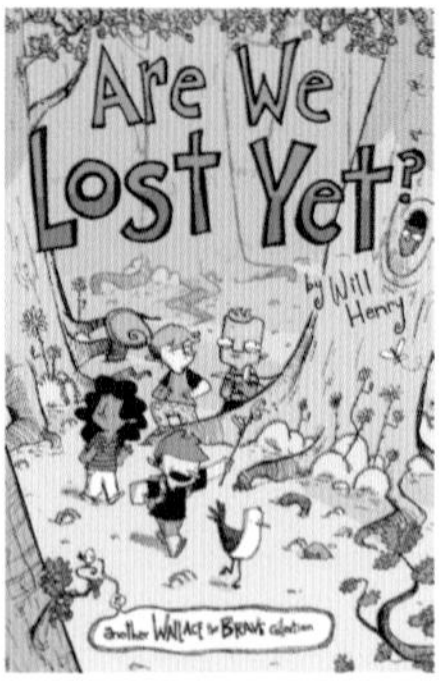
Are We Lost Yet?
by Will Henry